The
AGE
of
WITCHES

She had not laid curses upon her neighbors, only scolded them for stealing her apples. She had made a poppet or two, but they had done no real harm. She had never consorted with the devil.

She was, as she had told them, clear of offenses, but they would not hearken. They had taken the word of five girls and many more men, most of whom had tried for her favors at one time or another. They had judged her a witch and sentenced her to a dark death on this bright day.

The AGE of WITCHES

LOUISA MORGAN

www.orbitbooks.net

ORBIT

First published in Great Britain in 2020 by Orbit

1 3 5 7 9 10 8 6 4 2

A CIP catalogue record for this book
is available from the British Library.

ISBN 978-0-356-51258-7

Printed and bound in Great Britain by
Clays Ltd, Elcograf S.p.A.

Papers used by Orbit are from well-managed forests
and other responsible sources.

Orbit
An imprint of
Little, Brown Book Group
Carmelite House
50 Victoria Embankment
London EC4Y 0DZ

An Hachette UK Company
www.hachette.co.uk

www.orbitbooks.net

For Peter Rubie, agent, mentor, friend from the beginning.
Thank you.

I t was a cruel day to leave the world.

The sun shone with all the gaiety and promise of early summer. The new green leaves glistened with it, and the apple and pear blossoms, just past their prime, drifted in the warm air like white butterflies, powdering the orchard floor with their bruised petals.

Bridget paced in her cell, angry and getting angrier. It wasn't fair. It wasn't right. Those girls, those accusers, knew nothing of what it was like to grow old, to bear children and see them abandon you, to bury husbands you could not keep alive no matter how many potions you brewed or charms you concocted. Those girls—Abigail, Mercy, Elizabeth, Ann, and Mary—they were still young and fresh. They suffered no drooping of private flesh from having borne babies. No one mocked them for preferring a red bodice over a dull black one, or for enjoying a laugh with a traveler, or for keeping a pet goat to fuss over.

And the traitorous John Hathorne! He had visited her often and often after Thomas died. John liked the cider she made from her apples, and he liked even more the softness of her bed and the fragrance of her dark hair. Then, when her hair had gone gray and her once-sweet flesh had withered, he turned judge. He forgot those hours in the warm, secret darkness, forgot the special charm she'd made for him so his wife wouldn't know, forgot the words of passion he had whispered in her ear. He turned judge, and he allowed those silly girls, hysterical chits no better than they should be, to accuse her of all manner of evil doings.

She was innocent of the things they accused her of doing. She had not entered Herrick's bedchamber in spirit form and seduced him, though she knew he wanted her, even now. She had not laid curses upon her neighbors, only scolded them for stealing her apples. She had made a poppet or two, but they had done no real harm. She had never consorted with the devil.

She was, as she had told them, clear of offenses, but they would not hearken. They had taken the word of five girls and many more men, most of whom had tried for her favors at one time or another. They had judged her a witch and sentenced her to a dark death on this bright day.

Even now the cart waited outside her cell to take her to the gallows. She had listened, these two days past, to the sawing and hammering and the jests of the carpenters as they built her instrument of death. She had trembled in the darkness, then buried her terror under waves of fury at the unjustness of her fate.

The church bell clanged from the center of Salem Village. It was time. The clump of men's boots pounded across the cobblestones, coming toward her. Their voices rang through the sweet summer air, the voices of men taking pleasure in her punishment, of men who cared nothing for her now that she was old and alone. There was no one to speak for her. No one to defend her. She was lost.

John Hathorne appeared in the doorway, his weedy clothes dull and rusty in the summer sun, his hair sticking out like old gray straw from beneath his hat. He was stooped now, as aged as she was, but his voice still rang with thunder. "Bridget Byshop, your time has come!"

Her knees trembled, and she sagged against the wall, overwhelmed in the moment by terror. She pulled at her hair to regain control, to reignite her fury.

Her daughters were her only hope. Mary was a gentle sort of girl, loath to harm even the smallest creature. Christian was different in her inclinations, as angry as Bridget herself. Neither could save their mother now, but they would be her legacy, both of them. Freed of this tired flesh, inspired by her fury, she would watch over her descendants and see that each received inspiration in her turn. She would leave them the *maleficia*.

She might not be a witch—indeed, she was not sure precisely what a witch was—but she was not nothing. She was only a woman, but she was a woman with abilities. Woe to the ignorant men who thought they could silence her with a noose! They would learn that her power, whatever its source, was stronger than their cruelty. That would be her revenge.

When the door of her cell opened, Bridget Byshop stood tall, straightened her frail shoulders, and walked out to accept her fate.

Witch should be a beautiful word, signifying wisdom and knowledge and discipline, but it isn't used that way. It's been made an insult, implying evil, causing fear. The word has been perverted.

—*Harriet Bishop, 1890*

1

Harriet

1890

Harriet preferred foraging in Central Park just after sunrise, before the cyclists and equestrians poured into the Mall, and while noisy young families were still breakfasting at home. On the nights before her excursions, she slept with her curtains open so the first light of dawn could tease her awake, and she could be out in the fields before anyone else.

On a cold, clear morning in May she woke as soon as the light began to rise. She dressed in sturdy boots, a much-worn skirt, and a man's heavy jacket she had bought from a secondhand store in the Bowery. She took up her basket and slipped quietly out of the apartment so as not to wake her housekeeper. Grace worked hard, and she needed her sleep.

There were no other residents about as Harriet made her way down the corner stairs and out through the central courtyard of the Dakota. In front of the entrance arch she skirted the milk delivery van, its aging horse blinking sleepily beneath its harness. The milkman lifted a hand to Harriet in greeting. The ice cart rattled by as she crossed the road to the Women's Gate, and the driver, teeth clenched around a pipe, tipped his cap to her. She smiled at him, relishing the communal feeling of their fraternity of early risers.

The first rays of the sun charmed curls of mist from the grass of Sheep Meadow, fairy clouds that sparkled silver against the green backdrop of the pasture. Harriet slowed her steps to take in the sight, savoring the slant of spring light and the emerald glow of new leaves before she crossed the meadow into the chilly shadows of the woods.

Here was near darkness that made her draw the collar of her jacket higher around her throat. Thick boughs of white oak shaded the ground, sheltering riches of sage, red clover, sometimes mushrooms. Harriet breathed in the scents of the fecund earth as she crouched beside a patch of nettles to begin her morning's work.

It was a good day for her labors. She found a lovely bit of mugwort beside the nettles, and deeper in the woods she spotted burdock, which could be elusive. There was amaranth, too, the herb the shepherds called pigweed. She took care to harvest just what she could use and left the rest to propagate.

When she emerged from the shade of the trees into the brightness of the midmorning sun, she discovered dandelions growing among the Paris daisies, more than she had expected in mid-May. Their greens would make a nice salad. As she picked handfuls to toss into her basket, she noticed with a grimace how stained her fingers were.

She could have worn gloves, but she liked to feel the texture of growing things and sense the richness of the soil that nurtured them. She had inherited her grandmother's long, slender fingers, adept at threading the herb she wanted out of the tangle of vegetation protecting it. It gave her pleasure to select a stem of leaves, pinch it between her fingernails, and wriggle it free. If she wanted the root itself, as with burdock, she dusted the soil from it and replanted any part she didn't need. The process often gave her dirty fingers and grimy nails.

She breathed a rueful sigh. Grace was going to scold.

A herd of sheep had spread through the meadow to crop grass in the sunshine. Their shepherd, leaning on a stick as he watched his flock, doffed his cap as Harriet walked through the pasture. "Good mornin' to you, Miss Bishop," he called. "Bit nippy out today, ain't it?"

"Good morning, Tom. Yes, it does feel chilly now, but it will soon warm."

"That it will," he said. The sun was at her back, and he squinted against the light to see her. "My missus is grateful for that stuff you made. She wanted me to say."

"Is she feeling better, then?" Tom's wife had received a simple tincture, one that needed no magic to strengthen it.

"Right as rain, Miss Bishop. Right as rain. You did her a wonder."

The testimonial brightened an already fine day. It was hardly the first time Harriet had received such praise in her practice, but each instance lifted her spirit. Each moment diminished, ever so slightly, the burden of guilt she carried always.

With her basket brimful of her harvest, she set off across the pasture, pulling off her dilapidated straw hat to feel the balm of sunshine on her hair and her cheeks. At her age a few new freckles wouldn't matter. In any case, who was there to complain? Well, Grace, of course, but no one else.

Alexander had been fond of the faint freckles that dusted her nose and darkened in the sunshine. She remembered the feel of his hand cupping her cheek and the glow in his eyes as he teased her about them.

She sighed again, sadly this time. Alexander had been gone twenty-five years, but the passing of the decades had not diminished her grief. There was nothing like the pain of loss to teach a person that time was an illusion.

She put her hat on again as she reached the far edge of the meadow. The sheep had wandered on, Tom trailing behind them. Voices carried now across the morning air, the cries of children riding the carousel, the remonstrations of their nurses, the calls of the vendors selling ices and twisted papers of taffy. Harriet pressed on toward the drive.

Just as she reached it, a rider approached at a steady trot, a young lady mounted on a tall black horse. Harriet stopped. Her basket grew heavy on her arm, but she stood still to watch the striking pair pass by her.

The girl rode astride, which must cause comment, as would the divided skirt that made it possible. Strands of dark hair escaped from her straw hat and trailed over her shoulders. Her gloved hands rested low and easy on the reins, and she kept her chin tucked, her back straight as a spear. When she glanced up, Harriet caught a glimpse of light-blue eyes and thick dark lashes. She sat in the saddle as if she had been born to it, and Harriet felt a swell of pride.

The girl was Annis Allington, granddaughter of Harriet's sister. She didn't know it, but she and Harriet were the only ones left of their branch of the Bishop family.

She noticed Harriet standing beside the drive and acknowledged her with a courteous nod. Harriet nodded back, as one stranger does to another.

Annis Allington had no idea who Harriet was, of course. Her stepmother had seen to that.

Harriet passed over the dry moat and through the entrance of the Dakota with barely a glance at the building's facade. She preferred not to meet the glare of its gargoyles, and she found its wrought iron balustrades excessively baroque. She had moved there with Grace when it first opened, attracted by the open fields and farms that surrounded it, delighted by its nearness to her beloved park. She loathed the mansions being thrown up by New York's nouveau riche, ostentatious palaces that squatted along Fifth Avenue like the overdressed, overfed matrons who inhabited them.

Not that the Dakota wasn't ostentatious. It was designed to be. Still, Harriet loved the bright, airy rooms with their high ceilings and tall windows. She had space for her herbarium, and Grace had her own bedroom in the apartment, instead of on the cramped upper floor with the other staff. Grace had been thrilled to discover that the entire building was electrified, its own generator providing power for lights and heating and cooking. The Dakota was ideal for the two of them, and they owed their life there to Alexander's legacy.

As Harriet passed by the courtyard fountain and on toward the stairs, the fragrance of herbs from her basket made her raise it closer to her face to take an appreciative breath.

At just that moment, Lucille Corning, whose apartment was on Harriet's floor, appeared at the top of the staircase. She was dressed for shopping, a short cape over a full-sleeved shirtwaist. Her day skirt, fashionably long at the back, trailed behind her as she descended.

Harriet lowered her basket and stepped aside to make room, murmuring, "Good morning, Mrs. Corning."

Without pausing, Mrs. Corning picked up the train of her skirt with her hand and pointedly pulled it aside. She drew a long, noisy sniff as she reached the last tread, and she swept on into the courtyard without speaking a word.

It was the cut indirect. And it was not the first time.

Harriet watched the woman flutter away across the courtyard. A carriage was waiting for her, with a liveried driver who touched his cap as he helped her up the step. Her maid came scurrying down the stairs to clamber into the carriage while the driver stepped up onto the box.

Harriet chuckled and shook her head as she climbed the stairs to her floor. Mrs. Corning's disdain didn't matter, really. She had accepted long ago that she was meant for a lonely life.

She let herself into the apartment and set her basket down in the hall. Grace came bustling out of the kitchen, wiping her hands on her long apron. "Miss Harriet! Your skirt is wet to the knees!"

Harriet looked down at her bedraggled skirt and the bits of meadow grass that clung to its muddy hem. She pulled off her hat, dislodging the few pins she had stuck in her hair, and found that it, too, was littered with pine needles and the odd wet leaf. She tried to push her hair back into place with one hand, but to no effect.

She gave it up and bent to begin untying her boots. "Do you know, Grace, I saw Mrs. Corning going into the courtyard. She wouldn't speak to me, but she gave the most impressive sniff I've ever heard. I doubt if Queen Victoria could have outdone it."

Grace, whose own red hair was pinned into a tight knot at the back of her skull, tossed her head. "Mrs. Corning! Never you mind her, Miss Harriet. That woman is no better than she should be, I can tell you." She came to help Harriet out of her heavy jacket. "Her Patsy, the one that does for her three times a week, tells me all kinds of men go through that place when Mr. Corning ain't there. Their cook lives in, and she says the same. And the parties she gives! Why, you wouldn't believe the caviar and ices and champagne and…"

Grace rattled on with enthusiasm. Harriet nodded now and then, her usual way of dealing with Grace's chatter. Free of her jacket and having wriggled her wet boots off her feet, she started down the hall to her bedroom.

Grace pattered behind her. "Now, Miss Harriet, you get out of that wet skirt and into something dry and warm. It's only May, you know, not summer yet. We don't want you catching cold or something."

Harriet pursed her lips to prevent a smile of amusement. She had never, not once in their long relationship, caught a cold. Grace knew that.

She did as she was told just the same. As Grace went off with the wet skirt draped over her arm, Harriet settled into a comfortable shirtwaist and light woolen skirt. She tied an apron over it, a long one with deep pockets for the scissors and string she used for tying up swatches of herbs. Only then did she go to the mirror to try to do something about her disordered hair.

As she was trying to drag a brush through it, Grace tapped on her door and came in. "Your breakfast is almost ready," she said. "Oh, Miss Harriet, look at that hair! Give me the brush, now. Let me do it."

Harriet surrendered the hairbrush and settled onto the dressing table stool so Grace, a good head shorter than she, could reach. As Grace worked, Harriet mused, "I suppose Mrs. Corning has a point, Grace. I did look a sight. But then, I so often do. You would think she'd be used to it."

"I expect she wishes she could look like you do," Grace said. "She must have a devil of a time fitting herself into that corset, and here's you not even needing one."

"I have a corset," Harriet said, amused.

"Do you, now?" Grace eyed her in the mirror. "You don't never wear it, as far as I know. But never mind. Here's your hair all better."

"I'm going gray," Harriet observed.

"Perfectly natural. That Mrs. Corning gets her color out of a bottle, believe you me, Miss Harriet. A little bird told me all about it. Besides, this nice touch of silver in your hair looks dignified, if you ask me."

"You can say that, with not a single gray hair on your head." Harriet gave Grace an affectionate glance in the mirror. Grace, as she well knew, was vain about her hair.

Grace's naturally ruddy cheeks grew redder. "But you, Miss Harriet, don't suffer from this flock of freckles!"

"No," Harriet admitted. "It's true, my flock is considerably smaller, despite my being so careless about my hat."

"Yes, and you should do better," Grace said. She began inserting pins into the loose chignon she had created on Harriet's head. "You still have a lovely complexion, Miss Harriet, despite you not being so young anymore."

Harriet chuckled over this bluntness. "Yes, I think I bid youth farewell some time ago, Grace. Fifty! Hard to believe. But thanks for repairing my hair. It looks quite respectable now."

"Come on, then," Grace said, leading the way out of the bedroom. "I've got your coffee made, and I have eggs and ham, a good breakfast, since you've been out in the cold with your herbs and things. Do you want marmalade? I think there's some in the pantry. Or you could have honey, since I bought some down on Mulberry Street the other day. It looks good, and I think..."

Harriet let the flow of talk run over and around her, as comforting as a warm bath. And why, she wondered, as she sat down with her coffee, should she need comfort? A silly woman like Lucille Corning didn't have the power to hurt her. She didn't care about any of the things that sort of woman put store in, not clothes, or society, or a fancy carriage to take her shopping, or champagne parties. She had never cared about such things, but still—except for Grace, she had no real friends.

There was the woman who ran the herb shop down on Elizabeth Street. The proprietress was an aging Italian woman, Signora Carcano, a *strega* in her own language. She was a cranky old thing, and her shop smelled strongly of garlic and onions, but she and Harriet held each other in mutual respect. Harriet had never asked about the woman's practice. It was better not to know. They had much in common, and they respected each other, but they were friendly without being actual friends.

There were her patients, of course, but it would be unprofessional to think of them as friends.

She couldn't help wishing that once in a while someone would ask her to tea or to a quiet supper party. She lived in a fashionable building, paid her lease like anyone else, but she didn't fit in. She was, as she had been since girlhood, an outsider. All the Bishops on her side were, she supposed. Why should she be any different?

She sighed, sipped her coffee, and told herself to push the

whole nonsense out of her mind. Deliberately she recalled the pleasure of seeing her great-niece riding past on her beautiful horse. It had been lovely to see her. She needed to find a way to meet her. She could not trust Frances when it came time for Annis's instruction.

The time for that was coming very soon. She knew it.

2

Frances

Frances had argued with her stepdaughter that morning, and she regretted it. She had lost her temper again, but that was no excuse. Such disputes could undermine her plans. She must take more care in managing the girl.

She had no doubt Annis would come in for luncheon in her spattered riding habit, her hair a-tumble and her nails dark with stable dirt, as usual, but she would refrain from criticizing. Perhaps the whole thing could be forgotten.

George was at the factory, as he was most days, so the two of them would be alone in the dining room. She should ask Annis about her morning's ride and inquire about the health of Black Satin. She could pretend an interest, at least for now. Before long horse and girl would be separated, and that was for the best. Annis's obsession with the stallion was unnatural.

Frances had objected to the foal when it arrived, and Annis had made clear she meant to keep it for herself. Such a horse was completely unsuitable for a young girl, of course. Girls should ride mares, or geldings, or quiet ponies of an appropriate size.

Her complaints had gone unheard. Annis had won that argument, as she won so many others, by simply doing what she wanted. That was a luxury Frances had never enjoyed when she was that age. She had grown up with nothing, while Annis had everything any girl could want. Annis never waited for permission when she wanted something. In the case of Black Satin, the horse was in the stables almost before George was aware it was coming.

Annis was intelligent and spirited, which could be fine qualities if properly directed. It was unfortunate she wasn't prettier, but Frances thought she could work around that. It was for the girl's own good, after all. There was no future in being a gangly, horse-mad spinster.

When she and George had wed, she hadn't anticipated being in charge of a spoiled little girl, but her new husband had made it clear that Annis was now Frances's responsibility. He took no interest in the details. Such matters merely distracted him from his real concern, the Allington Iron Stove Company, and Frances had learned to accept that.

George had been mad about her in the beginning, but the feeling hadn't lasted long. She was forced to accept that, too. Fortunately, though she liked him well enough, she had not been so weak as to fall in love. She had not repeated her mother's mistake.

It would all have been easier if her stepdaughter took any interest in clothes or parties, but Annis cared for nothing but her horses. She more or less lived in her riding clothes and often came into the house covered in horsehair and other kinds of muck Frances didn't want to know about.

Well. She would put an end to all that soon enough. It was the kindest thing, in any case. Annis was nearly eighteen, old enough to understand that it was a man's world. A woman had to hide her strength beneath softness. She had to know her place.

Frances rang for her maid, and when Antoinette arrived, she said, "I'll want a walking dress. I'm going out."

"*Oui*, madame." Antoinette helped her out of her morning dress and carried it to the wardrobe while Frances sat at the dressing table in her corset and chemise, smoothing her hair. When Antoinette returned with a pink-and-cream ensemble, she shook her head. "Not that one. The gray wool."

"But, madame, there is sun today," Antoinette said.

"I can see that for myself, Antoinette. The gray, please."

Antoinette gave a Gallic sniff and went back to the wardrobe. Really, Frances thought, though having a French maid looked well in the eyes of society, she wished Antoinette were easier to get along with.

Antoinette had been trained by a titled Englishwoman living in Paris. That detail pleased Frances, but she couldn't shake the feeling that her maid's black-eyed gaze saw right through her mistress's facade of beautiful clothes and fine jewelry to the Brooklyn girl beneath. Antoinette had a trick of gazing at her with an unblinking stare, her brows lifted in disapproval. It made Frances's skin crawl.

Occasionally, uncomfortably, she thought Annis did the same, looking at her as if her exterior were no more than a wall of glass that couldn't hide what she had once been. Annis had no idea where Frances had come from or how poor she had been. Frances had every intention she should never find out.

She tried not to think about those things as Antoinette buttoned and draped and fastened the various parts of her ensemble. As Antoinette laid out her hat and gloves and cape, she asked, "*Moi*, I come with you?"

"No," Frances said. "Not today. That will be all."

It was a relief when she was gone. Frances smoothed her shirt-waist, taking consolation in her appearance. Her Royal Worcester corset made the most of her modest bosom and tiny waist. Her hair was shiny and soft, shaped into a perfect Newport knot. She usually arranged it herself, placing the knot in the most advantageous spot for her small features.

Annis's hair was another matter. She wished she could get Velma to do something about it. It was difficult, of course, thick and unruly, but it so often straggled every which way. It might be easier, in truth, to hire a new maid for her stepdaughter than to persuade her old one to change. Velma was as slow as she was plain, but maids were hard to find.

Annis's appearance would be a challenge in any case. A new maid would probably fare no better. There was only so much that could be done with a tall, angular figure like hers, and there was nothing to be done about such a long nose, however straight and fine. The freckles could have been avoided, of course. Only her eyes were good, that unusual pale blue she shared with her father.

Well. There were some men who liked tall women. Especially tall women with money.

Frances gave her hair a final pat and turned from the mirror. As she started down the staircase, she noted with satisfaction the gleam of the oak banister, the sparkle of the chandelier in the foyer, the elegant curve of the stairs. Her life was far from perfect, but who could have imagined that a girl from a dingy Brooklyn apartment would now live in a mansion on Riverside Drive?

Still, it wasn't Fifth Avenue. She was not one of the Four Hundred. There would be no invitations awaiting her on the breakfront engraved with the Astor crest or the Vanderbilt address. Her name would not appear in the society pages of that day's *Times*.

Yet.

She paused on the landing to smooth away the scowl she could feel gathering on her brow. She must be patient. Soon enough she would achieve her ultimate goal. She had already proved she could do whatever was necessary, and she would not balk at going all the way.

She swept on down the stairs, her head high and a cool smile on her lips.

The best thing about the Riverside estate was its size. Frances could stroll out through the front of the house and around to the side, where a sun-spangled path led through the manicured gardens and into the tangle of woods beyond. The early afternoon was warm enough to make Frances shrug out of her cape once she was out of sight of the house. The path was half-overgrown with sword ferns and blackberry vines, but she would never order the gardeners to clear it. The path and the cabin it led to were her secret.

The cabin was a near ruin, forgotten at the farthest boundary of the property. Once she had unlocked the door with its old-fashioned iron key, she had to wriggle it open, scraping it across the dirt floor. Its leather hinges had dried to the point of being nearly immovable, but she liked it that way.

She also liked the unglazed window, the cobwebbed ceiling, and the splintered table abandoned by some long-ago occupant. All of these things, so different from her rooms in Allington House, meant no one cared about this crumbling little structure, and no one disturbed her when she was about her business.

She wiped the veil of dust from the table, then opened her shopping bag to lift out the tools of her craft.

She laid a small, discolored compact on the table. It no longer held face powder, but her own carefully collected fingernail shavings. Next to it she set a tiny corked bottle holding drops of her blood suspended in a tot of port wine. She had pierced her finger with a sewing needle and squeezed it over the bottle, thrilling to the sight of her own blood, shining red with her personal power, dripping into the green glass.

She took out a packet of dried mandrake root purchased from the *strega* on Elizabeth Street. The crone had scowled at her when she asked for it and the other things she needed. She had shaken her finger in warning, but Frances had told her to keep her mouth shut about it, or she would see that her rich husband closed the shop down.

She shouldn't have crossed the old *strega*. That was dangerous, and she could lose her source of materials. She knew better than to do it, but she had lost her temper, just as she had with Annis that morning. When she got angry, when the fury simmering beneath her polished facade boiled over, she lost control. That was always a mistake. She must be more careful.

She pulled three long sulfur matches out of her bag and laid them next to the mandrake. She lifted dried leaves of mistletoe from a box, and the fragile stems of barrenwort. Last, taking care so as not to break it, she lifted out the manikin.

It was the sort of creation her ancestresses had called a poppet, and it was the finest she had ever made. She had found a large wooden bead with the lacquer worn off and used her fountain pen to paint two blue eyes on it. She had brushed on a dab of beetroot juice for the mouth. The body was sculpted of fine wax, as lifelike as she could make it, with small mounds for breasts, molded legs, a distinct vee where the legs met the body. She would need that.

She had fashioned the dress from a white cotton handkerchief, its lace edging forming a ruffle at the bottom. She had cinched the middle with a narrow ribbon and tied it in the back.

It was the manikin's hair that made it perfect. On a day when Annis was out riding and her maid was in the kitchen having a gossip with the staff, Frances had slipped into Annis's room. Her hairbrush lay on a silver tray on her dressing table, a handful of dark, glossy hairs still tangled in the bristles. Frances unwound them, wrapping the long strands around her fingers, and was back in her own room in less than three minutes. She had used her embroidery scissors to snip the strands of hair to the right lengths, and affixed them to the manikin's head with tiny drops of mucilage.

She propped the manikin in the midst of her other ritual objects and stood back to admire the effect. The poppet looked as if it were curtsying, the handkerchief skirt pooling around its feet, the bits of Annis's hair fluffed around its wooden-bead head. No one, Frances thought, could mistake this manikin for anyone but Annis Allington. It was superb.

Harriet would hate it.

3

Annis

"Robbie," Annis called into the open door of the stable. "Would you take a look at Bits's left forefoot? He's favoring it."

The stableman emerged from the tack room and crossed the aisle. Annis pushed off her hat and let it fall into the sawdust as she bent to lift the horse's hoof and prop it on her thigh. She couldn't see anything wrong. The shoe was new, since the farrier had been there the week before. She had cleaned all four hooves before setting out for her ride, but she picked at the frog and sole just the same, searching for a pebble that might have caused Bits to limp.

Robbie scowled above her head. "No job for a young lady," he said. "Dress all dirty, and that big horse like to crush your little foot."

Annis laughed. "My foot isn't so little! And Bits would never step on me. Don't worry. We know what we're doing."

She preferred doing everything herself, rubdowns, brushing, cleaning stalls, soaping her saddle. She oversaw Bits's feed, and she nursed his ailments, though she always sought Robbie's advice. She supervised his breeding, too, though it troubled Robbie even more for her to stand by, the lead in her hand, as Bits serviced a mare.

"Not seemly," he inevitably muttered, a phrase she had been hearing from him for years. "Lose my job if your papa finds out. It ain't easy for an Irishman to find work, see?"

Annis didn't want Robbie to lose his job. He was a wonderful horseman and a wizard with tack. Except for the breeding issue, he respected her capability, and he mostly stayed out of her way when she wanted him to.

"Don't worry, Robbie," she had said after the last breeding. It had gone well, with an experienced mare and Bits his usual gentlemanly and efficient self. It was a pairing Annis was happy about. The mare had a good balanced conformation and a record of throwing healthy foals. "Papa doesn't need to know," she had assured Robbie that day. "But *I* need to know everything's going well, as it just did."

"Not seemly," Robbie lamented. "A young lady, a breeding stallion—not seemly at all."

Despite his reservations, Robbie had always been happy to assist with her studies of bloodlines. She had a clear vision of the sort of mare she would allow to conceive one of Bits's foals, and she turned down as many requests for breeding as she accepted.

"You're a hardheaded lass," Robbie once said, when she rejected a Thoroughbred filly.

"A great compliment," she said, grinning.

He shook his head. "Pretty sure your papa would point out that a stud fee is good money. Lots of folks want a Black Satin foal."

"I know Papa loves money, Robbie, but this is about Bits's reputation. That filly's awfully highly strung. You saw her, rearing and stamping over nothing."

"That's as may be," he had answered. "But if the filly's owner complains to Mr. Allington, it'll be me pays the price."

"Don't worry, Robbie. I can handle Papa." She had patted his arm, the only affectionate gesture he would allow. He invariably pulled away, aghast, if she tried to hug him. He had done that even when she was small. He didn't say that such a display wasn't seemly, but she understood it just the same.

As to her breeding program, she was sure her father didn't notice what she did or didn't do. He never asked her about the horses. He hadn't ridden in years, but Annis made certain Chessie got his exercise and that all the horses were properly fed, shod, and groomed. The stables were her domain. Frances took no interest, except for wanting the carriage horse ready when she needed him. This arrangement suited Annis perfectly.

She had felt from the beginning that horses were easier to understand than people. They made their wishes clear. They bestowed their affection without conditions. They didn't love you for a time, then stop loving you for no apparent reason.

Annis knew Bits loved her. She sometimes thought the two of them must be connected by an invisible ribbon of emotion, one that drew her to the stables every day, to be in his presence, to savor the warmth of his big body, to breathe in the peppery scent of his hide, to bask in the trust shining in his eyes. Mounted on his back, she became one with his power and speed and beauty. No one scolded her while she was seated high in the saddle. No one nagged about her clothes or her hair or her manners. Riding Bits set her free.

She released Bits's hoof, and he put it down gingerly. She patted his shoulder in sympathy. Robbie said, "Walk him a bit, and I'll watch."

Annis led Bits down the aisle of the stables and into the paddock for a turn inside the fence. When they stopped, she stood stroking his neck. "What do you think, Robbie?"

"Not sure yet. Let me have a look."

Annis stood back, the lead rope slack in her hand, as Robbie lifted Bits's forefoot and inspected it. When he released the hoof, he ran his hand from the horse's shoulder to his knee, on down the cannon to the pastern. "Ah," he said. "Feel this, Miss Annis. See how warm it is?"

She reached past him to touch the back of the horse's leg with her fingers. "Oh, it is," she said. "I didn't notice that."

"Aye. It ain't that bad. Bit o' tendinitis, I'm guessing. Just need to wrap it and rest him for a few days. No canter or gallop."

"Should we ask the farrier to come? Or the veterinarian?"

"Only if it don't get better."

Annis straightened, and Bits dropped his head to bump his chin against her shoulder, asking for his treat. She dug a chunk of apple from her pocket and fed it to him. "It's going to be all right, Bitsy," she told him as he munched. "Robbie says it will be all right."

"A poultice should do it," Robbie said. He took off his flat cap to scratch at the gray bristle of his hair. "You can make that, lass, right?"

"Yes. I'll do it now." She handed off Bits's lead. "Will you put him in his stall? I'll be back in fifteen minutes."

Robbie touched the brim of his cap, then spoke a soothing word to Black Satin as he led him away. Annis picked up her hat from the ground and slapped it against her thigh to shake off the sawdust before she went indoors.

She let herself into the house by the door nearest the kitchen and hurried down the short hall to the pantry.

Robbie was her favorite servant outside the house. Indoors, Mrs. King, the cook, held that honor. She had been with the Allingtons since before Annis was born, and when Annis's mother died of a fever when Annis was not yet two, Mrs. King stepped in, though she was a servant. She always had a handkerchief for a little girl's tears or a plate of cookies to quiet her when she was anxious. She saw to it that Annis had clothes that fit, and she ordered new shoes as Annis outgrew the old ones. She listened to Annis's tales of triumphs and disappointments at school and helped her with her homework on the rare occasions that she needed it.

Mrs. King kept Annis as close as she could on the day of her father's remarriage, despite being needed in the kitchen and the dining room. That had been a hard day. Papa acted strangely, laughing at odd times, gazing at his new bride in a way that confused and embarrassed his little daughter. The people who came for the wedding breakfast cast such pitying glances at seven-year-old Annis that she thought something terrible must be happening.

But now she was seventeen. She had graduated from Brearley with good marks. She no longer wept into Mrs. King's handkerchief, and she didn't need cookies for comfort. What she needed from Mrs. King was her own corner of the pantry to make remedies for her horses, and Mrs. King provided it with good humor.

Annis wished she knew more about how to heal injuries and wounds. Her poultices and salves helped, but they hardly worked miracles. She would make the poultice for Bits with witch hazel and comfrey, but it was going to take time for him to heal. In the meantime she would content herself with riding Chessie or her old pony. Chessie was all right, but Sally was dull, with a slow, swinging trot and no canter to speak of. What Annis liked best was to gallop Bits around Central Park under the scandalized glances of passersby.

She had been startled that morning to see the dark-haired woman nodding politely to her as if there were nothing shocking in a young woman riding astride in Central Park.

Mrs. King came pattering toward the pantry while Annis was gathering her ingredients. She was quick and slight, not like any of the other cooks Annis had met, who bore the marks of their profession in full bosoms and generous hips. Mrs. King was no older than Frances herself, with a cloud of brown hair and bright brown eyes. When she was small, Annis had sometimes pretended to herself that Mrs. King was her mother.

"Miss Annis?" the cook said, peering around the corner. "Did you know Mrs. Frances is looking for you?"

Annis paused in the act of pouring dried witch hazel leaves into a clean mortar. "Oh no. Do you have to tell her? I need to make this poultice. Bits strained a tendon."

Mrs. King clicked her tongue. "Dear, dear. Poor Bitsy. You'll set him right, no doubt."

"I think so. Could you put the kettle on? I'll need hot water."

"I will, but if Frances comes in, don't tell her I saw you."

Annis said, "I would never do that!"

"I know, dear, I know. Just making sure." Off she went again, and as Annis ground the witch hazel leaves with her pestle and added comfrey and a bit of bay laurel, she heard the clatter of the kettle against the stove.

An Allington stove, of course. The Allington Iron Stove Company was the reason the Allingtons lived in this great stone house on Riverside Drive, with its gables and cornices and mansard roof dwarfing the more modest houses nearby. Annis was well aware how lucky she was to be able to afford her own horses, a private stable, even a suite of rooms all to herself. She was grateful for those things, because they set her free to pursue her ambition.

Her friends at Brearley had all planned grand marriages, with their pictures in the papers and their names in the society pages. They often invited Annis to their tea parties and shopping excursions, but Annis considered those things, and the constant flow of gossip that accompanied them, a waste of her time. She had gradually drifted away from her school chums. She focused all her energy on her ambition, which was to create a bloodline of fine horses. The line would bear Black Satin's name and bring honor to her beloved stallion. It was going to be respected everywhere.

Bits himself was a Thoroughbred, but neither as high-strung as other horses of his breed nor encumbered by the common fault of a ewe-neck. Annis constantly searched for mares and fillies with dispositions and conformation equal to his, Thoroughbreds or Arabians or one of the other light breeds. She had heard that the Spanish horses, sometimes called Andalusians, were calm and intelligent, but they were impossible to find. She didn't know anyone who owned one, and she had no one to escort her to the horse markets downtown. It was one thing Robbie refused to do, and she didn't dare ask her father.

She hurried the preparations for her poultice, wary of Frances coming in search of her. She thought it would be wise to avoid her stepmother until the heat of their argument had cooled.

Frances, clearly in a bad mood, had stopped Annis as she was on her way out to the stables and demanded she change her clothes. "How are we going to become part of the Four Hundred if you dash around looking like a hoyden?" she snapped.

Annis's own temper had flared at her being delayed. She pulled on her gloves as she answered. "Frances, that will never happen. The Allingtons are new money. We're shoddies. Arrivistes." She ignored Frances's growing frown, her mind already on her morning ride. "Mrs. Astor would turn a somersault in the park before she would invite us to one of her ridiculous balls, and even if she did invite us, I wouldn't go. I doubt Papa would, either."

Frances's cheeks turned pink. "Well! I will never agree with you about that, young lady. I don't know how you can be so selfish!"

"Selfish? Why is that selfish?"

"Because you think of nothing but your horses. You never consider how your behavior affects this family. I insist you stop parading through the park in that vulgar old riding habit, and for pity's sake, use a proper sidesaddle! I know you have one!"

"No, thank you. Sidesaddles are silly. Dangerous." A sidesaddle hung in the tack room, gathering dust, but Annis had never touched the monstrous thing, and she never would. As she turned toward the staircase, she had tossed a final remark over her shoulder. "Actually, I'm thinking of wearing trousers to ride."

"You will not!" Frances had stamped a foot, and Annis had laughed, which was not tactful. She had dashed down the stairs, leaving her stepmother fuming on the landing.

Frances had called, "I'll speak to George about this, young lady!"

It was true that Annis would have loved to wear trousers, and had even thought of talking Robbie into giving her one of his old pairs, but she didn't do it. Her divided skirt was as far as she dared go. She had meant the remark about trousers as a joke, but she should have held her tongue. Frances was not known for her sense of humor. She was better known for her hot temper.

Papa took no more interest than she did in Frances's longing to climb higher in New York society. He had no inclination to exchange his Riverside Drive mansion for a Fifth Avenue palace, and he would loathe summering in Newport as the members of the Four Hundred did. He might, however, object to such a public offense as his daughter riding astride like a man. So far he had not noticed, but if Frances pointed it out, he might put his foot down. Annis hardly knew her father anymore. It was hard to predict how he might react.

She worried over that as she finished the mixture for her poultice, then transferred her worry to the poultice itself. She had the feeling something was missing from it, but she didn't know what. It was frustrating to know so little. What there was of her herbal knowledge came from one slender pamphlet she had found in the library of Allington House.

Annis guessed the pamphlet had belonged to her mother. Mrs. King hadn't recognized it. Frances said she thought it was an odd thing for the first Mrs. Allington to have saved. Annis asked her father when she first discovered it, but he said only, "Throw it away. Looks like some kind of advertising."

It wasn't advertising. It was a marvelous little book, with pen-and-ink illustrations of herbs that grew wild in New York. There were descriptions of their uses and instructions for preparing various remedies.

Annis had nearly worn the pamphlet out reading and rereading it. She imagined her mother holding the little book, running her finger down the pages. The pamphlet convinced Annis she had inherited her passion for herbalism from her mother, though the little booklet was her only evidence.

Mrs. King begged Annis to take care using the remedies. Annis wouldn't use anything on her horses she hadn't first tried on herself, but she didn't want to upset Mrs. King, so she attempted them in secret. Sometimes they burned. Often they itched or stung, but the poultice for pain had felt marvelous when she applied it to her own arm. She was making that now.

She stirred drops of hot water into her mixture until she had a thick slurry, then spread the warm paste on a piece of old flannel. She folded it, wrapped it in a towel, and rushed back to the stable to apply it before it cooled.

Robbie helped her wrap it around Bits's foreleg and secure it with a strip of wool. "There you are, laddie," he said to the horse, patting his shoulder. "Miss Annis will let you rest now."

"I will, of course," Annis said. "How long do you think, Robbie?"

"Couple days, at least. Tomorrow you can ride one of the others."

"I guess I could take Sally out. She needs the exercise."

"That she does. Growing a belly, that one."

Annis kissed Bits's nose, fished in her pocket for another slice of apple, and gave it to him. It had gone brown, and it was fuzzy with lint, but Bits wasn't particular. She loved the feel of his soft, thick lips against her palm. She whispered, "I'll be back later. Don't you rub off that poultice, now, you."

She moved along the aisle to Sally's stall, scrounging in her pocket for another bit of apple. She gave one to the carriage horse, too, a thickheaded creature called Andy. Andy took her offering with no particular show of gratitude, but she patted him anyway. In the opposite stall, Chessie, named for his rich chestnut color, extended his neck in expectation of his own treat. Robbie's stolid gelding stood drowsing next to Chessie. Robbie called him Tater, for his dull brown coat, and he was even older than Sally. Robbie was supposed to accompany Annis when she went riding in the park, but once she had started riding Bits, poor Tater, with his lumbering trot, couldn't keep up. Annis told Robbie he didn't need to chaperone her, that no one could bother her when she was riding Bits. He had given in, lamenting as always that he would lose his job.

Bits was four now, and Annis had been riding him since he turned two. Under Robbie's guidance she had trained him in the classical fashion, the longe line first, with just a halter, then bits of tack and an empty saddle, and then, finally, Annis on his back. Robbie said he never saw a horse take so easily to a rider, but Annis wasn't surprised. Bits always understood what she wanted, from a slow walk to a trot, from a canter to a gallop. He was as eager as she for their more daring rides, the ones they made when no one could see them. He loved to run, and they both loved jumping. He sailed effortlessly over fallen trees, mane and tail rippling. He popped over rows of shrubs as easily as a leaping deer, making Annis feel as if she could fly. She definitely didn't want to take such jumps in a sidesaddle.

As she started toward the house, she reflected on her good fortune. She had her horses, and Robbie, and Mrs. King. Frances had been cross that morning, but maybe she had been right to accuse Annis of being selfish. It was true she thought of her horses more than she thought of anything else. Or anyone.

Whom did Frances have? Her husband spent no time with her. She didn't seem to have friends, not real ones. It could be that Frances, for all her airs and bad temper, was lonely. Impelled by a stab of compunction, Annis hurried her steps. She would explain to her stepmother that she had been joking about wearing trousers. She would clean up a bit before luncheon, perhaps get Velma to do something about her hair.

Frances would like that. Perhaps she would forget about complaining to Papa.

4

Frances

Frances didn't know how Harriet knew what she had done to George. Harriet did know, though. She often knew things she shouldn't. It was exactly like her to make an issue of it, to act superior, to pretend she had Frances's interests at heart.

Frances's mother had been a Bishop, like Harriet and her grandmother Beryl, but their familial connection was a distant one, traced over two centuries through the two lines of Bishops.

Harriet's upbringing had been as different from Frances's as could be. Harriet had lost her mother when she was five and had gone to live with her grandmother in a comfortable house in St. George. They employed a housekeeper and a cook, and a woman came in every day to clean. They had no idea what it was like to be poor.

Frances knew it all too well, and she bore the scars on her soul to prove it. Her mother had married badly, against her family's wishes, and her husband had abandoned her when Frances was an infant. She had worked as a laundress, or as a seamstress when she could get the work. She had barely kept a roof over her daughter's head, and there were times when they had no money left over for food. Frances had grown up in uncertainty and want. It was unfair for Harriet to criticize her desire for a better life.

Her wedding to George had been a quiet event, as befitted a second marriage, and that suited Frances well enough. Until her allowance began, she had no money for anything like a Worth wedding dress, such as one of the wealthy Manhattan brides would have worn. She had no trousseau to speak of, either. She had scraped together enough to order a traveling suit of blue silk with leg-of-mutton sleeves and a matching cape. For the ceremony she wore a modest gown of cream brocade with ecru lace on the sleeves and neckline. She decided it was best to go without jewelry until George put the heavy ruby-and-diamond ring on her finger. George's housekeeper arranged the wedding breakfast. The invitations were handwritten on the Allington engraved stationery.

After the wedding breakfast, Frances had gone up to her boudoir to change. Her brand-new maid, hired a week before the wedding, was pinning up her hair as she sat before the mirror.

Harriet came into the room without so much as a knock to announce herself. "I need a moment with Mrs. Allington," she said to Antoinette, and before Frances could stop her, the maid was out of the room.

"Wait!" Frances exclaimed, though it was already too late. Antoinette was gone.

People did that with Harriet. They obeyed every one of her orders, as if she were Queen Victoria herself. It was infuriating.

Frances's temper began to rise, her ready anger flaring. She wanted to jump up from her stool and stamp her foot, but her legs had gotten tangled in the lacy drapery of the dressing table. She felt small and weak, which made her even more furious.

She should be feeling triumphant! Even Harriet should respect what she had just accomplished, marrying a wealthy widower, becoming a cherished young bride despite her lack of dowry or family connections. Resentment drove her voice high, making her sound more like a complaining child than the new mistress of a Riverside Drive mansion. "Harriet, what—"

"You forced him, didn't you, Frances?"

Trapped by the swath of lace, Frances turned abruptly back to her mirror. She fussed with a strand of hair not yet pinned into place, endeavoring to hide her suddenly flaming cheeks.

Harriet had not bothered with a new ensemble for the occasion. Her visiting dress must be at least five years old, with flat sleeves and only a few jet buttons. It didn't surprise Frances, but it was a further annoyance. Harriet might be a forty-year-old spinster, but she could afford good clothes if she cared to bother. Her dead fiancé had left her enough for that and more. She could have worn an up-to-date gown for the wedding of a cousin, however distant. She was, after all, the bride's only family.

Frances scowled into her mirror. "I have no idea what you're talking about, Harriet," she said. She took one quick look upward and saw that the corners of Harriet's mouth were pinched with anger, drawing unattractive lines in her cheeks. The lines made her cousin look older than she really was, which gave Frances a brief feeling of superiority. She smoothed the strand of hair into place and adjusted a pin to hold it. She turned her head to assess the effect and was reassured by the smoothness of her cheeks, the unblemished line of her neck above the lace of her shirtwaist.

She preened a bit, twisting one of the expensive ruby earrings her groom had given her as a wedding present. "George is in love with me, Harriet. Anyone can see it. Why should you think I had to force him?"

"I don't know that you had to," Harriet answered with asperity. "I know that you did."

Frances dropped her hand to the dressing table, flexing the fingers to appreciate the sparkle of her wedding ring. "You can't know that, Harriet," she said. "You're just jealous."

"I'm not in the least jealous, but I'm worried about the welfare of my great-niece. She's lost her grandmother and her mother, and her father has rushed into marriage."

"Annis will be fine. I'll see to it."

"You know nothing of children."

"Neither do you!" Frances retorted, but her cheeks burned again.

"I do, actually, Frances. I often treat childhood ailments in my herbalism practice."

"Herbalism!" Frances spit. "You could do so much more."

"I could, and I do, when it's needed. I know the best uses for my ability, and I'm careful not to misuse it. You should do the same."

Frances finally freed her legs from the drapery of her dressing table and stood up. Her head came no higher than Harriet's shoulder, which she hated, so she moved away to the wardrobe, where her going-away cape waited, blue brocade with a white fur lining.

She lifted it down and held it in front of her as she turned back to Harriet. "I don't need you to tell me how to use my ability, Harriet."

"Grandmother Beryl warned you. I warned you. You should

have avoided the *maleficia*. It will always do more harm than good."

Frances tossed the cape onto the bed and returned to her dressing table. She would not give Harriet the satisfaction of an argument on this topic. It would not be the first between them in any case, and this was, after all, her wedding day. She should not have to defend herself.

She could have pointed out that her practice was every bit as ancient and powerful as Harriet's, but she would have been wasting her breath. Harriet would prate on about doing good and healing people, work that gave Frances no pleasure. Half the time, she knew perfectly well, Harriet didn't even use her ability. She just cooked up herbal concoctions and sold them, or, too often, gave them away.

Harriet was correct about George, though. Frances had forced him. Harriet might be maddening, but she was perceptive. She probably saw it in George's face. Others merely saw an older man in love with a young woman. Harriet no doubt took in the glassiness of his eyes, the urgency of his touch on his bride's arm, the hungriness of his hands when he encircled her waist.

But, Frances thought, Harriet was wrong about the *maleficia*. It had not harmed her. On the contrary, it had given her precisely what she wanted, and she had no intention of giving it up.

She settled herself onto the stool again, taking care to arrange her skirt around her ankles. "Harriet," she said, striving for a suitably commanding tone. This was her house now. Everyone in it must do what she wanted. "Call Antoinette back. I'm about to go on my wedding journey, and I have no time for this."

"I do wish you a happy honeymoon, Frances," Harriet said. Frances didn't believe she meant it, not for a moment. She went on, "But I fear you will regret what you've done."

"I won't. I already know that."

"Very well." Harriet turned and started for the door. With her hand on the latch, she said, "Treat Annis well, Frances. I mean to see to it that you do. And if she inherits the ability..."

Frances glared at her cousin's lean figure reflected in her dressing-table mirror. Anger gave her energy. It enhanced her own ability, and for once she felt as if the flow of her power was equal to Harriet's. Her fingers and toes tingled with the familiar feeling, with that vague hot thrill that was almost pain.

She said in a low, hard voice, "*I* mean, Harriet, to see that you stay away from us. I will make clear to George what a bad influence you are, associating as you do with the lowest classes, laborers and factory workers and their flocks of disease-ridden children. Imagine the illnesses you could bring into the house! My stepdaughter has no need of such an influence in her life."

Only then did Harriet smile, a cool, remote expression that made Frances's heart thud with fresh rancor. "We shall see about that, Cousin. It's your family now. But in the meantime—for this short time—enjoy your conquest." She opened the door, tossing her last comment over her shoulder lightly, as if it were too prosaic, too obvious, to be spoken gravely. "It won't last."

5

Harriet

Harriet heard the front door of the apartment open and close and Grace's running chatter greeting the housemaid who came to clean. The maids were all employed directly by the Dakota, and allowing one into the apartment was the only concession Grace made to the way things were done in the building. She flatly refused to use the kitchen service or even the laundry service. She had announced, at great length, that she was a better laundress and a better cook than any who would hire themselves out to a building of what she called "French flats."

The manager of the Dakota would be appalled if he heard the elegant dwellings of his building referred to as French flats. Fortunately, Grace had the wisdom not to refer to them that way in his hearing.

Harriet hurried her breakfast, then refilled her coffee cup and carried it to the herbarium, where she closed and locked the door against the clatter and bang of the housemaid at work. She was eager to begin sorting through her morning's harvest.

Harriet was of a precise nature, particularly when it came to the herbs and flowers she worked with every day. The herbarium was a space meant to be the fourth bedroom of the apartment, fitted with an iron sink and hot and cold running water. She had hired a cabinetmaker to line it with shelves and to install the two long stone counters where she could use scissors and knives without scarring the surfaces. On the shelves were dozens of glass jars of every size, pottery crocks, several mortar-and-pestle sets, and a fountain pen and ink bottle, with labels and mucilage for marking her remedies.

On a cabinet just inside the door, suspended on a triangular wooden stand, hung her most precious possession, when she wasn't wearing it around her neck. It had been her grandmother's, an amulet worked in silver and set with a large ametrine, its shades of lavender and yellow shot through with veins of deep purple. Harriet always touched the amulet as she passed it, and it always vibrated beneath her fingertips.

Magic? Yes. The best kind of magic, reminding her of her grandmother's love, still with her though Grandmother Beryl had died ten years before.

Harriet called on the amulet to enhance her potions and tinctures, her salves and poultices. Sometimes they needed to be stronger, their effects swifter, their results longer-lasting. The amulet was why Grace was not allowed in the herbarium. No one was allowed to touch it except Harriet herself.

Even the amulet had failed to help her heal Alexander when his time came. His injury had been beyond the power of either doctor or witch to heal. There had been no one to speak a word of blame to Harriet, but none was needed. She lived with the knowledge that his death was her fault, and with every remedy she created, every person she helped, she struggled to assuage her guilt.

Now, in the scented peace of the herbarium, she emptied her

basket, handful by handful, and spread her bounty across the stone counter. The dandelion greens she piled in a bowl to give to Grace for their dinner salad. She separated the stems of sage from the other greens and stripped the leaves to chop later for an infusion.

The shift from winter to spring often caused stomach upsets and inflamed chests. She kept remedies on hand for the people who sent requests up to her through the doorman. The doorman was a haughty creature, quick to reject anyone he deemed not of sufficient quality to enter his building. Fortunately, he had not forgotten his roots in the working neighborhoods of the city, and most of Harriet's patients were of that class. They couldn't afford a doctor, so they followed hearsay to the Dakota, where the doorman proved there was a heart beneath the copper buttons of his uniform.

Harriet tied the cut bunches of mugwort and hung them from hooks to dry. She tucked the stems and flowers of red clover into a pottery jar and did the same with the wild nettles, good for rebuilding the body after an illness. The burdock roots she trimmed and cleaned and set aside to make a decoction later for one of her patients, a girl of fourteen years who suffered from spots on her face.

Last she cleaned and chopped the leaves and flowers of the small amount of amaranth she had picked and added the bits to a glass jar. It was almost full now, and she would ask Grace to use it in a broth when the time was right. Someone was coming—someone always was—someone who couldn't afford food for her children or herself. A broth thickened with amaranth would be both healing and nourishing.

When she finished all these tasks, she shook out the detritus at the bottom of her basket into a bin. She wiped down her work surface with a damp cloth, then stood back, dusting her palms together, satisfied with the morning's work.

She was just untying her apron when she heard the tinkle of Grace's bell. It hung from a cord in the hallway outside the herbarium, far enough away not to disturb her if she didn't want to be interrupted, but close enough for her to hear. With mundane tasks an interruption would do no harm, but if a cantrip was needed, a disruption would mean starting over at the beginning. Now, however, she could hang up her apron, turn off the light, and answer the discreet ring.

She had been in the herbarium longer than she realized. She had worked into the afternoon. The housemaid had gone, leaving the floors and surfaces gleaming, and Harriet found Grace in the kitchen, wielding a cleaver to segment a chicken for dinner. Grace pointed toward the parlor with her greasy cleaver and gave a meaningful nod.

Harriet's parlor held two simple divans facing each other, with a low inlaid table between them. There were two straight chairs and a sideboard, but little else. She found a well-dressed woman of about thirty sitting on one of the divans, with a cup of tea on the table before her. She had the look of old New York, thick, fair hair above round blue eyes and pink cheeks.

She would be, Harriet guessed, a Stuyvesant or a Steenwijk or a Bleecker, one of the Dutch who had come here, made their money, and for decades dominated the city. She wore a walking suit of tweed, with a tightly fitted jacket over a high-necked shirtwaist and a graceful gored skirt.

Harriet absorbed all this in an instant, including the detail that the young woman had not touched her teacup, nor the small biscuit perched on the edge of the saucer. When the visitor spotted Harriet, she jumped to her feet and held out one gloved hand.

"Miss Bishop, I believe? I hope you don't object to my calling unannounced."

Harriet took the young woman's hand. "Yes, I'm Harriet Bishop. And you are Miss...?"

"Mrs. Mrs. Peter Schuyler. Dora."

"It's nice to meet you, Mrs. Schuyler." Now that she was closer to her visitor, Harriet saw that the pink in her cheeks was not from health but from embarrassment. Distress had intensified the blue of her eyes. It wasn't often that someone from the upper classes came in search of Harriet's help, and when they did, their need was usually desperate.

Harriet said, "Please, do sit down. You should drink your tea. Grace makes exceptionally good tea." And of course Grace had divined, in her best old-retainer way, that this was not a social call, despite the visitor's well-turned-out appearance.

"Thank you," Dora Schuyler said. She sat down again, perching nervously on the edge of the divan, skirts fluttering like the wings of a skittish bird. "This is the first time I've been to the Dakota. It's quite—quite a building, isn't it?"

Harriet sat down, too, linking her hands in her lap. She knew the process of getting to the purpose of Mrs. Schuyler's visit could be laborious, wandering through the lanes of polite conversation, twisting and turning until the end point was finally achieved, but she had little patience with small talk. The afternoon was getting on. It was best to move things along.

"I would say, Mrs. Schuyler, that there is no other building like it in New York. I haven't yet decided if that's a good or a bad thing. We are certainly well out of the city. You must have come by carriage."

"I did, Miss Bishop. My landau is waiting in the courtyard."

"Well, then. Let us not keep your driver waiting. How can I help you?"

As Dora Schuyler began to speak, Harriet bent her head to listen, not only to Mrs. Schuyler's voice but to her heart. Harriet was adept at hearing the truth beneath a person's words.

Mrs. Schuyler told her story in a hurried whisper. It was an echo of hundreds of others and as old as time. Her wealthy husband was a good bit older than she. Her marriage had no affection in it. They had two children but had not shared a bed in five years or more. She had met someone, had fallen in love, she had never meant to be indiscreet…

Harriet listened without judgment, and without curiosity for the details. She had heard it all before, though rarely from someone of Dora Schuyler's social position. She knew the end before her visitor said it, and she knew she would help. It was what she had been born to do, and it prevented women from seeking other, more perilous, frequently fatal remedies.

When the recitation stumbled to an awkward stop, Harriet asked, "Who sent you to me, Mrs. Schuyler?"

"My maid went to the Italian woman's shop on Elizabeth Street. Do you know it?"

"I do. Then I assume you understand the need for absolute discretion?"

"Yes, but…your housekeeper…"

"Grace has my complete trust, and she understands you and I are both at risk. You needn't worry."

The younger woman's eyes filled with sudden tears, and she groped in her small, soft purse for a handkerchief. She whispered, "I'm terrified, Miss Bishop. I will lose my children if I'm found out. My husband will find an excuse to send me to the asylum, to Blackwell's Island." She spoke the name with a shiver of pure horror. "I couldn't survive it!"

"I understand perfectly." Harriet spoke in a matter-of-fact tone, as if she were discussing a household shopping list. She would not indulge in sympathy, although she felt it. It wouldn't help. "You must come back the day after tomorrow, about this same time. I will have something for you then."

"You can't—you can't make it up now?" Dora Schuyler said tearfully. "I don't care what it costs, but it's so hard to get away . . ."

"I'm sorry," Harriet said. "What you need can't be rushed, I'm afraid. Do you know how long . . ." She let the question trail off and saw that Mrs. Schuyler understood.

The young woman's cheeks burned even hotter as she answered in an undertone, "About six weeks, I believe. Perhaps eight."

"You're in time, then, Mrs. Schuyler. Do your best not to worry."

Grace, hovering in the background, stepped forward to escort their visitor to the door. Harriet watched Mrs. Schuyler walk away, her shoulders hunched beneath her stylish jacket, her steps small and quick, the movements of an anxious rabbit.

Harriet sighed and went to make a cup of tea and find one of Grace's scones to fortify herself for the tedious task ahead. She had the ingredients on hand, because it was a tincture much in demand. Emmenagogues, herbs to stir the womb to clear itself. The making of the tincture itself did not require so much time or effort, but the cantrip to make certain it was effective did. She would be working late into the evening.

Harriet took the greatest care in measuring for her tincture. The wild carrot seeds and juniper berries were not likely to threaten Dora Schuyler's health, but pennyroyal and tansy could be deadly. Their amounts had to be precisely calculated. Harriet took pains with every step of the process and washed her hands thoroughly once the work was done.

When she had prepared everything and poured a precise amount of alcohol over the whole, she set the vial on the counter. The alcohol—she preferred to use port wine, which helped to mask the taste—would extract the essential, functioning elements of the herbs. For most herbalists, that would be the end of it. If she were an ordinary practitioner, she would cork the little vial, let it rest for two days, and it would be ready.

Harriet was no ordinary herbalist.

She arranged her ritual objects with the same precision she used in measuring powerful ingredients. A thick new candle in a brass holder rested behind the suspended amulet so that its flickering light would glitter on the stone's inner threads of purple. The vial of tincture she set at the center of the tableau, and she scattered a handful of sage around it to purify the atmosphere. She set a long match to the wick of the candle, nodding as the wick caught and flamed high, then settled to a steady glow. She turned off the electric lights, casting the room into shadows that shifted before the flame of the candle.

Harriet had only her grandmother's oral history to know how her ancestress, Bridget Bishop, had wielded her abilities. There were two separate and dramatically different traditions, derived from Bridget's two very different daughters, conceived of two very different husbands. The older daughter had been Mary Wesselby. The younger had been Christian Oliver.

Grandmother Beryl acknowledged the weaknesses of an oral tradition, but she was certain of one thing: she and Harriet were descended from Mary's line and had kept the Bishop name. Their practice, passed down over the two centuries since Bridget's execution, was one of beneficial herbs and healing cantrips, an art adapted and expanded according to the practitioner.

Christian's line was a different matter. Whether Christian herself had done it, Beryl could not be sure, but her descendants had added philters and manikins to their repertoire, both meant to manipulate minds and spirits, to persuade people to do what they did not intend to do. Beryl had warned against their use. Harriet wished she had listened.

Grandmother had also spoken, rarely, of the *knowing*. She herself had not possessed the ability. She was already dead when Harriet discovered she had inherited it and learned that it was sometimes a terrible thing.

With everything in order, Harriet recited the cantrip for today's purpose.

Root and stem, leaf and flower,
I command your deepest power.
Nature's strength unfettered be
To set one of her daughters free.

She stood in the dim room, a solitary, experienced practitioner. She bent her head as she waited for the sign that meant she had succeeded. The ametrine, its veins of purple vivid under the candlelight, grew cloudy, as if filled with mist. Harriet waited, five minutes, then twenty, then thirty, focusing her mind and her spirit and her ability on the need at hand.

The mist within the stone swirled, eddying like water in a brook. It grew thinner and thinner, as if evaporating before its own energy, and when at last it cleared, the ametrine sparkled with a light all its own, as if it had been washed clean. It shone with an inner brightness Harriet felt on her cheeks, on her forehead and lips, as if a stray shaft of sunlight had found her.

An instant later she felt it in her body. Energy shot through her bones and flesh, a jolt of power that sometimes threw her off balance. She had once inadvertently touched a wire that carried electricity from the dynamo in the Dakota's basement to a light fixture in her bedroom, and the feeling of working magic was much like that. The wire had stung her hand, and she had stumbled back, surprised by the unfamiliar bite of it. The power of a successful cantrip thrilled through her body in that same way, making her extremities tingle with a sense that was almost, but not quite, pain. She welcomed it as a sign she had achieved her intent.

Her tincture was ready. It would be thorough and effective, with a strength beyond that of any known medicine. It held power over life and death.

Harriet understood and honored the magnitude of her responsibility. Sometimes, as she whispered this cantrip or one of the others, she felt the presence of her predecessors, those wise women who had come before her. Often she felt Grandmother Beryl at her shoulder. Once she had sensed the shade of Bridget Bishop herself, and that one had unnerved her, a ghost still burning with resentment over her fate.

Harriet had been thirty when that happened, but twenty years had not diminished the impact of the memory. What had happened to Bridget was terrible, of course. She had been a simple hedge witch, pursued by the men in her town without mercy. They had convicted her as a demon and hanged her without remorse. Bridget Bishop had been different, odd, old, and alone. Her small ability was not enough to save her.

Still, Harriet considered that after two hundred years, Bridget's anger should have abated.

It had not. It had lived on in her daughter Christian, and then in the women who followed her. For them the art was not a tool. It was a weapon. It was, as Beryl had taught, the *maleficia*. Frances was of Christian's lineage, with all its dark practices, and though Harriet and Beryl had tried to prevent her from adopting dark magic for herself, they had not succeeded. The *maleficia* was in her blood. There had been nothing they could do about it.

Harriet's memories faded gradually as the light faded from the ametrine, leaving it an ordinary, polished, pretty stone. She was just reaching for the vial of tincture when that other, unpredictable element of her practice struck.

The knowing.

It was uncomfortable in a different way from the effect of working magic. It burst into being inside her mind with a force that made her heart thud and her skin prickle, and there was no resisting it. When it came over her, she *knew*, whether she wanted to or not.

6

Annis

The park was warm, even at this early hour, and the unseasonable heat brought prickles of perspiration to Annis's chest. She pulled off her hat to scratch an itchy spot on her head while Bits drank from the brimming fountain. It was too early for the carriages that used the concourse as a turnaround, and Annis thought she must be truly alone, a rare treat. She slid from the saddle, settled her boots on the edge of the bluestone basin, and steadied herself with a hand on Bits's neck so she could look around her.

The crest of Cherry Hill was a wonderful vantage point. To the west the lake gleamed sapphire blue in the May sunshine. To the east and south cherry blossoms blazed white against the green landscape. Annis said, "I wish I owned all this, Bits. I could walk anywhere I wanted, ride however I wanted to, with no one telling me what to do!"

She was free of school now. She had planned to spend her spring and summer riding, researching for her breeding program, helping with the mares who would come. Instead Frances kept her busy choosing shoes and hats, looking at fabrics and trims and buttons, standing on a stool for hours for dress fittings.

Frances was taking her to London. The whole summer would be wasted on tea parties and stuffy balls, boring people, endless empty conversations.

She had refused to go at first, but her father had insisted. "You'll go," he had growled at her. "Your stepmother has gone to a lot of trouble, acquiring a letter of introduction, finding a place for you, all that sort of thing. You'll see all the sights."

"I don't want to see the sights," she protested. "And Black Satin—"

"Behave yourself," he said darkly, "and Black Satin will still be here when you return."

It was a clear threat. She could lose Bits. Robbie could lose his job. She would go to London as ordered.

It hardly seemed fair, her father suddenly remembering her existence. It was Frances's doing, of course. For some reason Frances wanted to go to England, and she wanted Annis to go along, which was odd. It wasn't as if they enjoyed each other's company.

Bits snorted water, spattering her habit, interrupting her thoughts. Annis brought herself back to the beauties of the crystal morning. "I know, Bitsy. You want to run, but not yet."

She shook the water droplets from her skirt. Bits stamped, eager to be off for their canter. She stroked his neck, which had grown hot in the sun, and combed his silky forelock with her fingers. "Sorry, Bits. Walking only, until we're sure that tendon is healed." Which meant, sadly, that they wouldn't have their run until she returned from England.

She urged Bits closer to the basin so she could remount. She was just about to swing her leg over the saddle when someone spoke from the trees beyond the curve of the concourse. "Lovely morning for a ride."

It was a woman's voice, low in pitch, unusually resonant. Curious, a little embarrassed at having been overheard speaking to her horse as if he were a person, Annis bent her knees so she could peek under Bits's neck.

A tall, lean woman emerged from the copse. She wore a day dress every bit as worn as Annis's riding habit. She carried an ancient straw hat, and her uncovered dark hair was threaded with silver, like star streaks in a night sky. A basket full of greenery hung over her arm. She stepped out from beneath a canopy of cherry blossoms, and they sifted past her shoulders as if someone were showering her with flowers.

The woman walked through the drift of blossoms with a grace that belied the silver in her hair. Annis found something elegant about her, though Frances would have sniffed at the stranger's shabby clothes.

Intrigued, Annis loosened her grip on Bits's reins and inched along the rim of the basin to show herself. "Good morning, ma'am. I thought I was alone up here."

"Do you need help getting into the saddle?" the woman asked. Her voice carried easily through the percussive rustle of leaves, as musical as the birdsong filling the park.

Annis said, "No, thank you. I always stand on the edge of the fountain." She jumped down so as not to seem rude, and because there was something about this woman that made her want to meet her. To hear what she might say.

"Ah. How practical." The woman walked closer. "It seems your steed is cooperative."

"Oh, he is. He's the finest horse in New York City."

The woman's lips curved. "He must certainly be the most fortunate."

"I hope so," Annis said. "I do my best for him."

"Well, then. You are both fortunate. And what is your horse called?"

"Bits. That is, his proper name is Black Satin. I'm starting a bloodline with him."

The woman tilted her head to one side, and her fine gray eyes sparkled with interest. "Are you indeed? That's most interesting. A worthy ambition, I would say."

Annis grinned. "Thank you. Most people are shocked that I would be involved with such an activity—breeding horses, I mean. Everyone says it's unladylike."

"I suppose it is. But being ladylike is so tedious, don't you find?"

Annis laughed. "Oh, I do! Decidedly."

"And what do your parents think of your endeavor?"

Annis shrugged. "My stepmother thinks the whole thing is vulgar. My father says I'm a horse-mad girl and I'll grow out of it, but I won't. I'm young, but I know what I'm doing. Bits throws wonderful foals when he has the right mares. Everyone will clamor for one of them."

"Your enthusiasm makes me wish I were a horsewoman."

Annis said, "I do love horses. I love riding, too."

"And no sidesaddle, I see."

"Heavens, no! I only ride a cross saddle."

"I expect that draws attention."

"Oh yes," Annis said with a sigh. "Everyone is scandalized, but truly, the sidesaddle is a ridiculous invention. Dangerous." Annis pointed to her saddle. "This was custom fitted for Bits and me, and it's perfect. The balance is all wrong with a sidesaddle, both for the rider and the horse. It's fine for showing off fancy riding habits, but it's terrible for real riding."

It was a long speech, and something of a lecture. Annis's cheeks warmed at the realization, but her new friend was nodding with an expression of interest. "I've often wondered about that. It's a safety concern, surely. I wonder who thought of it in the first place?"

"Someone who hated women," Annis said with asperity.

The stranger laughed. "You're probably right."

Annis lifted her head and saw that the sun had risen above the woods. "Oh, it's getting late. Robbie will be worried about us."

"Robbie?"

"My stableman. Bits has a sore tendon. Robbie might think it has gotten worse and come looking for us."

"And what does one do for a sore tendon?"

"I made a poultice of witch hazel, with comfrey and a bit of bay laurel. I think it helped, but it takes time."

"You're quite right. Healing does take time, but that's a good combination. You might add some dried gingerroot, ground very fine. It's helpful for cooling inflammation."

Annis raised her eyebrows. "Do you know something of herbs?"

"I do, rather," the woman said. "As it happens, it's my profession."

"How wonderful! Gingerroot, then. Where can I find it?"

"Try the herbalist on Elizabeth Street. She seems to have everything."

"I will! Thank you for the suggestion."

"You're most welcome. And now perhaps you had best start back, since you have some distance to go. We don't want your Robbie to worry."

"Yes. You'll have to excuse me."

Annis maneuvered Bits closer to the fountain, stepped up onto the edge, and swung her leg over the saddle. She fitted her boots into the stirrups and lifted a hand in farewell as she pressed the reins against Bits's neck. She glanced over her shoulder just as the woman faded among the cherry trees, her dark silhouette melting into the curtain of white.

"I believe we've made a friend, Bits," Annis said. She felt the spring in his step, the urge to go faster, but she held him in. "Gingerroot, Bitsy. That will help."

She wished she had asked the woman's name, even asked where she lived. It had been marvelous to speak with someone of her own sex who was interesting. And now she was being dragged off to England for long, boring weeks and would probably never see her again.

Annis's bed was strewn with satins, silks, and brocades, with the occasional splash of organza. Layers of cream, yellow, and pink shimmered in the afternoon light, and jet and crystal beads flashed from the pile of tea frocks and day dresses. Frances had insisted Annis try on every single garment before it was packed, and Annis felt as cross as an alley cat.

Frances, seated on the dressing-table stool, didn't appear to notice her mood. She regarded the mound of clothes with satisfaction. "It will do," she said. She was cheerful this afternoon, with her cat-that-drank-the-cream smile, her lips curling at the corners, her eyelids half-lowered. "They aren't Worth creations, of course. George refused the expense of a trip to Paris, but my dressmaker did well, don't you think? Most of these are convincing copies."

"What does it matter? No one in England will care what one American nobody wears."

Frances looked up at her, her eyes narrow and cool, more catlike than ever. "You will not be a nobody, Annis Allington. I will see to that. We have a lovely letter of introduction, and I want you to look well at the teas and parties."

"I hate teas and parties."

Unperturbed, Frances rose and stroked one of the silk gowns. "But I do not."

"I'd rather see the museums, since we're going to be there. And Westminster Abbey and Buckingham Palace."

"We'll see all of that, in time," Frances said airily. "Didn't I say?"

"You didn't, Frances. Have you even bought a Baedeker or a Murray's?"

"We won't need guidebooks. The people we meet will show us about."

Annis waved a hand at the profusion on her bed. "I suppose all of this is going aboard the *Majestic*, and a matching pile for you? There won't be any room for us."

"Of course there will," Frances said. "We'll keep what we need for the voyage in our stateroom, and the rest will be stowed away until we reach Liverpool."

"But what about Antoinette and Velma?"

"They'll share a cabin in second class. Maids and valets have their own dining room. They'll enjoy themselves."

Velma was smoothing one of the tea frocks, readying it to be wrapped in tissue paper and folded into the waiting trunk. She glanced up and then quickly away, but Annis caught her look of anxiety. "Velma? What's the matter?"

Velma shook her head and stared, wordless, into the folds of powder-pink silk.

Frances said, "Annis, let it go if she doesn't want to talk about it." She pulled a cream-and-pink shawl from the bed and held it out to Velma. "This goes with the pink silk."

Velma, looking miserable, took the shawl and began to fold it.

Annis worked her way around the trunk to her wardrobe, where she slipped out of her dressing gown. She pulled out a shirtwaist and skirt and began to work her way into them.

"Velma, help your mistress," Frances ordered.

"She can't do everything at once!" Annis protested, even as Velma obediently laid the shawl on top of the trunk and came to help her with the buttons of her shirtwaist.

Frances gave a contented sigh and dusted her palms together as if she had just completed a job of work. Annis nodded to Velma to go back to her packing and bent to pull on her shoes.

Frances said, "Take care with your jewel case, Annis. You need to plan. You're going to want simple earrings and necklaces for daytime, but fancier things for the evenings. Do you have pearls? They would go nicely with the ivory brocade."

She was gone before Annis could tell her that she couldn't remember if she had pearls or not. She wore almost no jewelry, since it got in the way of her stable chores. Most of what she possessed had been her mother's. She wiped dust from the lid of her jewel case as she said, "Tell me now, Velma. What are you worried about?"

Velma was bent over the trunk, elbow deep in a layer of tissue.

She straightened and twisted the tie of her apron. "Don't like boats," she said.

"Are you afraid we'll sink?" Annis asked. "Is that why you don't like boats?"

Velma shook her head. "I'll be sick."

"Sick? Oh, you mean seasick? But how do you know?"

"Ferry." Velma shook out a chemise, smoothed it against her chest, then began to fold it. "From Brooklyn."

"You get sick on the ferry?" Velma nodded. "Then, Velma, why not use the bridge?"

"Don't like bridges."

Trying to talk to her was like walking into a wall, and Annis had to quell a flash of fresh irritation. She forced herself to speak in a mild tone. "I didn't know that."

Velma shrugged. "Never asked."

Annis gazed at her maid for a moment, thinking for the second time that perhaps Frances was right and she was too selfish. She promised herself she would try harder, at least where Velma was concerned.

At the very bottom of her jewel case, buried under other unworn pieces, she found a short string of pearls. The light in the room had begun to fade, so she carried the necklace to the window to see it better. She held it up to catch the sunset glow, letting the pearls dangle over her hand.

"Pretty," Velma said from behind her.

"They are, aren't they?" Annis let the smooth white gems slide between her fingers. There was a different stone in the middle, not a pearl. It was larger, shimmering white, with subtle layers of silver beneath its surface. Annis cupped the stone in her palm, then caught a sudden breath.

"You all right, miss?" Velma asked.

"Y-yes," Annis said. She stared at the stone, then closed her fingers around it. She had the odd sensation that she was holding something alive in her palm, something that vibrated against her skin, tingled through her hand, up her arm. It was as if she had picked up a live coal, but one that burned cold instead of hot. Her fingers tightened on it.

"Velma," she said, her voice suddenly hoarse. "Could you finish that later? I need a few minutes to—to rest."

It was a lame reason. She never rested in the daytime, but it was all she could think of. The maid was gone in seconds, and Annis, rapt, sank into the window seat. She opened her hand and gazed down at the creamy white stone. It lay quiescent, shining innocently up at her.

What had just happened? Annis struggled to understand the sensations that had stolen her breath. She hadn't imagined them. Her heart was pounding at the base of her throat, and her head swam as if she had turned a somersault. Her arms prickled with gooseflesh, and she closed her hand around the stone once again.

It spoke to her. She couldn't imagine how, or why, but there was no denying its message. The pieces of a puzzle fell into place in her mind, a puzzle she hadn't known existed. It was like finally grasping a mathematics problem or learning a difficult word in French. It flashed into being, an understanding that had not existed moments before.

She knew why Frances was taking her to London. It had nothing to do with tea parties or the British Museum or Buckingham Palace.

She tried to use her common sense, of which she possessed an abundance, to banish the idea, but she failed. She tried to rationalize it as the result of anxiety, or fear, but those emotions had never troubled her in her life.

She couldn't make the conviction fade. She knew. She understood exactly what Frances meant to do and why she was so determined to carry her off to England.

Frances meant to tear her away from Bits and all her plans. She meant to take her to England and leave her there. She intended to find Annis a husband, and not just any husband.

Frances wanted to acquire a title in the family, so the Four Hundred would no longer look down their old-money noses at the nouveau riche Allingtons.

Annis let the pearls drop into her lap, freeing her hands to rub her temples with trembling fingers. "I won't do it," she whispered to the gathering dusk beyond her window. "I don't care what she says. I don't care what she does. I'm not going." She leaned closer to the glass, straining for a glimpse of the stables, where her beloved horse rested in his stall. "Don't you worry, Bits," she muttered. "I'm staying right here with you."

7

Annis

So? You have to get married someday. Why not now?"

Annis stared at her father, rigid with hurt. He was seated at his desk in his private study, a room that had been one of her favorites when she still felt welcome there. Its two large windows looked out on the gardens and the river beyond. Bookshelves lined the walls, although there were no longer any books in them. Everything now was business, business, business, nothing but ledgers and piles of drawings, even two miniature replicas of the Allington Iron Stove. Annis had been allowed to play with those when she was small.

Things had been different then. Waking, she couldn't remember her mother, but sometimes in dreams a hazy scene came to her that felt like a memory. She seemed to be tiny, bundled in soft fur, snuggled between her mother and her father in the carriage. Snow was falling over the city, and a bell on the carriage horse's bridle jingled with each of his steps. She felt deliciously drowsy, lulled into sleep by the rhythm of the bell and the laughter of her parents above her head.

When her mother died, George Allington stopped laughing

and retreated into his business. Occasionally he thought of his little daughter, bringing home interesting scraps of iron from the factory for her to examine, or pulling a bag of roasted chestnuts, still warm from the vendor's brazier, out of his pocket. On birthdays he brought her saltwater taffy and arranged with Mrs. King to buy gifts.

On her sixth birthday, Papa took her hand to lead her out to the stables. Robbie was waiting there, and he had an enchanting fat brown pony on a lead. Papa said, "Happy birthday," but it was Robbie who lifted Annis into the saddle.

He said, "This is Sally, Miss Annis. She's going to teach you to ride."

Robbie held Annis in the saddle at first, but in moments she pushed his hands away. It never occurred to her to be afraid. She felt grand, sitting up high on her own pony. She kicked her short legs against Sally's ribs, urging her around the paddock as if she had been doing it all her life. Her father, satisfied he had fulfilled his paternal responsibilities, walked away, leaving Robbie to deal with Annis and her new passion. She remembered calling out to him, "Papa! Papa! Look at me riding!" but he was already gone.

In the ensuing months, she hardly saw her father. When he was in his study, the door was closed and locked. On nights he was home for dinner, he dined alone, and Annis ate in the kitchen with Mrs. King. She and her father had never spent a great deal of time together. Now they spent none.

Annis didn't know what she had done to lose her father's love. She wanted to ask Mrs. King, who watched over her with such affection, but she didn't know how. The change wounded and bewildered her. She fell into the habit of avoiding her father, trying to escape her confused feelings. She turned instead to Sally, letting the pony fill the empty spaces of her child's heart.

Annis poured herself into learning everything she could about riding and horses. She and Sally, with Robbie and Tater beside them, explored the meadows and paths of Central Park until they knew each tree and every shrub, where the ducks swam and where the rabbits hid. Annis spent every moment she could in the stables. She tagged after Robbie as he worked in the tack room or the hayloft. She pestered him with questions, demanding to know everything he did about how to care for horses.

She was thirteen when Bits arrived, a leggy Thoroughbred foal accepted as payment for a debt owed to her father. Annis claimed him immediately for herself. He was the most beautiful creature she had ever seen, and she loved him even more than she loved Sally, though she was careful not to let Sally see that.

There was only one person who could separate her from Black Satin, and at this moment he was glaring at her without putting down his pen.

She folded her arms tightly around herself, struggling for the right argument. "Why, Papa? Why do I have to get married?"

"Don't be foolish, Annis. What else are you going to do with your life?"

"What else? I'm going to breed horses!" she said. "I've told you!"

"Haven't you outgrown that notion yet? Women can't breed horses."

"Why not?"

"No one would buy horses from a woman!"

"They will when they see how marvelous mine are, Papa!"

"Foolishness. The whole idea is a waste of time and money."

"That's not true! The horse markets are doing a thriving business."

He snorted a laugh. "Horse markets! What do you know about horse markets, Annis?"

She thrust out her chin. "I know there were a hundred thousand horses sold in New York last year. Heavy horses, light horses, mules. I know the revenues were more than fifteen million. I know the market on Third, nearest Twenty-Fourth Street, specializes in horses bred for riding."

George lifted his eyebrows with something like respect. "You've done some research."

"Of course I have," Annis said. Encouraged by this slight advantage, she burbled on, "I expect I would need someone to make transactions for me at the Bull's Head, because some men won't care to negotiate with a female. Most of my sales would be private in any case, but I mean to make this a business. I will breed the finest riding horses and be famous for it."

The eyebrows fell, and the look of impatience returned to her father's face. "No. Much too indelicate a business for a girl. A well-brought-up young lady shouldn't have anything to do with—with such activities." He leaned back a little and tried a half-hearted smile of persuasion. "You should be thrilled by Frances's plan, Annis! You could be a titled lady. You won't have to do a jot of work your whole life!"

"Not a jot of work?" She bit the words out, her temper frayed to a thread. "You mean, except breed?"

George's temper broke completely. He slammed down his pen, spraying drops of ink across his desk blotter, and his face purpled. "How dare you speak to me in that disgusting manner!"

She was her father's daughter. She didn't flinch. "Disgusting? Why? Do you think I don't know how babies are created? Don't you think I *should* know?"

"You're too young to understand that sort of thing!" he roared.

"Don't be absurd, Papa. Everyone knows that sort of thing."

She thought it made a good argument, though it wasn't exactly true. The girls at Brearley tried to guess sometimes, wondering how it was between men and women, but they mostly got it wrong. More than one of her school friends had been convinced kissing caused pregnancy.

Annis, however, understood the biology perfectly well. She knew because she insisted on being present in the stable when Bits serviced a mare.

Her father's voice rose further. "I'm appalled, Annis! That's—it's—unladylike!"

With a curl of her lip, she quoted her morning's acquaintance. "Being ladylike is tedious."

"Tedious!" Her father gripped the edge of his desk with unnecessary force, and his jaw muscles quivered as he struggled to regain his temper. He turned his face to the window, where the gas streetlights ranged like tiny moons along Riverside Drive. "This is a phase, Annis. You'll grow out of it."

"A phase? I'm too old for phases. Do you know how old I am?"

He hesitated, drawing a noisy breath through his nose. "Of course I do."

He ran his ink-stained fingers through the thatch of his hair. It was nearly as thick and dark as her own, but a wedge of gray had developed at each temple. Annis remembered he had turned forty-eight at his last birthday.

She said, "I'm seventeen, Papa. I'm well beyond having phases. You were seventeen, as I recall, when you started your first business. You sold tools, and you made a success of it."

"That was different," he said. "I'm a man. You're a girl. You need a husband, and it might as well be one with a title."

"You knew all along!" she accused him. "You knew what she was planning, and you never said a word!"

"Frances knows what's best for you."

"Frances knows what's best for *Frances*!" Annis cried.

Her father turned in his chair and faced her directly. His eyes were her eyes, the same clear pale blue with a near-purple limbal ring encircling the irises. She felt oddly disoriented sometimes, looking into his eyes, as if she were looking into a slightly distorted mirror.

"Listen to me, Daughter," he said. With a qualm she recognized the flat voice. It meant he was no longer angry, but his mind had not changed. There would be no more arguing. She was going to lose this battle.

He said, in that toneless voice, "You're going with your stepmother to England. There will be parties and teas, the things girls like. You will meet a number of eligible young men, and you will choose one to marry, someone who will manage your money wisely."

"Why can't I manage my own money?" she asked, but weakly, defeated now.

"That's a silly question. Women can't manage money. I will not hand over your inheritance just to see you fritter it away."

"Fritter! Have you ever known me to fritter anything?" Angry tears began to burn in her throat. "Papa, I know how to handle money! I—"

"No more," he said coldly. "I'm not going to argue with a hysterical girl."

"I am *not* hysterical!" She knew even as she said it that it was a pointless protest.

He said, "You'll marry like every other well-bred young lady does. That's an end to it."

"I won't do it." She didn't look at him but out into the darkness, past the gardens to the distant gleam of the river. She let her chin thrust out in the same way his did. "I don't ever want to marry."

His temper erupted again, and this time it was as if a volcano had blown its top. "You will, Annis!" he shouted. The window glass shook under the volume of his voice, and it was then that he made his threat. "I'm tired of arguing. You'll do as you're told, as Frances bids you to do. Don't cross me further, or Black Satin and Sally will be gone. I'll have them sold in a day, I promise you that, and I will see Frances knows it!"

She turned back to him, horrified. "Papa, no!" But it was no use. He turned away, seizing up his papers and rattling them angrily in his hands.

She spun, her skirts swirling as she stamped out of the study and slammed the door behind her. She ran up the stairs, one hand over her mouth, managing to hold back her sobs of fury until she was in her bedroom with the door closed.

Velma was in the midst of laying out her nightgown and slippers, and she straightened, mouth gaping, Annis's dressing gown clutched to her chest.

Annis collapsed onto the dressing-table stool and turned her back to the mirror. Through a haze of tears she took in the expensive furnishings of her room, the wardrobe full of clothes, the elegant drapes, the satin and velvet pillows on her bed. "What good is all this?" she cried. "None of it is real! None of it matters! I'm for sale, like a filly at the horse market, and I hate it!"

Poor, slow Velma shed two tears of sympathy for her mistress, but she didn't say a word.

Annis spent a bad night. When she slept, she had nightmares of Bits being led away from her, sold off like a piece of furniture. When she lay awake, her thoughts skittered every which way, searching for a solution to her troubles.

By the time she rose in the morning, eyes burning from sleeplessness, she knew what she had to do. She would sail to England. She would go where Frances wanted her to go, meet the people she was supposed to meet. She would act the part of a young lady in search of a husband. She would do it for Bits, and she would do it for Robbie.

It would all be false.

Her father could force her to make the journey, but he couldn't force her to marry.

It was 1890, after all, not 1790. It was a new age for women. Women were becoming doctors and lawyers. Women were running businesses. They were fighting for full citizenship. Some even said women would one day be able to vote. A woman sat on the throne of England! She would have to make her father understand all of that, but she would start by pretending to be a dutiful daughter.

When Frances announced at the breakfast table that she had errands to run downtown, Annis seized the opportunity to begin her pretense. "I have an errand, too, Frances," she said. "May I come along?"

With her husband listening, Frances could hardly refuse. Indeed, the atmosphere in the breakfast room was thick with tension, and Frances seemed eager to ease it. She said, with a convincing attempt at gaiety, "Of course, Annis! What fun, just we two girls. We'll have luncheon in town! Do you have a shopping list?"

George looked skeptical at Frances's display of good humor, but Annis joined the subterfuge, resisting the urge to point out that "just we two girls" would mean Robbie to drive the carriage, and Velma and Antoinette in attendance. Frances was firm on the principle that ladies did not venture out without their maids. What she meant, Annis knew, was that she didn't want to be seen without her maid. Her Paris-trained French maid.

"Oh, thank you, Frances," Annis said, in her most innocent tone. "There's an herb shop on Elizabeth Street. I need something for Bits's poultice."

The carriage pulled to a stop in front of St. Patrick's on Mulberry Street. "Sorry, ma'am," Robbie said to Frances. "Like the last time. Elizabeth Street is too narrow. Afraid you'll need to walk around the corner."

As they climbed down, Annis gave Frances a questioning glance. "You've been to the shop before?"

"The proprietress carries a very good cream for the complexion," Frances said. "You should buy some while we're there. Hurry now, Velma, Antoinette. This is an unpleasant neighborhood, and I want to get to O'Neill's before luncheon."

The neighborhood seemed fine to Annis, but as they left the carriage, she saw Robbie glare at passersby as if daring them to come too close. The four women walked eastward, Frances with a hand under Annis's arm, the two maids close behind. They turned right, and Frances led them up Elizabeth Street to their destination.

The herb shop was tiny and dark, little more than a closet. It was wedged between a cobbler on one side, with boots and shoes littering the grimy front window, and a chandler on the other. The chandler's storefront was nicer, its polished window piled with candles of different sizes and an array of pretty holders. As Frances and Antoinette disappeared through the narrow door into the herbalist's, Velma paused in front of the chandler's display, gazing openmouthed at the shop's wares.

Annis, seeing, turned back. "Is there something there you like, Velma?" she asked. Velma shrugged, but Annis saw that her eyes were fixed on a cut-glass candleholder in the shape of a swan. "Is that it? Do you like that?"

"I like swans," Velma said. Her eyes, usually so dull, brightened with interest.

Annis was startled to sense, as if it were her own, Velma's longing for the little object. Velma wanted to touch it, to hold it. An odd little ache sprang up under Annis's rib cage, and she pressed an uneasy hand over it. Why should she share this feeling of desire? She had no wish to possess the candleholder, pretty though it was. It was Velma who had admired it, and Velma—

She made herself drop her hand to dig in her purse for a bit of money. "Go in and buy it," she whispered, pressing the money into Velma's fingers. Velma's eyes widened in disbelief. "I mean it! Quick now, before my stepmother sees you. Then join us in the herbalist's. Hurry!" She gave her a tiny push to encourage her.

A look of delight transformed Velma's plain face, and gooseflesh rose on Annis's arms. As Velma went into the chandler's, the money clutched in her hand, the ache in Annis's chest eased. She followed Frances into the herbalist's shop, telling herself she was imagining things. She couldn't have sensed Velma's feelings. She was not herself, truly. No doubt it was the stress of her argument with her father, and her worry over leaving Bits, that caused her to have such strange notions.

Inside the shop the scents of lavender and peppermint and eucalyptus wafted from shelves crowded with jars and bottles and baskets. The room was so narrow Annis could have touched both side walls with her outstretched hands. At the far end, a tiny, bent woman was wrapping a jar of something under Frances's watchful eye.

Frances glanced back as she approached. "Oh, Annis, there you are! What is it you want from Mrs. Carcano? I've forgotten. I'm buying you a jar of face cream, though. It has cowslip in it. It will help with those freckles."

Annis worked her way toward the counter, pulling her skirts aside so as not to upset the baskets piled on the floor. The proprietress peered at her from beneath an upswept mass of gray hair. Her eyes were black as coal, their lids sagging with age. "Freckles?" she said, with the rolled *r* of an Italian accent. "No, no, signorina, your freckles are perfect. No need, no need," and she immediately unwrapped the jar and placed it on a shelf beneath the counter.

Annis grinned. She had never understood why freckles were considered a fault, and hers were so pale they were almost invisible in any case. Clearly the old Italian lady thought the same, because she gave her a nearly toothless smile and a cheerful wink. "Signorina, you need something. Not for face, face is good. Skin is good, teeth is good. What, then?"

"My horse," Annis said. "A poultice. I'm told—that is, I think I need powdered ginger."

"Ah, *sì, sì, sì*," the woman said. "Ginger. Good for swelling. You know herbs, signorina?"

"A little."

"*Un po', un po'*. Is good." She turned and brought down a quart jar filled with oddly shaped roots. "Here is gingerroot. Is dried. You can grind?"

"Yes. Mrs. King—our cook—has a nut grinder."

"Good, is good. Clean first, though."

"I will."

"*Va bene*, I sell you two ounces, for poultice." Velma came in, the creak of the door announcing her presence. Mrs. Carcano looked up and gazed at the maid for a moment, her eyes narrowed. Annis and Frances and Antoinette all turned to see what she was looking at, then turned back, puzzled.

"You are going on a sea voyage?" Mrs. Carcano asked of Velma. Velma froze.

Annis spoke for her. "We are. We're going to England on the *Majestic*. How did you—"

"Never mind, Annis," Frances said, with an edge to her voice.

"Six ounces," Mrs. Carcano announced. "I sell you six ounces ginger. Is very good for upset stomach. Sea voyage, you take ginger to make tea."

Annis's lips parted to ask how she had known Velma had troubles with seasickness, but Frances forestalled her, saying hurriedly, "Fine, fine, Mrs. Carcano. Six ounces, if you say so. Now we must hurry. How much do I owe you?"

The transaction was quickly concluded. Annis accepted the little parcel from the herbalist, and they were on their way out the door and down the street.

"Frances," Annis said. "How did that woman—Mrs. Carcano—how did she know Velma gets seasick? How could she know?"

Frances avoided her eyes. "No idea. Perhaps it's something about Velma's complexion. We should have bought the face cream for her instead, I suppose. I didn't think of it."

"I'll go back," Annis said, slowing her steps, ready to turn back. She liked the idea of going back to the old woman's shop, of looking into those black eyes again. She would ask her how she had known about Velma.

"No, Annis," Frances snapped. She seized Annis's arm, her small hand surprisingly strong, and propelled her at a quick pace back toward Mulberry Street. "Come now, we have things to accomplish, and the morning is far gone already."

Annis frowned in confusion as she climbed back into the carriage. Velma sat beside her on the seat, hiding her package under her coat. Frances said to Robbie, "O'Neill's, please. Quick as you can."

Robbie clucked to Andy, and they were off. Though it was pointless, Annis couldn't help craning her neck, hoping for a glimpse of the herb shop as Andy pulled them away.

She couldn't see the shop, but she caught sight of a tall figure that looked familiar. She was better dressed this time, in a day dress and a white straw hat. Her hair was neatly tucked up, and she wore a short, slightly out-of-fashion cape. Surely, though her clothes were so different, that was the lady she had encountered in the park?

The woman paused, gazing toward the Allington carriage as if she knew who was in its plush seats.

Annis twisted to see her better, squinting through the bright sunshine. The lady's drooping hat brim hid her face, but not many women were so tall and lean...

Frances interrupted her thoughts, and she was forced to turn back. "Look there, Annis," Frances said, pointing with her gloved hand to a construction site in the early stages. "That will be the Siegel-Cooper emporium. It's going to be the biggest store in the world, and they're going to sell Allington Iron Stoves, which will make your father happy."

Annis, having no interest in stores, slumped back in her seat, frustrated and perplexed. Such an odd coincidence that she should see the tall woman on the street that way.

There had been something unusual about their visit to Mrs. Carcano, too, something even more perplexing. The Italian woman had refused to sell Frances the face cream, as if the sale didn't matter nearly so much as her opinion of Annis's appearance. She had tripled the amount of ginger in Annis's order on her own whim, as if she dictated her customers' purchases rather than the other way around. Strangest of all, Frances had objected to neither of these things.

That wasn't like Frances. She tended to be as imperious as the queen whenever she had the chance, reminding everyone that she was a woman of consequence.

Annis peeked up at her stepmother from beneath the brim of her hat. Frances's face was as composed as if she hadn't a care in the world. As if everything in her life was going just as she planned it. As if she was in complete control.

For a wild moment Annis envied her, which made the whole morning stranger than ever.

8

Frances

After Annis blurted out their plans for anyone to hear, and then Harriet standing on the sidewalk staring after them, Frances worried that Harriet would guess what she meant to do. Harriet was uncanny in that way.

She had learned that about Harriet when she was sixteen and Harriet a still-striking thirty-one. The two of them shared nothing beyond their Bishop heritage. Their familial relationship was so distant they couldn't measure it. They knew they were cousins, but at what remove no one seemed to recall.

Frances's mother had just died, and Harriet and her grandmother Beryl had come to visit. Cousin Beryl, as Frances had been taught to call her, was a tall, straight-backed woman with a shock of silver hair. Frances hadn't seen her in some time, and she was startled to see what age did to the Bishop face. Beryl's Bishop chin had grown more prominent than ever, and her long nose had begun to droop. Only the gray eyes remained sharp, with a diamond brightness Frances envied. Harriet had the same eyes.

Frances's own eyes were an ordinary brown, but fortunately

she had been spared the Bishop chin and nose. That was something, at least, to be grateful for.

"Well, Frances," Beryl had said, the moment she sat down. "We must think what to do with you."

"Do with me?" Frances asked. "What do you mean?"

"Now you're alone, we must decide how you're to go forward. We're sorry for your loss, naturally, but I'm afraid the Bishop women who deny their ability have a lamentable tendency to die young."

Harriet added, "Ignoring it is poison. It never ends well."

Frances looked from one face to the other, confounded by the conversation. "Ability?" she said faintly. "Cousin Beryl—Cousin Harriet—what are you talking about?"

"Grandmother," Harriet said. "You need to begin at the beginning. Frances doesn't know anything."

Beryl said, "I fear you're right."

"I can't think why Cousin Sarah didn't teach her," Harriet said.

"She was terrified," Beryl said, the two of them speaking together as if Frances weren't sitting right between them. "Because of her mother. Sarah's mother was always angry, cursing people, causing trouble. Using the *maleficia* drove her mad, I believe."

Frances had never met her grandmother and had no idea what they were talking about.

Harriet turned to her. "Frances, did you know your mother was a Bishop?"

"She wasn't. She was a Tyler."

"That was her married name," Beryl said.

"She said she was Sarah Margaret Tyler."

"Margaret was her middle name. You never knew her maiden name?" Harriet asked.

"No, she . . . no. She never told me."

Beryl's lips pursed with disdain. "Sarah was terrified of her Bishop heritage being exposed. I recall how thrilled she was to change her name when she married. She thought that would keep her safe."

Frances gazed at them in mystified silence. They were sitting in the tiny Brooklyn apartment Frances had shared with her mother ever since her father disappeared. It smelled of stew being cooked downstairs and laundry being boiled and starched next door. Its two small windows gave onto a narrow alley where rats and stray dogs scavenged for scraps. The windows were too small for the sun to penetrate, and mold and mildew grew in every corner.

It was a dismal place on a sad and dirty little street. Accordingly the rent was meager, but they had struggled to pay it just the same.

Their poverty didn't seem to be what Cousin Beryl was talking about, though. Ability?

Harriet said, "A cup of tea would be nice, Frances. I brought some, in case you didn't have any. This might be a long conversation."

Harriet didn't look craggy like her grandmother, but in her grief she had gotten too thin. Her cheeks had lost their youthful plumpness, and her bosom had shrunk to almost nothing. Even her lips were narrower than Frances remembered. Of course, she was thirty-one now, a spinster, still sorrowing over the death of her fiancé. Frances privately thought that five years of grieving was excessive, but she kept her opinion to herself. Alexander had been killed just at the end of the war. Such a pity! He had been a handsome man, and quite well off. Frances couldn't recall which battle he had been wounded in, but the name of it didn't matter. He was dead.

Listlessly Frances rose and crossed the kitchen to the range. She pushed bits of coal into a pile and lit them, then pumped the kettle full. As she did these things, Cousin Beryl began to talk. By the time the kettle whistled, Frances's entire life had changed.

"Seven generations ago," Beryl began, "our ancestress Bridget Bishop was tried as a witch, judged guilty, and hanged for the crime."

"A witch!" Frances exclaimed, with a little laugh.

Cousin Beryl put up her hand for silence. "It is no laughing matter, Frances. It is, in fact, a life-or-death matter. Now listen." She folded her hands on the table. "Bridget had two daughters, Mary and Christian. Both inherited some part of Bridget's ability."

Frances couldn't help interrupting. "What is this ability you keep talking about? I don't know what you're—"

Harriet said, "Frances, Grandmother Beryl is trying to tell you. Be patient."

Frances scowled at being spoken to as if she were a child.

Cousin Beryl took no notice. "Bridget did have a certain talent. She was just a hedge witch, an herbalist, a maker of potions and charms and tokens. She was good at simple cures, using her ability to make liniments and salves and tinctures.

"She was also, unfortunately, adept with manikins, and her daughter Christian chose that practice. Mary was a stronger practitioner, but it was Christian who did real damage. A manikin, before you ask, is a replica of a human being. Some witches call it a poppet."

"Witches! You've said that twice now. You don't mean, really—*magic*?"

"Yes, but I think of it as power, the power of intention. In conjunction with knowledge and study and discipline, it can effect wonderful things."

"What damage did Christian do?"

"She cursed people, they say, brought on illnesses, caused accidents, ruined romances. You and your mother are descended from Christian's line. Harriet and I are from Mary's line."

"What difference does it make what line I'm from? Would it mean I have the ability?"

Beryl said without inflection, "You do have it, Frances."

The kettle had begun to whistle, but Frances didn't reach for it. She stood frozen, staring openmouthed at Beryl. "How do you know? Mother never said anything!"

"Sarah watched her own mother go mad, probably from misusing her ability. Your grandmother was shut up in an asylum, a horrible place where she died in only a few months. Sarah spent her life trying to deny her legacy out of fear, and she didn't want to see it in her daughter."

"There are good reasons for that," Harriet put in. "Her line—your line—has suffered for their dark practices. They have been ostracized, put away, even murdered."

Frances turned to Harriet. "Do you have the ability?"

"I do. I use it sometimes in my work, if I need it to strengthen my remedies." She rose and went to lift the screaming kettle from the stove and pour the boiling water into the teapot.

Frances asked Beryl, "So why do you think I have it? You hardly know me!"

Beryl nodded. "That's true, Frances, and I'm sorry. I dislike speaking ill of the dead, but that is your mother's fault. Sarah didn't care for me. For us."

"Why not?"

"As we've said, she was afraid. She didn't want to be associated with us, even after your father abandoned her."

"She said," Harriet interjected, "that she didn't want us putting ideas in your head."

"But now you are putting ideas in my head!" Frances said, her voice strained by confusion and uneasiness. She wasn't sure she believed what these two were telling her. She hadn't yet puzzled out a reason for them to lie, but they must want something from her. People always wanted something. Men were the worst, but women could be more dangerous. More subtle, harder to read.

Harriet said, "We've talked this over." She had found a tray in the cupboard, and she set it beside the stove. As she arranged cups and spoons she said, "We decided, though we are sorry for it, to go against your mother's wishes. We are all that's left of your family, and we felt we needed to speak to you for your own sake."

Frances shook her head. "I don't understand."

"It's a shock, I know," Harriet said. "You must understand that it's not safe to have the ability and not develop it. Terrible things can happen. Have happened." She carried the tray to the table and set about pouring tea into cups.

Beryl said, "Come and sit down now, Frances. We'll explain it all to you."

It was a long explanation, and it took an entire pot of tea and the little sack of pastries Beryl and Harriet had brought to get through it. When it was over, Frances's head brimmed with family history, rules for practice, places to find what she would need, and warnings about the dark practices of her ancestresses, Christian's descendants.

"You must come and live with us, I think," Beryl said, as if Frances had no say in the matter. "I will teach you, as I taught Harriet. In my tradition, of course." She sniffed. "It would be just as well if Christian's line died out, in my view."

Frances considered. On the one hand, she would not be surprised if it turned out that all of this was merely the fantasy of a batty old widow and the delusions of a bereaved spinster. It might even have been concocted solely for the purpose of deceiving her, although she couldn't see the motivation.

On the other hand, she had longed for years to escape this dingy apartment, this drab neighborhood. Though she felt no familial affection for Beryl or Harriet, Cousin Beryl's home had to be an improvement on this place. Sarah had often complained that Cousin Beryl had been fortunate to marry a man of means who left her a comfortable widow, while her own husband had vanished from her life along with the few things of value they possessed.

Frances wanted to ask how many servants there were in the house in St. George. She wondered if she was to have a proper bedroom, or if she would be expected to sleep in the maid's quarters. Cousin Beryl might even give her an allowance, if she was to become her ward.

She kept these thoughts to herself. Even if she had chores to perform at her cousin's home, or perhaps would be compelled to serve as Cousin Beryl's companion as she got older, it would still be better than trying to survive in this place.

She had no place else to go, in any case. The only work available to her was the sort her mother had done, taking in laundry, cleaning other people's homes, backbreaking labor. Working in a factory, imprisoned all day in a room full of machines and other unfortunate girls, was unthinkable.

She decided to play the grateful younger relative and wait to see what would come of Beryl's invitation. She mustered the soft smile she sometimes used on gentlemen who held a door for her or retrieved her dropped handkerchief. "I'm very grateful, Cousin Beryl," she said, letting her voice be small and sad. "I didn't have any idea what I might do next, now that Mother is gone." She managed to produce a tiny tear and allowed it to slide daintily down her cheek.

"Of course," Beryl said briskly. Frances could see she was not the type to comfort crying girls. She wiped the wasted tear and dried her wet finger on her dress.

"It will be hard work," Harriet warned. "You have a great deal to learn, since your mother taught you nothing."

Frances ignored this. She resented Harriet insulting her mother, though she could understand it. Sarah had not been an impressive person. She had been both weak and passive. If there had been some ability she could have called on, to Frances's way of thinking she should have done it. Still, Frances hated Harriet looking down that long Bishop nose and giving orders Frances was obviously expected to obey without question.

She drew a breath that trembled a little, audibly, to show she was doing her best to collect herself. "Cousin Beryl? There is one thing you haven't told me."

"What did we forget?" Beryl asked.

"I still don't understand why you're so certain I have it. This— this Bishop ability."

"Oh," Beryl said, with a wave of her hand. She was putting on her coat and arranging her shawl over it. "That's Harriet's doing. It's a rare gift. I don't have it myself, but she developed it at an early age."

"What gift?"

Harriet said, "I think of it as the knowing. I don't have a better word. I often know things when I'm working. I can't explain it."

"And you believe I have the ability."

"I don't believe anything. I know you have it."

This had to be a good thing, Frances thought. Even if Harriet was wrong—and in this case she hoped she wasn't—she could pretend to have the ability. It would be worth it to live in a decent house and meet a better class of people. Perhaps Cousin Beryl would buy clothes for her. She said, in her most girlish voice, "You're going to teach me, Cousin Beryl? Really?"

"Yes," Beryl said. She was drawing on her gloves, but she paused and gave Frances a solemn look. "But remember, Frances—no one must know any of this outside of our family."

"Why?" Not that there was anyone Frances could tell, but she thought she should know.

"Because we can accomplish things other people can't. We can control our own lives and affect the lives of others. Such power frightens people, and frightened people can be dangerous."

"More specifically," Harriet added, "frightened men are dangerous to the women who have frightened them."

"Exactly," Beryl said. "Men control the government, the money, even the law. All we have is our ability, and too often it's not enough."

Frances knew how cruel men could be. She was accustomed to the screams of women being beaten by their husbands or lovers or customers, as the case might be. She saw them in the market and in the shops, their faces bruised, their arms in slings, sometimes leaning on sticks to relieve the pain of their injured legs.

Harriet was watching her, and those stone-gray eyes seemed to see right into her brain. "It's not just physical abuse," Harriet said. "A woman can be thrown out of her house. Separated from her children. Accused of hysteria or outright insanity. If a man speaks against her, no court will hear her side. She can be put away on the flimsiest of excuses, relegated to a hospital or a jail, even an insane asylum. It's how they deal with our sort in this new age, if we are exposed."

Frances said, "I will be careful, Cousin Harriet. Cousin Beryl."

"Good." Beryl settled her wide-brimmed hat on her head. It was old, Frances noted, but of quite good quality, perhaps even a Victorine copy. She would like one of those for herself.

Beryl asked, "Do you need time to get your things together, or will you come with us now?"

"I'll come now, Cousin Beryl." Faced with this new opportunity, there wasn't a single thing she cared to carry away from this hovel of an apartment. "I'll come right now."

9

Harriet

Harriet had tried to warn Frances. She had assisted Grand-mother Beryl in the instruction of their young cousin, the two of them introducing her to the practice as judiciously as they could. They had explained herbs and their uses and made Frances memorize dozens of them so she could recognize the leaves and roots by sight, both in the wild and in the herb shop. They taught her to make the simple things first, slurries and poultices, salves and ointments, before moving on to more delicate tinctures and potions.

Harriet often wished Beryl could have lived longer, and not only because she missed her. Beryl might have eventually convinced Frances to abandon the dark practice of her ancestresses—the *maleficia*—and embrace the disciplined purity of their own. Unfortunately, though Frances had done reasonably well at her studies, and she luxuriated in the comforts of Beryl's home in St. George, things had still gone wrong. After Beryl's heart failed her, Frances lost her way.

Harriet had tried to divert her from the darker path. She knew Frances envied her, but she could forgive that. She had enjoyed an easier life than her young cousin, despite having lost her mother even earlier than Frances lost hers. Grandmother Beryl had been a rigidly disciplined guardian, a product of her stern generation, but she had filled Harriet's young, curious mind with knowledge of all sorts of things: books, history, poetry, and music. She had imparted her deep understanding of the natural world and the uses of its miraculous products, and guided Harriet's first efforts to use her ability. Above all, when it became clear that Harriet's abilities outpaced her own, Beryl had rejoiced, not resented. She had encouraged her and inspired her.

Several weeks before her death, she bestowed her own precious amulet on her granddaughter, with a blessing. Harriet had objected, saying it was too soon, she must continue to wear the amulet for protection, but Beryl only smiled and pressed it into her hand.

"Come now, Harriet dear," she murmured. "You are the one who knows things. You must know it's time, or near enough to time as makes no difference."

Harriet hadn't known, though. Or perhaps some part of her soul had known but suppressed the knowledge. Beryl's death came as a shock. Harriet had done all she could, all she knew how to do, but Beryl slipped away from her, and that was a lesson in itself. She couldn't save everyone. She couldn't defeat death itself.

She could try, however, to prevent Frances from ruining Annis's life just to win entrée to the gilded world of the Vanderbilts and the Astors. She didn't know yet if Annis had inherited the Bishop ability, but she doubted a seventeen-year-old girl, however spirited, could stand up to Frances's dark practice.

How tempting power could be to a person of shallow character!

She turned out the lights in her herbarium and went to the kitchen, where Grace was slicing vegetables for soup.

Grace looked up. "All done? That's good. Mrs. Schuyler is due any moment."

"Her treatment is ready."

"I'm glad. She did look peaked, didn't she? Didn't look well at all. Pity, pretty young lady like that, a family and all, and plenty of money. You'd think she'd be happy, have anything she wanted, and there she is, looking for all the world as if she's lost her best friend. I thought—"

Harriet let Grace run on as she walked to the sink to run a glass of water. She drank it slowly, gazing through the window to the soothing vista of the park. When the doorbell rang, Grace went to answer it and to usher Dora Schuyler into the parlor. She came back into the kitchen and began filling the kettle.

Harriet smoothed her hair and skirt. "I don't think you need to bother with tea, Grace. I doubt Mrs. Schuyler will have a taste for it."

"You're probably right," Grace said. "She doesn't look a bit better today than she did before, circles under her eyes and her hands all trembly. She'll be glad of your help, that one. Just let me know if you change your mind about the tea, and I have some fresh biscuits I just made this—"

Harriet didn't hear the end of the sentence. She went quickly into the herbarium to collect the vial she had prepared, and carried it into the parlor.

Grace was right about Mrs. Schuyler's appearance. Her eyes were hollow and shadowed, and her lips were pale. She shot to her feet when Harriet appeared, and when she put out her hand, it was shaking. Harriet held it between hers to steady it.

"Good day, Mrs. Schuyler," she said, in a matter-of-fact tone.

"Oh, oh yes. Good day," Dora Schuyler said, flushing at the lapse in her manners.

"Do sit down."

"Thank you, Miss Bishop." Mrs. Schuyler didn't precisely sit, but perched on the edge of the divan, her slight shoulders hunched. She had a small velvet purse dangling by a cord from her wrist, and she placed it in her lap and opened it by its cord. "Do you have my—my medicine?"

"Of course." Harriet sat near her and placed the vial on the inlaid table. As Mrs. Schuyler counted out several bills, Harriet said, "Mrs. Schuyler. Dora, if I may call you that, since you have trusted me with your secret. Do you have someone to be with you when you take this tincture?"

"My maid will be with me. She always is. That is, not today, but almost always."

"And does she know you're here, and why?"

"No," Dora Schuyler said. She dropped her head and stared into her open purse. "No one knows but you."

"You can't trust her?"

Dora shook her head. "I'm not sure. She might—she's capable of telling my husband. She always seems to need money."

"How are you going to explain? This is going to make you very ill."

Dora shook her head again and raised a face full of misery to Harriet. "I thought—well, I hoped I could tell her my monthlies are particularly bad. They often are."

"Ah. There are some things that can help with that, but we can address the problem at a later date. In the meantime you will have to hide from your maid just how bad your pain is. I haven't experienced the effects of an emmenagogue myself—"

"A what?"

"An emmenagogue. An abortifacient."

"Oh."

"As I said, I haven't experienced the effects, but my patients have described it to me. It's a bit of a misery, I'm afraid."

"I've had two babies."

"Yes, I remember. It will be something like that." Harriet took a piece of tissue paper from a drawer under the table. She wrapped the vial and handed it to Dora. "Take it all at once. It's probably best if you take it in the late morning, so the worst of it will take place in the hours of darkness, when most of your household is asleep." As Dora accepted the paper-wrapped vial, Harriet warned, "If you seem to be in too much distress, I fear your maid will alert your husband, and he will call for a doctor."

"Oh, a doctor...oh no, I can't see a doctor."

"You're right. A doctor will most certainly recognize what is happening."

The flush on Dora's cheeks faded in an instant, and she swayed as if she might fall. Harriet moved closer to take the woman's arm to hold her upright. "There now, Dora," she said. "You have been brave in coming to me. Now you must be brave a little longer. Twenty-four hours, no more. Your confinements doubtless took more time."

"Yes," Dora whispered. "They seemed to go on forever."

"I should warn you, also, that you may never conceive again."

"I have two children already. It's enough."

"Very well, then. I think I've told you everything."

"You can't give me anything for pain, Miss Bishop? My doctors gave me laudanum when I delivered my children."

"There is a risk the tincture will not be effective if you counter it with a palliative. I'm very sorry."

Dora nodded, closed her purse, and pushed herself to her feet. Harriet stood with her, releasing her arm with reluctance. She recognized the pain in Dora's eyes. It was a pain that would last far longer than the suffering of the actual event. Dora Schuyler didn't want to do this. She had no choice, no other path. Harriet feared the young woman's spirit might never fully recover.

"I suppose you think I'm disgusting," Dora said in a thin voice.

"Of course I do not," Harriet said. "I think you're human."

"But ladies—nice women, well brought up—we're not supposed to be..." Dora's voice faltered, and she made a half-hearted gesture with her hand.

Harriet supplied, "Passionate?"

"Yes." The word was a breath, no more.

"Forgive me for being blunt, Dora, but that's nonsense. We are no less passionate than the men we love. The trouble is that when women love, they bear the greater burden. It has always been that way, I'm afraid."

"I suppose that's true." Dora's breath whistled in her tight throat, and her eyes sparkled with unshed tears. "I thank you, Miss Bishop. I was desperate."

"I know." Harriet put out her hand, and they shook. Dora Schuyler's hand felt heartbreakingly fragile in Harriet's strong one.

"Shall I—May I come to see you again?"

"Of course you may, and I hope you will, but wait a good while. Months. Neither of us benefits if someone makes a connection between us."

"I understand."

Harriet rang the silver bell on the side table, and Grace came to see Dora out. When she was gone, Harriet walked to the tall windows that looked to the north, where a gay sunny sky mocked the sorrow of the day. She stood with one hand on the amulet beneath her bodice and watched puffs of creamy cloud, propelled by the sea wind, scud toward the west. She breathed and reminded herself that she couldn't carry the burdens of her patients. It helped neither them nor her, and it hampered her ability to heal others.

She heard Grace return from the front door and move into the kitchen, but still she stood. She hoped the beauty of the fields and scattered farmhouses might soothe her, but her memories, never far from her mind, flooded through her defenses.

Alexander had been a gentleman, a throwback to a different time. She had wanted him. Had longed for him, her body throbbing with need, but he was a man of immense honor, and she was a lady. He would not give in, and then, when their wedding was only a few months off, he was shot and killed in northern Virginia. Their future died with him.

Harriet's body had never been satisfied, not once. She would never feel that quickening of the breath, that ecstasy of skin against skin, the bliss of two bodies becoming one. She would never feel the beginnings of life in her womb or the pains of childbirth. She was barren in every sense.

Not till she felt steady again, her heart beating evenly beneath the consoling weight of Grandmother Beryl's charm, did she turn from the window to take on the next task of the day.

She had to do something about Frances.

Harriet knew where Frances practiced. She had known for years, since her cousin first moved into Allington House. Frances was adept at her craft but naive in protecting her secrets. Her solitary outings, the only ones she made without her maid, caused her servants curiosity, which no doubt Frances never suspected. It had been simple to learn her schedule, whispered in exchange for a coin in a servant's hand. People told Harriet things they would not tell anyone else.

Harriet was very good at slipping in and out of a wood or a shrubbery without being seen. One day she had waited patiently in the shade of the strip of trees edging the Allington estate, watching for Frances. When she appeared, she walked quickly with only a cursory glance about her. A string bag bulging with supplies hung from her arm.

Once Harriet knew the spot, she could walk from the Dakota to Riverside Drive and turn north along the equestrian path, veering off into the woods as the trees thinned. She didn't go often, but it had become her habit, once or twice a year, to check on the cabin, to find out what Frances was up to.

It had shocked her to realize Frances had used the *maleficia* to force George Allington. His glassy eyes at the wedding breakfast, the quickness of his breathing when Frances touched him, the wetness of his lips, revealed clearly what had happened. Harriet didn't need the knowing to understand what Frances had done.

She didn't know whether Frances had used a philter or a manikin. She didn't learn about the cabin until Frances and George had returned from their wedding journey, and whatever Frances's means had been were gone. If there had been a manikin, she had no doubt destroyed it. If she had used a philter, a love potion, there was no evidence to prove it. She had the right ingredients, scattered on the bare shelves of the cabin, but Harriet had the same ingredients in her herbarium, each used for other purposes.

Now, with the future of her great-niece at risk, she set out for the cabin once again. The *strega* had told her what Annis said, that they were about to go on a sea voyage. There was no time to lose.

She had watched from a shadowed doorway as Annis pressed money into her maid's hand and sent her into the chandler's shop. She didn't know what the maid purchased, but the glow on her plain face when she emerged told her it had been something special to her, a gift from her mistress. Harriet's heart lifted at this sign of Annis's good heart. It was not too late to save her.

She hurried to reach the cabin while she knew Frances and Annis were out. When she reached it, she was out of breath, and her feet hurt from nearly running in her street shoes. The sun was past its zenith. The time for her search was short.

A heavy padlock secured the latch on the door, but Harriet had discovered a way to get in on her first visit. On that day she had pressed one hand to the wall of the cabin, the other on the amulet beneath her dress. She had concentrated, closing her eyes to allow her mind to roam around the old building.

As Beryl had said, hers was an unusual gift. Commonly, the knowing came upon her when she was creating a remedy of some kind in the herbarium, but occasionally—if she was patient and let it sift into her consciousness without obstacles, if she opened her mind and blocked all distractions—she *knew* things, things that were hidden.

Was it guessing? That was possible, but if it was, she was very, very good at it. That first time, she stood outside the cabin for nearly an hour, seeking, wondering, waiting for inspiration. She had known, at the end of that time, where the opening was. She could see in her mind the loose, rough-hewn boards. She sensed the weakness in the ancient rusted nails that held them in place. On the back wall were three such boards, side by side, making an opening wide enough for her to slide through without snagging her clothes too badly.

Now, hurrying, she went to the spot, removed the boards, and stepped through into the dim interior. A cobweb caught at her hair, and she brushed it out with her fingers as she looked around.

Frances had been terribly careless. Unlike Harriet's immaculate herbarium, this space was littered with discarded bits of leaves and stems and roots, and a clutter of glass jars and stoppered bottles lay every which way on her work surface, as if she simply shoved each away when she was done with it. In the middle of the chaos, propped against a roll of gauze, was a manikin.

There was nothing careless about the manikin. Its eyes were a startling blue. Its lips were convincingly red and full. It wore a dress, and a fluff of dark hair crowned its wooden-bead head.

It was Annis. No one could mistake it.

"Oh, Frances," Harriet murmured. "Beryl would be heartsick."

Her knowing, coming upon her as she completed Dora Schuyler's emmenagogue, had been correct. Frances meant to use Annis. She intended to force her into a marriage that would one day turn as cold and unsatisfying as Frances's own, and Annis, innocent, unsuspecting, would have no idea what was happening to her.

Thanks to the *strega*, she knew also that Frances was about to spirit the girl away to England, beyond Harriet's reach.

Harriet couldn't let that happen. She put a finger on the manikin and felt the faint echo of magic that clung to it. Dark magic. It made her fingertip ache.

She had to leave it where it was. It was an evil thing, but now that it existed, only its creator could destroy it. Only Frances, who had spent her energy and her intention on creating this pretty little golem, could undo it.

Harriet sidled back through her makeshift door. Taking care to avoid splinters, she fitted the boards back into their places. She shook the dirt of the cabin from the hem of her skirt and dusted her hands carefully to be certain she carried no residue of Frances's tainted practice away with her.

She melted into the woods, glancing behind her once to assure herself her presence had gone undetected, then set out at a brisk pace for home. Grace would not be happy about what came next, but there was nothing to be done about it. She must send a message to secure passage on the *Majestic*. She must visit the *strega* again, for supplies, and then she must set sail for England.

Frances was going to employ the *maleficia* against Annis, and Harriet was the only person who could stop her.

10

James

It was a relief for James to be on his own for a bit, though his mother would fault him for the indulgence. He couldn't blame her, really. He had left her on her own to deal with the last details. There were the funeral guests to manage, rooms to arrange for those who would stay the night, negotiations with Cook for more meals to see them through the last of the grim rituals. In the morning would be the reading of the will, and that exercise would undoubtedly involve unwelcome revelations.

Lady Eleanor would seize the opportunity to point out his various faults, committed on this occasion and others. She had a predictable tendency to catalogue his various sins, the list getting longer and longer by the year. His absence on this difficult afternoon would be added to the litany, but he couldn't help that. He needed air, and the sound of the sea, and the uncritical company of his favorite mare. He counted on these things to cleanse his mind, to sweep the sights and smells of death from his spirit.

He had, at least, spoken to Jermyn, ordered every guest's horse fed and groomed, ready to be put into its shafts. He had taken formal leave of the relatives and friends who had come to mourn with the family, and he had sorted through the pile of sympathy cards, now addressed to him with his new title. In a way he had done his duty, but as his mother would remind him, many more duties lay ahead. Perhaps he could persuade her to understand his wish for this moment of solitude, perhaps empathize with his need for reflection. Or perhaps not. At the moment he didn't care much either way.

He paused Breeze at High Point. There he gazed over her head to the sea tossing beneath the cliffs as he tried to comprehend how profoundly his father's unexpected passing had changed his life. His years as Lord James Treadmoor were over. He had become, in the instant of his father's death, James, Marquess of Rosefield, master of Seabeck Park and Rosefield Hall. He had always known it would happen one day, but not when he was twenty-one, in the midst of pursuing his passion for history and architecture, still working on growing up, still laboring through the insecurities and fears of his youth. Some men grew up fast, it seemed. They matured early. He was not one of them.

He loved Seabeck, and it had always been his plan to one day completely devote himself to its care and preservation. He had not expected that day to come so soon.

The funeral had been a misery. He envied the Catholics, sometimes, with their curated rituals and timeworn texts and hymns. In particular he loved their "In paradisum," which was both moving and formal, refining grief and loss into a moment of pure crystal music.

He could have requested they use it in their own service, he supposed. It hadn't occurred to him. Their service, at the chapel in Seabeck Village, had been one of raw emotion, sentimental hymns, and a somehow greedy devouring of this new stage of life, a marquess dead, a new marquess in place, a marchioness become a dowager in a stroke. There were changes ahead. There were frights afoot.

He would learn how bad the frights were when the will was read and the state of the Treadmoor finances, always held close to the old marquess's vest, was revealed. His mother had been walking about with a face of stone, which meant she already knew the news was not good. She didn't speak of it. James didn't ask. She would simply have said, lips pinched in that chilly way that told him he should have known better than to press her, "Everything in its time," and told him nothing.

Breeze tossed her head, making her wavy forelock lift in the wind. "You're right," he told her, lifting the reins. "We should go back and face it. But I'd rather run off, lass, wouldn't you?" Her ears flicked back toward his voice, then forward again.

Despite his declaration, he held her in place a few moments longer, looking out to sea, watching the rising tide splash the sea stacks with foam. It didn't show up on any map, but the locals had always referred to it as High Point. A cluster of boulders on the landward side of the road marked the spot, backed by a patchy copse of windblown trees. Sometimes James dismounted to sit on one of the big rocks to eat the sandwiches Cook packed for him.

There were no sandwiches today. He stayed in his saddle, letting the sea breeze pull at his hair and cool his face and neck. Behind him stretched the bit of land they called the High Point parcel, gentle hills rich with green grass. Before him the westering sun turned the waters of the English Channel the color of old emeralds, rather like a necklace his mother had but never wore.

He released a long breath as he turned his mare toward home. His mother might have to sell that necklace, and other old pieces.

And how could he justify the expense of his Andalusians? The hay and wool and milk production couldn't keep up with the mounting debt of Seabeck. Unless his father's will held some surprising good news, the estate was in deep trouble, and with it the livelihoods of more than a hundred people.

He feared even High Point would have to go, and that felt like the end of historic Seabeck's long life.

Breeze, happily ignorant of these worries, set out toward the stables at her best swinging trot, and James tried to give himself up to the pleasure of the movement.

It was satisfying to see the fields he passed through greening nicely between the hedgerows. Sheep grazed peacefully under the late-afternoon sun. A dozen columns of smoke rose from the chimneys of his tenants' cottages, promising meals for the laborers and their families. He knew those tenants. He knew how hard they worked and how loyal they had always been. He hoped they would remain loyal to their new lord. He hoped he could protect Seabeck, enable these farmers to support their families.

He lifted his gaze toward the sandstone facade of Rosefield Hall. At this distance he couldn't make out the damage to the tiles of the roof, or the gaps where stones had fallen from the southern parapet, or the upper windows in need of reglazing, but he knew all of that was there. Thinking of the work that needed doing, and what it would cost, set a bubble of anxiety rising beneath his breastbone.

For now he tried to be grateful that the mullioned windows gleamed in the sunshine and the stone balconies above them boasted pots of flowers. The phaetons and barouches of the visitors, freshly cleaned and provisioned, awaited their owners in the drive. The lawns and shrubberies were trimmed and weeded.

Dozens of servants labored to make all of that happen, servants who would now depend upon him for their livelihoods and their welfare.

He would do his best for them all, he resolved, his tenants and his domestic staff. He would do whatever it took.

He wished he knew what that might be.

James was barely awake the next morning when his mother gave her solid double knock on his bedroom door and came in without waiting for an invitation. She went straight to the window to pull the drapes open. Blinking against the flood of sunshine, James struggled sleepily to a sitting position and, since he invariably slept without a nightshirt, reached for the dressing gown his valet had left at the foot of his bed.

"Good God," he muttered, pulling the dressing gown across his bare chest. "Mother, what time is it?"

"You shouldn't sleep naked," Lady Eleanor announced. "You'll catch your death. I'll speak to Perry about that."

James could have retorted that unless Perry were going to climb into bed with him, that would be a waste of her breath, but he held his tongue. It was easier than arguing, and James much preferred, in all cases, the smooth path to the rocky one.

He didn't answer her, but he did thrust his arms into his dressing gown and pull it over himself as best he could beneath the coverlet. "Has something happened?"

"I want to talk to you before the reading of the will this morning."

He glanced at the gilt clock above the mantelpiece of his bedroom fireplace. "Mother, it's barely seven! What are you doing out of your own bed?"

"Seeing to breakfast, of course. We still have houseguests."

He swung his feet to the floor and tied the sash on his dressing gown. "Isn't that what staff are for?"

It was a slightly provocative thing to say. Lady Eleanor brooked no criticism, even of her working too hard, which wasn't unusual, but he wasn't fully awake. On this morning, however, she let the remark pass. She settled herself into the brocaded armchair beside the fireplace with a little grunt of effort. She was, he could see, wearing her corset too tight again. He knew she hated her thickening waistline. She fought it with admirable energy, but nothing seemed to slow the expansion except tighter and tighter corsets. He was sure that couldn't be good for her, but he knew better than to speak the thought aloud.

She leaned back in the chair, and for a moment her fatigue and worry showed on her plump features, normally schooled into rigorous composure. She said with a sigh, "The news will not be good, James."

"You know this already?"

"I fear so." Lady Eleanor toyed with the lace edge of the handkerchief she had tucked into her sleeve, flicking it with one blunt fingernail. "Your father was a good person but a bad businessman."

"To be fair," James began, but his mother interrupted him with a wave of her hand.

"Oh, I know, I know," she said. "It wasn't entirely his fault. American imports are cutting badly into Seabeck's output of wheat and corn. Your Andalusians are expensive, and not many people can afford them. You haven't sold a foal this season, have you? Seabeck's income isn't keeping up with expenditures."

"I had hoped there might be some source of income I didn't know about."

"Such as what?" Lady Eleanor straightened, and her face resumed its usual rather fierce nobility, as if none of the anxieties of ordinary people could trouble her. Her nose, short and blunt, thrust up like a terrier's scenting prey.

James squirmed on the edge of the bed, embarrassed about the nakedness of his long, pale shins. He wished he were dressed so he could pace around the room. "Well, Mother, I don't know exactly—I had thought perhaps some of the older paintings, furniture we don't use...Some of it is so uncomfortable, surely we could..." He broke off under the pressure of her narrowed gaze.

"James, listen to me. When a family begins to sell its heirlooms, all is lost. It's over. Everyone can see that it's the end for the family, no matter how noble."

"We could sell the London house," he ventured, but her eyes blazed with instant fury.

"No, we could not." She pushed herself to her feet and stood with her hands linked before her. The pose looked contained and calm, but he saw how her knuckles whitened. "The Marquess of Rosefield does not begin selling off his property. Nor—" Her eyes glinted with anger. "Nor does the dowager marchioness part with her jewelry, under any circumstances. These are acts of desperation. Everyone would know it. You're not even to consider it."

"Yes, Mother," James said meekly. He knew his lady mother's jewel case, and the safe in his father's library, were both overfull with rings and brooches and tiepins that were never taken out. The house in London maintained a staff year-round, even though they used it only during the season. He had to look away, lest his awareness of all that should show in his face. He wasn't nearly so good as she at disciplining his expression.

He should, he thought, as he fixed his eyes on the white clouds drifting across the sky beyond his window, stand up for himself. Point out that he was now the marquess and must do what he thought best.

He didn't have the courage. His father had never found it, either.

Lady Eleanor was not finished. "You," she proclaimed, her voice vibrating with the authority she had wielded his whole life, "will have to marry money."

At that his head snapped up, and he stared at her, aghast. "Mother!"

Her gaze never wavered. "There is nothing to be done for it. You're hardly the only nobleman in England facing the same... let us call it *choice*."

He stood up, careless of his bare legs and the inadequate coverage of his dressing gown, and gazed at her in horror.

She blew out a breath, but her posture did not relax. "You're old enough to face these things, James. My marriage to your father was hardly a love match. Our properties merged, which has been a good thing, a successful enterprise. At least," she finished, with just the slightest hint of defeat, "it was until the last decade or so."

He found his voice, although it was hoarse with shock. "But, Mother—you knew each other from childhood! You weren't strangers."

Lady Eleanor's expression didn't alter, but she stepped to the window to hold back a fold of heavy velvet drape and gaze out onto the raked gravel drive and the manicured gardens that spread all around the house. The gardens had been his father's special passion, and more than once he had seen his parents, his mother's hand tucked under her husband's arm, strolling together before coming in to dress for dinner. They were talking, sometimes. Other times they were just walking, side by side, enjoying the waning day.

James's throat tightened with the grief he had been suppressing. "Mother, I'm sorry. I know you're going to miss Father. I will, too."

"I know, dear," she said, in a tone so unaccustomedly mild that he almost went to put a comforting hand on her shoulder. He restrained himself, knowing she would hate it. He had never seen her weep. He was quite sure he never would.

He tightened the sash on his dressing gown and waited, aware that if there were tears in her eyes she wouldn't turn until they had subsided.

In less than a minute, his mother cleared her throat, jerked the velvet curtain decisively, as if she had gone to the window merely to adjust a fold of it, and turned to him. "You'd better ring for Perry," she said. "It's time to dress and join our guests in the morning room. The solicitor will be here at eleven."

She marched away from him toward the bedroom door, and he stood helplessly watching her. They were rarely affectionate with each other. That wasn't done in their social class. He had spent most of his youth at boarding school, and even when he was home on holidays, his parents were often abroad. Lady Eleanor was in many ways a hard woman, with old-fashioned principles and a spine as stiff as American iron.

Still, he admired her, and he certainly respected her. She was a fine example of a woman of her class, a true noblewoman who accepted her duties and responsibilities without demur. She would, of course, expect him to do the same.

He stood frozen in place as she went out and closed the door behind her with a decisive click. He wished he had found the words to tell her what he thought. A new century was coming, he wanted to protest. A new age was just around the corner. There had to be something he could do to save Seabeck, something practical, businesslike. Streamline farm production. Sell a parcel of land. Cut some corners.

The idea of putting himself on the marriage market, as if he were one of his Andalusian colts, filled him with self-loathing.

Other men in his position had done it, of course. They attended the balls and teas of the London season, singled out the richest heiress they could find, and secured their futures that way. There was a regular business associated with the process.

He wanted nothing to do with it.

He crossed to the bellpull and summoned his valet. He would go through the proper motions. He would listen to the provisions of the will and examine the finances of the estate.

As he waited for Perry, he moved to the window and took up the spot his mother had occupied. He gazed past the gardens and the drive to the woods beyond, and past those to the gentle slope of the coombe rising to the top of the hill.

If there was one sentiment he shared with Lady Eleanor, it was the love of Seabeck, of the house and grounds and stables and farms, the woods and hills and streams. Seabeck had been in the family since the Wars of the Roses. James felt his roots here as surely as if he were one of the great beeches growing in the woods. His heart seemed to beat with the rhythm of the life of Seabeck, and he wanted nothing more than to live and work right here, raising his horses, assisting his tenants, managing his estate.

The new Marquess of Rosefield would take his seat in the House of Lords as expected, but his heart would always be here, in Dorset, in the family seat. Surely, as the century drew to a close, a man should choose his own path.

If he could find it.

11

Annis

A nnis enjoyed the sea voyage despite herself. The *Majestic* seemed to her a wondrous vessel, with decks to explore and a bountiful library. Dinners were elegant affairs, with waiters in white coats and gloves, officers in their dark coats with shiny buttons, women in beaded gowns and long white gloves. She usually prided herself on her disdain for such luxuries, but aboard ship they seemed part of a different life, a separate life.

She worried about Bits, of course, but Robbie had promised to watch over him. She had made a fresh poultice, adding the recommended powdered ginger, and had wrapped it around his leg herself, with instructions to Robbie to see that it remained for at least three days. On board the *Majestic*, however, there was nothing further she could do. She had to trust that Robbie would see to Bits's welfare. She decided she might as well give herself over to the adventure.

And adventure it was. Frances, who found herself queasy at the slightest rise of the sea, spent most of her time in the stateroom, which set Annis free to roam the deck, breathing the pungent sea air, watching the waves splash against the hull. She spent hours in the library, dipping into history books and novels and a well-thumbed Baedeker. She took satisfaction in administering doses of ginger tea, which she made in her stateroom, to Velma, and watching her maid's greenish complexion turn back to its usual sallow color. She made tea for her stepmother, too, and received a nod of gratitude that made her feel, briefly, like a real herbalist.

She was surprised, on one of her exploratory tours, to discover half a dozen horses several decks below her own. They traveled in specially constructed stalls with padded walls and straw-covered floors. Annis watched their grooms struggle against the swaying of the ship, filling water buckets and scraping out soiled straw. When one of them slipped and fell, spilling a bucket of grain, she leaped forward, thinking she could help him, but he looked shocked at the sight of a girl from first class coming toward him across the soiled floor, and pretended not to notice her.

She hurried away with her cheeks burning, and she didn't visit that deck again.

She was not the only American girl being escorted to the marriage market of the London season. She encountered two others in the first-class lounge. One was a haughty-looking girl with a high forehead and a voice to match. Her maid was at her side every moment. The second was tiny and thin, dwarfed by her gowns and scarves and jewels, and accompanied by an overbearing woman who Annis guessed must be her mama. The girl had a frightened look that gave Annis a twinge of sympathy.

She made no attempt to meet either. She was not one of them.

When the rooflines of Liverpool came into view, she was surprised to feel regret that the voyage had reached its end. It had been a week of peace, of relative freedom from duty and obedience. She wondered if she should ever have another like it.

*   *   *

The train journey from Liverpool to London was another matter. Annis had no time to savor the scenery, to enjoy the variety of accents, to marvel at the different food, the wonderful tea, the excruciating courtesy of every servant and official.

Frances fussed endlessly, counting their luggage, ordering Antoinette and Velma back and forth from the dining car, making Annis check and recheck their documents. The peace of the ocean voyage vanished in the steam of the train's engines and was not restored by their chaotic arrival, the calling for porters to handle the trunks and valises, the hailing of horse-drawn taxicabs until one finally agreed to carry them to their hotel. By the time they reached it, Annis was tense and snappish, Velma was on the verge of tears, and Antoinette had gone silent, behaving as if she no longer understood English.

Their hotel, called the Swan, was a small one. Furniture crowded the lobby, crimson velvet settees and chairs upholstered in gold brocade. The suite was just as crowded, with wardrobes and bureaus filling every wall. Even the extra dressing room Frances had insisted on was jammed with furniture. The two maids had to stay on a separate floor, which Frances didn't mind, but when she realized she and Annis would be forced to share a bath, her already-frayed temper broke. The bellhop sent for the manager, who sent for the hapless clerk who had booked the rooms. Complaints and demands flew, and there was much running up and down the staircase as the staff tried to placate the American lady.

The hotel might not have met Frances's exacting requirements, but for Annis it was perfect. Just across the road was a park with sun-washed grass, stands of trees, and a broad, manicured drive.

She whispered a question to one of the bellhops and learned that it was called Regent's Park.

From the bit of it she could see, she thought it must be every bit as beautiful as Central Park at home. In the distance a fountain's jets of clear water sparkled in the afternoon sun. Horses trotted along the path, their riders wearing handsome jackets and tall hats. She spotted two female riders in sidesaddles, elegant habits draped over their horses' hindquarters. Small carriages bowled along with liveried drivers at the reins and well-dressed women seated behind them, holding parasols. It was a scene as bright and cheerful as the hotel was dark and grim.

Annis seized her moment while Frances was engaged in complaining about the linens. It wasn't quite fair to leave Velma unprotected, but she could scarcely breathe in the airless rooms. She yearned for the fresh air and sunshine.

She sidled out of the room while Frances was scolding a housemaid. She lifted up the short train of her traveling suit, that pointless extra fabric that always threatened to trip her, and dashed down the stairs, nearly colliding with the doorman. He hastened to pull the doors open for her, and she darted outside to dash across the road and on into the park.

She had expected London to be a cold place, beset by fogs and showers, but on this day the early-June sun poured over the stands of ash and cedar. A shrub she didn't recognize edged the raked ground of the path. She found a scrolled iron bench where she inadvertently frightened off a squirrel as she sat down to feel the sun on her shoulders and to watch people and horses enjoying the beautiful afternoon.

The horses appeared to be mostly Thoroughbreds, blacks and chestnuts and bays, with arching necks and the small, delicate heads typical of the breed. She eyed them idly, picking out the ones who might be a match for Black Satin, though there was an ocean between them. Content with this pastime, she stretched out her legs and leaned back against the bench, enjoying the familiar sounds of hooves on hard ground, well-oiled leather creaking, bridles jingling as the intermittent parade of equestrians passed by.

When a different horse appeared, she straightened in surprise. It was a heavier breed than the ones she had seen so far, a handsome white mare with a short, muscular neck, wide shoulders, and a hawklike profile that implied strength and nobility. Her mane and tail were golden brown, and wavy, as if they had been braided and then brushed. Her gait was clean and crisp, and she bore her rider, a tall man with long legs, as if he weighed nothing at all.

Suddenly England was interesting. This mare would be perfect to cross with Black Satin, if the obstacle of the Atlantic Ocean could be overcome. She was sturdy. She appeared to have a level disposition, paying no attention to the other mounts who passed her or the rattle and bang of the occasional landau. She carried herself beautifully, with a nice balance between the set of her head and the movement of her hindquarters. She held her silken tail high, a sure sign of joy and pride.

Annis jumped up, admiring the flex and stretch of the mare's hindquarters as she trotted past.

"I want that horse!" Annis exclaimed, making a gentleman and a lady strolling by look at her in surprise. Startled, she put her gloved fingers to her lips. In her enthusiasm she hadn't realized she was speaking aloud.

The horse and its lanky rider disappeared around a bend, leaving her gazing after them. She wished Robbie could have seen the mare. She would be interested in his opinion. She wished she had flagged the rider down so she could ask about the horse, perhaps even see if she might be for sale.

And she wanted to ride the horse herself, to feel that strong movement, that stout back, to know if the mare's mouth was soft or hard, if her gait was as smooth as it looked.

But it was a big park, and the path was long. There was little chance she could find the horse and rider if she went looking for them. The sun was beginning to sink beyond the trees, and though a few pedestrians still lingered on the grass, all the horses and carriages seemed to have gone. Frances would be looking for her, no doubt wanting her to dress for dinner. Velma would be getting anxious.

Annis took one last look behind her at the spray of the fountain glistening in the lowering rays of the sun. She was still watching it shimmer against the fading sky as she picked up her skirts to cross the path.

She heard the rattle of hoofbeats, but too late. She leaped back, out of the way of a horse coming at full gallop along the now-deserted path. The train of her traveling suit caught on her left boot, and she stumbled, then fell to the ground with a thump. Her eyes watered at the impact. Her hat flew off her head as if she had tossed it.

"Oh damn! Miss? Are you all right, miss?"

She struggled to a sitting position, fighting the tangle of her skirts and the constriction of her bodice. The rider of the horse dismounted in a leap and crouched beside her, one hand under

her right elbow, the other reaching for her left hand. He said
again, "Oh, do tell me you're all right! I didn't see you there! I
was sure this part of the park was deserted, now it's getting so
dark, and—oh damn!"

She leaned on him as she got to her feet and shook out the
troublesome skirts. "I'm not hurt," she told him. She was sure to
have an embarrassing bruise under her chemise, but there was no
need to admit that. "I'm the one who must apologize. I was looking at the—so silly of me—looking back at the fountain when
I should have been watching the path. I thought everyone had
gone, too."

Standing straight at last, she looked up and saw that the horse
who had almost run her down was the white mare she had so
admired. "It's you!" she exclaimed.

The man misunderstood. "Me?" he said. His voice was nice,
quite deep. She was surprised to find he was a full head taller
than she, something that didn't often happen. He said, "Have we
met? I'm sorry, but I don't—"

"Oh no, not you, sir! I meant the horse!"

He stared at her, openmouthed. She realized how strange that
must have sounded, and how odd she must look, hatless and
disheveled.

She straightened her jacket, bent to retrieve her hat, and tried
to regain some dignity. "I should explain," she said. "I saw your
mare earlier and wished I could see her again. I was startled and
spoke without thinking."

He closed his mouth and regarded her solemnly. He really was
very tall, rather young, and too lean for his height. He had a
shock of pale hair worn long on his collar, and quite good hazel
eyes, darkened now with alarm.

"I'm so sorry," she said again. She put out her hand, saw at the last moment that her glove was grimy from her fall, and retracted it. "I didn't mean to be rude. I just—I love horses, you see."

"Then we are well met. I love horses, too."

"What's your mare's name?"

"This is Breeze. She's an Andalusian."

"Is she? Oh, that's marvelous! I did wonder. I have the perfect stud for her."

The young man's eyes widened, and Annis couldn't resist a laugh. "Oh dear," she said. "I keep shocking people. I never intend to, truly. I'm a horse breeder, you see. I have a marvelous Thoroughbred stallion at home, called Black Satin, and I'm looking for mares exactly like this one to start my new bloodline."

"Ah. Well." He turned to his mare as if seeking refuge from Annis's barrage of words. "Well, here she is. I—This seems rather an improper topic to be discussing with a young lady, but perhaps…"

Annis was tired of being told she was improper, and thoroughly bored with people pretending she couldn't know about such a practical thing as breeding animals, but she tried to hide her impatience behind courtesy. "May I examine Breeze more closely?"

He stepped back a little, letting the reins go slack. Annis saw with approval that the mare didn't shy away from her in the least, although she twisted her head to see the newcomer. "Lovely girl," Annis murmured as she held out her hand for the horse to sniff. "Lovely big girl, aren't you, Breeze?"

She ran her hand under the thick mane, down the ridge of muscle to the point of the shoulder. She bent to feel the strength of the forearm and the knee, and the mare immediately lifted her hoof. Annis grinned at this familiar action and accepted the hoof, balancing it on her thigh, examining the pastern with her fingers. It was getting too dark to see, in truth, but she didn't want to miss a moment with this horse.

When she straightened, letting Breeze set her foot down, the young man said, "You do know horses. You surprise me."

Annis brushed at the smudge of dirt the mare's hoof had left on her skirt. "Why? Because I'm a female?"

"I don't know any girls who would pick up a horse's hoof that way."

Annis patted Breeze's warm shoulder. "I take care of my horses myself."

"Even the stallion?" His fair eyebrows rose.

"Especially the stallion," she said, with a lift of her chin. "I supervise everything that happens with Bits. I mean, with Black Satin."

"You don't mean . . . surely not everything."

"Yes," she said. "Of course! It can be a delicate process, don't you think? The servicing of a mare by a stallion can sometimes be complicated—"

He gave an audible gasp and actually drew away from her as if her crudeness might be infectious. "Miss," he began, and then seemed to have run out of words.

She exhaled an exasperated breath. "You're shocked. I told you I shock people."

"Oh no, no," he said, but he sounded as if he would choke on the words.

If she hadn't been afraid she would startle the mare, she would have stamped her foot. "Why should it shock you that

I understand how foals are created? If the horses do not join together—their bodies, I mean, so that…" She could see she had lost him.

He cleared his throat, probably to stop her speaking. He looked away from her, out to the road beyond the park, as if he were searching for something. "I—I must be on my way, I'm afraid. An engagement. Please excuse me."

"Of course. It's getting late." She stepped back to give him room to mount. When he was in the saddle, resettling his hat on his head, she couldn't help asking, "Do let me see Breeze again, though, when the light is better. Is she stabled nearby?"

He hesitated, just long enough that she knew he was choosing how to refuse. "I'm sorry," he said. "We're due to start back to our country house tomorrow." He lifted the reins and touched the brim of his hat.

"Wait, sir—could we—perhaps I could—"

"Sorry, miss," he said again. "Must dash. Very nice to have met you."

It was clear he couldn't wait to escape the American girl's blunt talk.

Annis could see she was not going to like Englishmen. This one hadn't even told her his name, and all she wanted was a closer look at his horse, perhaps a chance to bargain for her.

The horse and her tall rider were already gone. Annis stepped out into the path to watch as the mare moved from the trot into a smooth canter, her pretty tail rippling in the breeze. Annis's breast throbbed, first with desire to possess that wonderful horse, then with a surge of irritation over yet another man refusing to acknowledge her competence.

"Piffle," she muttered at the man's retreating back. "Who cares what some English stuffed shirt thinks, anyway?"

Frustrated, she stamped out of the park and back toward the Swan.

Velma met Annis at the door to the suite, and the relief on her face at seeing her mistress whole and safe filled Annis with compunction.

"Oh, Velma! You mustn't worry so. I just went out into the park. It's beautiful. When you have a moment you should go."

"Yes, Miss Annis," Velma said, in a voice that threatened incipient tears. "I didn't know where you was."

"I know, and I'm sorry. Where's Frances?"

Velma pointed at the door to the dressing room Frances had claimed for herself. "She's bin in that little room for ages. Don't know what she's doing, but Antoinette and me was getting awful hungry. Antoinette went to the kitchens to see if they will give us something."

"Frances is in there alone?" Suddenly brimming with curiosity, Annis started toward the dressing-room door.

Velma hissed a warning. "She said no one goes in there, only her! Don't, Miss Annis. She said!"

Annis stopped where she was, wondering what Frances was about. There was a smell in the suite, something like incense burning. And was that candle wax? It must be. But why should there be candles here? The hotel was fully electrified, though the lamps were so heavily shaded they cast hardly any light.

She took another step, hoping to hear something from the little room, but Velma's fresh gasp of horror stopped her. It wasn't worth upsetting the poor thing, so she turned away to her own bedroom. "All right, Velma. Come along. I need to dress for dinner." Still, as she and Velma went into her room to sort out an ensemble, she looked back, burning with curiosity about what Frances could be doing.

12

Frances

The little room was too small to be of much use. Its walls were too close, and the dressing table nearly filled the space. Though it was meant to be a dressing room, it was impossible for Antoinette and Frances to occupy it at the same time. It was perfect.

Frances locked the door before extracting her things from the string bag. She lifted out a pottery saucer and an unburned beeswax candle. There was the little vial of her blood, which would need refreshing. The tarnished compact with its trove of nail clippings came next, then mandrake root, dried mistletoe leaves, and stems of dried barrenwort, complete with the flowers, their lavender color faded to gray.

Last of all, carefully wrapped in tissue, was the manikin.

It had not been easy to hide the bag from Antoinette on the journey. Antoinette had packed Frances's valises and trunks and knew every item they held. Frances had been forced to slide the string bag into a small valise without Antoinette seeing, then remove it before her maid began the unpacking.

Now, on their first day in London, she made her start. She

planned to choose her target as soon as possible, and she needed Annis to be in the perfect frame of mind when the moment came.

Such work took time. It had taken her six weeks to magic George, administering her philter when they dined together. Here in England she had a scant eight weeks to bend Annis to her will. To force her, Harriet would say, but Frances didn't care what Harriet would say. A philter would not work, not in these circumstances. But Frances knew what would.

The *maleficia*.

"The *maleficia* may win a practitioner what she wants," Beryl had said. "But she pays a terrible price."

Frances smiled to herself, gazing down at the manikin. She remembered saying to Beryl, "Why do you keep saying 'practitioner'? Why don't you just say 'witch'? Isn't that what we are?"

Beryl had looked down that formidable nose. "We told you at the beginning, Frances. We take care with our words because we are at risk from the ignorant and the weak-minded."

Frances rolled her eyes. "I remember what you said."

"Yet I can see you're not taking it seriously. Have you heard of Blackwell's Island, the lunatic asylum?"

"Of course. It's a hideous place, but nothing to do with us. It's for—well, Blackwell's is for lunatics!"

"I know of at least three practitioners languishing there, women of our own kind imprisoned on Blackwell's Island. They were careless. They practiced the *maleficia*, and it redounded upon them in the worst way."

"What do you mean?"

"They were committed for 'aberrant behavior.' One was turned over by her husband, who paid a doctor to diagnose her as a hysteric. Another was reported by her neighbors for selling an abortion potion, and she was convicted under the Comstock Laws. Someone decided the asylum was better than prison, although I doubt that's true.

"The third, I'm sorry to say, was your grandmother. That was why your mother was terrified of the practice."

As Frances digested this bit of history, it occurred to her that Harriet and Beryl were afraid of the *maleficia*, too. That, she decided, was the real reason they refused to teach it to her.

But she, Frances, wasn't afraid of anything. She took pride in that and set about studying the *maleficia* on her own.

She spent hours in the library in Beryl's house, reading and memorizing the books assigned to her. She spent even more hours, when she was left alone, searching through the other books, the ones she wasn't meant to read but that she had known must be there somewhere.

They were older than any other books in the library, with cracked bindings and fading script. Someone—perhaps Beryl, perhaps someone even older—had hidden them behind less remarkable volumes, shelving them so high she had to climb on a chair to reach them. Their fragile pages held the secrets she wanted, the recipes for philters and the instructions for making poppets, also known as manikins. Some bore the initials of witches long dead. Some were so blurred with age they were impossible to read, but others—others were a treasure trove of forbidden knowledge. Of the *maleficia*.

Frances took great care with those books and always replaced them exactly as she had found them. Since Harriet often looked over her book of recipes, she wrote nothing down. She committed what she found to memory and then began to experiment.

She made a neighbor's cat follow her for days, tagging at her heels whenever she stepped out of the house. She caused a hummingbird to fly in manic circles, as if it had lost its little mind. When the bird bashed itself to death on the window glass, she felt a moment's regret before she told herself she had to learn somehow. Once she made a manikin of the rag man, just for the practice, and gave him a lame leg for a week.

After that success she decided it would be best to resist the compulsion of the *maleficia*. She had learned enough, and she resolved to do no more.

Stopping was more difficult than she had expected. The use of the power, the thrill of wielding her magic, was better than any drug she could imagine, more intoxicating than any wine she could drink. She struggled against it, pretending to be content producing the simples and salves her cousins wanted to teach her.

It was when she met the wealthy widower George Allington that her resolve failed. Fate had handed her exactly the prize she craved. She had only to reach for it, and the transformation of her life would begin. She would no longer be the poor relation from Brooklyn, destitute, dependent. She would be a lady.

She used everything she had learned to create the perfect philter. Persuading George to drink it had been simple, and its effect was gratifyingly swift.

The first step of her plan had been a great leap. The second step, acquiring a title in the family, was now within her reach. The third would be her acceptance into the Four Hundred, after which she meant to give up magic altogether. She would no longer need it.

It was unfortunate that she was having to bring Annis to heel through magical means, but the girl left her no choice. Surely

Annis would be grateful, in the end. She would have a wonderful life, titled, privileged. It would be, indeed, the very life Frances would have wished for, had the opportunity presented itself. Since it hadn't, her stepdaughter would be the beneficiary of her ability.

She dropped three of her fingernail parings into the pottery saucer and dripped a bit of the blood and wine from the glass vial over them. She shredded three leaves of dried mistletoe and crumbled the flowers, stems, and leaves of barrenwort on top. Finally she shaved a half inch of mandrake root, diced it fine, and mixed it in with the other ingredients.

She put a match to the candle and held the saucer above the flame until the mixture within began to bubble. When it had reduced to a speck of thick dark syrup, she scooped it up on her fingertip. She lifted the skirt of the manikin and rubbed the syrup on the little figure, down its belly, between its makeshift legs, whispering the cantrip she had devised for this purpose:

The power of witch's blood and claws
Bends your will unto my cause.
Root and leaf in candle fire
Invest you with impure desire.

It was at such times, she knew, that Harriet sometimes experienced the knowing. Frances had waited for years for it to happen to her, but she had been forced, finally, to admit it wasn't coming. She didn't have that particular gift.

Still, each time she completed a rite, so carefully prepared, her intention hard and clear as diamond, she closed her eyes, hoping. It seemed terribly unfair that Harriet should have the gift and not she. It didn't help that Harriet said it was not often a blessing. It was knowledge, and knowledge was power.

Frances needed power above all else. How else was she to erase the memory of the poverty-stricken girl from Brooklyn? How else was she to achieve her ambition, a lowly female in a world of men?

The simulacrum began to grow warm beneath her probing finger. Five minutes passed, then ten, until, ever so slightly, the thing wriggled under her hand.

Frances's eyes flew open. The manikin still stared up at her, its eyes empty, its little fluff of hair and its red painted mouth just as before. It lay still beneath her hand.

But it had moved. There could be no doubt. It had vibrated under her fingers, and the magic of it brought a deep ache between her hip bones, a pain like that of childbirth. The pain surprised her, stealing her breath and making her fingers shake.

Carefully she set the manikin down so she wouldn't drop it. She had not felt this way in the past, but she was wielding a far greater magic than she ever had before. She pressed a hand to her stomach. She had never given birth, but she thought this must be what it felt like, a sensation redolent with blood and pain and, in the end, triumph.

And sometimes death, of course. But Frances had no intention of dying.

She heard the outer door of the suite open and close, the voices of the maids chattering with Annis about dresses and dinner, cloaks and shoes, ribbons and necklaces.

Frances, breathing shallowly above the pain in her belly, rearranged the handkerchief dress on her manikin. She stoppered the vial and blew out the candle. When everything was restored to the string bag, its top securely tied with a knot only she knew how to undo, she tucked it into a drawer of the dressing table, closed the drawer, and locked it. She stood, smoothing her skirts and tidying her hair, waiting the few moments it would take for her eyes to cease their gleaming and her belly to ease its ache.

When she was sure nothing untoward would show on her face, she went to the door and opened it.

"Antoinette," she said. "We will have to dress in the bedroom. This room is far too small for both of us." She turned to see that Annis was already in her dinner dress, her pearls around her neck, but she was stretched full length on a brocade settee. "Something wrong, Annis?"

Annis made a face. "I don't know exactly. I felt fine, but suddenly—it's my stomach. I feel a bit queasy. Achy."

Frances schooled her expression into one of sympathy. "Ah, poor thing. I don't believe you ate a thing at lunch, did you? What you need is a good dinner. I will hurry to dress. The dining room is expecting us at eight."

It had taken a bit of persuasion and a substantial sum of money for Frances to acquire the letter of introduction to Lady Whitmore, who lived in Mayfair. "Not precisely on Grosvenor Square," Frances explained to Annis as they rode in the hired carriage for their first London call. "But close enough, I think, to be considered a good address."

Annis appeared to have recovered from the first effects of her rite. She was cheerful this morning. She liked the open carriage, which allowed her a good view of the stucco-fronted houses facing the park and a glimpse of the Gothic facade of the Houses of Parliament ranged along the river.

Annis protested at first over making a social call instead of going to the British Museum, but then, under the influence of Frances's newly established authority—*Witch's blood and claws*—she subsided. Frances smiled to herself and wondered why she had not made this happen sooner.

She thought Annis looked rather well, thanks to the choices she had made for her. She wore a visiting dress of white cotton trimmed with pink lace. Frances had personally overseen the dressmaker's work, and she was pleased with the results. There was a matching pair of gloves. Annis's waist was not as small as Frances's own, of course, but she was a good bit taller, and that was to be expected. Frances would have liked wider, more fashionable sleeves, and tighter at the wrist, but Annis had insisted she needed to be able to use her arms. Her hat was wide brimmed, with a plume of the palest pink Frances could find. There would be no more bent and stained straw hats.

Frances's own appearance was perfect. Her waist was tiny beneath her creamy printed cotton, the corset cinched as tightly as Antoinette could manage. Her hat was also of cream, with curling feathers that grazed her cheek, and her gloves were cream silk with threads of gold. She looked, she felt certain, expensive. A proper lady. No one would guess at her origins.

The carriage swept along the road at a good clip. The driver, a man recommended by the hotel, was respectably dressed in a long-skirted coat. When they reached the Whitmore house he jumped down to hand the ladies and their maids out of his carriage.

Frances shook the creases out of her skirts as Antoinette adjusted the feather on her hat. Velma stood idle, staring at nothing, making Frances snap at her. "For pity's sake, Velma! Don't just stand there. Check Annis's buttons. Tuck her hair back."

Velma's sallow cheeks went scarlet. She poked at Annis here and there, not to much effect, then stood back again, her head hanging. Annis stood limply, not even intervening to protect Velma from Frances's temper as she usually did. Frances gave an impatient click of her tongue as she turned to survey the house they were about to visit.

This one wasn't Georgian, like the homes nearest Regent's Park. It was newer, narrower, built of colored brick, with a bow window and an elaborate set of double doors.

Frances's catlike smile curved her lips. Allington House was much bigger than the Whitmore house, and far grander, with more elaborate ironwork and generous gardens. She would not feel intimidated in the least.

She straightened, patted her purse, where her letter of introduction waited, and said, "Come, Annis. Let us try our luck in London society."

13

James

"Not Americans, Mother," James said. "Please! They're so vulgar."

She pursed her lips. "Tell me, Rosefield, when have you met any Americans? Do you have a social life I don't know about?"

His mother had recently taken to calling him by his title. James knew other families did it, but it irked him just the same. It intensified his awareness that the title was not so much a mantle laid on his shoulders as it was a burden he could never lay down.

He and Lady Eleanor were alone, seated at the breakfast table in the morning room. There was no reason she couldn't call him by his Christian name, as she had always done.

He sipped his coffee and held his tongue. If he complained, she would lose her temper, scold him for lack of respect for his heritage, spoil the bright June morning, and still call him whatever she wanted to call him.

He swallowed the mouthful of coffee. He could have said that his social life was his own, but he didn't say that, either. "It was hardly a social encounter. As it happens, I met an American in Regent's Park. I was riding Breeze, and she was quite taken with her. We—"

"It was a woman?"

"Yes. Well, a girl. I have to say, Mother, she was distressingly blunt."

"About what?"

He set down his cup. "I don't care to repeat it. It would embarrass you. *I* was embarrassed."

"Well, of course one must have standards, but I think you will find the young lady I met at Lady Whitmore's to be quite modest. She hardly said a word, to tell you the truth, but her appearance was...acceptable."

Her hesitation was not lost on her son.

She went on, "Lady Whitmore knows a great many Americans, Rosefield, and not one lacks a healthy fortune."

"Gloria Whitmore has made an occupation out of introducing Americans to London society. She must make hundreds of pounds simply by holding tea parties."

Lady Eleanor chuckled. "I know, my dear," she said. "One might prefer she be less obvious about it, but since she isn't, we must take advantage." She put one plump hand to her throat, where she wore a cameo on a black ribbon. She was in deep mourning, a black shirtwaist and black skirt, black gloves when she went out. She seemed more comfortable today, though. She had evidently not felt the need to cinch her corset so tightly for breakfast at home.

She said, "Lady Whitmore is not someone I should normally socialize with, to be frank, but these are not normal times for us."

"But did you have to invite these people to Seabeck? Before I've even met them?"

"Don't fuss. It will mostly be the usual summer house party, except for them. Gloria Whitmore will be there, with that dour husband of hers. I felt I had to invite them, under the circumstances. The Hyde-Smiths are coming, as always, and the Derbyshires. You'll hardly notice the Americans."

"What's their name, these Americans?"

"Oh, I don't recall just now. There were so many guests at Lady Whitmore's tea. I've written it down somewhere."

James didn't believe this for an instant. His mother had a memory for names and titles like no one else. She could have consulted for *Burke's* if she cared to.

Clearly she didn't want him to do research of his own to determine who the Americans were, and that gave him a slight feeling of power over her, the first he had sensed. She must believe that if he put his foot down—as he could now that he was the marquess, he supposed—she couldn't refuse him. She was, after all, only the dowager.

It was a new and quite revolutionary thought, and his mind skittered away from it like a horse shying from an approaching train.

He finished his breakfast, excused himself, and headed out to the stables, where he ordered Jermyn to saddle Seastar, his Andalusian stallion.

The stableman gave him a doubtful look. "He hasn't been out in a while, my lord. Likely to be rambunctious, especially on a sunny day like this."

"Good. I will welcome the distraction."

Seastar was, as Jermyn had warned, restive and headstrong, much in need of a good run. As James trotted him up the coombe and out into the fields above Rosefield Hall, he was fully occupied with keeping the horse under control. A half hour passed with Seastar dancing and pretending to shy at birds and breeze-stirred bushes. When they reached an open pasture, James set him to the gallop to burn off his pent-up energy.

When the prancing and sidestepping eased, James slowed Seastar to a walk, letting his thoughts return to the problem of the London house. It had been built during the Regency, and it needed work as much as Rosefield Hall did. The window casings were beginning to splinter, and the brickwork on the upper floors was stained by coal dust. Here and there bricks had fallen from the walls, and rust grew on the ironwork balustrades.

Perhaps, he thought, he could find the courage to tell his mother they must sell it after all. He could stay at his club when he went up to town, and she—well, they would have to find a hotel or persuade a friend to accommodate her. They could save hundreds every year in upkeep and staff salaries.

He shuddered to think of Lady Eleanor's ire if he were to announce such a move, but her anger wouldn't last forever. He would just have to endure it. It was far worse to think of enduring a marriage made for money, and a marriage with a girl whose appearance was only "acceptable," to boot. Surely, in this new age, marriages should be chosen, not arranged.

He urged Seastar into a canter, for his own sake this time, hoping to push all of it out of his mind before it drove him completely mad.

14

Harriet

Harriet took a second-class stateroom on the *Majestic*. In second class no one would remark on the fact that she traveled without a lady's maid, and there was no chance whatsoever that Frances would venture below the first-class deck, so there would be no accidental encounter. She spent the voyage reading and resting as the ship carried her to Liverpool, gathering her strength for the conflict to come.

When they docked, it was easy to follow Frances and her frantic entourage. Harriet wore unremarkable clothes and a hat with a thick veil. She had laughed when Grace suggested she pack a tea gown. She dressed simply, a woman of no particular class, a tall, solitary American spinster come for a visit to England.

Secure in her disguise, she hired a cab to follow the Allington one, and she waited in an alcove of the Swan while Frances and Annis and the maids resolved their many issues with the staff. Once they finally disappeared upstairs, Harriet secured a room for herself, careful to ask for one much more modest than anything Frances might have considered. Her only request was a view of Regent's Park. She settled into a small single room on the fourth floor, where she could watch the comings and goings from her window.

She began her stay by lavishly tipping a bellboy and a housemaid, and this turned out to be a wise use of her money. Both were delighted to gossip about the hotel's residents, and in particular the demanding Americans on the second floor. Harriet knew when they were going out, knew when they were dining in, and knew when they were to travel down to Dorset for a long weekend at a marquess's country home.

"Such a fuss now, miss, you wouldn't believe it!" exclaimed the housemaid one day as she made up Harriet's bed. "Trunks turned out, wardrobes emptied, then filled again, everyone rushing here and there as if they was going to meet the Prince of Wales instead of some old marquess!"

"I believe a marquess is quite grand, though, is he not?" Harriet said, slipping a coin into the little woman's pocket. "Just below a duke, if I'm not mistaken?"

"Oh yes, miss, that's right, but still!"

"I gather you don't think much of marquesses, Violet."

"Nobs," Violet said instantly. "More money than sense, most of 'em."

"You meet a great many of them, then?"

Violet patted the side of her nose with a stubby finger and grinned. "Too many, in my line o' work, miss. Far too many!"

The bellhop was useful, too, because he had managed the hire of a carriage to take the Allington party to a Lady Whitmore's house, and he and the hired driver were friendly. The driver told the bellhop all about the conversation the ladies had on their way back to the hotel.

"It's that new one, the new marquess, Mrs. Bishop," he said as she tucked another coin into his palm. He hadn't seemed to grasp that Harriet was unmarried. "Rose-sumfin, can't quite remember the name. His daddy just died, and now he's got the title and the estate, too. Young gentleman, only twenty-one years old, I hear."

"How interesting, Sam. Rose-something? I wonder what his estate is called."

"Oh, I got that! Seabeck. Yah, Seabeck, funny kind of name, stuck in my head. Didn't never hear that word before, did you?"

"Why, no, I don't believe I have. I wonder what it means."

Sam, a lad of about sixteen, adopted a look of wisdom. "I fink," he said in a paternal way, "that it means the estate is by the sea."

"Oh, of course, Sam," she said. "That's so smart of you. Thank you."

"Anytime, Mrs. Bishop. Anytime. You need anyfing else, you just ring and tell 'em you want Sam."

"I will do that," she assured him. "As you can see, I'm a curious sort of person."

"So 'm I!" He laughed. "My mum allus said I was a curious sort of boy. Good fing to be in my job."

"Curiosity is a great thing," Harriet said. "It leads to all sorts of knowledge."

She meant it. She now knew, thanks to her new friends in service, exactly where Frances was taking Annis. There was no need to skulk around corners or hide behind a veil. She would simply buy a train ticket to Dorset.

She ordered a pot of tea and a sandwich to be brought to her, and she sat by the window as she ate, watching the road to choose her moment. When the Allington party appeared, with their trunks and valises on trolleys, Harriet held her grandmother's charm in her hand and concentrated.

Frances kept one small valise on her lap as they took their places in the carriage. That, Harriet felt certain, was where she had packed her materials. The herbs, the candle, the saucer, everything she had seen in the cabin, would be in that valise.

The manikin was there, too. Harriet sensed its presence, that tiny golem that should never have been created. It was a tiny shadow where there should be sunshine, a flaw in the bright afternoon. The wrongness of it made her fingertips ache with the memory of dark magic.

"You're making a terrible mistake, Frances," she muttered, gazing down on the group settling itself into the carriage. "I fear for you."

Four floors beneath her, Frances's head jerked up. She frowned deeply, gazing up at the facade of the hotel. Harriet hastily drew back, watching with just one eye through a tiny rent in the fabric of the curtain as Frances looked this way and that, scanning the windows. Frances pressed a palm to her breast.

"Yes," Harriet whispered. "Do you see, Grandmother? She feels it. She knows someone is looking at her."

Beryl didn't answer, but Harriet thought her grandmother must be aware. She had predicted it. "There is darkness in the girl," Beryl had said while they were still in the midst of Frances's training. "You will need to watch out for that, Harriet."

The cousins had not spoken since their argument at the wedding. Frances had never set foot in the Dakota. Harriet had never passed through the doors of Allington House a second time and observed Frances only from a distance.

She and Beryl had failed her, despite their best efforts. Nothing they did could relieve Frances's bitterness over the poverty of her childhood. Nothing they said could erase her resentment of the dingy flat she had grown up in, the ragged clothes she had worn, the low status of her mother. It seemed now, though she wore beautiful gowns and lived in a fine house, that she still carried that hungry, angry girl inside her. Nothing cooled the fire of her craving, of her drive to vanquish the memory of her younger self.

Frances had discovered on her own how to wield the *maleficia*. Harriet, cleaning out Beryl's library, had found the old books, hidden behind a dozen newer ones on a top shelf. She wasn't surprised her grandmother had saved them, since Beryl had cared so much about preserving the history of the Bishop witches. She was saddened to realize Frances had discovered them and learned what the worst of them contained.

Frances had experienced the power of the *maleficia* and succumbed to its temptation. Beryl had been right about the danger of the dark practice. It was, inevitably, corrupting.

Now Annis, innocent of all of this, had become Frances's most recent weapon.

Harriet sighed, tucked the amulet beneath her shirtwaist, and went to pack up her things for the trip to Dorset, and a place called Seabeck.

15

Annis

Lady Whitmore's tea party had been even more tedious than Annis had anticipated. Every guest seemed to her as stilted and shallow as the worst of New York society. The thin, hunched American girl from the *Majestic* was there with her mother, richly dressed but wan and hollow eyed, as if she were still seasick from the voyage. Annis shook her hand, and the hands of other women, young and old. There were, evidently, no gentlemen invited.

Annis wasn't feeling entirely well, either, although the ache in her belly that had begun the evening before had eased. She wondered if the air of the hotel might be draining her energy, or if it was the noise and bustle of London itself. The smell of coal dust clung to everything, spoiling her appetite and making her long for the fresh air of Central Park.

The lassitude helped her get through the boredom of the party, but it also blurred her thoughts. She had difficulty recalling the names of the people she met, which was not at all like her. Frances had taken charge of that, murmuring them in Annis's ear after each had moved away. "That's Mrs. Harlingford. Her daughter just became engaged to an earl." A moment later, she whispered, "Miss Smythe-Tobin, poor thing. This is her second season. Not a soul offered for her last year."

Annis roused herself to mutter, "How on earth do you know all that, Frances?"

"I read the London papers, of course. Oh, do sit up straight, Annis, and smile. That's Lady Eleanor, Dowager Marchioness of Rosefield, and she's coming our way!"

A stout, stern-looking woman dressed entirely in black approached them, her gloved hand extended to Frances. A conversation ensued. Annis couldn't remember a word of it, but it seemed Lady Eleanor had approved of the Allingtons. A handwritten note of invitation was in Frances's eager fingers before they went to bed that night. They were to travel to Dorset, to spend several days as houseguests of Lady Eleanor. Annis, lacking the energy to oppose Frances's wishes, offered no resistance.

At least, she told herself, as they chugged their way southward in the first-class compartment of the train, they would be out of the soot and crowds of London. She listened with indifference to Frances's description of the house party. A grand house, supposedly, and a great estate right by the sea. "Only the best people will be there," Frances said, almost purring with satisfaction. "It will be perfect."

She made no mention of a possible husband, for which Annis was grateful. In her half-dazed state she dared hope that a few days in the company of the aristocracy would satisfy Frances's ambition.

They were met upon their arrival at the train station by a footman in blue livery with gold braid on the shoulders. He assisted all of them into a carriage with an elaborate coat of arms on its door. A driver in the same livery sorted their trunks and valises. Frances was delighted by their attentiveness. Antoinette, looking as gratified as her mistress, settled herself on the bench seat. Velma was her usual stolid self, but she sniffed at the freshness of the salt air, and her eyes brightened a little as she gazed at the pretty houses of Seabeck Village.

Annis's ennui lightened, too, when she saw the matched pair of white horses in the traces of the Rosefield carriage. She thought they must be Andalusians, like the mare she had met in Regent's Park, though these were bigger, with heavier hindquarters, larger heads, and a more pronounced curve to the nose. They would have been bred to harness, she supposed. Their manes and tails were braided with gold ribbon, and the metal fittings on their tack sparkled. When they set out, she was delighted to feel their power and to note the steadiness of their gait.

She removed her hat and leaned as far out the window of the carriage as she dared, first to assess the movement of the horses and then to appreciate the low green hills they passed through, the prim white cottages behind well-kept stone fences. The breeze set strands of her hair whipping about her face. She caught an occasional whiff of burning wood, a relief after the smell of coal that permeated London. She inhaled a faint flowery scent, too, possibly from the small wild roses that tangled in the shrubs along the road. She wished she could ask the driver to stop and let her pick one to identify later.

She twisted to look at the footman clinging to the back of the carriage. He noticed and touched his forehead. "Almost there, miss," he called in an unfamiliar accent. He freed one hand to point ahead. "Just along that next coombe."

She had no idea what a coombe was. She turned forward in

time to see the roofline of Rosefield Hall come into view above the trees. Annis had expected an ostentatious sort of building, like the lavish Fifth Avenue mansions, but this was different. She was no authority on architecture, but it seemed obvious the central hall had been added to over long years, a wing here, a stable block there, but everything constructed with careful taste. The result was elegant and restrained, a big, graceful house unlike anything she had seen in New York. They drove past formal gardens, where a white pergola stood in a well-tended shrubbery. Gargoyles jutted from the roof of the hall, and a medallion, carved with the same crest that adorned the carriage, hung above the entrance.

As they drew near, Frances murmured an excited commentary on the grandness of the house, but Annis wasn't listening. Still with her head out the window, she had spied a stone-fenced pasture beyond the gardens. Half a dozen glorious white horses grazed there, the faint dapples of their coats gleaming like silver coins in the sunshine. As she watched, a coal-gray foal galloped in a circle around its elders, tossing its head and flicking its tail.

"Such beautiful horses!" she called to the footman.

"Yes, miss. My lord's Andalusians."

"Indeed! I thought they must be!"

Suddenly she couldn't wait to escape the confines of the carriage. For a moment she felt like her usual self, thrumming with energy, avid to run through the gardens to the pasture, to lean across the stone fence to admire those horses.

Frances tugged on the back of her jacket. "Annis! Stop acting like a child. Get back in here, and do something about your hair. Tuck your scarf into your bodice, for pity's sake, and put your hat on."

To Annis's dismay, the odd lassitude that had troubled her in recent days seized her again. She didn't want to obey Frances's order, but she seemed to have lost her ability to resist. She pulled back inside the carriage without argument. She repinned her hair, smoothing the disordered strands back into place. She settled her hat on her head, and Velma, under Frances's critical eye, resettled the pins.

Annis's joy at the sight of the horses evaporated. She folded her hands in her lap and gazed blindly forward, wondering what was wrong with her.

When the carriage rolled to a stop before a set of broad steps leading up to the front door of Seabeck Hall, Lady Eleanor was waiting for them. She sent their maids around to the service entrance and dispatched two footmen up the stairs with their trunks before she led Frances and Annis into a parlor to meet their fellow guests.

There was an awkward issue with the small case Frances seemed so reluctant to part with. Annis thought it odd, because her stepmother rarely carried anything herself if she could help it. In this case she did ultimately relinquish the little valise into the hands of a footman, but it had seemed for a moment she might carry it with her into the parlor.

A flurry of introductions enveloped them, and the ceremony of tea proceeded. The afternoon slipped away in a fog of small talk and formalities. Annis relinquished her urge to visit the horses and hoped, vaguely, that the morning would provide an opportunity.

The other guests were all terribly old. Lady Whitmore she had already met. Her husband was a gloomy man whose vest strained over a protuberant belly and whose nose was prominently veined. Annis had to pinch herself to keep from staring at it. The Hyde-Smiths were a gray-haired pair with a startling resemblance to each other, with thin, arching noses and vanishing chins. The Derbyshires were even older, and rather withered, like plants that hadn't had enough water.

The flame of resentment toward Frances for forcing her to endure such an afternoon burned lower in Annis's breast than she might have expected. She sat quietly, letting the innocuous conversation drift around her in bits and pieces. She repressed her yawns and tempered her usual bluntness out of respect for the advanced ages of the company.

As they climbed the stairs to dress for dinner, Frances remarked in an undertone, "You were charming with all those ancient people, Annis! I think the dowager marchioness was impressed. You surprised me."

Annis cast her a sidelong glance. Frances didn't look surprised at all. She wore her cat-who-drank-the-cream look, her lips curling, her eyes glowing beneath lazy lids.

Annis said, "Four days of this, Frances? Is that really what you want?"

"Oh yes," Frances said. She had reached her room, next door to Annis's. Her cat's smile broadened as she put her hand on the latch. "Yes, this is exactly what I want." She pulled the door open and spoke over her shoulder as she went in. "Do wear those pearls of yours, Annis. See to it you look your best."

In the cavernous dining room of Rosefield Hall, candelabras glowed on a long table laden with silver and crystal. Their yellow light glimmered on half a dozen sideboards but left the corners of the room in shadow. An enormous fireplace dominated one end of the room, with what looked like a small tree burning in it. The ceiling was decorated with creatures Annis couldn't identify in the gloom.

Lady Eleanor saw her gazing upward and came to join her. "It's Tudor," she said. "They're lions and griffins, heraldic figures, the same as the stone figures on the roof. The plaster paneling is even earlier, sixteenth and seventeenth century. It's all a bit dim in the candlelight, I'm afraid. One of these days we'll have electric lights so you can see them properly. A bit of a barn, this room, isn't it?"

"I love barns."

"Do you indeed, Miss Allington?"

Even in her bemused state, Annis recognized the humor in Lady Eleanor's voice, and her cheeks warmed. It had been an inappropriate response, born out of the odd feelings she had been having since yesterday. "I'm sorry, Lady Eleanor. That sounded silly. The mention of barns made me think of the beautiful horses in your pasture, the ones I saw when we arrived. I love horses."

Lady Eleanor smiled. "How fortunate. Horses are one of Rosefield's passions, too."

Annis wasn't certain who Rosefield was. She was afraid she was supposed to know, so she didn't ask.

Her hostess gestured to a chair at one end of the glittering table. "Here, Miss Allington. You'll sit here, on the marquess's right."

A uniformed servant hurried forward to pull the chair out, and Annis sat down. A heartbeat later, she realized no one else had taken their seats. They were all standing in front of their chairs, and several were watching the door. Her cheeks burned again.

The servant behind her, who could hardly be much older than she, whispered, barely moving his lips, "They're waiting for His Lordship, miss."

"Oh," Annis whispered. "Thank you." She came to her feet, resisting the urge to cover her red cheeks with her gloved hands. She glanced at the other guests and caught the eye of Mrs. Derbyshire, just across from her. The lady wore an evening dress of rather rusty black silk and an enormous diamond brooch. Both looked as if they belonged to a different age, just as Mrs. Derbyshire did. Annis was startled when the old lady lowered one eyelid in a wink and her wrinkled lips twitched.

Annis grinned, then ducked her head to hide it. It was a small gesture on the part of Mrs. Derbyshire, but a kind one. It seemed the old lady understood Annis's discomfort. Perhaps she even sympathized. The heat in Annis's cheeks subsided, and she was glad she had been patient during the interminable afternoon.

Annis's dress seemed embarrassingly bright compared with Lady Eleanor's mourning black. Her gown was cream silk, with pink embroidery on the sleeves and on the neckline. Pink beads crusted the bodice and the hem of the skirt. She wore her mother's pearls, and they felt cool and smooth against the bare skin of her throat.

There had been no more occurrences like the one in her bedroom in New York, no sudden flashes of understanding, but the pearls felt protective. She touched the center stone as she waited to see who this lordship was and why everyone had to stand waiting for him. She could see the first course already cooling on the sideboard. The butler, a stiff man of middle years, stood at attention beside it, his expression remote, as if the meal's growing cold didn't matter in the least.

The door to the dining room opened, and one of the servants hurried to hold it as a tall, slender man came through. He wore a black tailcoat and a high-collared white shirt with a black bow tie. His waistcoat was black, too, buttoned around his lean middle. As he crossed the room to the table, the ladies dropped tiny curtsies, and the gentlemen inclined their heads.

Lady Eleanor said, "Rosefield! At last. Where have you been?"

He said, "Mother, my friends, I do apologize. There is a problem with the roof of the stable block, and I lost track of time." He nodded to each guest in turn, saying their names. When he came to Frances, he paused, glancing at Lady Eleanor.

She said, "May I present Mrs. George Allington, Rosefield? She is our American guest. Mrs. Allington, allow me to introduce my son, the Marquess of Rosefield."

Frances curtsied. The marquess bowed. As he straightened, his gaze moved up the table to the place where Annis stood, wide-eyed, her breath stopped in her throat. The marquess stared back, his lips parted in surprise.

Lady Eleanor said, "And this is Mrs. Allington's stepdaughter, Miss Annis Allington. Miss Allington, my son, the Marquess of Rosefield."

Annis couldn't think what to say, so she dropped a curtsy and dropped her gaze at the same time.

His Lordship cleared his throat and started toward his place at the table on her left. When he reached Annis, he bowed. "Miss Allington," he said, with a hint of irony in his tone she hoped only she could hear.

"M-my l-lord," she managed, through a dry throat. She straightened and lifted her head to meet his gaze directly. Her heart thudded beneath her pearl-encrusted bodice. She didn't know what her response should be. Surely it was up to him to reveal—or not to reveal—that they had met. He was her host. He was a Lord Something or Other, for heaven's sake.

She decided in a heartbeat. It was his house. Let him solve the problem.

She looked away, and he stepped past her to his chair. A servant held it for him, and once he took his seat, there was a rustle of silken fabric and a scraping of chair legs on the tiled floor as the rest of the dinner guests settled into their chairs at last. Annis did, too, the footman sliding her chair neatly in behind her knees, then lifting her napkin from the charger before her. He managed, somehow, to flutter it open and let it drift across her lap without so much as brushing her with a fingertip.

Annis settled herself, smoothing the snowy napkin across her knees as she stole a glance at the young man to her left. His fair hair was carefully brushed, and it shone as if it had been smoothed with a bit of macassar oil. He had taken time to shave, or perhaps his valet did it for him. He looked younger in his dinner clothes, a bit like a boy playing at being a grown-up. Indeed, his shirt collar was ever so slightly too big, and it made his neck look boyish and vulnerable.

He was careful, she saw, to keep his gaze averted from her. As the soup was served, he engaged Mrs. Derbyshire in conversation, leaning toward her as if to emphasize how interested he was in what she had to say.

Mrs. Derbyshire spoke with him, but as the first course began, she pulled back a little and turned to speak to Mr. Hyde-Smith. Her message was clear: His Lordship was to speak with the girl on his right. The seating arrangement was deliberate.

Annis glanced down the table to where Frances sat next to

Mr. Derbyshire, with Mrs. Hyde-Smith opposite and Lady Eleanor on her right. Frances's elegantly coiffed head was bent as she respectfully listened to something Mr. Derbyshire was saying, but she managed to cast a sidelong look at Annis. Annis, with His Lordship ignoring her and Mr. Derbyshire engaged with Frances, had no one to speak to.

Annis lifted one eyebrow in Frances's direction, suppressed a sigh, and began on her soup. An excruciating evening stretched ahead of her, even more enervating than the afternoon had been. If His Lordship—what was she supposed to call him? Not Rosefield, as his mother did, surely? In any case, if he was not going to speak to her, her hopes of visiting the stables and getting close to those magnificent horses in the pasture were going to come to nothing. That was the only activity she could imagine that would alleviate the tedium of this visit.

The soup was taken away, and a small chilled salad took its place. The footman bent close to Annis and asked if he might pour her a glass of wine. She hesitated, then saw that everyone else had accepted. She murmured, "A half glass only, please," and he obeyed.

She passed the time, when she had finished the salad, watching the butler's flashing knives at the sideboard, carving a roast of some sort. It was served with a side dish of fresh buttered peas, and when she tasted them, she couldn't resist a murmur of appreciation. Mr. Derbyshire heard her and turned to speak to her at last. "The Seabeck farms are the best in the county."

"Are they?" she began, but was interrupted in this first conversational effort by Lady Eleanor, speaking from the far end of the table.

"Rosefield," Her Ladyship said, her voice echoing under the

high ceiling. "I understand Miss Allington has a great interest in horses. You must tell her all about your Andalusians."

It was not so much a conversational gambit as an order. His Lordship, whose Christian name no one had mentioned to her—perhaps no one used it—cleared his throat. A mannerism, Annis thought. He had done it in Regent's Park, too, when he was embarrassed—that is, when she had embarrassed him.

Obediently he turned to face her, but he leaned a little to his left, as if supporting himself on the arm of his chair. In truth, Annis thought he was keeping as much distance from her as possible without offending his mother. Perhaps he was afraid of Lady Eleanor. Perhaps he was afraid of women in general.

He cleared his throat again. "Miss Allington," he said, with an inclination of his head. "It would be my pleasure to show you our stables."

"Thank you," she said, and then added, since everyone else seemed to say it all the time, "my lord."

His cheeks pinked. His mother had turned her attention to the Whitmores, and conversation bloomed at the other end of the table. The marquess said, "I suppose you haven't brought a riding habit."

She put out her chin, though she knew it wasn't her most attractive gesture. "I always travel with a riding habit," she said.

He blinked, as if she had scolded him. "Oh. Oh, I see."

"Yes?" she prompted.

His cheeks grew even more rosy, and she experienced a wave of irritation. He really was rather a child, despite being so tall, and having a title and a huge estate all his own. She stared at him, waiting for the invitation he was now obligated to extend.

"Oh," he said again. "Well, that's lovely, isn't it? Perhaps you would like to ride out tomorrow morning."

"I would like nothing better," she declared, then withdrew her jutting chin and smiled. "Truly, my lord, I would be thrilled to ride one of your Andalusians, if you will permit it."

The pinkness of his cheeks receded, and he managed an answering smile. His posture relaxed a little. "Very good," he said. "I have just the horse, I think."

"Your own Breeze? She's glorious," Annis said. "I would love to—"

"Oh no," he said hastily. "No, I think Breeze would be hard to handle for a young lady. She can be headstrong, and at the gallop she's a bit rough. Also, she's never been under sidesaddle."

Annis sat up straight. "Sidesaddle! But I only ride cross-saddle, of course!"

He flushed again and cast a rather wild-eyed look toward his mother. Lady Eleanor, it seemed, was deep in discussion with Lord Whitmore and didn't look up. "I don't think—That is, ladies of our class—It is hardly genteel to—"

Annis couldn't resist a little rush of sympathy for him. He was rather like Velma, in a way. He had such difficulty expressing himself. He must be several years older than herself, but in this way he seemed much younger.

She leaned toward him, intent upon her argument. He shrank back, but she persisted. "I'm confident you will understand," she said, "that the custom of riding sidesaddle should have been abolished long ago. It was a bad idea to begin with, and now, in this age of more freedom for women and more practical considerations for our horses, it's archaic. Women should ride with the same security and control that men do."

"It's just—it's not decent," he mumbled, casting a desperate gaze down the table.

"Not decent," she repeated. The sympathy she had felt evaporated, replaced by a fresh flood of irritation. "So you subscribe, my lord, to the theory that riding astride is a threat to a woman's virtue?"

"Of course," he said. "Everyone knows that."

She leaned back in her chair to allow her plate to be removed and another set in its place. When this operation had been accomplished, she bent toward His Lordship once again. "There is not a shred of evidence for that, my lord. Not one bit of science has ever demonstrated that riding astride destroys a woman's—*virtue*."

His face flamed so she thought it must hurt. From the far end of the table, Lady Eleanor, who couldn't have heard their exchange, called, "So, Rosefield. Have you arranged a tour of the stables for Miss Allington?" On Lady Eleanor's left, Frances was smiling her cat's smile.

Annis's pearls suddenly, inexplicably, tightened around her neck, pressing the moonstone into the soft skin of her throat. A sign? Yes. She had not imagined it.

It was a warning. A warning to tread carefully, to resist the trap they were all setting for her, and for this poor hapless man as well.

It was no wonder this Marquess of Rosefield feared women. His life was being run by them—his mother, Frances, and now, although she had not intended it, herself. Her sympathy for him returned, and she sagged back in her chair, wondering how she had ever allowed herself to be maneuvered into this position.

16

Frances

By the time the guests and residents of Rosefield Hall retired, everyone knew of the argument between Miss Allington and the marquess. The footman who had served Annis at table told the cook, who told the housekeeper when the staff was having their dinner. The housekeeper ordered all the staff to refrain from gossiping, which meant that the ladies' maids and valets waited until they came above stairs to tell the tale. Even Antoinette, despite her difficulties with English, managed to relate a more or less accurate version of the story to her mistress.

Frances's first instinct was to storm into Annis's room and scold her, but she quelled the impulse. Her cantrip must have worn off. She needed to renew it, and quickly, before the rift between the two young people grew too wide to bridge.

She pretended only mild interest in the clash between Annis and Marquess of Rosefield. Antoinette, disappointed in the tepid reception, elaborated a bit, telling her how shocked the staff were by Miss Allington's assertion that she rode only cross-saddle. "Zey saying," Antoinette said, as she wielded the hairbrush on

Frances's hair, "zat Miss Annis must be a—hmm—a cowboy. *Non*, a cowgirl."

"A cowgirl? I don't think such a thing exists. Stop spreading gossip, Antoinette."

Antoinette fell silent, but she smirked at her mistress in the mirror. They both knew there was little Frances enjoyed more than a bit of gossip, especially about prominent society figures. The maid gathered up Frances's long hair and swiftly wove it into a thick braid.

When she finished, she moved to the bed to begin folding back the coverlet, but Frances shooed her out. "That's enough for tonight," she said. "You can go on to bed. Oh, and I'll want my white shirtwaist in the morning, to go with the gray silk skirt, the one with the little train. They'll both need to be ironed."

When the maid was gone, Frances turned the iron key in the lock of the door. She cleared everything from the surface of her dressing table, putting her brushes, perfume bottles, and jars of cold cream into the drawers. When she had a space to work, she knelt to pull the small valise from behind the wardrobe where she had hidden it.

She took out a lump of unformed wax, a half-used tube of mucilage, and a blank wooden bead of the same type she had used before. From the pocket of her dressing gown she drew out the things she had pilfered from the dining room.

It had not been easy. The ladies had withdrawn to a small parlor to have their coffee while the gentlemen sat on at table with a dusty bottle of port. When she heard the men scrape back their chairs and make a noisy progress to join the ladies, Frances pretended she had lost an earring and went back into the dining room to find it. The servants cleaning the room moved chairs and searched under the table while Frances stood beside the chair the Marquess of Rosefield had sat in.

No one saw her pick up the napkin he had used, which still bore the imprint of his lips in a port wine stain. There were crumbs of cheese on his plate, and she took those, too, folding the bits of cheese into the napkin and slipping the whole into her sleeve while the servants scrambled about under the table. As they began to back out, apologizing for their failure to find the mythical earring, she spotted a treasure, caught on the high back of the chair, gleaming against the purple velvet.

A hair. One single, very fair hair, long and curling, caught on the fabric. Swiftly, as she turned away, she snatched it up. As she made her way out of the dining room she wound it around one finger for safekeeping.

Now she unwound the hair and laid it in a careful curl on the surface of the dressing table. The napkin with its stain, and the crumbs of cheese she had scooped up, she set beside the hair, taking care so as not to brush the crumbs onto the floor. She took up the lump of wax and warmed it between her hands.

When it was malleable enough, she made a rude image of a man with stubby arms, longer legs, a middle. She pressed the wooden bead into the top and then used the mucilage to secure the single hair to it, curling it around and around the bead. She had no paint, but she drew eyes onto the bead by upending her pen over it and letting two drops of ink fall onto the wood. The eyes were rather blurred, but they were more or less in the right places. She drew a line for the mouth, straight and uncompromising.

Last she pressed the crumbs of cheese into the waxen middle

of her manikin and folded the napkin around the whole, so it looked more or less like a nightshirt. She propped the thing against the mirror and regarded it for a moment. It was inelegant and unconvincing, but it would do.

She sighed and stretched. It was going to be a long night.

She had thought it strange, when she first saw Rosefield Hall, that the house's facade faced the wrong way, looking away from the sea. Her bedroom faced in the opposite direction, with a beautiful vista of a narrow stone terrace, a shrubbery and lawn dropping down a gentle slope, and the English Channel in the distance.

Best of all, for Frances's purpose, was a small mock-Greek temple at the end of the lawn. It was pillared, open to the air, and partially hidden by some sort of large bush that grew beside its steps.

A folly. It was perfect.

Wearing her dressing gown and a pair of soft boots, and with the valise cradled in her arms, she crept along the corridor toward the servants' stairs. With an excuse ready on her lips should she need it, she slipped out through a baize door and into a narrow staircase. A half moon glowed through a single small window, shedding just enough light for her to pick out the treads. It seemed a good omen to her that she didn't encounter anyone, neither the butler nor the housekeeper nor any of the dozens of other servants. The house was peaceful, sleeping like a many-headed beast, quiescent under the moonlight. Her body throbbed with excitement, and though she felt as if she could have flown down the staircase, she forced herself to move with care, lest a tumble put an end to all her plans.

She had to unlock the back door. She left the door off its latch as she sidled through, her valise close to her chest. She kept to the shadows as she made her way across the terrace and down the steps.

Shards of moonlight striped the folly through its pillars. A few leaves littered the floor, and branches of a huge rhododendron, its blossoms spent but its leaves thick and dark, hung over it. A stone bench curved along the inside, and Frances laid out her things on it, one by one, herbs, vials, and the two manikins. Poppets, her ancestresses used to call them, but that word was too trivial for what she had created.

"It's a new age, grandmothers," she whispered, smiling into the dark. "A modern age of witches, one you could never have imagined."

She had brought a needle, and she pierced her left forefinger to harvest more of her blood. Her last rite had worn off too quickly, allowing Annis to flaunt her rebellious ways much too soon. This one would have to hold for the length of their visit, long enough to achieve an offer of marriage and an acceptance of the offer. A betrothal.

She squeezed her finger until the blood ran, half filling the little vial.

She mixed her ingredients, stirring in the wine and blood. She reduced her potion over the candle flame, tilting the saucer to test its thickness. As before, she painted the syrup onto Annis's manikin, and then, baring her teeth with the sheer joy of doing it, onto the manikin representing James, Marquess of Rosefield. She spoke her cantrip with relish, enunciating every word, feeling the power in every line.

The power of witch's blood and claws
Bends your will unto my cause.
Root and leaf in candle fire
Invest you with impure desire.

She added, to intensify the spell:

For each other you will yearn,
Your body will ache and your blood will burn.
Have each other you will, and must,
Nothing less will slake your lust.

It was a strong, clear cantrip. It stated her purpose and focused her mind, just as Beryl had taught her. Beryl would have hated this cantrip. Harriet would have been shocked by it, but that didn't matter. Harriet was half a world away.

Had Harriet ever employed the *maleficia*, she would understand the intoxicating effect it had, the irresistible pull of its magic. She would never do it, of course. She was too cautious, too fearful of what such power could do. She would never know this glorious sense of invincibility.

Giddy with the power of it, Frances held her manikins, one in each hand, and waited for their response.

It came with astounding swiftness. First the simulacrum of Annis began to warm and quiver against her palm. That made perfect sense, as she had already begun the process with it. It was attuned to her.

The manikin representing Rosefield took longer, but when it finally answered her summons, there was no doubting it. It grew so warm she feared the wax might melt, and its ugly, awkward limbs trembled in her hand.

Trembled before her cleverness. Her magic. Her *maleficia*.

The energy of the spell triggered the deep ache in her body, but she was prepared for it this time and barely noticed. Her heart swelled with pride in her achievement. She had done it again.

"You see, grandmothers," she whispered. "A modern age of witches, and I am the strongest of them all."

17

James

James went to bed that night in a foul mood, and woke up in an even worse one.

The American girl had humiliated him at dinner. He knew—Perry had confessed as much—that all the staff were talking about it. He had disliked the girl already, but this embarrassment was intolerable. It was mortifying.

The American girls who came to England husband-hunting had the reputation of being spirited, but Miss Allington was more than spirited, beyond outspoken. Her behavior was nothing short of scandalous.

Lady Eleanor came to his room before breakfast. "Rosefield," she said cheerfully. "Not dressed yet? Good. I want to talk to you."

He held the door for her and reluctantly followed her to the hearth, tightening his dressing gown around his waist. She took a seat by the fire and he sat opposite her, his hands on his knees, his head aching with tension.

She said, "Well? What did you think of her?"

James was too tired and too angry to be tactful. "Think of

her? I don't want to think of her at all, Mother! She's utterly unsuitable."

"What do you mean? Because she refuses to ride sidesaddle?"

"You've heard the story. I expect everyone in Rosefield Hall knows it by now."

"I'm sure they do." Lady Eleanor leaned back, pulling up the collar of her dressing gown. "You shouldn't have been so silly, Rosefield."

"Silly!"

"Silly. The custom of riding sidesaddle is ridiculous."

"It is not! What about—I mean, young ladies who are unwed—"

"Oh good God!" Lady Eleanor snapped. "Unwed? You don't really subscribe to the notion that riding cross-saddle destroys a girl's virginity?"

"Mother!" James gasped. "I don't want to have this conversation with you!"

"Why?" She leaned forward, and her eyes glittered with impatience. "Rosefield, when did you grow into such a prude?"

"I am not a—"

"Clearly you are! It's no wonder the staff are having a laugh at your expense!"

"You're hardly helping matters." James threw his head back against his chair and closed his eyes. "Surely you don't want such a—a *hoyden* bearing our name."

"Why is she a hoyden? She spoke the truth. I find it refreshing."

James didn't open his eyes. It was easier that way to speak his mind to his mother. "Everyone knows riding cross-saddle is a clear statement that a young lady has no virtue to protect."

"Stuff and nonsense!" Lady Eleanor snapped. "You know,

Rosefield, we expect girls to marry and produce heirs—to breed, if you will, like your precious Andalusians—but we don't expect them to understand how it's accomplished. Is that fair?"

"Oh my God," James groaned. "A man doesn't want to speak of these things with his mother."

"No? Then with whom will you speak of them? Your father is no longer here. You must marry, and I'd far rather embarrass you than have you make a muddle of things right from the start. Being coy about the facts won't help." She reached out her slippered foot and jostled his knee, making him open his eyes, though he didn't lift his head. "Too many marriages fail because neither the bride nor the groom understands what goes where, you know."

"Mother," James moaned.

"Son," she said. "Let us speak plainly. You have no male relative to advise you, so it falls to me. Not to speak ill of the queen, but her obsession with modesty is ruining the upper class of this country. I suppose I can't blame you, since all our set seem to think the same way, but I swear—the aristocracy will die out if we don't encourage more frankness."

"Well," James said sourly, "when it comes to Miss Allington, you won't have to worry about that. I suspect she knows more about what goes where than I do."

Lady Eleanor surprised him with an indelicate guffaw. "Does she, indeed! I do like that girl."

"She likes horses better than people, I'm fairly certain."

"So do you!"

He scowled at her. "I didn't like her in the first place, Mother. I like her less now."

"What first place?"

"She's the one I met in Regent's Park."

"What? She was?"

"Yes, and she had no manners at all."

"Manners can be learned. You and she share an interest in horses, which is no small thing." His mother's smile vanished, and she fixed him with a hard stare. "We need her, you know. Our situation is serious."

"I know that better than anyone, Mother. Just the same, I—"

Lady Eleanor raised a hand to stop his thought. "You'll have to give her a chance, Rosefield. Look at her again, without all your missish sensitivities. The girl may not be a beauty, but she has lovely skin, wonderful hair, brilliant eyes. She also has the body type that will never run to fat." She patted her own soft midriff. "Lucky."

She stood up and started for the door. "Give her a tour of the stables. If she wants to ride, indulge her. Remember what's at stake here."

She was gone before James could think of an effective protest. He sighed and rang for Perry. He would breakfast in his room so he didn't have to face the guests. He would dress for riding and have Perry take a message to Miss Allington.

It was not at all the way he wanted to spend his day. Irritably he kicked off his slippers, first the left, then the right. They both flew across the floor and slid under his bed, disappearing into the darkness.

Cursing, but not wanting Perry to have to hunt for them, the Marquess of Rosefield got down on his knees and scrabbled under the bed until he found the slippers. He set them side by side in front of the wardrobe.

When he straightened, he caught sight of himself in the mirrored door. "Damn," he said, shaking his head. Stubble covered his chin, and his hair stood out every which way, as if he had slept standing on his head. His neck, poking out of the wide collar of his dressing gown, looked as scrawny as that of a farmer's nag.

"Hardly an appealing figure," he muttered. "Chances are the dratted girl wouldn't have me anyway."

Two hours later a reluctant James walked down the main staircase, intending to await Miss Allington in the library as his note had promised. Instead he found her waiting in the foyer, pacing back and forth on the parquet floor. She caught sight of him and went to the foot of the stairs, gazing upward.

As he looked down on her, a strange thing happened. He had thought of her, at dinner the night before, and certainly in Regent's Park, as unremarkable in her appearance. She had struck him as boyish-looking, with her modest bosom and those narrow hips no bustle could disguise. Her eyes were good, the cool blue of the forget-me-nots that grew in the meadows of Seabeck, and her hair was dark and thick, but her nose was a bit long, and her chin too strong, almost masculine.

That had been his impression, but this morning—oh, this was indeed odd. He experienced a jolt of disorientation, as if he had opened the wrong door and gone into a room he didn't recognize.

Miss Allington stood in a shaft of sunlight falling through the leaded glass windows that flanked the front doors. Perhaps that was what made her seem, ever so faintly, to sparkle. Or perhaps it was that her riding habit, a severely cut deep forest green, suited her better than the pink-and-cream creation she had worn last night. Her hair was twisted up under a matching hat with no decoration other than a row of three large jet buttons. The same buttons adorned the riding jacket, running in two flattering rows from her collar to the points at her narrow waistline.

His step faltered so that he nearly missed a stair. She didn't look so different, surely, even with the tailored habit and subdued hat, the sunshine picking out the light freckles scattered across her face, but...

He cleared his throat. "Good morning, Miss Allington." His voice surprised him in its steadiness, because his stomach quivered and his pulse beat a swift rhythm in his throat. He felt, inexplicably, that he wanted to touch her. He wanted to take her gloved hand. He wanted to put his hand on her slender waist. Indeed...

He wanted to kiss her. He wanted to taste the texture of that smooth, freckled cheek, breathe in the fragrance of her hair.

What artifice could have created this change in his reaction to her? What alchemy could be wrought by a different dress, a comely hat, the glow of June sunshine?

There was no time to ponder the question. She said, "Good morning, my lord," and her smile, white and happy, flashed out. "I can hardly wait to see your horses. Thank you so much for the invitation!"

He managed, somehow, to take himself in hand. He gestured with his arm toward the doors. "We have a beautiful day, it seems."

"Yes, it's lovely! A perfect day for riding, don't you think?" He reached the bottom of the staircase, and she turned to walk at his side toward the doors. Her head easily reached the top of his shoulder, something he rarely experienced in a girl. "I admit, though," she said, "I ride in all weather. Unless the paths are too icy for Bits, of course."

It was an unremarkable comment, but somehow one of the most charming things he had ever heard a young lady say. He glanced down at her and was stunned by the clarity of her eyes, glistening like sapphires. He just stopped himself from clearing his throat again. Such an irritating habit. He said, "I don't mind weather, either. Rain or sun, I would rather be astride a horse than languishing behind a desk."

The word *astride* should have recalled their argument, but somehow it did not. It seemed foolish now to have fallen out over something so trivial. His mother had been right, and now, to his great surprise, he found himself eager to give Annis Allington a chance. What had been shocking at dinner, and in Regent's Park, now seemed wonderfully bold, delightfully daring. The girl who had seemed unfit for the company at Rosefield Hall now cast the elderly couples as staid and out of touch. Surely this tall, slender girl, with her modern ideas and outspoken ways, was a young woman perfectly suited to the coming new century.

He couldn't guess how the change in his perception might have happened. He also couldn't resist, as he escorted her down the broad front steps to the drive and around to their left, where the stable block and paddocks beckoned, putting his hand under her elbow.

She glanced up at him, her lips curving. "I'm in no danger of tripping, my lord."

He dropped her arm, and his cheeks burned. "No, of course not. I can see that, Miss Allington." They walked on, James lost in a cloud of bemusement.

What, he wondered, had happened to him? What did this overnight transformation of his feelings mean? It had brought with it, he was appalled to realize, a strange and shameful feeling in his groin.

It was as if he had been bewitched.

18

Annis

Annis was grateful for the distraction of the horses. She had woken that morning with the sick feeling in her belly once again. It was an odd, yearning ache, utterly unfamiliar to her. She felt hot, too, not feverish, but heated, with an excruciating awareness of every part of her body.

She couldn't have described the feeling to Velma, nor would she have tried. It was embarrassing, somehow—not an illness, exactly, but an uneasy discomfort, as if she were hungry, although not for food. She hungered, it seemed, for...

Well. She wouldn't name what she hungered for, even to herself. It made no sense. It was, in a way, repulsive.

It also confounded her that the marquess seemed a different person this morning. The figure she had thought so painfully thin the night before now seemed merely lean. It was nice that he was so tall, too. She was often self-conscious about her height. She could appreciate the autumn color of his eyes today, because he appeared to have overcome his distaste for her, looking directly into her face, even taking her arm as they left the house.

She didn't know how to manage the confusion of her feelings. Fortunately, there was no confusion when it came to the Andalusians.

There were a dozen of them. Four were in the pasture, grazing in the summer sunshine. Eight were still in their loose boxes, their big heads hanging over the half gates to inspect the visitor.

The marquess spoke their names and stroked each of them in turn. "This is Seastar, our stallion. That big fellow is Shadow, our only black. It happens among Andalusians, though not often. Here's Dancer, and across from her is Isabella. You've met Breeze already, of course." They went on down the rows. Annis pulled off her gloves to feel each satiny coat, to caress the wide cheeks and strong noses, to rub the warm necks beneath those rich, wavy manes.

She stepped up on a crosspiece in Isabella's gate for a better view of the horse. Like Breeze, she was stout of leg and chest, with a short, powerful neck. The mare nuzzled at her jacket pockets, looking for treats, and Annis chuckled. "I'm sorry, Isabella. I had no opportunity to get anything."

"She's a beggar," the marquess said with an indulgent smile.

"Your horses have easy dispositions, I see," Annis said.

"They do. They're known for that."

"Bits—that is, Black Satin—is easy with me, but he can be testy with other people. Well, not with Robbie, but—"

"Robbie?"

"Our stableman." She glanced around the stables. "Where are your other horses? Those were Andalusians in harness yesterday, I think."

"Yes. Come this way, I'll show you the carriage horses. And my old pony."

"Your pony? That's sweet. I still have mine, too, though she's getting a bit slow, poor old thing."

The two of them walked on to another wing of the stable, side by side. Annis had forgotten, until that moment, her odd feelings of the morning. Now they came back in a rush. The sweet, pungent smells of horses and fresh straw, leather and sawdust, mixed with the scent of soap and shaving lotion that clung to the marquess. Her belly contracted strangely, and she cast him an uneasy glance, as if he could guess.

His eyes were brighter today, alive with enthusiasm. His hair was unoiled, and it fell every which way over his collar and over his forehead, which suited him. He sensed her regard and turned. "Are you well, Miss Allington? You look a little flushed."

They had reached the corner of the aisle that led to the other wing of the stables. Several horses looked out of their boxes. Annis turned sharply toward one of them, as if especially interested. "I am quite well, my lord," she said. Her voice sounded strange in her ears, husky, a little hollow. "Is this your pony?"

"Yes. An Icelandic pony. Quite old now, twenty-two or -three, I think."

"He's a darling." She let the fat pony nuzzle her palm, and she scratched behind his ears. He had once been coal black, she thought, but now his coat was grizzled here and there with gray. "I wish I had something for him."

She left the pony as the marquess came to her side, and she moved on down the aisle, glancing at the heavier horses, who gazed incuriously back at her. She wanted distance from the marquess, even as she found herself, unaccountably and distressingly, wanting to be close to him.

This was not natural, she thought. There was something

wrong with her. Perhaps, in truth, she was not completely well. But what illness would cause such strange sensations, such conflicting emotions?

Something was definitely the matter, but she didn't know what to do about it, and there was no one she could consult.

She wanted to be her usual independent self, even though being herself so often got her into trouble. At this moment she felt as vulnerable as a newborn foal. She loathed the sensation of weakness.

She felt better once she was mounted. The stableman had pointedly placed a sidesaddle where she could see it, though he had prepared a horse for her with a cross saddle. The sidesaddle was ugly, with its hideous double pommel, one to put a leg over, and one to trap the other leg beneath. An extra cinch dangled under its skirts, which she knew was the balancing strap. Such nonsense. With a cross saddle none of that was necessary. She pretended not to notice the thing as she stepped up on the mounting post and threw her leg over the horse's back.

She heard the stableman's indrawn breath of disgust, and she didn't know whether to laugh or to reprimand him. She decided that as he was not her employee, and as she would probably never lay eyes on him again, the better course was to ignore him, too, and focus on the elegant horse the marquess had chosen for her.

She was called Patience. She was smaller than Breeze, with a well-cut head and small ears and beautifully turned hocks. "She has the look of an Arabian," Annis said.

The marquess, already astride Breeze, nodded. "You have a good eye, Miss Allington. There is an Arab stallion in Patience's pedigree. She's the only one at Seabeck. All the other horses here are from the pure Spanish bloodline." He lifted his reins and indicated a direction with his chin. "There's quite a nice path through the coombe. It runs up to the crest of the hill, where there's a view of the sea. Shall we?"

"Yes, please." She urged Patience forward, and the mare set out at a smooth walk that matched Breeze's speed perfectly.

The last of Annis's discomfort fell away as the two of them rode in silence out of the drive and turned into the well-trodden path. The breeze from the Channel helped to dissipate the cloud of confusion that had enveloped her all morning. The wind set the boughs of the trees dancing and made Patience's mane ripple like silk.

It was pure pleasure to be riding, to be silent, to be free of deciding where to stand, when to sit, what to say to a marchioness or any of her stodgy guests. Annis felt comfortable for the first time since arriving at Rosefield Hall. She was grateful for the sounds of water and wind and horses' hooves. She relished the view that opened before her as the horses made the shallow climb out of the coombe, which turned out to be a sort of valley, and up to the crest of the slope.

They reined in before an ancient beech tree. Its trunk and branches leaned inland, bent by many years of ocean breezes. Half-buried beneath a root that arched out of the ground was a rectangular slab of stone that didn't seem to fit the landscape. Annis pointed to it. "What is that stone doing there?"

"It's a menhir," the marquess said. At Annis's puzzled expression, he explained. "One of the standing stones—well, this one has fallen over, but there are several stone circles in Dorset. If there was once a circle here—a henge, it's called—it's gone now. The stones have probably been pressed into other uses, fences or walls. I expect this one was too large to move."

"I don't know what a henge is," Annis said. Intrigued, she swung down from her saddle and bent to put her hand on the cool, rough surface of the stone. "Have you touched it? It feels alive!"

He laughed and slid down to join her beside the stone. He laid his own hand on it, right beside hers, then shook his head. "It doesn't feel alive to me, I'm afraid. It just feels cold and rough and old. A henge is a stone circle, you know, from ancient times. A ceremonial circle, we think. No one knows exactly what it was for."

Easy together for the moment, made comfortable by the presence of the horses and the glitter of the wide sea below the fields, they turned together, looking from east to west. The marquess pointed out the farms of his estate, the sheep grazing in their pastures, the first golden haystacks of summer beginning to blossom here and there. The crenellated roof of Rosefield Hall was just visible beyond the gentle green of the hills and the darker green of the woods.

Annis turned in a half circle, admiring the view and breathing in the sweet air. "There's a scent, something I don't recognize."

"The sweet one, rather cloying?"

"Yes. I first noticed it from the carriage. Is it those white flowers, the ones with the yellow centers? They grow all through the shrubbery, I think."

He smiled. "Those are my favorite wildflowers. They grow all over this land, in the woods and in the hedgerows. They're called field roses."

"Oh! Is that where your name comes from? That is, your title?"

"In part. The title goes back to the Wars of the Roses, which you have probably never heard of."

"I have, though," she said, intrigued now. "I learned about them in school. The Yorks and the Lancasters."

"Precisely! Well done, Miss Allington." His smile grew, and he gestured again to the expanse of the estate, from the wooded hills in the north to the blue sea in the south. "My ancestor fought for Henry VII and was granted all this land and created Marquess of Rosefield when it was all over. Although," he added, "the field rose is white, and the York rose was red. I suppose they thought it didn't matter, or perhaps it was symbolic of the end of hostilities. Peace." His smile faded as he gazed over his lands. "Seabeck is a peaceful place. I like to think the people who work this land are happy here, that they love it as much as I do."

"Why does that make you sad?"

He looked down at her. His eyes darkened, and a crease appeared between his brows. "I am responsible for it now," he said. "I don't know if I'm up to the task."

She nodded gravely. "Yes. I can imagine it's a daunting responsibility."

"Indeed." He looked away again and sighed. "So many people rely on me."

"Would you rather do something else?"

He glanced at her again, his brows lifted. "I beg your pardon?"

"I mean, perhaps you would rather be a scholar, or a lawyer, or something."

"I have no choice in the matter," he said. "I am my father's only heir."

"But what if you didn't want it?"

He shook his head and straightened his shoulders as he gazed out again toward the sea glittering in the morning light. "It's not a matter of what I want. It's my duty."

"Oh, duty!" she said. "Other people deciding what we must do or must not do!"

"I don't understand," the marquess said.

"I mean," she said, "that I don't want anyone telling me what I have to do! What if you decide you don't want to be the Marquess of Rosefield? What if you want to be plain...Oh dear. I don't know what your name would be if you weren't Lord Rosefield."

That made him laugh, and she was glad to see the crease disappear from his forehead. "I would be plain James Treadmoor. That's the family name."

"James Treadmoor. That sounds nice," she said. She grinned. "James Treadmoor, lawyer. Or teacher. Or farmer."

"Farmer," he said. "I like that. I'm pretty much that already."

"And I," she reminded him, "am going to be a horse breeder."

He turned away from her again. She looked up at his spare profile and saw how his mouth turned down and his chin tightened. He was, once again, the stiff, disapproving man he had been in Regent's Park and again at dinner the night before. "I don't think that's going to happen, Miss Allington," he said. "I think you should give up thinking about it."

She said, decisively, "Never."

He didn't respond. She sniffed and turned away, back to Patience. She was sorry their moment of camaraderie had been broken so easily, but it was his fault. She wouldn't let her father stop her, and she certainly wasn't going to let this snobbish aristocrat stop her, either.

Her discomfort didn't return until he held out his hand to boost her up into the saddle. At that moment, at the touch of his gloved hand on her knee as he lifted her up, the ache in her belly and the heat of her blood returned tenfold. It caught her by surprise. For a moment she gripped the low pommel of her saddle, as if she were about to fall. She couldn't find her stirrups with her boots.

"Miss Allington?" The marquess was standing at Patience's shoulder, his hand on her bridle as he looked up with a frown of concern. "Are you unwell?"

She gazed helplessly at him as she suffered an urge to simply release the reins and slide out of her saddle into his arms. It was a horrible feeling, utterly unlike her. She didn't even *like* him. He didn't like *her*, and yet he was standing there, his eyes fixed on her face, as if he wanted what she did.

Annis drew a sudden, much-needed breath. She jammed her boots into her stirrups with a rough motion, making poor Patience startle and take a nervous step to the side, forcing the marquess to let go of her head. The distance between them helped to soothe Annis's feverishness, to ease the ache in her belly. She said, more sharply than she intended, "I'm perfectly well, my lord. Isn't it nearly time for luncheon? We should be on our way."

It occurred to her, as she watched him leap easily up into his own saddle, that he was as relieved as she was. He didn't look at her again, or speak. He put his heels to Breeze's flanks and led the way back down the path toward the coombe.

Could he be experiencing the same weird brew of feelings she was? Did it mean something? None of it felt natural. None of it felt right.

Annis let Patience have her head to follow Breeze as she gazed off toward the sun-bright sea and wondered what could possibly be happening to her.

Once luncheon was over, the company disappeared, each to their own preference. The elderly couples went up to sleep until tea. Lady Eleanor excused herself to meet with her housekeeper. Frances vanished without explanation, and Lord Rosefield did the same, bowing to the company, departing without ceremony. Annis felt a terrible moment of disorientation, glad to see the back of the marquess and at the same time wishing she could run after him.

She hesitated in the foyer. The servants all seemed to be busy elsewhere. The sun was already on its westward journey, leaving the house sleepy and dim. Annis didn't feel sleepy in the least. She felt—she didn't know what she felt. Itchy. Restless. Wanting something without knowing what it was.

As she hesitated at the foot of the staircase, she experienced a sudden, inexplicable urge to go outside. The impulse surprised her, building into a compulsion. She felt as if someone had called her name, though she had heard nothing.

Swiftly she slipped out through the doors, closing them behind her as quietly as she could. The impulse felt like a command, one she couldn't refuse. It drew her to her left, along the stone porch to a short stair leading to the west lawn. There she turned left again, pulled as surely as if she were on a longe line. Her skirts in her hands, her uncovered hair flying in the afternoon breeze, she dashed down the sloping lawn behind the house, where a narrow gravel path led to a funny little building. It was round, pillared, open to the air.

A folly, she thought. Though she hadn't seen one before, she had read of them in novels. She had the impression they were usually bigger, but this one was charming, with an enormous rhododendron shading one side and weeping roses growing opposite. The inside was fitted with a stone bench running half the circumference.

A woman rose from the bench as Annis approached. She wore

a plain walking suit with a thick jacket, and she was tall, dark haired. Familiar.

Annis slowed her steps and released her skirts so she could push her hair out of her eyes. Her heart began to pound with this new, confounding development.

"It's you," she breathed. "It's you! Whatever are you doing here?"

19

Harriet

Harriet hadn't issued a summons in a long time, and she had worried it might not work. But here was Annis, breathless from having run down the lawn, her pupils expanding with shock at finding Harriet waiting for her. Annis looked as if she might crumple in a faint, if she were that sort of girl.

She made it instantly clear that she wasn't at all the sort of girl to faint. She steadied herself with a hand on one of the pillars as Harriet said, "Yes. It is I. I should introduce myself at last."

"You're the herbalist!" the girl breathed. Her color rose in a wave and then receded, leaving her cheeks ice pale beneath her smattering of tiny freckles.

"I am that," Harriet said, trying to speak in a bracing manner. "I'm also a relative of yours, Annis."

"You know my name?"

"I do. Perhaps you should come and sit—"

Annis blurted, "You're a relative? Are you an Allington?"

Annis had already, Harriet could see, suffered some confounding emotions. She wished she could put her arms around the girl, but that would hardly be welcome. She was still, essentially, a stranger. She said, "No, I'm not an Allington. My name is Bishop. Harriet Bishop."

"My mother's name was Bishop."

"Yes. My sister Lily was your grandmother. You are my great-niece."

"Oh! Am I? Why—I don't—Are you here because of me? You came all this way?"

"I did. I think you need me."

Annis lifted her hand from the pillar and came slowly up the two steps into the folly. She sank onto the bench and twisted her hands in her lap. "How did you know, Miss Bishop?" Her words tumbled from her, stammering, confused. "How—how did you know what's happening? Everything is so—so strange. The oddest things... There's no one for me to talk to!"

"I understand. As it happens, I know all about it, and I'm going to try to explain." She sat next to Annis but took care not to sit too close. She felt the girl's tension radiating from her as if she were a wary bird who might fly away at any moment.

Harriet had rehearsed her explanation in her second-floor room in the Four Fishes Inn of Seabeck Village. It wasn't much of a room, but then, the Four Fishes wasn't much of an inn. There were only four bedrooms, fanning out from a steep, rickety staircase. She had to share her bathroom with the guest next door. Fortunately, the occupant of that room was rarely present. She had paced in circles, from the dormer window to the old-fashioned door with its iron fittings, practicing what she would say to Annis, but the words she had prepared seemed woefully unequal to the task. How in the world do you explain such things to a girl who has never even heard of them? And probably doesn't believe in them?

Still, there was intelligence in Annis's eyes, and courage in her stance, despite her state of mind. Her color had begun to return, and her breathing to ease. She touched the choker at her throat, a string of white pearls with a cream-colored stone in the center. A moonstone, Harriet realized, with layers of silver beneath its pearly surface. It was a jewel known to produce calm and balance. To emphasize feminine energy and wisdom.

Harriet remembered this necklace. "Your choker...," she began.

Annis dropped her hand. "It was my mother's, I think. She died when I was small."

"I know. Such a tragedy, and so hard for you to grow up without a mother."

The girl shrugged. "I had our housekeeper, Mrs. King. And then I had my horses."

Harriet considered horses a poor substitute for a mother's love, but she kept the thought to herself. She pulled her grandmother's amulet from her bodice and lifted it up in her fingers. "This was my grandmother's. Your necklace once belonged to your grandmother. I remember the stone—a moonstone."

"Is that what it is?"

"Yes. Moonstones have wonderful properties, and this one has a special power."

Annis caught a breath and touched the stone again. She whispered, the words almost inaudible, "I thought I imagined it."

"Has it spoken to you?"

"Well, I suppose...you could say that, I guess. I didn't know what to make of it."

"Perhaps I can help with that." It was a good introduction to the subject of witchcraft. Harriet gave Annis a tentative smile as she slid her amulet back inside her dress. "I have a great deal to tell you, my dear. I hope you're comfortable. This will take a while."

"But how can you be sure," Annis asked, "that I have any ability at all?"

Harriet had finished telling the story. Their story. Annis had listened, her lips open in wonder at first, then set with determination when Harriet reached the part about Frances and what she had done.

Harriet had left nothing out. She explained the Bishop heritage, the divergence between the practices of Mary and Christian, and the difference between her own practice of enhanced herbalism and Frances's *maleficia*. She had talked for nearly an hour. Annis had barely moved in all that time, watching Harriet's face intently, as if to see beyond her features and into her soul. As if to decide whether to trust her. Harriet hoped that their family resemblance would help to convince her.

In answer to her question, Harriet said, "It's a gift of mine. I think of it as the knowing, for lack of a better word. Insights come to me, usually when I'm working, sometimes when I'm not. They have never been wrong." She added, with a twist of her lips, "It can be a mixed blessing, but I'm glad to know you have inherited the ability. Knowing how your pearls affect you is confirmation."

"I thought they would strangle me last night at dinner."

"But not now."

"No. Now they're—they're comforting."

"Very good. Last night, they were warning you."

"Warning me about Frances?"

"Yes."

"Are we—then are we—" She swallowed, as if it was difficult to speak the word. As if it felt alien in her mouth. "Are we—witches?"

"Don't be afraid of it. Today, when women have little power that is not granted to them by men, to be a witch is a very good thing."

Annis drew herself up, as she did in the saddle, her chin tucked, her spine ramrod straight. She said, her voice deepening, "This is all true."

"Yes, my dear. This is all true."

"You must know how hard—I mean, it must have been hard for you to grasp it all, the first time you heard it."

"I don't think I ever learned it, exactly. Lily and I simply knew, from an early age. It was easier with a sister."

"She was older?"

"Yes, much."

"I can hardly believe you came all this way just for me. No one else—I don't think there's another person in the world who would have done that, not for me."

"And yet I did," Harriet said. She let her tone soften, now that the hard part had been accomplished, now that she could admit to the emotion welling up in her heart. "We're Bishops. Family."

Annis touched the moonstone. "I'm grateful, truly, just still . . . it's hard to grasp. Things have been so odd."

"There's no need for gratitude. We Bishops must support each other."

"What happens now?"

"Now," Harriet said, "we have to undo a work of *maleficia*, and it will be both difficult and dangerous."

"Dangerous for me?"

"For you. For me, for Frances. Also for the young marquess."

Annis shivered, suddenly, involuntarily. "The marquess? Why is he in danger?"

"Because Frances has included him. I haven't seen his manikin—I told you what that is—but I have no doubt it exists."

The girl's upright posture suddenly sagged, and she put her hands to her cheeks. "Oh no," she groaned. "You mean the marquess has been feeling the same things I've been feeling? It's awful, Aunt Harriet! It's embarrassing, and—oh, this is terrible!"

Harriet put her hand on Annis's shoulder. It was a surprisingly sturdy shoulder for such a slender girl, the bones and muscles strong under her fingers. "Annis, we're going to do our best to fix this. That is, I am, and you're going to help me."

Annis dropped her hands and squared her shoulders again. "Tell me what I need to do. It was I who brought these troubles to James's door."

"It was not your fault," Harriet said firmly. "It will only weaken you to think that way. Now I'm going back to the village, and I would imagine you need to dress for dinner. Behave as normally as possible, but once everyone is in bed, change into something warm and join me here. I will be back at midnight. Can you manage that?"

"I *will* manage it," the girl said.

"Wear the moonstone."

"I will."

Lily would have been proud of this girl, the granddaughter she had never known. Harriet would ask Lily's intervention in their work this night, and Beryl's, too. They would need all the support they could get.

*   *   *

The problem with the *maleficia* was that once employed, it was difficult to undo. Dark magic had a crude force her own practice lacked. She had always believed it was because its practitioners were untroubled by conscience. With nothing to distract them, all their energy could be poured into the thing they wanted to make happen. Her own practice, by its nature, divided her attention in a hundred ways.

It was a warm evening, the height of summer. Harriet had no lantern, but the path from Seabeck Village to Rosefield Hall was brightened by the field of stars shining from a clear black sky. Off to her right, the calm sea glistened in the starlight. Ahead of her, the house bulked against the stars, a great dark lady skirted by sleeping gardens.

She had gauged her time well. As she descended the slope to the folly, the village church bells tolled midnight.

Annis, brave girl, was waiting, alone in the darkness.

Harriet gave her a nod of greeting. "This is not the way I would have preferred to begin your instruction, Annis. Needs must, I'm afraid."

"It's all right," Annis said. She reached to help Harriet with her basket and set it on the bench where she had been sitting. "You can't imagine what a relief it is to understand what's happening to me. Even at dinner tonight, I—I mean, I have to sit next to him, and I have these awful feelings. Animal feelings. I don't even *like* him, Aunt Harriet."

"Do you not? He seems all right to me, but I'm an old woman. It's different."

"When have you met him?"

"I haven't, not properly. I watched you this morning. He appeared to be polite to you."

"He thinks I'm unladylike. Worse, he thinks I'm immoral, and only because I refuse to ride sidesaddle. He's a stuffed shirt!"

"Ah. An unforgivable sin."

That made Annis smile. "I'm supposed to call him *my lord*. It's stupid."

"What does he call you?"

"Miss Allington, of course. Truly, we hardly know each other, which makes this so much more disturbing. All wrong."

"The good thing, though," Harriet reminded her, "was that you sensed it was unnatural, though you didn't understand. You must trust yourself about such things."

"I will try."

Annis took the two thick candles Harriet handed her and set them behind a pillar, to protect them from the wind. She lit the candles as Harriet unwrapped the herbs she had brought from New York.

She laid them out between the candles, naming them as she did so. "These are flowers of the linden tree. They help to calm the nervous system. This is starwort, to restore proper bodily function. This is wormwood, a purgative. Honey, from the village. It's always better to use local ingredients when you can." She reached into the pocket of her skirt and brought out a tiny bunch of mistletoe sprigs. "I found a nice cloud of mistletoe in the woods," she said. "Mistletoe is beneficial for a suffering heart, but it can be toxic. You must use only a tiny amount."

Annis repeated each name and touched each with her finger.

"These are all useful taken alone," Harriet told her. "In combination, we hope they will reverse the *maleficia*. You'll have to ingest the mixture."

"Ingest? You mean swallow it?"

"Swallowing it is the easy part, I'm afraid."

"It's going to make me sick?"

"It might, depending on what Frances does. James needs to take one, too."

"James!"

"Oh yes. He is no less affected than you are."

"I hope I can find a way to give it to him."

"We'll create an electuary, and that will help." At Annis's blank look, she said, "I usually make electuaries for children. The honey helps to mask the taste of the remedy."

Harriet took the jar of honey, a mortar and pestle, and her herb scissors out of her basket and set to work. When the linden flowers, the starwort, and the wormwood were thoroughly crushed and blended, she cut a sliver of mistletoe leaf and mashed it in the mortar with the other herbs, then dripped a generous dollop of honey over everything.

Finally she drew a fold of thick paper from the bottom of the basket. Inside was a single sewing needle that gleamed silver in the candlelight. She held it in her right hand and positioned her left over the mortar. With one quick motion, she pierced her finger. She ignored Annis's gasp and concentrated on counting the drops of blood as they fell. Three might have been enough, or five, but she knew Frances's strength. She shed seven dark drops of her blood into the mixture.

"Is that necessary?" Annis whispered.

"It is. Frances uses it in her rite, and my blood must answer hers." She wrapped her wounded fingertip with a bit of cloth. "I am the stronger practitioner, Annis. Believe that."

"Yes, Aunt Harriet."

"Good girl." Harriet used a tiny silver spoon, darkened with age, to blend the drops of blood into the herbs and honey. When the mixture was as smooth as she could make it, she scooped up a fingerful and rolled it in her palm until she had a small, pungent ball. She held it out for Annis to see. "This is our remedy. You do the other one. Then our rite begins."

Annis did as she was told, and they set the two electuaries side by side on Harriet's clean handkerchief. Harriet cleared away the remnants of the ingredients, stowing them back in her basket. She moved the candles a bit closer to each other, then drew out her amulet and held it in her hand. "This is our practice—our art, as I like to think of it."

"Our magic?" Annis asked.

Harriet nodded. "Yes. Magic is wisdom and power, wielded well. That's what we're going to do, wield power."

"How?"

"We will speak a cantrip. A verse, rather like a chant, always with a specific purpose."

"Like a prayer? We chant prayers in church."

"It's a bit like a prayer." Harriet considered, cradling Beryl's amulet in her palm. "Words have strength, and spoken words have the greatest weight. They express our intent, and for such as we—"

"You mean, witches?"

"You've noticed, I suppose, that I avoid saying that."

"Why is that?"

"Ah. You're making me think about it." Harriet lifted the amulet so it caught the candlelight directly, its two halves glowing gold and violet. "*Witch* should be a beautiful word, signifying wisdom and knowledge and discipline, but it isn't used that way. It's been made an insult, implying evil, causing fear. The word has been perverted."

"Will it always be that way?"

"I can't claim to know the answer. It would mean seeing rather far into the future, which is a magic I don't possess."

"And the cantrip?"

"We speak the cantrip to express our intent. The intentions of our kind have more force than those of ordinary people. If we're successful, we make things happen."

"So if we're witches, a cantrip is a spell."

"You prove my point. Words are powerful things."

Harriet lifted the amulet's chain over her head and bent forward to set the ametrine between the two electuaries. When she stepped back again, she watched Annis unclasp her choker and lay it next to the amulet. The jewels glistened in the flickering light of the candles, the creamy moonstone, the yellow and violet of the ametrine.

"Now," Harriet said softly. She and Annis stood shoulder to shoulder. Harriet felt the power flowing between them and around them, the beginning tingle in her belly and her bones as she gathered her energy.

"Now," she repeated. "Let us begin."

She recited:

Stem and leaf and root and flower,
Witch's blood and witch's power,
All the wicked art unmake,
And, in its place, the good awake.

She felt Annis's shoulder brushing hers, and her throat tightened with emotion. How long since anyone had touched her, beyond shaking her hand? Grace brushed her hair sometimes, but it was not the same. No one had really touched her in years. Despite the grim circumstances, it was a blessing.

This was not the time to think about it, though. There was work to be done, work already begun. She swallowed away the constriction of her throat and fixed her gaze on the amulet, waiting for the sign that her rite had been accomplished.

She tried not to think of the risks, but she knew they were there. Two powers were about to go to war with each other, with two innocent young people caught between them. It was a conflict she would have preferred to avoid. It was a conflict, she feared, that had been building for a long time.

She felt the faint tremor of Annis's shoulder against hers. She supposed the child was anxious, and that was proper. She should be.

Harriet waited for the sign, but the ametrine did not respond. When she had waited fifteen minutes, twenty, with nothing happening, she repeated her cantrip. Annis stood steady beside her, watching, listening, her eyes glinting ice blue in the candlelight.

The waiting began again. It had happened before with difficult rites. The sea whispered through the darkness. Night birds called now and then. The breeze through the folly grew chilly, but the thrill of energy through her blood kept Harriet warm.

Annis was a different matter. Harriet became aware that the girl was shivering. Although it meant starting again, Harriet said, "Annis, get your shawl. There's no need to catch a chill."

Annis, her eyelids dragging with fatigue, nodded, and stepped to the side of the folly where she had left it.

"You can sit," Harriet said. "You can watch from there."

"But I want to know when it's done," Annis said, hesitating.

She pulled the shawl around her shoulders and knotted the ends together. "How can you tell?"

"It's easier to show you than to describe it," Harriet said. She hadn't thought about the cold or her tiredness until this moment, seeing them in Annis. Now her feet felt chilly, standing on the stone floor of the folly, and her neck began to prickle with the predawn mist. She found her own shawl in her basket and wrapped herself in it.

"One more time," she told Annis. "Don't despair. Sometimes it's like this."

Annis came to stand beside her once again. They were of a height, the two of them, similar in their dark hair, their slenderness, both with the prominent Bishop chin. It occurred to Harriet that this could have been her daughter, hers and Alexander's. She had once longed for a daughter of her own, a daughter to love, a daughter to teach.

She straightened her shoulders. She knew better than to allow random thoughts into her mind at such a moment. She needed to concentrate, to focus all her energy on her rite.

To make magic.

Stem and leaf and root and flower,
Witch's blood and witch's power,
All the wicked art unmake,
And, in its place, the good awake.

She spoke the cantrip in a steady voice, standing as still as one of the sea stacks in the bay below Seabeck. The magic would happen. It *must* happen.

Annis seemed to sense the intensity of her concentration. She, too, stood very still, no longer shivering, her eyes fixed on the amulet shining in the candle flames.

Before a full minute had passed, the ametrine filled with a shifting, trembling mist. It began to glow from within, as if it had its own flame, illuminating the purple veins in the stone. Harriet's fingers and toes began to ache as the light brightened until even the purple threads disappeared.

Annis gave a soft cry and clasped her hands before her. Harriet put up a finger to ask her to be silent. The girl pressed one hand to her lips, her eyes brilliant in the dimness.

By the time the light in the stone began to fade, the stars were also fading, the eastern sky turning gray. When the ametrine was itself again, a simple stone of yellow and violet, Harriet spoke in a voice dry with fatigue. "It's done. We'd better get you back to the house."

"But what about you?"

"I'll walk back to the village. Here, put on your pearls. Don't take them off." She lifted the choker and passed it to Annis. She carefully wrapped the electuaries in her handkerchief, folding in the corners to protect them. "You need to take one of these, Annis, but wait until you're in your room, alone, in case you have a reaction. Focus on the intent as you do—concentrate on undoing the *maleficia*."

"I will," Annis said gravely. She accepted the handkerchief and tucked it into a pocket.

"You'll have to find a way to get the marquess to swallow one."

"That could be hard."

"Don't take chances, like dropping it in his wineglass. He might leave it there."

"I'll look for an opportunity."

"Don't wait too long. The electuaries will last only a few hours before they lose their effectiveness. Less, if Frances is quick. You need the remedy before she tries again."

"All right." Annis tightened her shawl and glanced out through the folly's pillars. "It's getting light. I need to hurry."

"Yes. Go. Good luck."

Annis started for the steps, but she paused, looking back. Her face was tired, but her eyes were still bright. "When will I see you, Aunt Harriet? I have a hundred—no, a thousand—questions to ask you."

"I'll be nearby. I'll be watching."

20

Frances

When Annis emerged from the folly, Frances jumped back to take cover behind the ancient rhododendron. Harriet followed Annis, a basket on her arm. The two made their way up over the lawn to the servants' entrance, where Annis went inside. Alone, Harriet strode away in the direction of the village. Frances stepped into the open to watch her cousin's lean figure disappear behind the stable block.

She was going to have to go inside, too, lest the servants catch her on the stairs or in the corridor. She waited until she guessed Annis had reached her room before she hurried up to the servants' door, cursing Harriet's interfering ways at every step.

She ran up the stairs as quickly as she dared and let herself into her own bedroom. She locked the door from the inside. For extra security, she pulled a straight chair to the door and wedged it under the handle. She would tell Antoinette she was ill or something, perhaps say she hadn't slept well and was going to stay in bed. Now, before Annis swallowed Harriet's electuary, and before she managed to slip the other one to the marquess, Frances had work to do.

She slid the little valise out of its hiding place and opened it. The manikins were intact, though the smears of her potion had gone dark on the wax. The candle was the problem. It was burned more than halfway down, its energy depleted. She cast about her bedroom, wondering where the maids might keep a supply of fresh candles.

There was a candle on her bedside table and one on the dressing table, but both were little more than stubs. She wasted precious minutes searching in cupboards and bureaus and cabinets. The room was enormous, and it seemed every corner held a curio cabinet or an étagère, every one of them crammed with china and glass ornaments. Where would there be candles?

She was on the point of giving up, though that would mean the further delay of having to ask for a candle—and explain why she needed a fresh one—when she spied a wide drawer under the wardrobe. She opened it and found a full supply of dust cloths, tins of wax, and a fresh box of candles. Hands shaking now with her need to hurry, she pried open the box and took out a new taper.

In haste she shoved the things on the dressing table to the floor. A vial of perfume she hadn't noticed fell and spilled its fragrant contents onto the rug, but she ignored it. She stabbed her finger much too deeply in her haste, and her blood spattered the openwork cloth that covered the surface. It was probably ruined, but she couldn't worry about that now.

She added her fresh blood to the vial with the other ingredients and clipped a nail as well. She lit the candle and heated her potion as before, watching it until it thickened. When it was ready, she anointed the manikins, using every bit of the potion. She held them, one in each hand, and drew a deep breath to focus her mind. In a low voice, wary of being heard, she chanted:

The power of witch's blood and claws
Bends your will unto my cause
Root and leaf in candle fire
Invest you with impure desire.

She closed her eyes and squeezed the manikins tighter.

For each other you will yearn,
Your body will ache and your blood will burn.
Have each other you will, and must,
Nothing less will slake your lust.

The simulacra warmed in her hands and began to quiver. She let them tremble in her hands for several minutes, savoring their struggle for vitality, before she opened her eyes to watch them twitch and shake. The pain returned to her belly, the ache of life striving to be. It intensified until she began to tremble as strongly as the manikins.

She had done this. *Her* magic had brought these bits of wax and cloth and ink to the brink of real life. The *maleficia* was singing in her blood now, echoing through her bones, and the feeling of power was better than any drug.

This time, her magic would work. This time, she would have what she needed. It might startle or even frighten James and Annis, but they were young. They would get over it. They would become accustomed to their changed feelings and, in time, to each other. They had things in common, after all. They just needed encouragement.

And Harriet—imperious, high-and-mighty Harriet—would understand that she, Frances, was the strongest of the Bishop witches.

When Antoinette knocked on her door, Frances exhaled, long and slowly. She laid the manikins on the stained openwork cloth, and their quivering ceased the moment she released them. On dragging feet, exhausted now, she went to the door and spoke through it.

"Antoinette, I didn't sleep well. I'm going back to bed."

"You do not want your coffee?"

"I don't want anything. Just silence. This house is so noisy."

"*Oui, madame.* When shall I call for you?"

"I will come down for luncheon. Come an hour before that to do my hair."

"*Oui, madame.*"

Frances put her tools and the manikins in the valise and hid it once again. She moved the chair she had propped beneath the latch and unlocked the door, leaving the key in the lock. She stripped off her skirt and shirtwaist, draped them over a chair, and fell into bed wearing just her chemise and stockings.

For a few moments she gazed up at the painted ceiling, a tired but satisfied smile curving her lips. She had done what she must. She was a mistress of the *maleficia*, and it would not fail her.

She turned on her side and slept without moving or dreaming until Antoinette came to wake her.

21

Annis

Annis took off her clothes, put on her nightdress again, and lay down, but sleep eluded her. She couldn't keep her eyes closed, no matter how she tried to squeeze the lids together. Her brain buzzed with fantastic tales, a flood of information that was all but impossible to absorb. She kept seeing Harriet, such an imposing figure, her gray eyes shining like silver in the candlelight. Her deep voice had made Annis's very bones vibrate as she spoke her cantrip.

Cantrip! One of the many singular things spinning through Annis's mind, keeping sleep away. Herbs. Blood. Cantrips. Magic. *Witches*.

She wouldn't have believed any of it had she not felt so odd, so out of control, these past days. She had known something was amiss with her, something inexplicable. It made her skin crawl with shame to think that James must have had similar unwelcome feelings.

She hugged herself beneath the coverlet, chilled by fatigue, head swimming with strangeness. Witches. Frances was a witch. Harriet was a witch. She herself—if Harriet was right, if her knowing was accurate—was a witch.

It was beyond implausible, beyond any fantasy she had ever entertained. She half expected to startle awake and discover she had imagined all of it in a feverish dream. A nightmare? No, not a nightmare. If it was all true, if she really was—was *that*—she would have power. Real power. Power over her life, over her father, over Frances. Power to live her life the way she wanted to live it.

She suddenly remembered the electuary. She was supposed to take it the moment she was alone in her room. The swirl of new ideas in her brain had distracted her.

She jumped out of bed and found the folded handkerchief in the pocket of her skirt. She opened it carefully. The two little balls of remedy lay side by side, unappetizing chunks of green and yellow. She was supposed to concentrate, to invite the concoction to do its work.

She took one of the balls and put it in her mouth. She meant to swallow it straightaway, but she hesitated, caressing it with her tongue, pressing it against her palate. It tasted of honey and of the herbs, which had a piney sort of flavor. She closed her eyes, thinking of clearing her body of the *maleficia*, of having her own sensations and thoughts and desires restored to her. She concentrated on breaking the hold Frances had exerted on her, envisioning herself shrugging off her stepmother's hand on her shoulder.

The tidbit of remedy dissolved swiftly in her mouth. She swallowed, but there was little left to go down. She opened her eyes and gazed at herself in the dressing-table mirror. It was still dim in the room, the early sunlight just beginning to filter through the drapes. She couldn't detect any difference in her appearance, nor in her feelings. The moonstone lay quiescent in the hollow of her throat.

She yawned, suddenly unable to keep her eyes open a moment longer. She went back to the bed, folded herself into the sheets, and was asleep before her head settled into the pillow. She was still lost in a hot, heavy slumber when Velma came in with the coffee tray.

Annis woke to the sensation of a war being waged inside her body. It seemed to be centered in her belly, but it radiated outward, to her head, to her fingers, to her toes. Every piece of her seemed to be at odds with every other piece, as if each of her organs were following a different rhythm. She couldn't draw a decent breath, and her heart fluttered unevenly beneath her breastbone. Her mouth still tasted of honey and pine. Her skin itched, and she shoved the blanket away from her.

Velma, setting the tray beside the bed, gave her a worried look. "Miss Annis? You don't got the influenza, do you?"

"What—uh—I don't think so." Annis struggled to sit upright, and as Velma plumped a pillow behind her back, she realized her nightdress was soaked with perspiration. "It's much too warm in this room, don't you think? And so close. I wonder if anyone bothered to air it before we arrived?"

"I dunno. I could try to open that window, I guess," Velma said, though she gave the drape-covered window a doubtful glance.

"Could you try? Please."

The drapes gave every sign of not having been drawn back in a long time. Dust puffed from their folds as Velma dragged at them, pulling first one and then the other all the way to the side. The glass looked old, as if the window had been installed decades before. Annis worried for a moment that if Velma opened it, it would crack.

Velma labored over the heavy iron window catch and finally, with a grunt, succeeded in releasing it. She pushed the window open, and though its hinges creaked alarmingly in protest, fresh summer air flooded into the bedroom.

"Thank you, Velma," Annis breathed. "Much better."

Velma came back to pour her coffee and hold it out to her. "You're looking real peaked, miss," she said, frowning. "You want I should call someone?"

"No, you don't need to do that. Run me a bath, will you? A cool bath. I'm burning up."

Velma, her plain face creased with anxiety, went off to fill the big claw-foot tub. Annis took a sip of black coffee and held it in her mouth for a moment. The coffee washed away the lingering taste of the electuary, but she still felt as if her stomach were doing battle with her heart. Her skin prickled as sweat dried on it, and though she breathed the fresh air as deeply as she could, she felt as if nothing was working as it should. She drank more coffee, afraid to try to stand. If she stumbled, or was faint, Velma would call for help, and then what would she say?

It wasn't like having influenza. She didn't ache, exactly, and though she had been so hot under the blanket, she didn't think she was feverish. She was just—she didn't know. It reminded her a bit of having fallen from Bits's back once when he took a jump. Her head had spun with black stars, and for long moments she couldn't catch her breath. There had been no one to pick her up then. She had been as helpless as a baby, and Bits had dropped his head to nose her again and again while she tried to recover her wits.

Velma returned, silent now with worry. She put her hand under Annis's arm and lifted her from the bed. Annis tried to walk steadily toward the bath, but she didn't shrug off Velma's hand. It was comfortingly steady. "I'll be all right," she said. "I just need to rest in the bath for a bit."

Fearful tears gathered in Velma's eyes as she helped her into the tub. To distract her Annis said, "You can lay out my clothes. Choose whichever dress you like. That will be good."

Velma sniffled as she went back to the bedroom. Annis lay back in the cool water and closed her eyes. As her skin cooled and her breathing steadied, she tried to examine what was happening in her body, to track the battle to its source.

It was in her belly, of course. That was where she had first felt the effects of the *maleficia*, those unaccustomed sensations in her middle. Now Harriet's electuary was braced against the *maleficia*. They were warriors, the icons of two powers facing each other across a battle line, about to charge—and Annis was between them.

It helped to picture it that way. She sank deeper in the water, letting it rise about her shoulders and up her neck until it reached her chin. She made her arms relax, and her legs, flexing her toes and her fingers. She pictured the remedy coursing through her blood, clearing it of the *maleficia*'s poison. She imagined the warrior of the electuary as her champion, her protector, her hero. She saw the soldier of the *maleficia*, Frances's creation, driven to its knees.

Her breathing eased, and she stopped controlling it. Her heart settled into a normal rhythm. Her skin was soothed by the cool water and, she hoped, by the defeat of the *maleficia*. She supposed she would discover soon enough who had won this war.

She climbed out of the bathtub and was pleased to find her legs steady and her head clear. She dried herself and went into the bedroom to let Velma dress her hair, lace her into her corset—but not too tightly—and button her into a dimity shirtwaist and gored skirt.

Velma held up the Eton jacket that matched the skirt, but Annis shook her head. "I won't bother with the jacket."

Velma looked alarmed. "Mrs. Frances says—" she began.

"Never mind," Annis said. "It's too hot for a jacket this morning. If we go out walking, I'll come and fetch it, I promise."

She felt almost herself again, and really, it had taken her longer to recover from her tumble from Bits. With her hair pinned up and Harriet's handkerchief in her hand, she went down the staircase to the breakfast room.

James was already there. He leaped to his feet when he saw her and pulled out the chair next to his. His hand brushed her back. When he leaned over her to adjust a fork into the proper position, she felt the warmth of his body on her cheek, but she experienced no reaction to his nearness, or to his touch through the fabric of her shirtwaist. Her belly felt normal. Her mouth didn't dry, nor her heartbeat speed. She was in control.

She nestled the handkerchief safely in her lap as the breakfast began with a clink of silver on china. The sun was brilliant through the window, which in this room appeared to be much newer glass, without the ripples and faults of the one in her bedroom. The crystal on the table winked with sunlight, and Mrs. Derbyshire's snowy hair glowed silver. The light was cruel to Mrs. Hyde-Smith, accentuating the wrinkles on her heavily powdered face, and Mr. Hyde-Smith blinked, owl-like, against the brightness. Lady Whitmore wisely kept her back to the sun, as did her husband. There was only one empty place at the table. Frances had not come down.

Three servants were arranging a series of chafing dishes on

a sideboard, lighting small, flat candles beneath them to keep the food warm. The guests took turns leaving their seats to help themselves to various meats and grilled tomatoes.

James said, "Do let me get you something, Miss Allington. Do you prefer ham or bacon? Coddled eggs? I can order a boiled egg for you if you would prefer it." He looked down on her, a smile on his lean face, his autumn eyes sparkling as if she was just the person he most wanted to see in the world.

His Lordship was in desperate need of Harriet's remedy. Annis had a bad feeling it would come too late.

Since he was so eager, she asked for bacon and eggs and a slice of toast. When he came back, he brought a bowl of porridge for himself, liberally dotted with chunks of stewed fruit. It looked as if it might be apple and raspberries.

Annis said, "Oh my. That looks delicious."

He gave her a boyish grin, which made him seem much less stiff. "Favorite of my childhood," he said. "Would you like some? Our Dorset porridge is famous."

"Yes, please," she said.

He set down his bowl and crossed to the sideboard. Swiftly, after a glance told her the other guests were busy with their meals, she plucked the electuary from the handkerchief and added it to the bits of compote on James's porridge. By the time he came back to the table, she was innocently cutting a rasher of bacon into bite-size pieces.

She watched him from beneath her lowered eyelashes. He ate with good appetite, starting with the porridge. She tried not to hold her breath as he spooned up a mouthful, then another, and a third. By that time the bits of stewed fruit were gone, and with them the remedy.

To distract him, lest he notice that one of his bits of compote tasted different—tasted more like a compote of pine needles than one of apples and raspberries—she said brightly, "Shall we ride again today, my lord?"

His mouth was full, but he turned to her, on the point of swallowing. Suddenly his lips puckered, as if he had tasted something sour. He lifted his napkin, and she feared he was going to spit out the electuary. To stop him she leaned very close, widening her eyes. "Could I ride a different horse, my lord, please? I wish I could ride them all!"

He took a small, choked breath, and she worried he might cough out the remedy. Instead he picked up a water glass, washed down what was in his mouth, and dabbed at his lips before he answered. "I will let you choose, Miss Allington. But please, for the sake of my horsemaster, not the stallion. Jermyn will have a nervous fit if I allow a young lady to mount Seastar."

She sat back, satisfied. There were no more bits of fruit in his bowl. It was done.

"I wouldn't want to upset your horsemaster, my lord." The title was coming more easily to her tongue, probably because everyone else used it all the time. It was still rather silly, in Annis's view, but that didn't matter.

With luck the electuary would do its work, and in a few hours the Marquess of Rosefield would be himself again—stiff, old-fashioned, repelled by an American girl with no moral standards. With some luck she would have put him off so thoroughly that she would be set free, allowed to go home to Bits and resume her life.

And, she hoped, learn everything her great-aunt Harriet had to teach her.

22

James

James marveled once again, as he went up to change into his riding clothes, at the abrupt change in his feelings. He had considered Annis Allington a wanton. Shameless. Her disregard for convention went against every principle of ladylike behavior he had ever understood. Annis Allington as the chatelaine of Rosefield Hall had been unthinkable.

Yet now he could hardly wait to see her again. He was eager to ride out with her, though she would refuse the sidesaddle Jermyn would set ready and might choose an inappropriate mount. Why had he said she could choose? Why, indeed, had he fawned over her at breakfast, fetching her food, insisting she sit beside him, fussing with her flatware as if he were a servant?

That had been a ruse, of course, the silverware, and the chair, too. He had simply wanted an excuse to bend close to her, to touch her through her shirtwaist, to breathe in her scent. She wore no perfume, but she smelled deliciously of soap and shampoo and clear skin. She seemed irresistible. It was as if he had lost control of his sensibilities. What had happened to him?

He had one boot on, and the other was waiting in Perry's hands, when the nausea struck. It came all at once, out of nowhere. One moment he was extending his foot for his second boot, and the next he was doubled over the commode. He had never felt so sick, and certainly never so suddenly, or so thoroughly.

Perry, alarmed, knelt beside him, a towel in his hand. "My lord? Shall I send for the doctor?"

Still gagging, James shook his head. It was a minute or more before he could say in a choked voice, "Give me a minute. I must have eaten something—" He had to pause as he choked again and spit. The taste in his mouth was vile, and oddly tainted with something like pine needles, which made no sense at all. There had been nothing like that in his breakfast.

It wasn't until Perry had helped him up and aided him in washing out his mouth and bathing his face with water that he remembered there had been something—some odd taste that had been in his mouth for only a second, but had that tinge of pine in it. He had been on the point of spitting it out, he remembered, but Annis had spoken to him, leaning forward so he could look directly into her amazing eyes, that forget-me-not blue, and...

He had swallowed it. Whatever that was that had tasted like a tree instead of proper porridge, he had let it slide down his throat. Thinking of it made his stomach contract again, and he pressed his fist to his lips.

Perry said in alarm, "My lord? Again?"

James shook his head. He couldn't speak until the spasm eased. "Tell Her Ladyship," he croaked. "Something at breakfast—see if anyone else is ill."

"I'll bring up some tea."

"Help me get this damned boot off first. I'm going to have to lie down. Oh good God." He gritted his teeth against a fresh wave of sickness. He was sure there was nothing left in his stomach. He said hoarsely, "Give my apologies to Miss Allington, will you, Perry? We were to ride—we will have to postpone."

"Yes, my lord. Of course. Here, into bed with you. Let's get your jacket off."

James lay back on his pillows and closed his eyes as Perry pulled the coverlet over him, clothes and all. "Best bring me a basin," James said miserably. "I don't know if this is over."

Perry hadn't been gone more than ten minutes when a firm knock sounded on the door. Sure it was his mother, and knowing she wouldn't be kept out if she had decided her presence was required, James called weakly, without opening his eyes, "Yes. Come in."

He had stopped being sick, at least for the moment, but he felt as weak as a newborn puppy. The room was too hot, the air fouled, but he didn't have the strength to get up to open the window, nor even to cross to the bellpull to ring for Perry. The door opened, and quick, light steps approached his bed. Those steps did not belong to Lady Eleanor.

James forced his eyes to open. When he saw his visitor, he groaned, "Oh my God. Miss Allington—too humiliating, really—I—"

"Nonsense," she said. She set something down on the nightstand and began fussing with his pillows. "Here, my lord, see if you can sit up. I've brought you some ginger tea. That might ease your stomach."

"Ginger?" he said, feeling more like a sick child than the man he wanted her to see.

"Yes, do try it. I had some in my things, because my maid suffers from seasickness."

"I'm not—I'm never sick on the sea—"

She was urging him into a sitting position with surprisingly strong hands. "No, of course not, but you have the same symptoms, Perry says. Now, I'll hold the cup for you. Try a sip."

It was, of course, utterly improper for her to be alone with him in his bedroom. She had, in her typical careless way, closed the door. Anyone could think anything, but...

The tea felt marvelous in his mouth, and even better as it began to soothe his aching stomach. He drank it slowly, unsure if it would cause another bout of sickness. It didn't. He didn't feel well, precisely, but he felt strong enough to say, "Thank you, Miss Allington. But you shouldn't be here, in a gentleman's bedroom with no chaperone."

"Don't be silly," she said briskly. "I knew what you needed, and I brought it. You're feeling better, isn't that true? That's what matters." She bent forward to place her hand on his forehead. "You're much too warm, my lord. Let's get some air in this room."

She crossed to the window and pulled back the drapes, then opened the window with impressive ease. James knew how stiff that latch was. She exclaimed, "There! So much better," as fresh air poured through, replacing the staleness with the scents of summer flowers and freshly cut grass.

She came back to the bed to take the empty teacup from his hand and replace it in its saucer. She stood by his bed for a moment, her hands on her narrow hips, assessing him.

She was in her riding habit, her hair pinned up, ready for her hat. She was wearing a pearl choker with a large moonstone in the center. It was out of place in her ensemble, of course, but he didn't care. Her skin glowed in the sunshine from the open window, her pale freckles like gold dust on her fine straight nose. He couldn't imagine he had ever thought her plain.

Annis was nothing like the rosy, beribboned girls he so often met in London. She didn't fill every silence with torrents of words no one needed to hear. She stood looking quietly down at him, elegant in her height and slenderness, her eyes full of intelligence. She was better than pretty. She was much, much better than pretty. Even as shaky as he was from having been sick, as discomfited from being found lying in bed like a hapless boy, he wished she would stay with him so he could see her, talk to her. He wished she would touch him again.

He suspected it wasn't her ginger tea that had eased his illness. It was her presence. It was the matter-of-fact touch of her fingers, the glisten of sympathy in those forget-me-not eyes, the musical sound of her voice.

He still didn't know if he liked her. The stunning thing, despite that, was how much he *wanted* her.

Of course he couldn't possibly say that. Even the idea of it embarrassed him. He had the odd thought that she knew what he was thinking, and that embarrassed him even more. He hoped very much he was wrong.

She said, "If you feel ill again, have Perry send for me."

"Very kind, Miss Allington," he said.

She suddenly grinned, her face lighting, her freckled nose crinkling. "Couldn't you call me Annis? Now that I've been in your bedroom?"

His cheeks warmed unbearably. "I—well, of course, if you wish it, I—"

"Good. And I will call you James. That's settled, then." With the teacup and saucer in one hand, her skirts lifted in the other, she turned to the door. It opened just as she approached, and a scandalized Perry stood back, eyebrows lifted and mouth open, watching her stride past him. Over her shoulder she said, "Remember, James. Send for me if you feel ill again."

Then she was gone, leaving Perry staring after her and James groaning in confusion.

23

Harriet

In her slant-ceilinged room at the Four Fishes, Harriet slept for no more than two hours before a jolt of anxiety woke her. Her heart thumping, she got out of bed and went to kneel in the window nook to look out.

The roof of the inn was a thatched one, glittering now with drops of morning dew. The early sunshine illuminated the weave of wheat straw and reeds and gave her glimpses of other things here and there—heather, perhaps, or sedge. She gazed into the thatch's pattern, one hand at her throat as she tried to slow her breathing.

What had gone wrong?

She tried to convince herself she had imagined this rush of unease, that the late night and her fatigue had caused it, but the effort failed. Any Bishop witch worthy of the name knew better than to ignore her instincts. Something had happened.

Hastily she cleaned her boots and put on a fresh walking dress, worrying all the while. If the electuaries had not worked, Frances was stronger than she had suspected.

Harriet stopped at a tea shop in the high street, where she

bought a cup of tea and drank it so quickly it burned her tongue. She also bought a scone, wrapped it in a napkin, and carried it with her to eat on the mile-long walk through the woods to Rosefield Hall.

She skirted the stable block and hurried across the bottom of the lawn to the folly. She knew, as soon as she set foot on the step, that her feeling had been right.

Annis was already there, pale-faced and pacing.

"What's happened?" Harriet asked, without a greeting.

"He threw it up," Annis said, also wasting no time on pleasantries. "I put it in his porridge, and I saw him eat it, but then—he was really ill, his valet said, so I took him some ginger tea, and he looked awful."

"Were you ill?"

"Yes." She was frowning, but she didn't look afraid, only worried. "I felt as if I was going to come out of my skin for a little while. I wasn't sick, though. I was fine by breakfast."

"How long between when you consumed the electuary and the marquess did?"

Annis pressed her lips together, thinking. "It must have been four hours. I took it when I got back to my bedroom, which was—I think it was about four. They breakfast at eight-thirty in Rosefield Hall."

"Did you see Frances at breakfast?"

"No. She stayed in her room."

Harriet sank onto the cold stone bench, her arms folded. "She did it again, then."

"You mean Frances?"

"I do." Harriet breathed a long, tired sigh. "You took the electuary in time. He didn't."

"So she did the—the *maleficia*—again?"

"The *maleficia* is in the manikin itself," Harriet said. "She repeated her rite, to renew the spell." A spurt of anger made her clench her jaw until it ached. She wished she had Frances in front of her right this minute so she could give her a piece of her mind. "The electuary came too late for James. He couldn't tolerate it."

"I think I understand," Annis said. She sank down beside Harriet and leaned back against the pillar. She was dressed in her riding habit, and with her slender waist and long legs in the divided skirt, she looked as elegant as any Fifth Avenue society girl. "Frances repeated her rite, so the electuary was poison for poor James."

"'Poor James' is correct. He's caught in a struggle he doesn't even know is happening."

"What do we do now? Can we try again?"

"We must, Annis." Harriet linked her hands in her lap and thought about it for a moment. "Can you get some rest this afternoon?"

"Oh yes. All the other guests are terribly old. They always sleep in the afternoons." She added, with a moue of disappointment, "We were going to ride this morning. I was going to be allowed to choose my own horse."

"You were?"

Annis nodded. "I suppose James was still—um, still influenced by the—by Frances. That part was rather nice, that feeling that my wishes mattered. I suppose that wasn't real."

"It's hard to know," Harriet said. "You do have to account for the effects of the *maleficia*. If that's what it was, it wouldn't last."

"Aunt Harriet—do you think that's what Frances did to Papa? Do you think she made a manikin and created a cantrip to make him fall in love with her? I don't think he is anymore."

"The trouble with the *maleficia*, used like this, is that it doesn't actually create love. It creates—" Harriet paused, not sure how to explain such a thing to seventeen-year-old who knew nothing of the world, or of relations between men and women.

Annis said, "I understand. It's not love, it's that other thing. Lust, I suppose. The way a stallion wants a mare, but when he's done his work, he doesn't care if he ever sees her again."

"Oh my," Harriet said. "Annis, you..."

Annis thrust out her chin. "Please, Aunt Harriet, don't tell me you're shocked, too!"

"Oh no, no," Harriet said hastily. "Not shocked at all. Surprised."

"Because young ladies aren't supposed to know anything about sex?"

"Exactly!" Harriet gave a small chuckle. "I'm pleased, though. I don't agree at all with the custom of keeping young girls in ignorance until they marry. I suspect many a marriage that might have been happy is spoiled by that."

"Well," Annis said. She sat up, her back straight, her hands in her lap. "I will confess to you, Aunt Harriet, I don't actually know much about men and women. But I know all about horses, and I can guess. Extrapolate," she added, with a little shrug.

"Excellent. The more you know—about everything—the better practitioner you will be."

"I've been thinking about that," Annis said. "When we're back in New York, I want to learn everything you can teach me. I want to be what you are. To do what you do."

"To be an herbalist?"

"To be a *witch*," Annis declared.

"Just be certain you want that for the right reasons."

"I want it because it will set me free," Annis said.

Harriet answered, "That is the best possible reason."

The beautiful weather broke in the afternoon, swiftly and dramatically. A roll of thunder rattled the old-fashioned windowpanes in the Four Fishes. Harriet startled awake just in time to see the rain begin, great sheets of it that splattered her window and began to drip on the windowsill. She jumped up, taking care not to bump her head on the low ceiling, and found a towel to tuck beneath the leaking sash. Beyond the rooftops of the village she could see the rain-pocked bay, the water turned gray as lead.

She found her shawl and wrapped it around her shoulders, then curled herself into the window nook to watch the storm drench Seabeck Village. In moments the dry street ran with muddy rivulets, and the shopkeepers hurried out to take down their awnings. The avalanche of rain slackened to a steady drizzle that showed no sign of easing any time soon. Harriet supposed she would have to borrow an umbrella from the innkeeper. She hoped he wouldn't ask too many questions.

First she needed food. The scone of this morning was all she had eaten. She had walked a good distance and was going to have to do it again. Her empty stomach made her long for one of Grace's big breakfasts, meals always accompanied by a stream of innocuous chatter. She suffered a momentary bout of homesickness at the thought.

"Stop it, Harriet Bishop," she told herself. "This is no time for self-pity." She made herself wriggle out of the nook and go to the wardrobe to find her warmest clothes.

In the dining room downstairs, which was little more than an extension of the kitchen, with its big wood oven and open hearth, she was the only customer. The innkeeper, no doubt persuaded by her ready cash, seemed to have adjusted to the idea of a woman traveling alone, although he spoke to her as little as possible. He brought her a bowl of hot lamb stew and a loaf of fresh bread. He set a dish of butter on the table and stood back, his hands under his apron.

"Need anything else, miss?"

"No, thank you. This smells marvelous."

"The wife is known for her lamb stew."

"Do thank her for me." Harriet hadn't laid eyes on "the wife." She supposed the woman labored in obscurity, as so many wives did, while her husband dealt with the public.

It was, in fact, a quite respectable stew, although Grace would have found fault with the faint tang of meat kept too long. Harriet didn't mind it, hungry as she was. She ate all the stew and half the bread, liberally spread with butter. Grace would not have approved of the butter, either, with its strong sour taste, but Harriet found it delicious. The rain continued to sluice from the thatched roof. The windows in the dining room leaked even more than the one in her room. Without apology, the innkeeper placed rags and buckets where they were needed.

As Harriet rose, she asked, "Will this rain continue all night, do you think?" His answer was a shrug. "Well, then," she said briskly. "I must borrow an umbrella. I hope you have one."

He gave her an odd look but didn't comment. As she started for the stairs, he went behind the front desk and brought out an enormous, rather ragged umbrella. He handed it to her without speaking. She thanked him and carried the thing upstairs with her. When she came back down, swathed in her coat, he was nowhere to be seen.

It was a dark, wet hike back to Rosefield Hall. The drizzle continued, and a wind came up from the sea to blow droplets of rain past the shelter of the umbrella. By the time Harriet reached the folly, her coat was dripping and strands of her hair were glued to her cheeks.

Annis was waiting for her. She shot to her feet the moment Harriet appeared, and she held out her hands for the umbrella. "Are you cold? Such a surprise, this storm, after the hot weather."

Harriet handed over the umbrella as she stepped up into the folly. "Thank you, Annis. No, I'm not really cold, just damp."

"I thought you might not come. Walking through those woods in the middle of the night, in a rainstorm—you're a brave woman."

"Not so much brave as cautious. I say a cantrip for protection at such times. I'll teach it to you." She had, in fact, recited it several times on her long walk.

"I would like that, Aunt Harriet," Annis said. "Here, let me take your basket."

Together they laid out the ingredients for the electuaries, prepared them, and rolled the remedies into tiny balls of herbs and honey. Annis had to block the wind so the candles would continue to burn. They laid their charms between them, Annis her moonstone, Harriet her amulet. Harriet spoke her cantrip, and this time Annis spoke it with her. They watched, side by side, as the ametrine responded. Even the moonstone glowed, silvery layers rippling beneath its surface. When Annis replaced her choker around her neck, she caressed the stone with obvious pride.

Harriet folded the electuaries into a fresh handkerchief. "You may feel ill again, if Frances is still trying."

"I'll be fine," Annis promised.

"I hope James keeps this one down."

"I'll do my best."

Harriet repacked her basket and took up the umbrella in preparation for the long walk back to the Four Fishes. "Was James better today? Did he come to dinner?"

"He did. Dinners are terribly grand there, everyone wearing evening dresses and masses of jewels. James wears a dinner jacket."

"Did he seem recovered?"

"He was pale. Rather quiet. But if I've been sick, I feel that way, too."

Harriet looked out to the dull shine of the nighttime sea under the gradually clearing sky. It would be nearly dawn by the time she reached the village. "And your stepmother?" she asked.

"The same as always, I suppose. I don't pay much attention to her."

Harriet turned back to her, saying gravely, "You should, Annis. A witch willing to wield the *maleficia* is dangerous."

"But I'm protected now, aren't I? The remedy worked."

"It's not over yet. Take the electuary as soon as possible. And as you walk up to the hall, speak this cantrip:

Mothers and grandmothers, guard my way
Every night and every day.
Let no danger me befall,
Nor evil catch me in its thrall.

She made Annis repeat it, and Annis said, "Why do cantrips rhyme?"

"They're easier to remember if they rhyme. Remember, don't take off the moonstone."

"I won't. Thank you, Aunt Harriet."

"Rest well, child. Good luck."

Annis flashed her a quick smile and dashed up the slant of the lawn toward the hall. More slowly, feeling every one of her years, Harriet set out to walk back to the Four Fishes.

24

Annis

Annis popped the electuary into her mouth the moment she was safely in her room. She put on her nightdress, but she left the choker around her neck, and as she lay back on her pillow, she touched the moonstone with her fingers. It felt warm beneath her fingertips. She wondered if, after lying neglected in her jewel case for so long, it was pleased to be coming back to life. The weight and smoothness of it reassured her, and this time she fell asleep quickly, not waking until Velma came in.

"Velma," she said sleepily. "Have you seen my stepmother this morning?"

"That Frenchie said she went out early. For a walk, she said."

Annis bolted upright, a tremor of anxiety speeding her heartbeat. James needed to take the electuary, and soon. She had no doubt Frances would repeat her rite as soon as she could. Was perhaps doing it even now.

Obviously she had taken her remedy in time, because she felt no ill effects at all. But poor James—a repeat of yesterday's misery was not to be thought of.

"I need to dress, Velma," she said. "Hurry. And stop calling Antoinette 'that Frenchie.' I've told you before."

"Sorry, miss," Velma said, without the slightest sign of compunction.

Annis glanced at the clock. It was eight, and breakfast would be served in half an hour. Could Frances perform her rite before that time? Surely she wouldn't dare miss breakfast a second day in a row. "Hurry, please, Velma," she said, as she took her seat at the dressing table. "Just do something quick with my hair. I'll be wearing a hat most of the day anyway."

With her hair in a simple figure-eight knot, and wearing her white walking dress, Annis hurried down the staircase to the foyer and on to the breakfast room. The three old couples were already there, drinking coffee and chatting. The servants were just setting out the chafing dishes, and Annis saw there was porridge again, with a dish of stewed fruit next to it. She hovered by the table, though a servant frowned at her. When James came in, she dished up some of the porridge, dotted it with stewed fruit, and surreptitiously added the electuary, stirring it into the mix. She dished up a bowl for herself and carried both to the table.

She set his bowl, with its remedy, at his place. He glanced up, and brightened when he saw her. "Oh! Good morning, Miss Allington," he said. "You look lovely today."

She set her own porridge at the place nearest to his and sat down, saying, "Come now, James. I thought we were going to use Christian names?"

He blushed a little. "Yes, indeed. I forgot. Annis."

She gave him a smile she hoped was indulgent. Friendly. "You see, James, I noticed yesterday how much you enjoy porridge. I thought I would have some myself, so I brought it for you as well."

She was aware that the Hyde-Smiths and the Derbyshires had ceased their conversation and were watching her and James. Their regard made her neck prickle.

James was staring at the porridge before him in evident dismay. His cheeks paled and reddened, and paled again, and when he looked up from the bowl, his eyes showed real distress. "Oh, Miss Allington—that is, Annis—so kind, but—"

"What's wrong?"

"I can't—this is so embarrassing, but—I fear it was the porridge that made me ill yesterday. I can't risk it happening again."

"The porridge?" she said faintly. "Do you really think that was it?" She stared helplessly at his bowl, where the spoonfuls of stewed fruit now made swirls of color against the creamy porridge, and her heart sank. The electuary was gone. She couldn't even protest that it couldn't have been the porridge, because, in fact, it had.

He cast her a look of pure misery. "I am so sorry, Annis."

"Oh, James, it doesn't matter," she said, although, in cold fact, it mattered such a great deal. "It's only a bowl of porridge."

He said, "Perhaps you shouldn't eat yours, either. In case."

She managed a shaky smile and pushed her own bowl away. "You're right. I don't want to be ill."

He rose from his chair and signaled to one of the servants to remove the bowls. "Let me get you something else for your breakfast."

"Of course."

He paused, standing beside his chair. "And we missed our ride yesterday. Perhaps you would like to ride today?"

Resigned, she smiled more broadly. "I would like that, James. I believe you were going to let me choose my horse from your stables."

He returned her smile with relief and enthusiasm. "Yes, of course. Yes, just as you like."

While James was at the sideboard, dishing up eggs and ham for Annis, Frances appeared. She was wearing a day dress of apple-green pique with leg-of-mutton sleeves. Her waist was cinched so tightly Annis wondered how she could breathe. She paused in the doorway, taking in the scene of James carrying a plate to Annis and setting it before her.

Everyone had turned to watch Frances's entrance, and Annis could see the effort it took her to greet them all casually while restraining her triumphant smile.

When Annis looked up at James, the feverish spark in his eyes made her stomach quiver with something like revulsion. She felt sympathy, too, and a distressing sorrow at being the cause of such shameful feelings.

Perhaps Frances had won after all.

It was easy, once she was walking down the freshly groomed aisle of the Rosefield stables, to put aside the problem of Frances. Annis wanted to linger at each stall, to enjoy the pungent scents of these enchanting horses, to touch the sleek hides and feel the muscles beneath. She wanted to choose a mount with spirit and strength, and of course beauty—but all of these horses were beautiful, from the magnificent Seastar down to the aging pony.

James behaved normally enough at first, although he did seize every opportunity to touch her hand or her back. She tried to keep her distance from him without being too obvious about it.

Jermyn had once again set out a sidesaddle. Annis was tempted to shove the monstrosity off its support into the straw, but she resisted. She was a guest and wanted to be courteous, but Jermyn's sour expression gave her a pang of longing for Robbie's cheerful face.

James hung on every word Annis uttered about his horses and their special qualities. He led out Dancer when she had made her choice, and went into the tack room for the cross saddle Annis had used before. He saddled the mare himself while Jermyn, stony faced, stood by.

When James helped her up into the saddle, his hand lingered on her calf and slid down over her ankle, fingers trailing over the bones and heel. She caught a breath and turned to look down at him from her perch on Dancer's back. His cheeks flamed, and he averted his eyes.

"I—forgive me, Miss Allington," he stammered. "Please, I—it was unintentional."

It had not been unintentional. She knew that. She decided not to correct his address, to remind him they had agreed to use their Christian names. It was best, perhaps, that they return to formality until she and Aunt Harriet could resolve this situation.

He said again, "Do forgive me."

She said, "Of course, my lord. Shall we go?"

In embarrassed silence he mounted Breeze and led the way out of the stableyard. This time he didn't take the path up the coombe but turned to the right, cutting across an empty field to reach a road that led south, past the tenant cottages and on toward the sea.

25

James

James rode ahead of Annis, hoping to hide the flare of heat in his cheeks. What on God's green earth had he been thinking? He had touched her leg, felt the turn of her ankle, imagined the feel of her skin beneath her stocking...

It was as appalling as it had been thrilling. He had touched her as if she were one of his horses. As if he had a right. As if he were no gentleman at all.

James supposed he wasn't the cleverest Marquess of Rosefield there had ever been. He was certain, having grown up with the portraits decorating the great hall, that he was not the best looking. He disliked most pursuits generally regarded as manly ones—hunting, boxing, gambling—but he had never doubted that he was a gentleman. Now his base instincts had overcome his gentility, and that filled him with shame.

He glanced back at Annis. She had a beautiful seat in the saddle and nicely balanced hands on the reins. Dancer had earned her name by her tendency to prance at odd moments, but her spirited gait obviously didn't trouble Annis Allington. They made a handsome pair, the tall, slender girl and the sturdy white mare.

Perhaps, James thought, it was Annis's skill as an equestrienne that drew him to her, but he entertained the idea for only a moment. Whatever his other faults might be, he did not usually indulge in self-deception. He couldn't pretend to a more respectable reason. He just wanted her, in the basest, most carnal way, as if he were some sort of animal.

He urged Breeze into a trot, and Annis and Dancer followed close behind as he led the way toward High Point. Impulsively, without warning Annis, he let Breeze break into a canter. As if it had been rehearsed, as if the four of them were a team, Annis and Dancer did the same. It was stunning to see the high-strung Dancer obeying Annis's light hands and soft heels without resistance. The girl was a remarkable horsewoman.

They could be magnificent together, the two of them. They could make Seabeck, and the Seabeck Andalusians, into something spectacular. What other young lady would share James's passion for his horses? He had never met one.

He decided, on the instant, to speak to her.

They reached High Point in a short time, walking the horses the last half mile to cool them down. James had cooled down by then, too. Though his blood still pounded uncomfortably at Annis's nearness, he managed to assist her to dismount without doing anything discourteous. She thanked him, behaving as if nothing had gone amiss.

His cook had packed a basket, and he untied it from the back of his saddle and set it on the flattest of the boulders that marked the spot. Annis looped the horses' reins over a branch of one of the wind-deformed trees and came to stand at the peak of the cliff, gazing down at the waves rolling up the narrow strand beneath.

Herring gulls swooped and soared above the beach, raucous in the wind.

When he joined her, she said, "What a lovely place! What did you call it? High Point?"

"The farmers call it that. They use this road for their wagons." He followed her gaze down to the beach. "I often ride this way, just for the view." He pointed to the west. "If you follow this road far enough, you reach Seabeck Village. In the other direction, you can reach Golden Cap, the highest cliff on the southern coast. It's worth a visit, but too far for a day's ride."

"I see you've brought a picnic," she said. "Do you often do that?"

"Sometimes. I thought you would enjoy it."

"I would," she said with a smile. "This is so much nicer than being indoors." She took off her hat, and her hair tumbled out of its pins, falling to her shoulders, shining in the sun.

James took a deep breath and looked away from her, out to the glistening sea. He must keep his head about him and not be led astray by these untoward feelings.

He had never joined his university classmates on their outings to the city brothels. If he had, perhaps he would be more worldly, have more understanding of this newly awakened passion, but he had never been tempted. The lads always came back laughing, bragging, much the worse for drink, and also—none of them ever admitted it, but he could see it—more than a little sick at what they had done. Few of them ever wanted to repeat the experience.

He was, he feared, the most naive of men. He knew how the whole thing was supposed to work. He just had no experience of

it, nor had he cared about that until now. It had always seemed
to be something he could think about later, when the right time
came. He had always believed his fastidiousness proved his good
breeding. The idea of a brothel, of lying in a bed where so many
had...

The very thought made him shudder.

"Are you all right, my lord?"

He cleared his throat to compose himself and made himself
turn his blandest expression toward her. "Perfectly, Miss Allington. Shall we see what temptations Cook has packed for us?"

The boulder they sat on was warm from the sun, and the breeze
was barely strong enough to ruffle the manes of the horses. The
lunch basket held three kinds of sandwiches and a packet of
almond cakes, one of James's favorites, as well as a jar of cider. The
two of them devoured everything, appetites sharpened by fresh
air and exercise. When there wasn't a crumb left, they folded
their napkins and the tea towel that had protected the cider and
repacked the basket.

As James thought of how to phrase his proposal, he glanced
around at his beloved Seabeck to build up his courage. The
gentle hills rose like folds in a quilt, green and yellow and brown,
dotted with wildflowers in a riot of colors. The sea below shimmered in the sun. The herring gulls chuckled overhead, and
below the cliff, sandpipers darted across the wet sand. It was, he
thought, the best possible setting to appeal to a sporting girl like
Annis Allington.

He hoped it was, in any case. With all his being, at this
moment, he hoped so.

Annis had shaken the crumbs from her riding habit and moved
to the edge of the cliff. She stood shading her eyes with her hand,

peering out over the water. She made a lovely picture, with her mass of dark hair lifting in the sea breeze. His heart leaped at the sight of her, and his belly contracted with the desire—no, the *need*—to possess this quicksilver creature.

It wasn't just that he wanted to possess her physically, although he had been unable to quench that feeling. He felt more than that. He wanted her company. He wanted her on his arm when he went out in public, and he wanted her in his parlor in the evenings, reading by the fire. He wanted to see her giving orders to the housekeeper, visiting the tenant farmers, walking the streets of the village.

He cleared his throat. "Miss Allington? I have something to ask you."

She turned slowly to face him, and he saw with a quailing heart that she knew what he was going to say.

And that she was going to refuse.

He asked her anyway. There was nothing else he could do, though his spirit faltered at the prospect of her answer. He took her strong hand in his, looked into her forget-me-not eyes, and said, "If your father were here, I would speak to him first, but as that's not possible, I will take the liberty of speaking directly to you."

"Oh, James," she began, but he shook his head. He was committed now. It would be cowardly to give up before he began.

"I will come to the point," he said. "I would like you to do me the honor of becoming my marchioness. Of being my wife."

"James, I—"

"Truly, Annis, you must let me finish my speech," he said, pulling a wry mouth, and pleased at the dry humor he managed to produce in his voice. "I rehearsed it, you see."

Her little smile of comprehension and sympathy melted his heart, and he had to restrain himself from crushing her into his arms. He stood even more stiffly than before, holding her hand at a little distance from his body. He pulled in his chin, fortifying himself against the disappointment to come.

"I have never met a young lady like you," he said. "And while at first I was—somewhat surprised—"

"Shocked, you mean to say," she said. "Perhaps even revolted."

"No, no, not that. Well, perhaps, a little bit. But in these few days of our acquaintance, I've come to admire the very qualities that—uh, startled me. We share many interests, especially our passion for good horses. Your life would be comfortable. Although there are duties that go with the title, I think you would not find them onerous. And," he added, with a self-deprecating lift of his shoulder, "my mother would be pleased."

"You mean, because she believes Papa will settle a lot of money on me."

"I'm afraid your stepmother has made that clear to her."

"Oh yes, my stepmother will surely have done that."

He blew out a breath. "Money is a consideration for us, I'm afraid, but it's not by any means the reason for my proposal. I promise you that. I thought, under the circumstances, that frank speaking between us would be best."

"Of course," she said. "I much prefer it." Gently, she withdrew her hand from his. "I will speak frankly, too, James. I thank you for your offer of marriage, but I must decline on two counts." She stepped back a little and met his eyes with her unnerving blue gaze.

"First," she said. "I have no intention of marrying anyone. I don't think the restrictions of marriage would suit me. Second," she said, a little hurriedly, as if expecting him to interrupt, "I would hate to think that someone—anyone—should marry me for Papa's money."

"I've tried to make clear the money is not everything, Annis."

"You've done a fair job of that, but still, as you say, it is a consideration."

"I suppose I haven't presented my suit in the poetic way that might persuade you."

She exclaimed, with a laugh, "Poetic! I would hate that!"

He laughed, too. "Yes, probably. And I would be terrible at it, but do let me make a clean breast of everything. There's no doubt that Seabeck needs an infusion of money. Marriage, I believe, is an economic agreement as well as—for the most fortunate—a romantic one."

"I understand that," she said, nodding. "Money can be useful. I intend to use mine for my bloodline, for example, to acquire more mares, expand my stables—"

"But you could do that here," he said.

Her eyebrows lifted. "Here?"

"Of course." He waved his arm to indicate the expanse of Seabeck all around them. "We have adequate stables, but we could make them bigger. We have an abundance of pasture and some excellent seed stock right here in Dorset."

"But, James, everyone here in England is so—so old-fashioned. So *stuffy*. They would never let a woman like me breed horses!"

James could see he had no hope of convincing her, and he was dismayed at how much it hurt. It was physical, an ache deep in his solar plexus. He struggled to hide it from her, to maintain some remnant of his dignity.

He said, "You forget that there is the title. I'm a marquess, and only a duke—or Her Majesty and her children, of course—rank higher. We are often the ones who break the rules."

"I don't see you as the kind of man who enjoys breaking rules."

"Ah. You think I'm stuffy, too." He managed to produce a grin, and took pride in it.

She answered, in her blunt way, "Yes. A bit."

There seemed to be nothing else to say. No other argument he could make. He cleared his throat again and immediately regretted it. He had been trying to rid himself of the habit. "Well. Thank you for hearing me out, Annis."

"Oh, James, I do thank you for the honor," she said. "I do. And I hope—That is, could we be friends?"

"Of course." He turned away to begin untethering the horses, adjusting saddles and checking cinches, glad of the excuse to look away from her penetrating gaze. He was afraid she would recognize the pain in his eyes. "We had better start back. We'll be expected for tea."

She came to take Dancer's reins from him and placed her foot in his cupped hands for a boost into the saddle. He held her boot, gave her the needed lift, guided her boot into her stirrup with care, making no contact with her skin or even the hem of her divided skirt. He avoided her eyes as he stepped up on the flat boulder to mount Breeze.

His throat tight and his heart burning, he let Annis and Dancer lead the way down the winding road so he could give in to his misery.

26

Annis

Annis was gripped by an acute sense of unhappiness as she and the sprightly Dancer led the way back toward Rosefield Hall. She couldn't understand it. She had felt completely free of Frances's *maleficia* this morning. She had no doubts about refusing James's proposal, because it was her conviction that only the *maleficia* had driven him to make it. So why did she feel this welling of regret in her chest, this sorrow for what could not be?

She stripped her glove from her right hand and pressed her palm over the moonstone nestled at the point of her collar. The stone seemed to pulse against her hand, and beneath it a physical pain rose from her breast into her throat. Was she imagining that? She didn't think so.

With her left hand, she lifted the reins to urge Dancer into a trot. She needed to think about this. It was nothing to be laughed off. Perhaps Aunt Harriet could explain it.

She glanced back to be certain James and Breeze were behind her, and caught a breath at the look of woe dragging at James's eyes, his mouth set in hard lines of unhappiness. His hurt look made her chest ache even more. She swallowed, trying to release the ache, but without success.

It struck her, all at once, that there was a reason she couldn't swallow these feelings away. They weren't her own feelings. They were out of her control. But why should she experience James's emotions, feel them as sharply as if they were her own?

She was utterly confused, and at first that frightened her. A moment later her fear gave way to anger. She said, "Let's go," to Dancer and pressed her heels against the mare's ribs. Dancer broke into an eager canter, and then, when Annis pressed her calves tighter, a gallop.

Annis didn't look back to see if James and Breeze were keeping up. Recklessly, relieved to be in motion, even if she was in danger of falling, she gave Dancer her head.

The mare was magnificent. Set free, she stretched her body into a flat run, ears back, tail streaming in the wind. Annis bent low over the pommel of her saddle, and strands of Dancer's mane whipped against her face, stinging her cheeks. The wind brought tears to her eyes, but she didn't care. She clung with her hands and her thighs and her heels, giving herself thoroughly to the thrill and the risk of racing an unfamiliar horse full out on a strange road.

She arrived at the Rosefield stables a full five minutes ahead of James and Breeze. Jermyn met her with a disapproving scowl. She barely restrained herself from sticking her tongue out at him.

Jermyn was one person, at least, she thought, who would be delighted to know there was no chance of Annis Allington becoming the marchioness.

"You. Did. *What.*"

Annis gaped at her stepmother, stunned at the fury that

blazed from her. It made her take a step back, as if Frances might strike her.

She said, her voice trembling just a little, "You heard me. The marquess asked me. I refused him."

Frances's lips pulled into a thin line, and white spots appeared beside her mouth. Annis had seen her stepmother lose her temper before, but not like this. This rage felt primal, ancient, as if a long-banked fire had suddenly blazed into an inferno and any pretense of sophistication had vanished in its flames. Frances leaned forward as if she might seize her stepdaughter by the throat. She hissed, "You will go back to him. Apologize. Tell him you've changed your mind."

Annis took another step back, but she managed to say, though her mouth had gone dry, "No. I will not."

"Lady Eleanor and I—"

"It doesn't matter, Frances. This is between James and me."

One of Frances's hands had tightened into a fist. The other was a claw, the fingers curled, the nails sharp, and Annis braced herself for the attack that seemed imminent.

"You will do as I say," Frances growled, in a voice Annis didn't recognize. The cat's smile was now a tiger's snarl.

Annis shook her head, though inwardly she trembled. "I'm not going to marry him."

"Any normal girl would leap at the chance to become a marchioness. I would be thrilled if I were you!"

"You're not me, Frances! We're different. I will apologize, but I'm going home."

"You will do no such thing."

"Do you think you can stop me? I have my own means, you know." That was a slight exaggeration. Annis guessed she had enough money in her purse to buy passage for herself and Velma, but not a penny more.

Frances spun away from her, facing the wardrobe, her shoulders high and tight, one fist still clenched against her hip. Annis watched her, her own hands clasped before her breast, fighting a sense of terror that was out of all proportion. She was bigger than Frances. She was younger, and stronger, and yet...

She heard Frances draw a long, noisy breath. She watched her drop her shoulders and release her hand. Frances gave a tiny, almost undetectable shudder, and turned back.

Annis gaped anew at the change in her.

Her stepmother's eyes no longer burned with that terrifying wrath. Her cheeks were smooth, and her lips curled. Her hands were relaxed by her sides. She said sweetly, "You know, Annis dear, there's a telegraph office in Seabeck Village. Should you decide to go through with your mad little plan, I will wire your father. Black Satin will be sold before you reach New York."

"No!" Annis cried. Her hand dropped from the moonstone. "You won't do that! If you do, I'll—I'll tell Papa—" Her voice broke, and she twisted her fingers together so hard they ached.

Frances's kittenish smile intensified, and her eyelids drooped lazily. "What?" she purred. "What will you tell him?"

"I'll tell him that you—that you've been—"

"Oh, come now," Frances said, just showing her little white teeth. "Let's have it all out in the open, shall we? You're threatening to tell your father I'm a witch."

Annis gaped at her stepmother. "You—you—*spied* on me! On me and Harriet!"

"I observed you. Of course I did. What you were doing concerns me, after all."

"So you admit it!" Annis cried, her composure in shreds. "You're a witch! You magicked poor James, and you tried to magic me!"

"And what do you think your father would say if you told him that, you idiot girl?"

Annis didn't respond. Breathing hard, as if she had run a mile, she turned to her dressing table and started pulling the pins out of her hair.

She knew the answer to Frances's question, of course.

Her father wouldn't believe a word of it. He would think his daughter had lost her mind.

Tea was an ordeal. Annis was again seated at James's right, but neither of them spoke a word to the other, nor did they touch their food. Annis felt Lady Eleanor's sharp gaze throughout the meal, and she knew there was trouble ahead. She should never have come. She should never have allowed herself to be used this way. When she had given in to Frances's scheme, she had thought only of herself and getting home to her horses. It had never occurred to her that some young man might be harmed.

And now she had to fear for Black Satin as well. Frances didn't make empty threats. She might be vain and selfish, but she was no weakling. She had proved that already. She was capable of doing just what she had said.

And Papa? She couldn't trust him. He had been content to let Frances use her however she wished. What else might he do to keep Frances from pestering him?

When the meal ended at last, she and James parted without a word or a glance. James went into his library. The rest of the guests followed Lady Eleanor out to the garden to observe the midsummer flowers in bloom. Annis followed, but at the first opportunity she slipped away into the woods to be alone, to try to think what she might do to save herself, to save Bits, to soothe James's wounded heart.

She wandered for a bit, finding deer tracks that wound through the shadows of the trees and around the tangles of brush and berry vines. The moonstone throbbed against her throat, and instinctively she chose her direction according to its intensity. She didn't think about where she was going but simply walked, turning beneath an ancient elm, pressing through a narrow spot where brambles caught at her clothes, following a track that widened and then forked. She took the left turning, urged by the vibration of the moonstone. It had begun to feel familiar, and she trusted it. The way was rough, with occasional stones and tree roots that threatened to trip her. She watched her step and, despite the uneven path, felt better and better as distance grew between her and Rosefield Hall.

When the path suddenly broadened and smoothed, she looked up to find that she had reached the outskirts of Seabeck Village. To her left was a cottage with an oil lamp glowing in its single window. Ahead the sun was just setting beyond the thatched roofs. Long violet shadows stretched across the high street. A horse and cart waited outside a greengrocer's. Two women in long coats, carrying laden wicker baskets, walked in a westerly direction, away from Annis.

She stopped where she was, uncertain what to do next. It would be full dark soon. She should be dressing for dinner. Velma would be in a panic. Frances would be irate, and it was rude to miss dinner without warning her hostess. She should turn around instantly, hurry back to Rosefield Hall.

She didn't do it. Aunt Harriet hadn't mentioned the name of her inn, but there was only one. A sign swung on an iron shaft projecting from the thatched eaves, featuring a crude painting of four leaping fish. The legend read "Four Fishes Inn," and as Annis started toward it, the moonstone gave one last, affirming pulse.

A tall figure stepped out of the inn's entrance and stood waiting on the stoop. Annis hurried forward to seize her aunt's proffered hand. "Aunt Harriet! Were you waiting for me?"

"I was."

"But—I didn't even know I was coming! How did you?"

"I summoned you, Annis," Harriet said, as calmly as if this sort of thing happened every day in her world. "Fortunately, you heard me."

"I think the moonstone heard you."

"Only because you were open to its message. Come inside, it's beginning to get dark."

"Frances is going to be furious if I don't appear for dinner."

Harriet arched one dark eyebrow. "Does that matter?" She pulled open the door and led Annis into a small, dark foyer with a reception desk at one side. Straight ahead of them was an uncarpeted, crooked wooden staircase, and Harriet started up it.

Hurrying behind her, Annis said, "It does matter, I'm afraid. She threatened to send a telegraph to my father, to tell him to sell Black Satin!"

Harriet turned right at the top of the stairs and produced a key from her pocket to open a door. The lintel was so low she had to duck to go under it. Annis did the same.

Once inside the room, as Harriet held a match to the wick of an oil lamp, Annis said, "I have never seen Frances so angry. It was horrible—one moment she was so furious I thought she was going to strike me, and the next she was like ice."

"What made her so angry?"

"James proposed marriage, and I refused him."

"Ah. That must have been upsetting for you both."

"James doesn't want to marry me, not really. It's just the *maleficia*, not—not *love*."

"It can be both," Harriet said mildly. She pointed to the only chair in the tiny room. "Have a seat. You've had a long walk."

"At least my electuary worked," Annis said glumly as she sank into the chair. "I'm not having those revolting feelings anymore."

"That's good."

"Why did you—what did you call it?—summon me?"

Harriet sat on the edge of the bed, stretching out her long legs. She folded her arms and regarded Annis. "I know what happened this morning."

"You do? How?"

"It's something I do sometimes. Something that is part of my ability. Often I can't do anything about what I know, but sometimes I can, and this is one of those times."

Annis said wonderingly, "I know things sometimes, too."

"Do you? Tell me about that."

"I knew what Frances intended, when she and Papa made me come to England."

"Ah. Any other times?"

"Yes, this morning. I knew James was going to ask me to marry him."

"I see." Harriet tapped her arms with her long fingers. "The knowing can be a powerful thing, Annis. Usually it comes to me when I'm working, as it did this morning."

"You were working?"

"Oh yes. I made another electuary for you. Actually, I made two."

"You did it without me?"

Annis's disappointment must have shown on her face, because Aunt Harriet smiled and pointed to a small box on the table beside her bed. "I didn't feel we could wait until tonight. Frances will keep trying, and we must resist her. It won't hurt you to take one more remedy, and I want you to have an extra, just in case."

"What about James?"

"It's too dangerous. He's under the influence of the *maleficia*, and the remedy made him ill once already."

"Oh, poor James! None of this would have happened to him if I hadn't come to England. I feel—I felt—" She made a helpless gesture.

"Yes? Do tell me what you felt, Annis."

"I felt all of his emotions after his proposal. His sadness. His pain. It was awful."

Harriet regarded her for a long moment, her eyes shining silver in the lamplight. "Have you felt such a thing before?"

"No. Well, maybe once or twice." She thought of Velma, outside the chandler's shop, and how she had sensed her maid's yearning for the cut-glass swan. "Is it—is that because of the magic?"

"I'm not sure. We all experience our abilities a bit differently. In my case it's just the knowing. In yours it may also be empathy."

"I had a terrible argument with Frances. She spied on us, in the folly. I told her I know all about her, and I threatened to tell Papa. She said he would never believe me, and she was angry because I refused James, and that's when she said—" Fear made

Annis's voice break on a sob. "I'm so far away from Bits, and I can't do anything about any of it! I'm afraid I'm going to lose him, if I don't marry James, and if I do—I'll lose him anyway! I'm trapped, Aunt Harriet!"

"You're not," Harriet said. "Or at least you won't be."

She went to the bedside table to take up the little box. She set it on the bed and lifted the lid. Annis bent to see inside it.

There was a white handkerchief, neatly folded, which Annis assumed held the electuaries. Next to the handkerchief, resting on a cushion of cotton batting, was a figure fashioned of cloudy white wax.

The simulacrum was a simple construction, as if it had been made by a child. It had a rudimentary torso, and its legs and arms were mere stubs of wax. A tuft of what looked like dark moss was glued to the waxen head. Two dark pebbles had been pressed into the place where eyes should be, and a chip of something like bark represented a mouth. A makeshift dress fashioned out of a bit of flannel was pinned around the thing, somehow making it even more ugly.

Annis gaped at it. "Is that—Aunt Harriet, is that a—a *manikin*?"

Harriet spoke in a low tone. "It is, Annis. It is a manikin intended to be Frances, but it's not finished."

"But you said—about manikins, you said that was the *maleficia* and we should never—"

"I meant it, too," Harriet answered. She stood, her hands folded before her, and gazed at the hideous little thing in the box. "I wish it weren't necessary, but there is no other way to undo what Frances has done. Once the *maleficia* has succeeded, it must be answered in the same way it was accomplished." She took out the handkerchief and gave it to Annis. "I think you should take one of these right away, to be certain you're safe. I hope it doesn't make you feel ill. If she's working her cantrip even now, you may feel the effects."

Annis took the handkerchief and unfolded it. The electuaries lay within, perfectly round, smelling of pine and honey. She popped one into her mouth and swallowed it as Harriet watched her. "Do you feel anything?"

Annis pressed a hand over her stomach. "Not yet," she said.

"Perhaps she's waiting until tonight. Take the other one with you, and keep it somewhere safe." Harriet replaced the lid on the box with care.

"I'd better hurry back. Things will be worse if I miss dinner, and we're only to stay at Rosefield Hall one more day before we go back to London."

"Do you want me to walk with you?"

"No, I'll be fine. I know the way, and it's not completely dark yet. You must be exhausted, in any case."

"I'm a bit tired, yes. Now, I have to ask you to do something for me."

"Anything."

"I need something of Frances's. Something personal, to add to the manikin. A bit of hair is best, but a piece of jewelry will work, or a snippet of fabric she has worn close to her body, such as a chemise or a corset."

"I can do that."

"I'm very sorry to involve you in this, Annis."

"I want to help."

"I know you do, but I must warn you that the *maleficia* is not only dark but dangerously powerful. Such power can be intoxicating. It can corrupt the practitioner."

"You think that's what has happened to Frances."

"The darkness was always within her, I'm afraid. It's in her Bishop line. The *maleficia* brought it out, and now that she has tasted it, I don't know if she can turn away. I want you to understand."

"I think I do."

"Good. Best hurry now. You have a long walk ahead of you. I'll meet you tomorrow in the folly. Come after breakfast."

Annis bid Harriet farewell and hurried out of the room and down the narrow staircase. She walked as quickly as she dared up the street, and when she reached the path to Rosefield Hall, she broke into a run.

27

Harriet

It was the dinner hour, but Harriet couldn't face the smoky dining room of the Four Fishes. She wasn't very hungry, but she was, as Annis had said, exhausted. She decided on an early night, the first since her arrival at Seabeck Village. It would be good to have one full night's sleep.

As she laid out her clothes for the morning, she lamented Grace's absence. None of her shirtwaists were particularly clean. She had washed out her smallclothes as best she could, but there was little she could do about her other things. Grace would be appalled at the state of her meager wardrobe.

Harriet sighed. She would be glad, just at this moment, to be bathed in a flood of Grace's soothing, inconsequential chatter, to be free of the anxiety that gripped her, her worry for Annis, her fear for James, her horror of the *maleficia*. She remembered how difficult it had been to resist its appeal once she had felt it thrill through her body and her mind. Beryl had been right about that. She had been right about Frances, too.

Annis's description of Frances's rage brought back the memory of the shade of Bridget Bishop, still furious after two hundred years. It boded ill for them all.

Harriet closed the little wooden box, hiding the manikin from view. Her belly had roiled as she shaped the figure, added the pebbles and bark and fur, and wrapped it in flannel. It was still a dead object, nothing but a collection of oddments. With nothing of Frances added to it, it could be discarded without a thought, and with all her heart, she wished she could leave it that way. If Frances would only stop now, give up her assault on the marquess, let him and Annis be, Harriet would not have to take this perilous step.

She extinguished her lamp but left the window open to let the night birds soothe her troubled soul, to be lulled by the distant swish and pull of the sea. She fell asleep watching the stars begin to sparkle, one by one, tiny distant jewels coming alive in the darkness.

Far into the night a nightmare woke her. It was a dream she had suffered before.

It was of her beloved Alexander on his deathbed, grievously wounded through the chest by a rifle bullet. His injury had been beyond her skill to heal. She could do nothing but watch as his life slipped away.

He had, they told her, hesitated at a crucial moment. He had been leading a charge, his men behind him, the enemy dug into their places, waiting. Just at the time he should have taken cover, leveled his own rifle, he stopped. His men raced on, but he stood, an officer frozen on a hillock where anyone could see him—the perfect target.

She had tried to stop him going into battle. She had made a manikin of him and created a cantrip to make him crave peace instead of war. She had tried to extinguish his wish to fight, but she had succeeded only in weakening him, making him vulnerable. It had cost him his life. She had lost her only love.

That manikin, decorated with a button from one of his uniforms and a tiny, precious lock of his beard, she had tucked into his coffin, to be safely buried with him. He was dead, and the manikin with him.

The dream was always the same, Alexander's eyes on hers as he breathed his last, his grip on her hand weakening, little by little, until she held only his lifeless fingers. Always, at the end, when she felt his life slip away, she woke. Always there were tears on her face, and a pain deep in her chest that took a long time to ease.

This time, in a strange bed, in a strange country, she woke with a clenching in her stomach. Something was terribly wrong, something that had nothing to do with her nightmare.

She reached for the amulet resting on the bedside table and held it up in the darkness. It caught the starlight, glittering faintly, but only in reflection. She pressed it to her heart and whispered into the darkness, "What is it? What's happened?"

There was no answer, but of course it must be Annis. It could only be Annis.

Annis had summoned her. Annis, who knew so little, who had only begun to learn who and what she was, had summoned Harriet in a stunning demonstration of nascent ability. Under less frightening circumstances, Harriet would have been thrilled.

She threw back her covers and began unbuttoning her nightdress. She didn't bother lighting the lamp, but hastily pulled on her shirtwaist and skirt and her jacket. She thrust her feet into her walking boots, tying them as quickly as she could in the darkness.

She caught up her basket and laid the wooden box inside, along with a package of herbs and scissors, matches, and candle. At the last moment she hung her amulet around her neck, gathering courage from the weight of the jewel against her breast.

The inn was silent around her as she crept down the stairs, clinging to the banister so as not to miss a step in the dark. She slipped out the front door, closing it softly behind her. No one was on the street. No lights showed in any of the houses. Clouds had gathered, and only a shrouded half moon lit her way. She set out with urgent steps, worry driving her.

Her mind burned with questions. What could have happened? Annis had seemed fine when she left. Surely Frances wouldn't harm her physically. Had the electuary made her ill? Had she lost her way in the woods?

Harriet walked as fast as she dared in the darkness, reciting her cantrip just for Annis:

Mothers and grandmothers, guard her way
Every night and every day.
Let no danger her befall,
Nor evil catch her in its thrall.

28

Frances

Frances thought the great Sarah Bernhardt could not have given a better performance than the one she herself gave that evening. She had quelled her simmering temper, despite seeing Annis tumbling in for dinner at the last possible moment, her hair barely pinned up and a great crease in her dinner gown. Lady Eleanor, clearly aware that her son had offered for Annis and been refused, barely spoke to Frances when she came into the dining room. It was hardly the cut direct, but it was a decided snub.

Frances sought out the Hyde-Smiths for conversation. She forced herself to be charming, to make bright conversation, to be quick to laugh, outwardly merry while white-hot fury raged inside. She drank a full glass of champagne straight down, hoping to cool the fire within her.

Annis hadn't appeared until they were all trooping into the dining room. It didn't help Frances's mood to reflect that only a young girl could look that well when she had made no effort. She had come flying down the stairs like a hoyden with no breeding. Her cheeks were pink, and the disordered state of her hair made her look girlish and appealing.

It wasn't fair. It wasn't fair at all.

Fighting her fury, Frances played the role of vivacious American. She pretended to be unperturbed by the coolness of her hostess and the distraction of her host, though the Whitmores looked puzzled and the Hyde-Smiths and Derbyshires seemed taken aback by Lady Eleanor's grim demeanor. They made a heroic effort to join in Frances's gaiety. They barely managed to keep a conversation going through the multiple courses of the meal and the coffee hour. Frances forced herself to wait until one of the elderly couples proposed going up to bed before she, too, made her way up the staircase.

She allowed Antoinette to take down her hair and brush it, though her skin prickled with impatience. She rubbed cold cream into her hands as the maid fussed with hanging up her dinner gown. She didn't hurry Antoinette out, though anger burned in her stomach and her muscles tensed with the need to hurry. Time was running low. Only one day remained of their stay.

Antoinette tidied the dressing table, mounding the hairpins on their enameled tray, scooping up the hat pins to stick them into the waiting cushion. She settled Frances into bed, turned down the lamp, and left the room at last.

The moment the door closed, Frances scrambled from the bed and dived behind the wardrobe for the valise that held her supplies. She turned up the lamp just enough so she could see to work. She propped her two manikins against the mirror and set a match to her candle. She clipped a fingernail and set it in the saucer on top of the mistletoe and the last of the mandrake root and barrenwort. She pierced her finger and dripped fat dark drops over the whole, then held the saucer over the candle flame.

When the concoction was reduced to a few thick drops, she

squeezed her finger to force out half a dozen more drops, soaking the mixture with fresh, undiluted blood. She needed every bit of magic she could call upon.

She painted the manikins as before, swiping up the last bits of the concoction, wasting none. She sat back, one simulacrum in each hand, and recited a new, stronger, more provocative cantrip.

Witch's blood and witch's claws
Witch's power and witch's cause
Heat your blood, inflame your brain
Till no usual sense remain.
Lust now fills you with its fire.
Be you maddened by desire.

The manikin representing Annis lay in her left hand like a dead thing, unresponsive, still. Her cantrip had no effect at all.

It was different with the manikin of the marquess. Her cantrip brought it to life with a jolt of energy that stung her hand. The simulacrum quivered and shook so hard she nearly dropped it. The pain of the *maleficia* shot through her belly, a great cramp that blurred her vision and made sweat break out on her chest.

"So be it," she gritted, shaking the trembling manikin as an angry parent shakes a disobedient child. "Do what you must to win her. Hold nothing back! This is your last chance."

29

Annis

Lady Eleanor stopped Annis as she was about to mount the staircase to go to bed. "Will you speak with me a moment, Miss Allington?" she said. "I would consider it a great favor."

Frances's laugh bubbled from the parlor, where she was playing cards with the older couples, but it couldn't dispel the strained atmosphere that had marred the entire evening. Annis yearned to escape to her room, but she said politely, "Of course, my lady." She turned away from the staircase and followed Lady Eleanor along the hall to a small room she hadn't seen before.

As they entered, Lady Eleanor said, with a wave of her hand, "My personal study. This is where I write letters, manage accounts, and occasionally have a few moments to myself."

"It's a beautiful room," Annis said with sincerity. Its walls were lined with bookshelves, every one of them full. A small ebony desk rested beneath a window, with a well-used blotter and an inkstand on it. There was a framed photograph of a younger, thinner Lady Eleanor, with a tall, distinguished-looking gentleman at her side. A lamp on the desk was already burning.

"Please take a seat," Lady Eleanor said, gesturing to one of two upholstered armchairs arranged beside a piecrust table. Annis sat down, and Lady Eleanor settled opposite her. "I expect you're tired after such an exciting day, Miss Allington."

"A little," Annis answered warily.

"Yes, indeed. A rather strenuous ride, I'm told by our stable master. And a proposal of marriage as well. Not every day a girl has such experiences."

"No, my lady," Annis said, resigned now. She should have known Lady Eleanor would be aware, and the strange thing was that she didn't mind. Her hostess appeared more matter-of-fact than angry, which was a relief. It was best, surely, to have everything out in the open.

"I have nothing to say about your riding," Lady Eleanor said. "Although I hope you will take thought for your safety. It might surprise you, but it's my view you're wise to forego the sidesaddle."

"It does rather surprise me," Annis said. "I thank you, though. Someone has to put an end to the silly practice. It might as well start with me, because I don't care what people think."

"You are fortunate in not needing to care. Your father's wealth insulates you. Not every young lady is so lucky."

"Yes, I know."

"Well. As the hour is so late, I will come right to the point." Lady Eleanor fingered the long loop of pearls and diamonds that hung around her throat and all the way to her waist. Her bosom mounded above the décolletage of her black satin gown, and the tightness of her corset meant she could neither sit back in her chair nor relax her stiff posture. Annis wondered how she could breathe.

"Rosefield told me he spoke to you today," Lady Eleanor said.

"You refused his offer, I understand. I hold out hope that I may change your mind."

"I'm sorry, Lady Eleanor, but no," Annis said. "Forgive my bluntness."

"You're direct. I tend to be that way myself."

"Yes. I assure you it's not James's—Lord Rosefield's—fault. The truth is that I do not wish to marry."

"I think many of us wish we did not have to marry," Lady Eleanor responded, startling Annis anew. The older woman gave a tiny, flesh-trembling shrug. "We're females. Marriage is our lot. What else can we do with our lives?"

"I intend to breed horses. Establish a fine bloodline."

"Do you indeed? How ambitious you are. And how will you do that without a husband?"

"I will have money of my own. I have a home, and stables to work from."

"I fear you will learn no one will buy horses from a woman, or trust that she knows what she's doing."

"I do know what I'm doing, though. I have made a study of it."

"I believe you, but the men who run the world will not."

"But James believes me!" Annis protested, and realized her error immediately.

Lady Eleanor's smile was restrained, despite the minor victory Annis's admission gave her. "Yes, Miss Allington, I believe he does. Wouldn't that be an excellent solution to your problem?"

Annis folded her arms around herself and looked away from Lady Eleanor's plump face with its pompadour of graying hair. She was clever, James's mother. Annis struggled for something to say to her that would not offend but would make her own intentions clear.

Carefully she said, "I was surprised by Lord Rosefield's proposal. I have no reason to believe he cares for me."

"That was true," Lady Eleanor said. "But that has evidently changed."

"I don't think he would be happy with me."

The older woman emitted a gentle laugh. "Happiness is overrated, my dear, and hard to define. Most of us settle for contentment in our marriages. And for some of us lucky ones, friendship. The late marquess and I were the best of friends. I do think you and Rosefield could be friends, too."

"Lady Eleanor, I am delighted to be your son's friend, but I will not marry him. It was a kind offer, and I assure you it was courteously made, but I want only to go home to my horses and my life in New York." She glanced up to see how Lady Eleanor had taken this statement.

Lady Eleanor looked terribly weary. No doubt she longed to be free of her cruel corset, free of the weight of her jewels and the black mourning feathers in her hair. No doubt she longed to be free of the burden of worry she carried.

Annis said sadly, "My stepmother has misled you."

"Yes. She has."

"She wants a title in the family."

"Oh, they all do," Lady Eleanor said, with a quirk of her lips. "It's the bargain we make. An heiress's dowry in exchange for a title for the bride."

"But I don't care about the title."

"So I gather." Lady Eleanor started to push herself up from her chair, then fell back with a little grunt. Annis, seeing this, jumped up to take the older lady's hands and assist her to her feet. "Thank you, my dear," Lady Eleanor said. "I do wish you might reconsider. This is a fine place to live—or it will be, with some repairs and a few modern conveniences."

"I can see that," Annis said with sincerity. "Seabeck is beautiful, as is Rosefield Hall."

Lady Eleanor drew a shallow breath, and when she started toward the door, she stumbled. Annis took her arm. "Please let me assist you, Lady Eleanor. You're tired, I think."

Her Ladyship didn't answer, but she leaned on Annis's arm as they climbed the staircase. At the top her lady's maid met them, and Annis released the older woman into the maid's care.

"Good night, Lady Eleanor," she said, as the maid led the older woman away.

Lady Eleanor paused, changing her grip on her maid's arm so she could turn back to look up into Annis's face. Her eyes, autumn hazel like her son's, glistened in the low light of the gas lamps. "You know, Miss Allington," she said, "I would very much have liked a girl like you for my daughter-in-law."

"S-so kind," Annis stuttered, startled and touched. The only other woman she had ever known who spoke so plainly was Harriet.

"Not at all," Lady Eleanor said, with a small, regretful smile. "I'm not a particularly kind person, I'm afraid. I meant what I said, all the same."

Annis met Antoinette in the corridor on her way to lay out Frances's nightdress. With sudden inspiration Annis said, "Do you know where Velma is? I suspect she's still in the kitchen. I want to have an early night."

Antoinette frowned over the extra steps she would have to

take and gave a noisy sigh, but she went through the baize door to the servants' staircase without argument.

Annis could still hear Frances's voice from the parlor below. She seized her moment. She slipped into Frances's bedroom and moved hastily to the dressing table. Antoinette had already cleaned the hairbrush, but there was another brush, carelessly dropped onto the openwork cloth. Its bristles were white with the pearl powder Frances used. Hastily Annis wrapped it in her handkerchief and hurried out of the bedroom.

In her own room, Annis found Velma drowsing in a chair. She checked the drawer in her bedside table to make sure the folded handkerchief was still there, with its precious remedy. She felt no need of it at the moment, but it reassured her to know she had it.

She roused Velma with a gentle shake of the shoulder just as Antoinette peeked in to say she hadn't found her. As Velma yawned and got up, Antoinette sniffed and backed out of the room, closing the door with unnecessary force. Velma ignored her, beginning to help Annis out of her evening dress and the stays beneath it. Velma yawned again as she hung up the clothes, then brushed out Annis's hair.

"Tangled," she complained.

"Sorry," Annis said. "I had to do it myself, and I was late."

"Out walking?"

"Yes. I walked farther from the hall than I realized."

It was what she had told everyone at dinner. She said she had wandered away from the gardens and out into the woods, lured by the wildflowers, and had lost track of time. She described a white flower with a yellow center, much bigger than the field roses she had noticed on her ride with James. Mrs. Derbyshire, with a forgiving smile, told her they called it a moonpenny in Dorset, but it was properly named an oxeye daisy. A lively discussion between Mrs. Hyde-Smith and Mrs. Derbyshire ensued about the correct names of local wildflowers. Amid the chatter Annis's infraction was forgotten.

Not by Frances, of course, who looked daggers at her whenever she wasn't playing at charm and vivacity.

And not by James, whose intense gaze followed her the entire evening.

With her hair braided and her gown exchanged for a nightdress, she said good night to Velma. She settled herself into bed with a novel she had found on the bedside table. It was a vapid, pointless tale of a peasant girl and a prince, and it didn't hold her interest. She closed it, turned down the lamp, and settled down to sleep.

Her door burst open with a bang just as she started to close her eyes.

Annis gasped and bolted upright, the coverlet clutched to her chest. James loomed in the doorway, tall and dark against the low light of the corridor. He still wore his evening clothes, but his jacket and waistcoat were unbuttoned, and his tie hung loose beneath his collar. He stood, one hand on each side of the doorjamb, and gazed at her, slack lipped and glassy eyed.

"James!" she cried. "Whatever—why, what's the matter with you?"

He lurched into the room, much as if he were drunk. Annis had little experience with intoxicated men—her father drank very little—but she had read descriptions. James had that look, his face suffused, his step unsteady. He advanced toward the bed, and she could hear his rough breathing, as if his throat were constricted.

"James," she said. "I think you must be ill."

"Not ill," he said, his deep voice rough.

"What is it, then? Have you been drinking? What can you be thinking, coming into my bedroom this way?"

"You came into mine," he said, with no humor at all in his face. "You came into my house, my stables, my bedroom, tempting me, bewitching me—"

At that she gasped again, a gasp of pure horror. This was Frances's doing. This was the *maleficia*. James was in the grip of her cantrip, in neither his right mind nor his normal nature.

He reached her bedside and fell sideways, his chest landing heavily on hers so she couldn't catch a decent breath. He scissored his legs, trying to press her down, to hold her in place. One of his hands, fever hot, gripped the back of her neck, while the other tugged at the neckline of her cotton nightdress, ripping it from her arm and her left breast. He clutched her upper arm before his hand slid to her naked breast and pressed it, kneading it greedily, as if its touch could satiate the hunger that drove him.

"James! No! Stop!" Annis hissed. She could scarcely believe any of this was happening, and the shock of it threatened her own sanity. She batted at his hand as she twisted her neck, trying to get free. She suffered a moment of real panic as she struggled to push his hand away from her breast.

It felt so strange, a man's hand on her flesh, flesh that was usually hidden from everyone but herself and her maid. It made her feel as if her breast—her body—were no longer her own, as if it had become some sort of object to be used without her volition.

She hated the feeling, and the shock of it, the wrongness, gave her strength.

She gritted her teeth to suppress the scream that built up in her throat. Her cry would bring the household, the maids, the valets, the butler—James would be ruined, and for something that wasn't his fault. This was all Frances. James was Frances's victim.

Still, if she didn't stop him, prevent the violation that was clearly intended, she would be a victim, too. She refused to be a victim, ever. She could not let this happen.

She gathered all her strength and broke free of his groping hand. She pushed herself backward, kicking at him with her bare feet. She wished she still had her shoes on. Her toes weren't hard enough to get his attention. She hissed, "James, stop it! You're not yourself!"

James was a tall man, and strong, but Annis was a strong girl. James was heavier, but he was in the grip of madness, and it weakened his muscles as well as his mind. Half the coverlet was caught between their bodies, but Annis could grasp the other half with her left hand. She pulled it up and threw it across his legs, twisting it beneath his feet. In the same movement, wriggling from beneath him, she scrambled from the sheets and stood on the far side of the bed, panting, as she tried to tug up the torn neckline of her nightdress.

James's attempts to kick the coverlet off made the tangle around his long legs worse. The more he fought it, the tighter it held. Annis, seeing this, became aware that the moonstone at her throat had begun to throb, as if it were part of her battle.

The bedroom door still stood open, as James had left it. Anyone could walk by and see His Lordship in Miss Allington's

bedroom—in her *bed*—and come to the most damning of con-
clusions. Annis didn't want that for herself, but just as much, she
didn't want it for James.

She ran to close the door, then put her back to it, facing him.
The room was in near darkness now. She had only the light of a
cloud-filtered moon to help her see that James had managed to get
the coverlet from his legs, though it caught on the tail of his coat
and wound around his dress shoes. He shoved the whole thing to
the floor, tearing off his coat in the process. Sitting up on the bed,
he began to shrug out of his waistcoat as Annis stared in horror.

The power of the *maleficia* had turned this gentle, courteous
man into an animal, a beast. She hated Frances for doing this to
him. He would hate himself when he realized.

He was tearing at the buttons on his shirt now, off the bed, on
his feet, coming toward her even as he yanked his arms out of the
sleeves.

Annis gripped the moonstone. She had no time. In seconds
he would take hold of her, and she didn't know if she could fight
him off a second time. Swiftly she whispered the words of Harriet's cantrip, the lines tumbling over one another so quickly she
didn't know if they would mean anything.

Mothers and grandmothers, guard my way
Every night and every day.
Let no danger me befall,
Nor evil catch me in its thrall.

James paused, one foot in front of the other, his ruined shirt
dangling from his hand. He gasped for breath as he peered at her
through the dimness. "What—" he began.

One more uncertain step brought him so close to her she could feel the unnatural heat radiating from his body. His long arm reached toward her, the trembling fingers outstretched.

The moonstone pulsed beneath her palm as if it had a heartbeat of its own, pounding in synchrony with her own panicked heart.

She repeated, louder now, faster,

Let no danger me befall,
Nor evil . . .

She didn't finish. James's momentum faltered. His arm dropped to his side, and his eyes rolled back in their sockets. He fell to his knees and then, with an awful groan, to one side.

Annis couldn't restrain a soft cry, fear for herself giving way to fear for him. She knelt beside him, taking one of his hands to chafe the wrist with her fingers. "James! James?"

He didn't respond. His eyelids were open, but his eyes were as vacant as if he were dead. She felt the pulse in his wrist and heard the whistle of his breathing. He was alive but senseless.

This tall, heavy man was unconscious on the floor of her bedroom, and there was no one she dared call for help without revealing her secret, and his.

She had never in her life felt so helpless. Clutching the moonstone in her closed fist, she bent her head and focused on calling for assistance. On summoning Harriet.

30

Harriet

The silhouette of Rosefield Hall loomed against the pale, cloudy sky. The sea whispered to Harriet's right, and to her left the stable block stretched toward the pasture. She could see the folly from her vantage point at the edge of the woods, but she felt the pull of Annis's summons. She needed to go inside the hall.

Undoubtedly the staff locked the doors at night. She detected no flicker of light in any window, not even on the third floor, where she guessed most of the servants slept. If anyone was watching, she would be visible as she crossed the lawn, but she did it anyway. Whatever awaited within those walls, there was urgency about it. She knew it by the trembling of the ametrine against her breast, and by the sense she had of being tugged, as if she were attached to a rope.

As she hurried across the lawn to the small door in the back of the house, the one she had seen Annis use, she glanced up at the blank, dark windows. Was there a face, there at one of the mullioned windows on the second floor? She slowed, just for a step, but it was gone before she could be certain.

She reached the door and tried the latch. As she had expected, it was locked. How many such doors were there? Could she count on any servant having been careless, forgetting one? It seemed unlikely.

She drew a slow breath to calm her heartbeat and focus her mind. She placed the flat of her left hand on the chilly wood of the door, bent her head, and closed her eyes. She placed her right hand on the amulet as she called upon her special gift. Upon the knowing. She couldn't hurry it. She had to let the knowledge seep into her mind at its own pace.

She waited. Off in the darkness the breakers rolled against the shore. In the shrubberies night birds twittered. Filtered moonlight gleamed on the gables above her head, and a horse stamped in the stables. Harriet observed all these things, but at a distance. She kept her mind as blank as she could, as open as she could, and—

There it was. A window to her right, left open to allow fresh air into a stuffy room.

She had never understood how the knowing worked. Did part of her mind break free from her physical self? Possibly. Or possibly it was that all minds, if they were open enough, sensitive enough, could perceive things not obvious to the eye.

She found the window without difficulty, open just far enough for her to put her fingers underneath the sash. She pushed it all the way up and wriggled through the window frame on her belly. She swiveled and set her feet down inside a dark room crowded with boxes and trunks and unused bits of furniture, the flotsam and jetsam thrown up by a house long occupied. She pulled the window down again, leaving it open as she had found it. She felt her way through the cluttered room and, when she reached a wall, ran her hands along it until she encountered a door frame.

This door was unlocked, its iron key hanging, unused, in the keyhole.

The corridor outside was a shade brighter than the storeroom. A window at one end allowed moonlight to fall on the floor and the lowest treads of a narrow staircase. Harriet moved to the stairs and started up, tiptoeing in her boots. On the second floor, she pushed through a baize door and into a much broader corridor, with closed doors set far apart. She saw the head of a grand staircase leading down to the foyer. A set of double doors stood open to an enormous room that might have been a ballroom.

She turned in the opposite direction, moving cautiously, her fingertips trailing over each door as she passed it. When she reached the right one, the ametrine gave a pulse that made her skin tingle. Cautiously, as silently as she could, she eased the door open.

Annis was kneeling beside the limp body of the marquess. She lifted her head at the soft scrape of the door, and even in the darkness Harriet saw how pale the girl's stricken face was.

Annis gave a low cry. "You're here! Oh, Aunt Harriet, you're here!" and burst into tears.

"Is he going to die?"

Annis's tears didn't last long. She gulped them back, apologized, and was ready to address the crisis.

Between them they managed to hoist James's lanky body from the floor to the bed. Annis patted his hands while Harriet tried to get him to swallow a bit of water. He couldn't do it. The water dribbled down his cheek and onto the pillow, and she gave up the exercise for fear of drowning him. None of their actions roused him in the slightest.

"I don't know if he's going to die," Harriet said, "because I don't know what's wrong with him."

"It's the *maleficia*."

"I assumed that. What happened?"

"I was in bed, and he came in looking like—like I don't know what. He tried to—that is, he acted as if he were drunk, but he wasn't, and then he—he attacked me." Annis sniffled back fresh tears, and her face reddened. "He ripped my nightdress, and he tried—he was going to—" Her voice broke.

"Yes, I understand his intent," Harriet said briskly. "He didn't succeed, I gather?"

"No," Annis said, her voice steadier now. "I got away from him, and then—I used the cantrip, the one you taught me, and I was holding the moonstone, and this happened!" She gestured to the senseless form of the Marquess of Rosefield. "Now I'm afraid I killed him!"

"He's not dead yet," Harriet said, trying to speak with confidence. In truth, the young man looked ghastly. Even in the dim light, his color was gray, his breathing shallow. His body felt cold under her hand, as if the spirit had already gone from it. "Come now, don't spend your energy blaming yourself. We have work ahead of us."

"What can we do?"

"Did you find something of Frances's, something we can use?"

"I did. I hope it works." She turned to her dressing table for her handkerchief and opened it to show Harriet. "It's the brush she uses for the pearl powder she puts on her face. It still has powder on it."

Harriet leaned forward to look at it. It was a pretty thing, as much ornament as tool. The brush handle was sterling silver, and the bristles were dark. Mink perhaps, or goat hair, something soft, and nicely saturated with the white powder. "Perfect," she murmured.

"But we can't leave James here," Annis said. "Everyone will think he—that he tried to violate me!"

"He did, didn't he?" Harriet said, without thinking.

"But it's the *maleficia*! He would never do such a thing! Poor James. It's not fair to him."

Harriet straightened. "Of course you're right, Annis. This isn't fair to either of you." She turned back to the senseless young man on the bed. His lips were parted, his eyes not quite closed. She didn't want to alarm Annis more than necessary, but the sense of urgency returned to her in a rush. "Do you know which is his bedroom?"

"I do. It's just past the great chamber. That big room with the double doors."

"Good. Not too far, then."

"Do you think we can move him?"

"I think we must. We're strong, you and I, and he's a thin man. We have to hurry, though, before the servants are up and about."

Annis went to open the door before positioning herself at James's head. "You take his knees," she said, in a voice as steady as if she were suggesting they move a table. "I'll lift his head and shoulders."

It was a practical suggestion, made by a practical girl, and Harriet was glad of it. She was also glad of Annis's youth and strength in this moment of crisis. She did her best to carry her share of James's weight, but her knees and shoulders felt every one of her fifty years as they struggled through the first door, then maneuvered down the hallway, past the great chamber and the head of the staircase, and on to a door that had been left open.

"This is it," Annis whispered. She backed into the bedroom, and with relief they deposited James onto his bed, tugging at his arms and legs until he was securely in the center.

Not that he seemed likely to roll over and fall. James didn't so much as flicker an eyelid, which worried Harriet. There truly was no time to lose. The longer this death-like state lasted, the more danger he was in.

She saw Annis's anguished glance at the unconscious man as they closed his door. They hurried back to Annis's room, where Harriet collected her basket and Annis the handkerchief-wrapped powder brush. Annis pulled a coat over her nightdress and thrust her bare feet into her walking boots. They closed her door, and the two of them hastened to the servants' staircase. Dawn was not far off. They paused at the top of the stair, listening for any movement, but there was only silence.

Harriet descended cautiously, fatigue making her feel unsteady. Annis flew ahead, her steps light and sure, and waited at the bottom with her hand on the outer door. They didn't speak. The breeze from the sea cooled their heated faces as they crossed the lawn, damp now with dew. The moon had set and the eastern sky was brightening as they ducked past the thick branches of the rhododendron and stepped up into the folly.

As she took what she needed out of her basket, Harriet said, "I wish we didn't have to do this. I hoped Frances would relent."

"I know, Aunt Harriet. But James—"

"Of course. We have to help him. This is the only way I know to do it."

She laid out a candle she had taken from the inn, along with the packet of mandrake root and mistletoe and barrenwort, all things she had brought with her from New York and had hoped she would not need. She had pared her fingernails the night before and added the slender bits to the packet. She lifted the amulet on its chain from around her neck and set it beside the candle, along with three sulfur matches.

Finally she brought out the simulacrum that would represent Frances. Her own cousin. Frances, who had made all of this happen through her selfishness and ambition.

"Do you have the brush?" she asked in a low voice.

Annis unfolded her handkerchief and held it out on her open hands. Harriet struck one of the matches and set it to the candle wick, then laid the manikin within the circle of candlelight. Taking the silver-handled brush from Annis, she dusted the ugly little thing's head. The grains of pearl powder glistened with iridescence. Harriet tapped the end of the brush until she had extracted every bit of the powder. She hoped it held enough of Frances's essence to be effective.

She handed the brush back to Annis before she brought a saucer out of her basket and filled it with the ground herbs. Last she took out a long sewing needle. It flashed silver as she lifted it in her right hand and plunged it into her left thumb. It was the part of the ritual she hated the most, not because it hurt—it did—but because it was the wrong way to spend the power of her witch's blood. Because it broke the vow she had made after Alexander's death. Because it dragged her down to Christian Oliver's level. It was the dishonorable part of the Bishop legacy, and she loathed employing it.

Needs must, she reminded herself. This was not the time for doubt.

She held her left hand over the saucer and let the drops of her blood, black as coal in the weak light, drip over the herbs. She

watched, swirling the saucer, until the mixture begin to steam,
tiny tendrils of moisture that flickered and evaporated in the predawn air. "Now hand me the brush again."

She dipped the brush into the sticky stuff in the saucer and
painted the manikin with it. She daubed the poorly shaped head
and then the chest. She spread what was left on the hands and
feet. When she was done, she took a step back, gazing down at
the ungainly little creation.

"It's hideous," she muttered.

"Does that matter?"

"It does not. It's just not the way I want my practice to be."

31

Annis

Annis agreed with Harriet that the manikin was ugly, a distortion of a human being. It looked nothing like Frances, and yet it seemed to reflect what her inner self had become, twisted and stretched and corrupted, a woman she didn't recognize. Was that because of the *maleficia*?

As the light beyond the folly rose, the sounds of the sea grew more intense, and the breeze died away. Harriet, striking in her dark skirt and heavy jacket, stood with her head bent, gazing at the manikin in her hand. Candlelight picked out threads of silver in her hair, and shadows hollowed her cheeks and darkened her eyes.

She looked magnificent, every inch a witch, an embodiment of wisdom and courage and authority. Her voice echoed from the stone floor to the domed top of the folly, each word clear and commanding.

By my witch's blood I say
You will yield to me this day.
Release the victim of your spell.
This I swear I will compel.

Her cantrip's results were so quick and so dramatic that Annis cried out. The ametrine awoke, glittering and glowing, and the manikin jerked to life. Its head pulled back, and its misshapen hands flailed so violently Annis feared it would rip itself from Harriet's hand.

She shivered, not with cold but with awe. She whispered, "What's happening?"

Harriet said in a low, tight voice, "Frances knows. This is Frances fighting me."

"Will she release him?"

In Harriet's grip the manikin writhed, a grotesque imitation of a struggling human being. Harriet said, "I fear not." She held the manikin with both hands now, and Annis saw her knuckles whiten as she fought it. "She has lost control of herself. There was always darkness in her, but using the *maleficia* has made it worse."

"What can we do?" Annis breathed.

"It's going to take both of us." She wrapped the fingers of her right hand around the manikin's throat, and the left around its rudimentary legs. "We need your blood, Annis. The blood of two witches—and a lock of your hair, a tiny one, to add to the slurry. Can you do that?"

"Of course. Do you have more of the herbs you need?"

"There's another packet in my basket. The needle is there, too. You'll have to do it by yourself. I can't let go of this damned thing. If it breaks free, she does, too."

"Oh!"

"I'm sorry about this. It makes you part of the *maleficia*."

"But I already am. If it were not for me, James would not have suffered so."

"We'll talk about that later. We must hurry—mustn't give Frances a chance to work her own rite."

Annis stepped around Harriet, who swayed with the effort of controlling the manikin. She delved into the basket for the packet of herbs and the silver sewing needle. The saucer had cooled but was stained with the remnants of Harriet's slurry. Annis crumbled the herbs into it. She gritted her teeth and pricked her thumb as deeply as she dared with the needle.

Her blood flowed more swiftly than Harriet's. Perhaps she had gone deeper with the needle, or perhaps it was her youth, but the blood, ruby red in the growing light, flowed in a steady trickle into the saucer. She watched, fascinated by the way it shone, by the way the herbs soaked it up, as if they thirsted for a witch's blood.

"Hair," Harriet said, between gritted teeth. Her hands jerked and shook with the antics of the manikin. "There are scissors."

"Yes! Just a moment." Annis's thumb continued to bleed, staining her coat as she dug out a pair of tiny ivory-handled scissors. She pulled a strand of hair from its braid, more blood dripping over her wrist. She snipped the end and clipped the lock into the smallest pieces she could, letting them fall into the saucer.

"Now heat it," Harriet said.

Annis did just as Harriet had done. She held the saucer over the candle flame, tipping it this way and that, until it began to bubble and thicken. "Now?" she said, glancing up at Harriet.

Harriet's eyes had narrowed, and she held the manikin with a brutal grip. "Yes," she answered, in a grating voice. "The brush. I'll hold the thing, you paint the slurry onto its head and feet. I can't let go."

Annis dipped the brush into the gluey mixture and spread it across the head of the manikin. It made her skin crawl to see it cover the face of the thing, even though it wasn't much of a face. The dark mixture blinded the pebble eyes, smothered the wood-chip mouth. She smeared the last of the slurry onto its feet.

"There's no more, Aunt Harriet," she whispered.

"Very well." Harriet held up the manikin and drew breath.

Annis said, "Wait! Wait just a moment." Hurriedly she unclasped her pearl choker, with the moonstone in its center, and set it beside Harriet's amulet. "There."

"Excellent," Harriet said. She drew a long, noisy breath and expelled it. "Come stand beside me." Annis did, and Harriet held up the manikin again. This time she chanted in a louder voice, one Annis feared might carry up the lawn to any open window:

We command you in this hour
Bow before our greater power.
Witches two to witch just one
Order your spell to be undone.

Annis gasped at the sensations that gripped her. These were different from the ones Frances had caused. Her body began to ache, belly and bones and skin. Her eyes burned, and her blood seemed to run hotter. It was painful, but it was also exhilarating, a rush of power and energy that excited her mind and made her wish it would never end.

She had to force herself to focus on joining her intention to Harriet's. Their rite must succeed. It had to succeed, for James's sake. She watched the ametrine and her own moonstone and chanted with Harriet when she repeated the cantrip. Her soul

thrilled to the currents of magic flowing through the folly and
out, all the way up the lawn to Frances.

We command you in this hour
Bow before our greater power.
Witches two to witch just one
Order your spell to be undone.

She thought perhaps, when the ametrine began to glow and
the moonstone to shimmer, that they were finished.

"Not yet," Harriet said. And when they had repeated it, she
said, "Again. Until the manikin is still."

32

Frances

Frances woke feeling as if someone had placed a pillow over her face. She struggled to sit up in bed, and she clawed at an obstacle that wasn't there. Gasping, sucking in desperate breaths, she threw off her coverlet and put her bare feet on the floor. She tried to stand, but her feet had gone numb. They wouldn't hold her. She crumpled to the rug beside the bed, dragging the coverlet with her.

She had left her window open for the fresh sea air, and she saw that it was nearly dawn. She tried to crawl to the window but collapsed before she reached it, her legs at an awkward angle. She struggled to push herself up on her hands, choking, unable to force a single good breath into her lungs. What was happening to her?

On hands and knees she dragged herself to her dressing table. She pulled herself up onto the stool, where she slumped, nearly nerveless, her body refusing to obey her will. She peered into the mirror with half-blind eyes. What should she do? Was she ill? Should she ring for someone to wake Antoinette, and—

She caught sight of the two manikins still propped against the mirror, next to the cushion bristling with hat pins. Suddenly she knew exactly what was wrong with her.

It was Harriet. Harriet, who swore she would never use the *maleficia*, who pretended to be too pure, too high-minded, to ever create a manikin and work a spell with it. Harriet was attacking her, and Annis was helping. Frances didn't need to go down the corridor to Annis's room to check. She sensed the two working together, aligned against her.

Of course she knew what they wanted, but she wouldn't give it to them. Why should she?

Her temper began to rise, that suppressed fountain of rage that never truly died down. It simmered in her blood and burned in her brain.

Why shouldn't she, Frances Allington, have what she wanted for once? They had everything their way. Harriet had been born to comfort. Annis was indulged and spoiled and had never wanted for anything.

The unfairness of it fanned the flames of her anger. It grew hotter, deeper, stronger than ever before, and before its ancient fire her self-control fell into cinders. She would have her way no matter what it cost.

This was no longer about a marriage, or a title, or the Four Hundred. This was about taking her rightful place in the line of Bishop witches. This was about showing high-and-mighty Harriet what she, Frances, was capable of.

It was time for a final victory, and she could allow no one to stand in her way, not Harriet, not that spoiled brat of a girl, not even Beryl from beyond the grave.

She fumbled for matches to light her candle. She had left her case at the foot of the dressing table, and she opened it with fingers gone clumsy, as if the nerves and muscles no longer functioned.

She hadn't anticipated Harriet's attack. She needed a remedy, the same one Annis had taken, but she didn't have the right ingredients. At this moment she couldn't quite remember what they were. Mistletoe, she thought, which was also in the *maleficia* mixture. She had a bit of that left, and she could take it as a nervine, to ease blockages. There was a bit of mandrake root still in the bottom of the case, which could be a stimulant. Either herb could also kill her, but at this moment of sublime fury, she didn't care.

She had no starwort or wormwood. She couldn't remember what else was in the remedy against the *maleficia*.

There had to be another way.

Suppose Annis had more than one of the remedies? It might be in her bedroom, even now. If Frances could manage to get there.

She had to do it. The light was rising, and the staff would soon be abroad in the corridors. Swiftly she broke off a fragment of dried mistletoe and swallowed it. Her breathing still felt sluggish, as if her lungs were full of mud, but sensation began to return to her feet and ankles. Awkwardly she stumbled out of her bedroom and limped down the corridor to Annis's.

She could see easily now as dawn broke over Seabeck. As she had suspected, Annis was not in her room. Frances cast about for where to look for the remedy she hoped was there. It *had* to be, or all this was for nothing. She began the search, starting with Annis's jewel case—the pearl choker wasn't in it—then moving on to the drawers in the dressing table. Finding nothing, she straightened and cast an urgent glance around the room.

The bedclothes were pulled back, even tumbled onto the floor, which was strange. There was no time to think why that should be. A shallow drawer in the bedside table was open, just a little. Her breaths coming hard now, Frances staggered across to the table to pull open the drawer. It was empty, except for a single white handkerchief, folded into quarters. Frustrated, she started to push the drawer closed, but while her hand still rested on the knob, a faint smell rose from inside it. It was the scent of pine and the flowery smell of honey. She stopped and stared at the folded handkerchief.

With care she lifted it out and gently unfolded it, layer by layer. There were initials embroidered on the edge of the handkerchief. H. B. Harriet Bishop.

It was there. What she needed, the electuary created for Annis to fight Frances's *maleficia*. And now it would help her, Frances, to fight the *maleficia* being visited on her by Harriet.

The rightness of it, the justice, made her give a low, bitter laugh. She plucked the little ball from the handkerchief and popped it into her mouth.

It tasted just like it smelled, sweet, piney, and tart all at the same time. She swallowed it whole, dropped the handkerchief into the drawer, and turned to make her clumsy way back to her own bedroom.

With every step her feet and ankles felt a little better. Her breaths began to come easier, too, and she spared one generous thought for her cousin: Harriet was very, very good, as an herbalist and as a witch. None of her own philters or potions had ever worked as swiftly as Harriet's electuary, and the admission did nothing to cool her anger.

She slipped inside her bedroom and locked the door from the inside.

As she settled at her dressing table, she felt as if there were two of her. One was imprisoned in Harriet's manikin, tortured, smothered, bound. The other was preparing to do battle. To protect herself. To win.

She would be ruthless. She would have to be. The *maleficia* dictated it. Its power was greater than any she knew, and she would wield it however she had to. There would be pain, but it wouldn't last. Every battle caused pain and suffering, but victory demanded it.

She set a match to her half-burned candle and took up the manikin of the marquess. It hung limply in her hand, all the fire that had energized it the night before expended. She set it back against the mirror.

Hastily she blended the last of the mistletoe and barrenwort and mandrake in her saucer. Her forefinger was still sore from the piercing of the night before, so she stabbed her thumb instead. She squeezed the drops of blood over the ground herbs, and finally, inspired, she plucked three of her eyelashes to add to the mixture.

She held the saucer over the candle flame, too close, because she was hurrying. It grew so hot she almost dropped it, but she gritted her teeth against the burning in her fingers and waited for it to bubble.

When it was ready, she picked up the manikin of Annis.

For the briefest of moments, she admired it anew. It was uncanny, really, how much it resembled her stepdaughter. Perhaps, she thought, her initial success had transformed it, made its little beetroot-dyed mouth more natural, its painted eyes look so real they might blink. Even the wooden-bead head seemed almost alive, its roundness softened by the fluff of Annis's hair. It was perfect, and it radiated magic. Her magic.

She dipped her finger into the saucer and rubbed the syrupy mixture on the simulacrum's chest, on its belly, between its legs, and then, turning it over, on its back. She chanted as she did so, her voice throbbing with fury:

Witch's blood and lashes three
Bring obedience to me.
What is done in candlelight
You will suffer full this night.

She laid the manikin down and took up the cushion with its array of hat pins. She chose an amber-beaded one for its length and slenderness and for the sharpness of its tip, meant to penetrate the thickest straw, the most elaborate hairstyle. She chanted her cantrip again, and when she reached the final line—

You will suffer full this night

—she plunged the hat pin into the very center of Annis's manikin.

33

Harriet

The last of the stars had retreated before the steady march of morning light, and Harriet was so tired she could barely stand. She wished she had forced herself to eat something the night before. They had repeated their cantrip half a dozen times before, at last, the manikin representing Frances went limp in Harriet's hand.

"It's done!" Annis said.

"It looks that way," Harriet answered. She set the thing beside the candle, but she watched it warily. Something about it troubled her, some sense of work unfinished, though she couldn't say why.

She was about to blow out her candle when Annis emitted an anguished cry. Harriet whirled and reached for the girl just as she doubled over. She had both arms wrapped around her middle, and she was groaning and gasping for breath. If Harriet had not been there to support her, she would have fallen.

"What is it?" Harriet asked, and at the same time, she knew. Her ametrine was on fire, and the knowing gripped her with sickening surety.

It was Frances. She had surrendered completely to the darkness. She was lost in the miasma of her own witchery.

And she was torturing Annis.

Annis moaned again, and Harriet led her to the bench, where she huddled in obvious misery. "I must be sick," she grunted. "My stomach..."

"You're being magicked," Harriet said in a hard voice. "Breathe, Annis. Do your best to release the pain."

As Annis drew a ragged breath, Harriet strode back to the manikin. She seized it up in her left hand, gripping it hard. There was no time to make a new slurry, nor to paint the thing. There was no time to create a cantrip. There was only her strength to counter Frances's, and it was a deadly duel they were fighting.

She took her amulet with her right hand and awkwardly looped the chain over her head so the ametrine settled against her breast. She took the moonstone and pressed it into Annis's hand. The girl's forehead was beaded with sweat, and she writhed on the bench, trying to find a position that didn't hurt.

Harriet said, "Keep the moonstone in your hand. Call on your grandmother Lily to help you. I'll work as fast as I can."

The candle was burning down, the wick almost drowning in a pool of melted wax. Harriet held the manikin in both hands over the sputtering flame, lowering it until she could feel the heat of the candle on her skin. She hissed,

Sister witch, it is your turn.
Release her now or you will burn.

Nothing happened. Annis groaned in agony.

Harriet lowered the manikin still farther, letting it dangle from the head, dropping it closer and closer to the flame until the waxen feet began to drip. As the wick hissed and flared, Annis breathed a sigh of relief.

Harriet lifted the manikin again, but it was damaged now, what remained of the bottom of it misshapen and lumpy. "Is your pain gone?" she said in a low voice.

"Almost," Annis said. "I thought—it was as if a sword had pierced me right through!"

"Yes. She did something horrible to your manikin."

Annis straightened, her eyes wide with horror. "What if she does it now to James's? He's unconscious! We have to—"

"Yes. We do." Harriet thought fast. "Tell me, Annis—can she see the folly from her bedroom? It's light now. Can she see me?"

"I think so."

"Good. Stay there. Hold the moonstone close."

The knowing washed over her again, a terrifying image of blackness overcoming them all, of evil building to a horrible end. Harriet sensed the other witch's fury as if it were a hot tide pouring out of Rosefield Hall and down over the lawn, and her own anger, cooler, more controlled, rose to meet it.

Frances would be in pain now, her feet and legs on fire. She would be beside herself with rage, all integrity devoured by the intoxicating power of the *maleficia*. She would use James. She would abuse his manikin as she had Annis's. She was beyond conscious thought.

Harriet couldn't fail. She didn't dare. Frances's judgment was gone. If Frances won this battle, both young people could be lost.

Carrying the manikin, Harriet dashed out of the folly and onto the lawn. Annis, ignoring her command, followed to the steps of the folly, still hunched over her middle. "Which window is it?" Harriet asked.

Annis pointed. "It's that tall one, the third from the front. It's open, can you see?"

"Oh yes," Harriet gritted. "I can see. And she can, too."

Frances's strength shocked her. She had never known her cousin had such ability. She glared at the open window Annis had pointed out, willing her cousin to appear. Ordering her, with all of her power, to appear.

Frances responded at once. She pulled back the drapes and stood in the open window, fully revealed in the morning light. She wore a flowing nightdress and a peignoir over it. Her hair tumbled around her shoulders. She looked taller than usual, her back very straight, her head thrown high.

Harriet held up the manikin for Frances to see.

In response, Frances held up two of them.

"Don't do it," Harriet whispered. "Please, Frances, don't do this."

Annis had stumbled onto the grass, and she clung to one of the pillars of the folly as she peered up at Frances in the window. "What is she doing?" she asked. "Are those the manikins?"

"They are," Harriet said. "I don't know what she's going to do, but this isn't about you anymore, or about James. This is between us."

"But she doesn't have a manikin of you!"

"No. She will use yours, and James's, as weapons against me. She is in the grip of the *maleficia*, without conscience or control. Courage, Annis. This might be—" She broke off as Frances, with a deliberate motion, turned one of the manikins upside down and shook it.

Annis, with a long moan, collapsed to the grass, senseless.

Harriet couldn't help her. She focused on Frances, not with her eyes but with her mind. The ametrine grew hot against her breast as she brought all of her power to bear in this moment, and proclaimed,

Sister witch, let her be,
Or you will have to deal with me.

Annis didn't make a sound. Harriet didn't look back at her, couldn't allow her concentration to waver.

She tried one more time, although in her heart she knew it was pointless.

What we were taught was always true.
This evil will redound on you.

She opened her eyes then, cast one swift glance back at Annis, and saw that she still lay on the dew-damp grass, her head at a terrible angle, her hands thrown out. Her slender bosom rose and fell, but shallowly. And how long would that continue?

Harriet squinted up at the hall again. Frances, fixing her with a gaze she could feel even at this distance, held both manikins far out her open window. One, which she was sure must be James's, was limp, unmoving. The other was still upside down, its make-shift dress falling around its wooden bead head, its poor legs helpless in Frances's grip. If Frances dropped the manikins from the second floor, they would be smashed. Even if she regained consciousness, Annis would never walk again. And James? He was already weakened, unresponsive, with no way to fight this attack. He might never wake.

Frances called, in a carrying voice,

I will do it, this I swear.
The guilt will then be yours to bear.

Harriet had done her best. She had tried to avoid the worst thing. The fatal thing. Frances would not expect it. She would be sure Harriet could never bring herself to do it.

The entire crisis was proof of everything Harriet had ever believed about the *maleficia*. All of them—Frances, Annis, James, Harriet herself—were caught in its dangerous web.

There was only one thing left to do, though it offended all her principles, and despite her awareness that it would haunt her always.

She feigned surrender. She lowered the manikin and hung her head as if in defeat.

Peering up from beneath her eyebrows, she saw Frances pull her two manikins back, away from the drop that would destroy them. When they were safely inside the window again, Harriet muttered a swift, impassioned plea: *May all the Bishops aid me to save one of our daughters.*

She closed her eyes and opened herself to the ancient magic. It throbbed in her bones and burned in her bloodstream. A savage and familiar pain shot through her belly, and her head pounded. Her mind felt as if it would break free of her skull, rise above the physical essence that was Harriet Bishop. She could command the power of her ancestresses, their wisdom and learning, their suffering and endurance. She felt as if gravity disappeared beneath her, and the sky opened above her, a universe of energy.

She kept her eyes closed as she lifted Frances's manikin in her left hand. Swiftly, the way a farmer might wring the neck of a chicken, she twisted the head of it with her right hand. It was mercifully quick and utterly awful. She wrenched the head from the body of the manikin.

With the head in one hand and the body in the other, she opened her eyes. She looked up just in time to see Frances's head lift high, proud in the moment of her triumph. An instant later she dropped out of sight.

Still prone on the grass, Annis suddenly, noisily inhaled. She groaned, "Is it over?"

Watching Frances's window, Harriet responded with bitter conviction. "I believe so."

"I looked up, and I saw—" Annis took another noisy breath and coughed. "I saw—"

"What?"

The girl's voice shook with wonder. "Aunt Harriet, you—you were *flying*."

"I—what?" Harriet tore her gaze from the window and stared down at Annis. "What do you mean?"

"I mean—" Annis dropped her hands and pushed herself up to her knees, then, unsteadily, to her feet. She clung to the nearest pillar, the rhododendron leaves drooping over her shoulder. She said, breathlessly, "I looked up from the grass where I was—why was I there?"

"You fainted." Harriet thought it would be best to explain the details later. "But, Annis, what were you going to say?"

Annis pressed her back against the pillar, as if she hadn't the strength to stand upright. In a trembling voice she said, "You rose from the ground, Aunt Harriet. You—it wasn't flying, exactly, but—your feet didn't touch the grass."

"You must have been dreaming."

Annis shook her head. "I wasn't. I saw you rise above the grass, and then you—" She grimaced. "You ripped the manikin in two. I saw you do it."

"I did." Harriet looked down at the two halves of Frances's manikin. With distaste she crumpled them together. She walked back up the folly's short steps and laid the mess of wax and pebbles in her basket.

The sun had risen, and its slanting rays set the waters below Seabeck gleaming like pewter. It woke the gulls, who swooped above the shore, announcing the new day with joyous squawks. The damp grass steamed in the morning light, and Harriet saw, looking up beyond the lawn, the first ribbons of smoke curling from the chimneys of Rosefield Hall.

"They'll all be awake, Annis," she said. "Do you feel strong enough to get back to your bedroom? There will be staff about."

Annis was supporting herself on one of the pillars of the folly, but she nodded. "I feel fine," she said, which Harriet was certain was not true. "I'll say—if I see anyone, I'll tell them I went out for an early-morning walk."

"There will be a shock this morning."

Annis straightened with obvious effort. "What is it? Frances?"

"Yes. I think—perhaps you could say she and the marquess contracted the same illness."

"Will she recover? Will James?"

"I'm sorry, but I don't know. I had to do something, because you—she threatened to drop both of those manikins from her window. I was convinced she would do it."

"She would have *killed* me?"

"Or crippled you. Crippled you both."

"But she wanted us to marry!"

"She was as much in the grip of the *maleficia* as you and James. She was no longer rational." Harriet picked up her basket. "I wish I didn't have to leave you, but I can't risk being discovered here, an uninvited guest. Will you be all right?"

Annis drew herself up and straightened her shoulders. "Of course, Aunt Harriet. What will you do?"

"I'll go back to the inn and sleep. I'm exhausted."

"Will I see you?"

"If you need me."

"We were supposed to leave today."

"That may not be possible now."

"I want to go home," Annis said. "But I'm worried about James."

"I'm afraid there's going to be an uproar. Whatever condition Frances is in . . ."

Annis's eyes went wide. "Could she be—could she be *dead*?"

Harriet exhaled a long, tired breath. "I don't know," she said wearily. "But I have to leave you to deal with it, I'm afraid. Whatever it might be."

"I can do it."

Harriet gave her a last, tired smile. "I know. I'm proud of you." She buttoned her jacket and picked up her basket. "You must find those manikins and keep them hidden."

"I will."

"Let us promise to see each other again in New York."

"I promise."

Harriet, with her basket over her arm, went back down the steps to Annis. She pressed her cheek to hers, and the feel of the girl's sweet, smooth skin was like a balm on the fresh wound in her soul. "Take care, dear heart. Be safe."

Annis nodded, whirled, and dashed up the lawn as if none of the stresses of the past hour had affected her in the least.

Harriet smiled after her, but wearily. She was tired enough for both of them. She pulled her hat over her forehead against the brilliance of the rising sun and set out on the long walk back to the Four Fishes.

34

Annis

Annis opened the door of the servants' entrance and was greeted by a cacophony of cries and calls and running feet. A maid was dashing down the staircase at breakneck speed. She barely paused even to curtsy to Annis, much less ask her where she'd been. Annis hurried up the staircase, and when she pushed through the baize door leading to the upper hallway, the noise intensified.

James's valet was just backing out of James's bedroom, a pile of linen in his hands. He barely glanced at her as he trotted toward the back staircase, though she was dressed so oddly, a coat over her nightdress, her unstockinged feet in boots gone dark with dew.

Lady Eleanor, wearing a dressing gown, appeared in the door-way of James's room, bellowing for the housekeeper, something about beef tea. Another maid, one of the young ones, ran past Annis on her way to the stairs, a steady stream of Lady Eleanor's orders on her heels.

Lady Eleanor caught sight of Annis, who was hesitating at the turning of the hall. She beckoned, and Annis ran to her.

"There must be influenza in the house," Lady Eleanor said. She was, Annis guessed, too distracted to notice her odd attire. "Do you feel ill, Miss Allington? No one else does, but my son fell sick in the night, and now your stepmother—"

At Annis's indrawn breath, she put a hand on her arm. "Oh, my dear, I'm so sorry. I shouldn't have told you like that. Forgive me, but…Rosefield can barely open his eyes, he's so weak, and Mrs. Allington…" She pressed her plump hand to her lips. "Oh my. I do hope none of the older guests become ill. Some of them are already frail."

"And Frances?" Annis choked, though her heart had begun to beat so hard she thought Lady Eleanor must hear it.

"I don't—oh dear, Miss Allington, I'm so sorry. We've sent for the doctor, of course. He'll be here in an hour or two, I should think."

"Thank you, my lady," Annis breathed. She stepped back, gently releasing her arm from the older woman's grasp. "I had better—I suppose I had better go to her."

"No, my dear, please don't! Send your maid, or have her maid come to describe her condition to you. It would be terrible if you fell ill, too." She pulled at the neckline of her dressing gown and straightened her shoulders. "I'm going back in to my son, if you will excuse me. I must be at his side."

"Of course," Annis said. "Of course you must. Do send someone for me if there's anything I can do."

She hurried to the other wing of the corridor and let herself into her own room, where she found Velma, white-faced and nearly inarticulate with fear. The maid jumped to her feet, twisting her hands in the folds of her apron. "Oh, Miss Annis! You're in your nightdress! Oh, oh, I thought you were—You must be—"

"Velma, you goose! I'm fine. It's all going to be fine."

"No, no, Miss Annis," Velma gabbled. "No, no, it's—Mrs. Frances is—She looks—I think she's dead!" She collapsed back into the chair and buried her face in her hands. "Mr. Allington's gonna be mad! I'll lose my—There won't be any—" Her thought was extinguished in a torrent of sobs.

Annis hurried to her and seized her hands, pulling them away from her tear-streaked face. "Velma! Come now, pull yourself together. What's wrong with Frances?"

"Sh-sh-she isn't b-b-breathing!" Velma gulped. "Sh-sh-she w-w-was on the f-f-floor, and that F-F-Frenchie f-f-found her—"

"Antoinette? Is she with her?" Velma only wept harder and louder. Annis despaired of getting an answer.

She caught sight of herself in the dressing-table mirror, hair tumbled, nightdress wet to the knees, coat buttoned wrong. Hastily she stripped off the coat and nightdress, and she wriggled as quickly as she could into a skirt and shirtwaist. "Velma, please," she said. "You have to stop crying. Help me with my hair so I can go and assist Antoinette."

Velma wiped her streaming nose with the back of her hand as she came to stand behind Annis. "Oh, for pity's sake!" Annis exclaimed. She took a handkerchief from the drawer in the dressing table and passed it over her shoulder. While Velma snuffled into it, Annis undid her braid and began to pin up her hair by herself.

This offense apparently brought Velma to her senses. She blew her nose, stuffed the handkerchief into the pocket of her apron, and pushed Annis's hands away. "I'll do it," she said. "No more tangles."

Dressed properly, if not stylishly, Annis said, "Thank you,

Velma. You can stay here. I'll come for you if I need you." She let herself out of her room and went next door to Frances's.

She didn't have to knock. The door stood partly ajar, and when she pushed it all the way open, she saw Frances on the bed, on top of the coverlet, her head on the pillow. Antoinette had a sponge in her hand, and a basin was set on the bedside table. She was mopping Frances's face, more roughly than Annis would have thought necessary.

Annis moved to the opposite side of the bed and stood, heavy-hearted, gazing down on her stepmother's still, white face. Drops of vinegar water from Antoinette's ministrations dripped down her forehead and into her hair. Frances's mouth was open, and her lips were as pale as her cheeks. When Annis touched her hand, it was ice-cold.

Frances was not, however, dead. Her bosom rose and fell, shallowly but steadily.

Annis said, "Antoinette. Stop that for a moment. We should cover her."

The maid dropped her sponge into her basin and helped Annis work the coverlet and sheet from beneath Frances's unmoving form, then spread it over her, up to her shoulders. "She was collapsed," Antoinette said. "I found her in a pile by the window, and I thought—*peut-être*—*elle était morte*."

That much French Annis understood. "No," she said quietly. "She is not. But she is terribly ill."

"*Oui.*" Antoinette looked up. "Perhaps she is going to die."

"I don't know, Antoinette. A doctor is coming."

"If she die, you give me money. I go back to Paris."

Annis glared at her. "*Très bien.* Now run down to the kitchen and ask the cook for some tea. We'll try to get her to sip it."

The moment the maid was out the door, Annis was on her knees, searching. She looked under the bed and beneath the dressing table, even lifted up the edge of the rug, with no luck. She had to find them. She couldn't leave them here, in case Frances woke, in case she tried again.

She moved to the bed and put her hand on Frances's shoulder.

There was no reaction, no movement or recognition of the touch, but Annis sensed, in some hidden part of Frances's mind, an awareness. A consciousness.

This was, Annis supposed, the empathy Harriet had spoken of, and it was terrible. Frances was still there. She could feel her. She was there, but she was trapped, a captive in her broken body, imprisoned like a fly in a bottle. Annis's throat closed with horror.

Despite that, she needed to find the manikins. She bent forward, bracing herself against the cruelty of pressing her stepmother in her moment of profound weakness. "Where are they, Frances?" she whispered. "What did you do with them?"

There was no response.

Time was speeding by. Antoinette would return, and her chance would be gone.

Annis put her hand on Frances's slender shoulder and closed her eyes. With the other hand she touched her moonstone, making a bridge between it and Frances, who knew where the manikins were, though she couldn't speak of it.

The image came to Annis a moment later. She didn't know if Frances had given it to her, or if it was the moonstone that had made it possible, or if it might be simply her newly discovered ability. Whichever it was, she saw the manikins in her mind. She knew where they were.

They were behind a cushion on the window seat. When Harriet

defeated Frances's *maleficia* with such a surge of power it lifted her right from the earth, when Frances collapsed as if she had been struck, she must have dropped them. They had tumbled behind the square of scarlet silk brocade and were caught in its gold tassels.

Annis opened her eyes, jumped to her feet, and crossed to the window in two swift steps. The manikins were exactly as she had pictured them. She untangled them from the tassels and thrust them into the pocket of her coat.

When Antoinette returned bearing a cup of tea. Annis took it from her and spooned a little into Frances's mouth. Frances swallowed some, although most of it dribbled from her lips. Antoinette dabbed at Frances's chin, murmuring French words Annis couldn't catch. There was no sympathy in them that she could hear.

"Don't leave her, Antoinette," she ordered. "I don't want her to be alone."

"Non, mademoiselle. D'accord."

Annis, exhausted and drained, left her to it. She plodded back to her own room, kicked off her slippers, and fell onto the bed.

Velma's tears had dried. As she bent to pick up Annis's slippers, she asked in a hushed tone, "Is Mrs. Frances dead?"

"No," Annis said tiredly. "But not well, either."

"What do we do?"

"Rest for now," Annis said. "I'm too tired even to think. We'll decide later."

Velma pulled a comforter over her mistress, tucking it around her shoulders before she drew the curtains over the window. Annis was asleep before the door clicked shut.

Annis woke heavy eyed and dazed from having slept through a hot morning. She had dreamed of Frances pacing in circles in a tiny prison cell, and then of Harriet floating inches from the earth as she ripped the head from a manikin.

Annis threw off the coverlet and set her bare feet on the floor, rubbing her eyes with her fingers. Her mouth was dry, and her tongue felt swollen. Velma had left a glass of water already filled beside the bed, and with a silent word of thanks for her fore-thought, Annis took it up and went to stand by the window to drink it.

Between the water and the fresh air from the window, she began to feel more like herself. She tugged the bellpull before she went to the ewer to splash water on her hot cheeks. Velma arrived, out of breath from having hurried, the last morsel of her luncheon still in her mouth.

"Worried," she said, once she had swallowed. "You don't never sleep so long, miss."

"I know. Run me a bath, please, Velma."

As Velma started for the bathroom, she said over her shoulder, "You wasn't in your bed this morning."

"I went for a walk."

The maid stopped, turned, and stared at her, hands on her hips. "In your *nightdress*?"

Annis settled onto the stool of the dressing table. "Bath, Velma," she said. She knew she sounded cross, but she couldn't think of any way to explain.

Velma frowned, wrinkling her forehead beneath the band of her cap. Her lips parted, and she ran her tongue over her bad teeth. It was painful to watch her trying to think things through, and it gave Annis a pang of compunction.

"Velma, I'm sorry. I had a reason, but I can't talk about it. Just run my bath, will you please? Unless Mrs. Frances needs it."

"Mrs. Frances ain't awake," Velma said, on certain ground now. "She ain't waked up at all, not like His Lordship."

"Oh! Is the marquess awake?"

"Awake, but still in bed. If he had a fever, it's broke."

"Does Mrs. Frances have a fever?"

"Don't know. I'm not going in that room, in case it's that there influenza. That Frenchie says she's probably going to die." She went into the bathroom, and the taps squeaked as she started the bathwater.

Annis seized the opportunity to take the manikins from the pocket of her coat and hide them in her jewel case. By the time Velma came back she was untying her plait and brushing the kinks from her hair. Velma took the brush from her, and Annis gazed into the mirror as she brushed, thinking hard. If Frances died, should she say it was the influenza? Would Papa want her to bring her home or bury her here? If Frances didn't die but continued as she was... What should she do then?

Lady Eleanor would know. She was the sort of woman who always knew what was best.

Annis took care in dressing, in hopes that perfect propriety now might erase the multiple signs of impropriety from the night before. She allowed Velma to do her hair in a Psyche knot, though it took extra time. The pink dress had irritated her at first, but now, when she wished to appear as an innocent young girl, she was glad of it. Its puffed sleeves and gored skirt accentuated her slenderness. Frances had deplored her meager bosom, but Annis suspected Lady Eleanor would envy it. She pinned a girlish pink ribbon to her hair, and over the embroidered neckline of the bodice, she wore her pearls with the moonstone in the center.

Before going in search of Lady Eleanor, Annis peeked into Frances's bedroom. The only difference she could see in her stepmother was that Frances had closed her mouth, or her maid had done it for her. Antoinette still sat beside the bed, but she was drowsing, her chin on her chest. Annis let her sleep. She gazed at her stepmother and wondered if she, like James, would eventually waken.

But James's manikin had not been destroyed. It was safe in her jewel case, next to the one meant to represent herself, while Frances's manikin was irreparably broken. Harriet had lumped the shattered bits of it into her basket. Did that mean Frances was broken, too?

She had no answer. She withdrew in silence and closed the bedroom door.

At the suggestion of one of the footmen, Annis knocked lightly on the closed door of Lady Eleanor's study and heard a peremptory, "Yes?"

Annis opened the door and stepped inside, but not too far, in case she wasn't welcome. With a careful curtsy, she said, "Lady Eleanor, if I may, I've come seeking your advice."

Lady Eleanor waved a hand to a chair opposite her. The tray holding the remains of her lunch was on her desk, and Annis could see she had eaten almost nothing. Her plump cheeks looked sallow, and her eyelids were swollen. She wore a loose-fitting gown with no corset beneath, and no jewelry at all.

"How is Lord Rosefield?" Annis asked as she sank into the upholstered armchair. "I'm told he's awake, which is the most wonderful news."

"Yes. He's awake, but the doctor says he will need weeks of rest. Perhaps months."

"Oh dear. He must have been very ill indeed."

"No one seems to know what it was, but of course, Mrs. Allington has it, too, so we must assume it's infectious. I feel terrible for her. I was so fearful—" She pressed a hand to her chest. "I could say I feared for the estate, and for the title. It would go to some cousin or other, someone I don't even know, but I don't care about that. I love my son very much. A ridiculous amount, actually. It's something I don't speak of often. I suppose, if I had had other children—"

She closed her eyes for a moment, and Annis almost reached for her hand in sympathy. She was sure Lady Eleanor would hate that, so she resisted the urge.

When Lady Eleanor opened her eyes, she gazed at her linked fingers in her lap, saying softly, "I don't believe I've ever expressed those feelings to Rosefield. I expect he thinks I'm a hard woman. A cold woman."

Annis didn't know what James thought of his mother, beyond her wish that he marry money, so she said nothing. She couldn't think of anything to do but sit and listen.

Lady Eleanor drew a small, shuddery breath. "He's a dear boy, truly, Miss Allington. A dear man, I should say. An admirable one. He's smart. Studious. Disciplined in every way. He's never been athletic—hates most of the things other young men do for sport—but he's devoted to Seabeck, and I'm so very proud of him for that."

"As you should be, Your Ladyship. It's clear in everything he says."

"I was terrified, when Perry found him this morning…" Her lips suddenly trembled, and she put a finger to them. "Well, never mind that," she said, with an attempt at her customary briskness.

"He's going to make a full recovery. We must believe that. Hold to it."

"Yes, of course."

"And now," Lady Eleanor said, unfolding her hands and spreading them on her knees. "Now we must speak of your step-mother. Ghastly business, all this."

"Did the doctor see her?"

"He did. It seems to be the same ailment, but she shows no sign of coming round. James awoke almost immediately when Perry shook him by the shoulder."

"I've just stopped by Frances's room. I could see no change at all."

"You must be terribly worried."

"I am. This is the day we were to leave, but I don't see how to manage that."

"Obviously you can't leave until she is much better."

"This is why I've come to you," Annis said. She folded her own hands and sat as straight as she could in the overstuffed armchair. "I don't know how to prepare for the chance Frances may die."

"I'm afraid that's possible. I'm very sorry, but it's wise of you to face it straight on."

"If that happens, what do I do? I suppose I could wire my father for instructions, but I hate to alarm him."

"I would say that's a bridge you don't need to cross until you come to it."

"We can't impose indefinitely on your hospitality."

"I assure you, it is no imposition. However, our other guests are going home this afternoon, and with Rosefield confined to his bed, this will be a dull place for you."

"That isn't important," Annis said. "All that matters is that

James—I mean, Lord Rosefield—gets well. And that my step-mother does, too, of course."

"Allow me to invite you to remain with us as long as you need," Lady Eleanor said. "At the very least, until Mrs. Allington has recovered. Please say you will, Miss Allington. That will relieve my mind greatly. I feel responsible for what has happened."

"I accept with gratitude, my lady," Annis said. "Although I'm confident you bear no responsibility. I'm accustomed to being occupied, however. You must tell me if there's anything that needs doing, if you're busy, or you're tired . . ."

"Very kind." Lady Eleanor's brief spurt of energy seemed to dissipate all at once, and she sagged back in her chair. "I am tired, Miss Allington," she murmured. "First the death of my husband, so unexpected. The debts—the worries about Seabeck's future—and now Rosefield's illness. I confess I feel quite done in."

Annis doubted Her Ladyship had forgotten her son's rejected marriage proposal, which might have solved one of her problems. It was kind of her not to include it in her list of concerns. On an impulse she sprang up from her chair. "Why don't you go and rest this very minute, Lady Eleanor? I can see to your guests' departure. I can speak to Jermyn for you, make certain the carriages are ready, that the horses are properly in their harness—I'm very good at that. I know precisely what needs to be done."

"Why, Miss Allington," Lady Eleanor said, her words coming slowly, as if she wasn't quite sure of them until they were spoken aloud. "That's very generous of you. Do you know, I believe I will accept your offer." Her Ladyship pushed herself from her chair and rang a little silver bell that rested on her desk. "A lie-down will do me the world of good. I'll tell my housekeeper you're going to step into my shoes, at least for today. Please make my excuses to the Hyde-Smiths and the Derbyshires and the Whitmores, will you? I'm sure they will understand."

"Yes, of course I will," Annis said. "I'll go to the stables now, shall I? Perhaps the housekeeper could send word to Jermyn through one of the footmen. Tell him to expect me—that you have deputized me."

"How very kind. I will do that, and thank you very much." Lady Eleanor's smile was more gentle than usual as Annis curtsied again and let herself out of the study.

She was halfway to the front doors when the thought occurred to her that Lady Eleanor had accepted her offer with no resistance at all, though it must be an unusual suggestion for such an ordered household. Despite everything, Annis found herself smiling over Her Ladyship's cleverness.

James's mother had put Annis in the post of the mistress of Rosefield Hall, however briefly. Annis could guess Her Ladyship hoped she would like it. Would change her mind, accept James's offer of marriage. Solve the problem of Seabeck's debts.

She would have to be careful around Lady Eleanor. She had secrets now, secrets that must be protected.

She hugged the thought to her as she hurried out to the stables. She wasn't sorry to have something so marvelous, so remarkable, to hide. She was a Bishop. A woman with abilities. She was a witch, and she thought the word was a marvelous one, with connotations of knowledge and power and independence.

Despite the sadness of the day, Annis felt a surge of joyful freedom, a feeling she had never before experienced. It was the best feeling in the world.

35

Harriet

At the Four Fishes, Harriet went straight to her room and rested all through the day. She didn't rise until after five, and though she was still bone weary, she was also ravenous.

She found the two pieces of Frances's manikin in her basket, mashed together into a shapeless lump. As the creator of it, she could dispose of it. It had done its damage, of course. There was no more harm in it, but she wanted to make certain it could not be put back together. She crumbled the wax into fragments. She separated the pebbles and moss and the bit of bark from the pile and tossed them out onto the thatch for the birds to take. She wrapped the now-formless wax in the flannel that had served as its dress. There was no longer any danger in the crumbled wax and scrap of cloth. Her fingers told her that, sensing no electric tingle of magic.

With a sense of mingled relief and guilt, she set the bit of flannel in her basket and went to run a bath.

She presented herself downstairs for dinner at about seven. The innkeeper, with his hands linked under his apron, came to say that "the wife" had made shepherd's pie. "Salad, too, if you like that sort of thing," he said. "The wife uses her own lettuce from the garden out back, with radishes and some watercress she bought this morning."

"I will have both," Harriet said. "And bread and butter, please."

"Ale?"

"No, thank you. A pitcher of water."

He nodded and disappeared into the kitchen. Other patrons came in and settled at the other tables. The villagers had gotten used to Harriet's presence. They nodded, and two of the men touched their forelocks. When her dinner arrived, she ate hungrily at first, then at a more moderate pace once her appetite began to ease.

And she listened.

It was amazing, she thought, how swiftly news flew through the houses and shops of an English village. By the time she had finished the excellent salad, she had heard that "the influenza or some such" had struck Rosefield Hall. As she worked on her serving of shepherd's pie, which tasted unpleasantly of old mutton, she learned that only two people had fallen ill. There had been, the gossip said, three old couples there who had departed in haste, eager to avoid infection. Since then, no one had been allowed in or out.

Harriet waited, toying with her fork, to hear more details of who was ill and if they were recovering, but those weren't forthcoming. Surely, she told herself, as she pushed away the unappetizing remains of the shepherd's pie, if someone had died they would know. Evil news always had wings of its own.

There was an hour left of daylight. She went up to her room to retrieve her jacket and her basket and hurried out of the Four Fishes and down the short high street. Beyond the green she pressed on into the copse on the western boundary of Seabeck.

The light was beginning to fail in the shadow of the trees by the time she had finished burying the remains of the manikin. Despite the gloom, she managed to find mullein flowers, for discernment, and bilberry, to enhance her vision. She still had a bit of starwort, which was helpful for freeing the imagination. Alone they might not have added up to much. Together she hoped they would give her the insight she needed.

As she carried her trove back to the Four Fishes, she felt a stirring begin in her solar plexus. The thrill spread in shallow, distinct waves that flowed up to her heart and down into her belly, the familiar near pain of magic. Her hands and feet began to tingle with it.

This was the aftermath of the power she had wielded in her battle with Frances, and she knew enough about it to be wary. Misuse of such singular power could have destructive side effects, and there could be no doubt she had misused it. That her motive had been pure made no difference to the source. There was a darkness about her now. It would take a long time to disperse.

Nevertheless, since the current of magic was running high, she would use it.

She opened the window of her cramped room before she dropped the crumbled shreds of herbs, bit by bit, into her candle flame. As the fragrant smoke drifted up into the shadows to waft through the open window, she laid her amulet beside the candle and muttered her cantrip:

Reveal to me the fate of the one
Whose manikin is late undone,

And of the innocent lying ill
Cruelly magicked without his will.

The flow of magic in her body sharpened, its energy sparkling through her bones and stinging her toes and fingertips. She
caught a breath at its intensity, and at the same moment the ametrine flared. The violet above shimmered with waves of color.
The yellow below glowed as if it had caught fire. The veins of
purple burned in lines so intricate they appeared to become an
arcane script, some ancient words no human could remember, no
tongue pronounce.

The knowing seized her, filling her mind with the knowledge she sought. There was no foretaste, no foreshadowing, no
warning. It was like a blow, but one that struck inside her head,
between her temples, and it rocked her backward as if it had been
physical. She *knew*.

The marquess would recover. It would be slow, and he would
chafe at the pace, but he would one day be whole again and pick
up the scattered pieces of his life.

Frances would survive, but she would not thrive. She would
not speak, nor live independently, ever again. Her body would
function, after a fashion, but her mind...

Her mind was no longer part of the whole. It was ruined.

The knowing was often uncomfortable, but this was ghastly.
Harriet rarely shed tears, but she found they were spilling down
her cheeks now, dripping on her clasped hands. She leaned forward and blew wetly at the burning candle. It took three tries
before she succeeded in extinguishing the flame.

The ametrine continued to glow, the power that had ignited
it not so easily doused as the wick of a candle. Harriet gazed

at the amulet through the sheen of her tears, helpless before an onslaught of guilt and confusion and regret.

Many moments passed before she could dry her face, take up the amulet, and go to sit by the window. With the ametrine clasped against her heart, she gazed up into the cold stars and whispered a message to Frances, who would never hear it, nor understand it if she did.

"I am sorry," Harriet murmured, "so very sorry for what has happened to you, Frances. Poor little cousin, never content, never happy." Fresh tears choked her as she thought of Frances's pretty face, her craving to belong. "Oh, Frances," she murmured. "You will never be one of the Four Hundred. You will never practice your art again. Your wealth and privilege will mean nothing. Your future is wasted. I am sick at heart, but I had no choice. It was you or it was Annis and poor innocent James."

A different kind of knowing came over her as she sat there, gazing over the sleeping village. What she had said was true. There had been no choice. If she had not been here to fight for Annis and for James, there would have been two tragedies instead of one. Two lives destroyed instead of one.

There had been nothing else she could do. She understood that, but still grieved that it had to be so.

She rose to get into her nightdress and to lay out her things to pack. Tomorrow she would go back to London, book passage to New York, return home as soon as possible. It would be good to see dear Grace, to be back in her herbarium, to walk again in her beloved park. She folded herself into bed, closed her eyes, and welcomed the deep sleep of exhaustion.

She suffered no nightmares, despite her sadness. She slept soundly, comforted by a dream of Alexander, who touched her cheek with his big, gentle hand. She found no judgment in his eyes, no criticism for anything she had done. She saw only love, the kind of love that comes once in a lifetime, the kind that can never die.

She woke with more tears on her cheeks, but these were tears of nostalgia and of longing for the life she could not have.

36

James

James was confined to his bed for a full week before he felt strong enough to sit up in the armchair, his feet on a hassock. He had Perry pull the drapes so he could gaze out over the gardens and catch a glimpse of the summer-blue sea. His bedroom faced east and south, with a view of the Seabeck farms. The rain of a few days ago had revived the browning fields. White sheep grazed along the hillsides, and a herd of red dairy cows browsed in their pasture.

The doctor had said it could be weeks before he would be well enough to ride out on the estate. James had to settle for the view and for the scents of summer-blooming flowers and shrubs borne to him on the sea breeze.

The doctor had not been able to identify the illness that had come over him so suddenly. The same ailment had evidently struck Mrs. Allington, and that troubled James. He worried that it might attack some other resident of Rosefield Hall. Most especially he worried that it might strike Annis.

It had been a bizarre sort of sickness. He couldn't remember anything about the night he fell ill except for a strange sequence of nightmares. They still haunted him, though he couldn't bring himself to speak of them, either to Perry or to the doctor. They had been violent, disgusting, lurid as passages from the penny dreadfuls sold on railway station racks. He would never want anyone to know the inventions his fevered mind had been capable of. He could only hope the nightmares would eventually fade from his memory, the way normal dreams did.

Perry had just removed his luncheon tray, leaving the door open so the air could circulate. James dropped his head against the back of his chair and contemplated a pair of bullfinches darting from tree to shrub at the edge of the garden, their plumage glowing rose and silver in the bright sun. He envied their freedom and their energy, while he sat here, weak as a newborn lamb. As an infant. The doctor said he would recover, but since the same doctor had no idea what was the matter with him, it was difficult to place confidence in his prediction.

A light knock on the open door roused him. He lifted his head and twisted in his chair. It was Annis.

She was dressed in her riding habit and offering him a tentative smile. "James," she said. "I'm delighted to see you out of bed."

"Yes, at last," he said. His voice, hoarse from disuse, creaked like an unoiled hinge. He cleared his throat. "Do come in, Miss Allington."

"Annis, please." She crossed the room and came to sit on a straight chair beside the hassock. She looked as bright and glowing as the bullfinches, the opposite of his own condition. He was infinitely glad she could never guess at the role she had played in his nightmares.

He tried to sit up a bit straighter, distressed at looking feeble. "Tell me," he said. "How is your stepmother?"

"I'm sorry to say she is still in her bed. Her eyes are open, and she takes a bit of nourishment. My maid, Velma, is particularly good with her, persuading her to swallow some soup and sometimes a little toast. She hasn't spoken a word since she fell ill, though. The doctor doesn't know why. I'm terribly worried."

Annis's worry didn't show on her face. Her wonderful eyes were as bright as the summer sky, and her skin shone with health. There were several new, tiny freckles scattered across her nose. The jaw he had once thought too masculine now appeared merely well cut, a decisive feature in a strong face. It was ridiculous to think he had once found her plain. "You look as if you've been riding, Annis."

"Oh yes! Lady Eleanor encouraged me, since we remain here, to take advantage of your stables. I do hope you don't mind."

"Which horse did you ride?"

"Why, I've ridden them all, James—well, all except Breeze, because she's yours. And of course Jermyn flatly refused to let me ride Seastar, which I very much wanted to do."

"You've even ridden Shadow?"

"Oh yes, Shadow is easy, isn't he? I mean, he's a stubborn boy, but once he knows you mean business, he's perfectly fine. His trot is a bit rough, but his canter is lovely."

James had nothing to say to this. Shadow was a horse only he and Jermyn were ever able to persuade past a stolid walk. They had given up trying to use him for guests.

Annis burbled happily on. "Today I took Dancer out. She practically begged me to, nodding over the stable gate and whickering at me when I came in. I felt quite honored! She has the most delightful running walk, doesn't she? We went along the coombe, then had a lovely gallop in the upper pasture." Her cheeks went pink as she described the wildflowers she had seen and the many birds that were unfamiliar to her. "Do you know there's a bed of mallow along the stone fence in that pasture? Mallow is good for inflammation. I would have picked some if I had thought of taking a basket with me."

She seemed to become aware that she had been chattering, and sank back in her chair, wrinkling her freckled nose. "I didn't mean to rattle on so," she said. "I will tire you."

"Not at all," he said. "I'm glad of the diversion. Tell me what else you've been doing."

"I helped Cook with the kitchen garden. There were root vegetables ready to be pulled, and the pea vines were more than ready for the picking."

"You didn't pick them yourself, surely?"

She laughed. "Well, a few. The kitchen maids did most of it. Our kitchen garden at home is a marvel, because Mrs. King—that's our cook—is insistent on only the freshest produce. She knows a great deal about cultivation, and she taught me. I also made two calls on your mother's behalf, which was great fun. One was to one of your farms. There's a brand-new baby, the most precious darling, called Rosemary. Lady Eleanor wanted to send a gift for the little one but was too busy to go herself. The other was in the village, a few things she needed at the greengrocer's. I was going there anyway."

"I'm sure my mother is grateful for your help."

"She's been so good, since my stepmother's illness, insisting we stay on until Frances can travel. She's been very kind."

James didn't answer that. He put his head back and let his gaze drift out again to the emerald fields and the sapphire sparkle of the sea. It wasn't usual for him to hear his mother described as "very kind." Annis's youth and energy must be helpful to her just now, with two invalids in the house, but she had never wanted help before. He had no doubt his mother had a motive. She invariably did.

He said, "I'm glad you've found things to occupy you, since you've been stuck here through no fault of your own."

He heard her small, sharp intake of breath and cast a quick glance her way. Her cheeks paled, and she dropped her gaze as if she were embarrassed by something. Or ashamed of it.

A little silence stretched between them until he said, "I believe, Annis, that you didn't want to come here in the first place."

Her color returned, and she gave an apologetic shake of her head. "All of this was my stepmother's idea, James. I did object, but my father ordered me. I'm so sorry you were deceived. I have explained this to Lady Eleanor and apologized on Frances's behalf."

He knew she was trying not to hurt his feelings, but they were wounded just the same, all over again. He couldn't speak past the knot suddenly tightening his throat.

He wished he could start again with her. He wouldn't be upset by her free-spirited ways. He would try to be less old-fashioned—less of a prig, as his mother had said. He would make an effort to charm her. He would demonstrate to her what a good life she could have as Lady Rosefield. It seemed his mother had succeeded where he had failed.

He remembered how glorious Annis had looked racing away from him on Dancer after his awkward proposal. Her seat in the saddle had been as steady and secure as any man's, her hands low on the reins, her posture well forward, in perfect balance. She had lost her hat, and her hair had streamed in the wind, a dark, rippling flag of farewell.

He was in love with Annis Allington. The embarrassing and shameful fires of lust had died down, thank God, but he still wanted her. Not her money. Herself, with her freckled nose and boyish figure, her cascade of dark hair, her forget-me-not eyes, her stubborn jaw, and all her rebellious, unabashed modern ways. Why in heaven's name had he not told her that in the first place? It was far too late now.

His eyes stung, and he had to look away. She would think, he hoped, it was the illness that reddened his eyes and rendered him mute. No doubt that was best.

Annis told him she had sent a wire to her father while she was in the village, and that she had just received his response, delivered to Rosefield Hall by a boy on a bicycle.

"I'm going to take Frances home," she said. "That's what I came to tell you, James. I wrote to Papa, and he has booked our passage to New York. The *Majestic* again."

"How will you manage, with your stepmother so ill?"

"My maid and I can cope," she said. "Velma's strong and remarkably patient. Once we're aboard, it will be simple."

"I wish you would stay until Mrs. Allington is better," he said.

Her expression turned somber. "Lady Eleanor said the same thing, but I don't think Frances is going to be better. Something has happened to her mind."

"But just you and your maid...What about Mrs. Allington's maid?"

"Vanished," Annis said. "She took two pieces of Frances's jewelry and ran off yesterday. Probably back to Paris."

"Oh! Shall we summon the sheriff?"

"No. Antoinette wanted me to give her money, and I didn't have enough to satisfy her. It's good riddance, truly. I didn't care for her much in any case, and I don't care at all about the jewelry. She's welcome to sell it and use the money for her passage home." She patted her hands together, as if dusting the issue away. "She will have no reference from us, of course."

James, so concerned about money himself, thought it must be very nice not to care about the loss of two pieces of expensive jewelry, but he didn't speak the thought. There was no point.

He let his gaze drift back to the rich green pastures of Seabeck and the tidy cottages of his tenants. How was he going to hold it all together? He had no idea.

When he turned his head back to Annis, he saw that she had gotten to her feet and was standing with her left hand on her pearl necklace as she reached toward him with her right. "I will miss you, James," she said, in a sisterly fashion. "And I will miss Lady Eleanor, and Rosefield Hall, and Seabeck. And most especially your Andalusians! Thank you so much for allowing me to ride them."

He took her hand in his and shook it. He wanted to press it to his lips. He wanted to say something, anything, that would stop her going, but no words would come.

"I've tired you," she said quickly, releasing his hand. "As I feared. I'll come and say goodbye before we go. Rest now."

When she was gone, James closed his eyes and tried to pretend that his throat didn't ache with sadness.

37

Annis

The look on her father's face when she and Velma shepherded Frances down the gangplank of the *Majestic* made Annis's blood run cold. She and Velma had done their best to make Frances presentable. They had brushed and pinned up her hair and dressed her in her simplest suit and hat, though they had given up on her corset because she couldn't stand without them supporting her. They had managed to pull gloves on over her nerveless fingers. She walked well enough, if each of them held an arm and balanced her between them, but there was nothing they could do about the expression on her face, or rather the lack of it.

Her pretty mouth was slack, as if she couldn't remember to close her lips. Velma had fallen into the habit of holding a handkerchief ready to dab at the little rivulet of saliva that so often dripped down Frances's chin. Frances's bright eyes had turned muddy. Her cheeks were hollow, as she ate only what Velma could get into her mouth and persuade her to swallow. Velma had proved to be very good at this, coaxing Frances to take nourishment as if she were a recalcitrant infant.

Papa's countenance was rigid as a stone sculpture by the time the three of them reached him, but not before Annis recognized his look of horror at the sight of his wife.

She had become used to that look as they sailed from Liverpool to New York. She and Velma had all their meals brought to the stateroom to avoid the curious stares and the fuss of trying to manage the dining saloon, but even that didn't protect them. The stewards gaped at Mrs. Allington's blank features and slumped posture. A ship's officer came by once, resplendent in his white dress uniform, to invite them to sit with the captain at dinner. He took one look at Frances and backed out, bowing and apologizing. The porters who managed their luggage in the train stations and at the docks were just as disturbed, although they did their best to hide it, and to avoid looking at Frances whenever possible.

Annis had written to her father, trying to warn him, but the cold reality was a shock. Frances had left New York a chic, self-possessed, bright woman. She had returned barely human.

There had been a moment, though, on board the ship. Annis was helping Velma with Frances's nightdress when a feeling of shame filled her, making her heart flutter and her stomach sink. It wasn't her own feeling, Annis knew. It was Frances's emotion, one she had no way to express. Annis had put a sympathetic hand on her stepmother's shoulder. It was heartbreaking to think there was no way to undo what had been done.

They had docked under a burning August sun. The air of New York felt heavy and sluggish, almost too thick to breathe, as Annis steered her charge down the ramp, then left Velma to support Frances while she went to embrace her father. Their eyes met, but they didn't speak. There was nothing to say.

Not until they were in the carriage, with Robbie on the driver's seat and the boxes and valises piled in the back, did George say anything beyond giving orders. "It's worse than your letter said, Annis."

"I'm sorry, Papa. I didn't know how to describe it. One day she was fine, and the next she was so ill we thought she might die. I hoped she might improve during the crossing, but now—well, now you see."

"Better she had died," he said.

Annis cast him a horrified look. "Papa! You can't possibly mean that!"

His features were still stony, showing no emotion at all. "Look at her," he said in a low tone. "She's as good as dead, isn't she? Can't speak. Can't walk on her own. Doesn't recognize me, or anything, as far as I can tell."

Annis could hardly breathe for the cruelty of it. She looked across at Velma, seated on the opposite side of the carriage, trying to keep Frances from slumping to one side. Velma looked no more anxious than she usually did. Perhaps she didn't understand George's comments. Perhaps she thought he didn't mean them. Annis wished she could convince herself of that.

Her father had not spoken his wife's name, not once. He hadn't touched her, either, but allowed Robbie and Velma to assist her into the carriage and settle her on the plush seat. Now he stared out the window as the carriage made its way through the city streets, as if he couldn't bear the sight of his stricken wife.

Annis turned her head in the opposite direction, watching the grand hotels and sprawling department stores flow by on the other side of the road. What would become of the ruin that was Frances Allington? Her stepmother had done this to herself, provoking Harriet into the battle that destroyed her, but that didn't ease the pity Annis felt. She didn't want what was left of Frances to suffer.

In the misery of the moment, enervated by the thick hot air of New York in August, a longing for Seabeck's fresh, sea-scented breezes surprised Annis with its intensity. The second cutting of hay would be almost ripe. The Andalusians would be frolicking in their sunny paddock. Would the field roses have finished their bloom? She wished she could see them transform into the scarlet hips James had described to her.

It was all terribly confusing. She had wanted nothing more than to be home again, and now she was missing Seabeck and Rosefield Hall. And James, too, but she shied away from that thought.

She needed to see Bits, to bury her face against his warm neck, to feel him nibble at her shoulder. He would stamp and whicker, happy to have her home. She would examine him from nose to tail to assure herself he was healthy. When they were reunited, she would feel like herself again.

She found her hands twitching in her lap, as if she could slap the carriage horse's reins and make him go faster.

Robbie pulled up the carriage at the top of the curved drive in front of Allington House. Annis stayed to see Velma and Frances on their way up to the front door, where Mrs. King was waiting, before she picked up her skirts and ran around the side of the house to the stables. She heard her father call after her, but she pretended she hadn't heard. She couldn't wait another minute to see Bits. The weeks of their separation had felt like an eternity.

She could smell the stables before she stepped into their welcome

shade. She gladly sniffed the scents of fresh straw and hay and sawdust. Careless of the hem of her traveling suit, she trotted to Bits's
box and leaned over the gate.

The stall was empty. Sally's was, too. Only old Tater put his
head out over the gate to blink at her. Down the aisle Chessie
eyed her with disinterest.

She hurried to the paddock behind the stables. Bits must be
there, having a bit of a walk, though the air was so hot and close.
She would find him, bring him into the coolness of the stables,
refresh his water trough.

He wasn't in the paddock, either.

She heard the creak and jingle of the carriage coming up the
lane from the house and ran to meet it. Robbie was climbing
down from the driver's seat, and when she saw his face, her heart
clenched in her chest.

"Robbie! Where's Bits? Where's Sally?"

Robbie looked so sorrowful she thought he might burst into
tears. "Sold, Miss Annis," he said. "Mr. Allington sold them right
after the wire came."

"Wire? What wire?"

"The telegram," he said, as if that would explain it. When
she only stared at him, he added, "The telegram saying you was
going to be married."

"Married? I'm not going to be married!"

"Mr. Allington said you was, and so he sold Black Satin, and
threw Sally in as a bonus."

"S-sold?" Annis cried. "Robbie, no! It can't be! Frances said—
We hadn't—"

Panic seized her. On a normal day she would have lent a hand
with the carriage horse's tack, rubbing him down, seeing to his

feed and water. Now, with a cry of pain, as if she had been stabbed, she spun away from Robbie and dashed back to the house.

She burst in through the front doors, pushed past Mrs. King without a greeting or an apology, and ran to her father's office. The door was closed, but she banged it open without knocking. He was at his desk, his back to her. He didn't turn at the sound of her precipitate entry.

She shouted, so loudly he winced. "Papa! How could you?"

He still didn't turn. With a deliberate movement, he closed the ledger lying open on his desk. He didn't pretend not to know what she was asking. "Her telegraph said you were going to marry a marquess."

"She lied!" Annis stalked over to her father and stood hugging herself to keep from bursting into childish tears. "I never said I would marry him! Where's Bits? And Sally?"

Slowly her father turned in his big leather chair so he could look up at her. His face was drawn. "Annis," he said heavily. "I can't worry about horses just now. I have to think what to do about Frances."

"What do you mean, what to do about her?"

"Her maid didn't come back with you."

"Antoinette stole two pieces of Frances's jewelry and disappeared. Where's Black Satin?"

"I can't manage Frances without her maid."

"Don't be stupid, Papa! She has Velma, who has been wonderful with her. Mrs. King will find a regular nurse. I want to know where Bits is! I'm going after him!"

As if he hadn't heard her, her father said, "You should have left Frances in England."

Annis's mouth fell open, and for a frozen moment she couldn't think of what to say. Even her distress over Bits receded in the face of her father's heartlessness. "Papa!" she breathed.

"What difference would it make? There's no point in her having made the journey. She's—she's like a dead woman."

Annis dropped her arms to her sides and gazed in horror at the father she thought she knew. His eyes, so much like hers, were the blue of winter ice on Azalea Pond. "Don't look at me like that," he growled. "It was her own idea to go, to get a title. Not my fault she got sick."

"You made me go along," she said. Her voice was flat, and she deliberately jutted her chin forward. "You wanted both of us out of your way."

"It wasn't like—" he began.

She interrupted. "And now you've sold Black Satin to spite me. Who bought him, Papa? Where is he?"

Her father put his hands on his desk and pushed himself up. She took a step back. She couldn't help herself.

He made no move toward her. "I'm not going to tell you, Annis," he said. "There's no point. The stallion is sold. I've been paid for him." He gave a slight shrug. "I'll give you the money if you want."

"Money!" she spit. "I don't want the money! I want my horse." She whirled in a storm of swinging skirts that spattered sawdust over the floor. At the door she cried, "I will never, ever forgive you! You are no longer my father! I am no longer your daughter!"

It was an uncomfortable walk from Riverside Drive to the Dakota in the stifling August heat. Anger propelled Annis's first hurried steps. By the time the gray bulk of the apartment building came into view, anxiety had taken over, and she was near tears by the time she was allowed into the main courtyard and ascending the corner staircase.

She knocked too loudly at the apartment door, her muscles charged with emotion. The door opened almost at once, and a redheaded, much-freckled woman stood in the doorway. "I would guess you're Annis Allington," she said by way of greeting.

Annis gripped her hands together to stop them shaking. "Yes, I am. You couldn't have—I mean, you weren't expecting me, surely."

"Not me." The woman stepped to the side and gestured her into the elegant entryway and on into a high-ceilinged, spacious apartment. "I'm Grace, by the way, and very nice to make your acquaintance." She shut the door and made a little shooing motion. "That way, if you please, Miss Annis. It's Miss Harriet is expecting you. The *Times* said you and your stepmother would be on the *Majestic* this very day. I said surely you wouldn't come so quick, not when you'd just arrived, but Miss Harriet was that certain, just knew you would be here. I know better than to argue, so I made some fresh scones, just in case, though I still wasn't convinced, but here you are, and I know she's eager to see you."

Annis barely heard the last words of this recitation. She found herself in a charming room, sparsely furnished, with tall windows facing the park. Two comfortable-looking divans faced each other, with an inlaid table between them and two straight chairs at the sides.

It was such a relief to see Aunt Harriet turn from the windows and stride toward her, hands outstretched, that Annis burst into the tears she had been holding back for two hours.

Harriet took her in her arms, and as she held her, she gave instructions. "Grace, a pot of tea, please, and your scones. Annis, dear heart, cry it out. You'll feel better. Then we'll get to work."

★　　★　　★

Still sniffling, but fortified by two cups of tea and one of Grace's tender scones spread with fresh butter and fragrant honey, Annis followed Harriet into her herbarium.

She felt instantly soothed, and the last of her tears receded. The herbarium was scrupulously ordered, with tools and containers neatly arranged. The room was long, with the high ceilings of all the Dakota apartments. The fragrance of drying herbs and beeswax candles tingled in Annis's nose, and she wanted to know the names and uses of everything. Harriet pulled back the drapes on the window at one end, and the last sunlight of the hot afternoon fell across the tiled floor. Dust motes gleamed like gold dust in the light, spinning gently in the faint air current roused by the closing of the door.

"Oh," Annis breathed. "Aunt Harriet, this room—it's magical!"

Harriet smiled. The sun gleamed on the strands of silver in her dark hair, and her gray eyes glistened like well-polished silver. "I'm glad you like it."

"I don't ever want to leave!"

"It does rather give one that feeling, doesn't it? But we must recover Black Satin, and Sally, too. I know where they are. We'll need to persuade the buyer to sell them back to you."

"I don't know if my father will give me the money if he knows that's what it's for."

Harriet's smile gave way to a fierce look of determination. "Oh, we'll persuade him, too. We already know he's vulnerable to the Bishop style of persuasion."

Harriet, Annis learned, had been following all the news about the Allington family in the *Times*, in the *Herald* and the *World* and the *Sun*. She had seen a tiny announcement on a back page of the *Herald* about George Allington's sale of a breeding stallion. The buyer had begun advertising his stud services already.

"Is it—is it right, to persuade the buyer?" Harriet raised her eyebrows, and Annis added hastily, "Of course Papa shouldn't have sold Black Satin without telling me! That wasn't fair."

"No, it wasn't fair." Harriet put down the mortar and pestle she had lifted from a shelf. She put her back to the counter and folded her arms. "But we should talk about this."

"We're still going to do it, aren't we?"

"I believe we can do it, but as to its being right or not, I would say that whether an action is right or wrong depends greatly on your viewpoint."

"I think you know what my viewpoint is."

"Yes. And mine is the same. I did give this some thought, Annis, because it matters how we use our ability. It seems to me, though, that the man who bought Black Satin has hundreds of horses to choose from. They are his business, not his passion. As long as he is repaid, we're not going to cause him any harm. Further, I suspect your father sold your horse to offset the considerable expense your dowry was going to be."

"And now there won't have to be one."

"Evidently not."

Annis thought Harriet sounded amused, but it didn't show on her face. Annis said, "This isn't the *maleficia*, then."

"No, most definitely not. Just a tiny spell of persuasion, for a horse and a bit of money. It doesn't need the *maleficia* to succeed. Were you worried?"

"I remember you said the *maleficia* can corrupt the person who uses it."

"As you have seen."

"I was part of it, wasn't I? I worry that it's still inside me, in my blood, in my mind."

"I know that feeling, Annis. The choice will be yours to make, as it was hers. She gave in to it. You don't need to do that."

Harriet turned back to her work, pulling down swatches of herbs. She laid a cutting board and knife next to the mortar and pestle.

Annis asked, "Does your housekeeper know what you do?"

Harriet sliced a twig of dried rosemary with the knife. "Grace has been with me for a long time. She knows I'm an herbalist. I sometimes think she suspects I am something more, but she never says so." She went back to her task, smiling over it. "She would tolerate it, I think, out of loyalty, but she's an old-fashioned woman with a prosaic turn of mind. She might not even believe it."

Annis pondered that as she watched Harriet grind leaves of wormwood and chop a bit of mandrake root. As her aunt began to gather the prepared ingredients in a small copper bowl, she said, "I wonder how many other women are like us? They wouldn't dare to say, would they?"

Harriet spoke without looking away from her work. "Women like us don't reveal themselves as a rule. That's why we try to track the Bishop descendants, so we can watch over them, nurture their ability."

"Do you think there are others—not Bishops—who have the ability?"

"I know there are." Harriet dusted her fingers over the bowl, then set it on the counter next to a fat white candle. "They keep to themselves, out of necessity. I met one once, though. At the herb shop. We just—" She smiled at the memory and finished in a voice of nostalgia. "We just recognized each other."

"Did you speak of it?"

"I wish we had. I would have liked a friend who understood. A colleague to share with."

Annis sighed. "So many secrets. It's sad."

"You're right. Secrets are kept because people—men in particular, but women, too—are quick to judge. To condemn." Harriet lifted her amulet from around her neck and settled it against the candle. "Frightened people are dangerous."

Annis took off her moonstone and set it opposite the ametrine, with the candle between them. It made a pretty tableau, the yellow-and-violet ametrine in its puddle of silver chain, the creamy moonstone surrounded by pearls, the white candle in the center. It looked as innocent as a decorative display in a curio cabinet, but she could imagine that someone observing what she and Harriet did, seeing the effect they were about to create, might be frightened by it. It was a shame. How many people denied their ability out of fear? How much magic was wasted?

She reflected, as she and Harriet began their rite, that Frances would never again do this. She would never again employ her knowledge or her ability to affect events or manipulate people, for good or ill. Frances's power—Frances's magic—was gone forever.

38

Harriet

With a freshly concocted and magicked salve in a tiny jar in Annis's pocket, Harriet and Annis rode in a hired carriage to the commercial stable on Third Avenue and Twenty-Fourth Street. The *Herald* had reported that one Mr. Albert Neufeld had added Black Satin to his breeding stock. Sally wasn't important enough to warrant a mention in the newspaper report, but they hoped to find out something about her when they arrived.

They had chosen their clothes deliberately. Annis wore her most expensive suit, cream linen with a peach-colored vest, a jacket embroidered in peach thread, and an elaborate hat with a peach-colored feather. She appeared the very picture of a wealthy young socialite. Harriet wore a walking dress in a summer print, clearly not new, with a modest straw hat.

Mr. Neufeld was the proprietor of a hired-carriage business, with an office adjacent to his stables. He clearly assumed, as they were ushered by his clerk into his private office, that Harriet was Miss Allington's chaperone, and that the daughter of the owner of the Allington Iron Stove Company had come to rent a carriage.

He bowed to Annis and nodded to Harriet. "Miss Allington," he said, actually rubbing his plump hands together. "A pleasure to meet you, after my happy association with your father. How can I help you? A landau? A brougham, perhaps, and a pair? I understand you have a grand wedding coming up!"

Annis curtsied prettily. "Thank you, Mr. Neufeld," she said, skirting the issue of her wedding. "I've learned you bought my horse while I was abroad. I long to see him one more time, and I thought—I hoped—you might be kind enough to let me visit his stall."

"Well!" This request evidently startled Mr. Neufeld, and the eager expression on his round face sagged into one of bewilderment. "Well, Miss Allington, of course I—I mean, the black *is* a stallion, and I'm not sure a young lady—"

"I do realize it's unusual, Mr. Neufeld," Annis said, with impressive smoothness. Her upbringing, Harriet could see, had prepared her for dealing with tradespeople. "It's just that since I gave up riding my dear little pony, Sally—"

"I have your pony, Miss Allington!" Neufeld exclaimed, with an air of relief. "Her stall is just up on the second floor. Would you like to see her? I've already rented her out for two birthday parties, and all the children found her most amenable."

"Of course, I would love to see Sally," Annis said. "But, Mr. Neufeld, truly—I've been riding Black Satin for three years, almost every day. He knows me well, and he's no danger to me. I promise you it's perfectly safe for me to say hello, stroke him a bit. I just—I do so long to see him one more time!"

It was clear Neufeld was still uncomfortable, but after a few more exchanges, during which Annis became more and more tremulous, and Neufeld's thick features drooped in confusion, they were on their way, up a cleated wooden ramp to the third floor of the stables. Neufeld stood close to the gate as Annis approached the stall, adopting a protective stance, as if he was afraid the horse might try to break free.

Tears glimmered in Annis's eyes as she stepped forward, holding out her gloved hands to the horse. Black Satin threw up his head and whickered, and then, in a movement that startled Neufeld, he pressed his chest against the gate so he could stretch out his neck and drop his head into Annis's waiting hands.

Annis slid her hands up over Black Satin's cheeks and onto the arch of his neck. She pressed her forehead to his, and the two stood there for a long moment, the beautiful black horse and the tall, slender girl. It was an embrace between two creatures devoted to each other. Harriet could have shed a tear or two herself.

Neufeld was not so sensitive. He cleared his throat and tugged his jacket over his protuberant belly. Harriet guessed he wanted to intervene but was wary of offending the daughter of George Allington, soon to make a brilliant marriage.

Nervously Neufeld turned to Harriet for reassurance. She gave him a frosty nod, even as she saw, beyond his shoulder, Annis stroking a palmful of their salve onto Black Satin's neck, beneath the fringe of his mane.

Annis, as they had planned, took charge. "Mr. Neufeld, I believe there is a scratch on Black Satin's neck. A wound, perhaps from a protruding nail or a splinter. It might be bleeding. Have you ascertained the safety of this stall?"

Neufeld, with a grunt of anxiety over the condition of his expensive purchase, reached to examine the spot Annis had just smeared with their salve. He slid his hand beneath Black Satin's mane and ran his fingers along the horse's neck. Neufeld stepped back, looking curiously at his fingers. They shone, as if with sweat, or oil.

He said, "I don't find any wound, Miss Allington. This is not blood, but—well. I don't know what it is. It is very hot today, and perhaps…" He rubbed his fingers together, then wiped them on his trousers.

"Oh, what a relief," Annis said coolly. Still with one hand on Black Satin's neck, she said, "Mr. Neufeld, please. Will you consider selling my horse back to us? My father misunderstood my situation. I want to have Bits back in our stables. Black Satin, I mean."

Neufeld licked his lips uncertainly. "I don't—Miss Allington, this is—does your father—"

As the salve took effect, the change in Neufeld was neither subtle nor slow. His frown of confusion transformed into a genial, avuncular look. His eyes brightened, and his brow smoothed. He said, as if it gave him pleasure to do so, "But of course, Miss Allington! Anything I can do for the bride-to-be! Anything that will make you happy! There's to be a title, I understand? Now, I am sure we can come to an arrangement that will please both you and Mr. Allington, and—"

He burbled on for a bit, happy now that his anxiety had eased, eager to do anything Miss Allington asked of him. Harriet stood silent as Annis made the arrangements.

A plan was easily agreed to. Black Satin, and Sally as well, would be delivered to the Allington stables the following morning. The payment for the horses would be refunded by Mr. Allington, with an allowance for their care and feeding during the period of Mr. Neufeld's custody of them. Miss Allington, of course, would recommend Neufeld's carriages for hire to all her friends and wouldn't dream of using any others for her wedding arrangements.

They stopped for a brief visit to Sally before making their way out of the stables, Neufeld making jolly comments all the while. The alteration sat oddly upon his thick features and stolid manner, like a costume that didn't quite suit. Harriet contained her amusement until she and Annis were safely in the privacy of their hired car.

Once the carriage horse had begun to trot northward, she began to chuckle. "You, Annis Allington," she said, "were born for this! You must have confidence in our work now, I hope?"

"I do, Aunt Harriet, I do!" Annis glowed with relief and joy over her reunion with Bits. "Mr. Neufeld seems perfectly happy, and as you say, he has a stable full of other horses! I will see to Papa's dose of our salve the moment we're home."

"I wish you good luck with that. We'll drop you there, and I'll go on to the Dakota."

Annis turned glowing eyes to her. "When do we begin my apprenticeship, Aunt Harriet?"

"Why, my dear Annis," Harriet said, still smiling, nearly as joyful as her great-niece at the success of their mission. "It has already begun."

39

James

Autumn wound to its close with clement weather that brought an abundant harvest from every sun-drenched Seabeck farm. The spring foals were thriving, bounding around their pasture with all the joy of youth and health. The fall foliage painted the hills and the coombe with red and gold and bronze. James had at last fully recovered from his strange illness in the summer.

There was no peace, though, for either the Marquess of Rosefield or the dowager marchioness. Despite the good harvest and the prompt rents of their tenants, expenses spiraled upward. The roof of Rosefield Hall sprouted two new, serious leaks. A hundred-year-old chimney gave way under the unusual bout of heat, its bricks tumbling over the gutters and nearly decapitating a gardener. One wing of the stable block suffered a small fire that destroyed the tack room and ruined half the hay stored in the loft. A bank loan with a steep rate of interest, taken out by the old marquess, seemed to grow larger every month. Lady Eleanor and Lord Rosefield were falling further behind than ever.

Though the London season was over, Lady Eleanor managed to invite a dwindling stream of young heiresses to Rosefield

Hall. James did his best to be polite, to take an interest, but to no avail. Even the prettiest face, the most delicate waist, the loveliest curls, seemed bland and uninteresting to him in comparison with the height and athleticism and carelessly freckled nose of Annis Allington. If the hair was fair, he wished it were dark. If the eyes were brown, he longed for forget-me-not eyes that looked so coolly onto the world. Mostly, the flow of inconsequential small talk made him yearn for the frankness of an American girl now lost to him.

"Rosefield, you must choose someone. You're twenty-one. It's time."

"I don't think, Mother, that my age has anything to do with it."

She sniffed and wriggled a bit against the strictures of her corset. "Perhaps not. But our finances have everything to do with it. I'm not sure we can survive another year." They were lingering over their coffee in the morning room. The weather had turned at last, causing Lady Eleanor to order a fire built.

"It's the debt that's holding us back, Mother. If we can't pay down the principal, we'll never get ahead."

"I know. I warned your father this could happen."

"Did you? You knew?"

"It was the house in London. Its roof was falling in, and your father was short of cash, so he took out a loan. He wasn't a practical man, I'm afraid. He may have ruined us." She sat stiffly, as always, and her face was as impassive as if she were reciting someone else's history. "That," she added, in a hard voice James had come to understand hid her real distress, "would be a shame, would it not? When all we need is an infusion of cash."

"Well, Mother," James said, trying to speak as evenly as she had. "I'm going to sell the High Point parcel. I can get a good price for it from Hemmings."

"I'm against it."

"I know. But unlike Father, I'm a practical man."

"I've brought you a half dozen suitable brides, Rosefield. Any one of them would have a generous settlement made on her by a father who will hardly notice the loss."

"I would rather lose the land than marry someone I don't care for."

"Care for! What does it matter if you care for her?"

"It matters to me." He rose abruptly and went to the fireplace. He put one hand in his pocket and the other on the mantel as he gazed down into the flames. Did he dare confess the truth to his mother? He heard her draw breath to press her argument, and he spoke in haste to forestall her. "I'm in love with Annis Allington, Mother."

"Goodness." Lady Eleanor, with a grunt, pushed herself to her feet. "Not that I think being in love is a real condition, Rosefield, but if you feel that way, why did you let her slip through your fingers?"

"She was never in my fingers," he said bitterly, staring down into the dancing fire. One of the small logs fell into two pieces, sending a drift of sparks up the chimney. He felt a bit like that log, falling into two pieces. One was here, arguing with his mother. The other was on a ship to New York to try again to woo his American girl.

"It's a figure of speech," his mother said. She smoothed the skirt of her morning dress as she came to stand beside him.

"I know. But Annis—between Mrs. Allington and you, and

me, I suppose, she felt trapped. Manipulated. She never wanted a titled husband. She never wanted to leave New York."

"You'll get over her," Lady Eleanor said. She didn't reach out to touch him. That was not a gesture that often passed between them. She did, however, allow a bit of warmth to creep into her voice, a tinge of sympathy. "But I'm sorry, Rosefield. I believe I understand. I liked her very well myself."

He straightened, facing her. "Did you? You haven't told me that."

"She's a clever girl, and not afraid of hard work. She's reasonably attractive, and though her stepmother is rather obviously nouveau riche, Annis is not. She has—I would say she has substance. And dignity." Lady Eleanor spread her hands. "I suppose it makes no difference, if she won't have you. My own feelings are of no consequence."

James smiled down at her. "Mother. Your feelings are absolutely of consequence, even though you pretend you don't have them."

Her lips twitched, as if she might smile back, but she evidently suppressed the urge. "What are we going to do, Rosefield?"

"Well." He cleared his throat and made himself hold her gaze. "You won't like it, but I've made decisions. Selling the High Point parcel will catch us up with the bank, although it won't reduce the principal. I would like you to sell some of the old jewelry you don't wear. I won't order you to do that, though. I'll leave it up to you. I'm afraid, however, we have to sell the London house." He didn't allow his doubts to show in his face or in his voice. The title was his, after all. It was time he behaved like it.

She didn't pull herself up and glare as if she were the queen and he were an unruly subject. She had done that often enough, but this time she didn't scold or repeat her stance that families who began to sell things off were doomed. She only gave a small, resigned sigh and said, "Yes, of course, Rosefield. I've set out a diamond brooch and those hideous rubies, and I'll take them up to Marsden in the city. Of course if we must sell the London house, then we must. It will all be just as you wish."

He had prepared for an argument, and he was a bit disconcerted by her acquiescence. He said, a bit too eagerly, "I can go with you to Marsden's."

"Not necessary." Lady Eleanor reached for the bellpull. "I'll go tomorrow. No point in delaying."

"I'll set the sale in motion. Hemmings has been asking for years to buy that land."

"I hate giving in to that old reprobate," Lady Eleanor said, but without heat. "He'll leer at me every time he sees me, as if he knows all our business."

"Do try not to let him bother you, Mother. Rosefield Hall is two centuries older than that hovel of his, and Seabeck..."

"I know," she said. Her offhand manner didn't fool him. The pretense that she didn't care was her protection. "Even without the High Point parcel, Seabeck is twice the size of his estate."

"And twice as productive."

"Is it? Excellent. Well done, Rosefield."

She was gone a moment later, sweeping out of the room with her customary regal bearing, leaving her son blinking at the unaccustomed praise.

James went to his study to write to Hemmings after luncheon, but when he stood beside the window, watching the foals kick up their heels in the autumn sunshine, he felt an irresistible urge to be out of doors. One more day would make no difference, he told himself. A good gallop with Seastar might help to drive the taste of failure from his mouth.

The brisk, bright air agreed with the horse, too, it seemed. As James mounted, Seastar sidestepped and swished his tail in his eagerness. James held him in until he was sure his muscles were warm enough, which was no small feat. When he thought it was safe, he let Seastar canter, then gallop.

James hadn't intended to ride to High Point, but Seastar's liveliness commanded all his attention, and he hardly realized they were on that road until they were halfway there. He wasn't sure which of them had made the choice, but he gave in to it. He let Seastar gallop out his coltish energy, then slowed him to a steady trot as they wound along the cliffs.

He hadn't ridden in this direction since the day he had proposed marriage to Annis Allington. As the three ancient boulders of High Point came into view, he felt a wrench of nostalgia for the day he and she had spent here, though it had ended in such humiliation.

He slid from the saddle and dropped Seastar's reins to let him crop the sparse yellow grass around the wind-stunted trees. James recalled laying out the picnic and remembered Annis's unabashed enthusiasm over the food. Not for her the dainty appetites of the well-bred English girls he knew. She had an appetite for life in general. She loved horses, and flowers, and birds. She was intensely interested in plants, especially herbs. She had such a vital presence in his mind that it seemed impossible she was not standing beside him.

They had made their peace after his ill-fated proposal. They had become friends in the aftermath of his illness, and in the generosity of Rosefield Hall as she dealt with her stepmother's sickness. She had exclaimed over the little parting gift he had given her, a daguerreotype of Seastar, which she promised to show to her stableman. In return she had left him a novel she finished on the voyage to Liverpool, for him to read while he recuperated. They had said farewell as friends.

He longed for another chance with her, but the moment had come and gone.

He walked up to the peak of the cliff and stood looking down at the strand beneath. The gulls cried overhead, and the waves murmured below, all the sweet things he loved about this spot. All the things he was going to lose.

Of course he could still come here. Hemmings wouldn't mind, but it would be a painful reminder of how low Seabeck had sunk, selling off land that had belonged to the family since the Wars of the Roses.

James stood still, his hands in the pockets of his jacket, his overlong forelock lifting in the wind. He closed his eyes and breathed the salty air, hoping it might soothe his injured spirit.

When it hit him, his eyes flew open. He froze in place, staring unseeing out to sea.

What was this? It didn't feel like anything he had experienced before. It was more than an idea. It was a conviction. A compulsion. It came to him fully formed, inarguable and irresistible. His blood sang with it, and his body tingled all over.

He was going to New York. He was going to see Annis without the distractions of maternal pressures and weird illnesses and bizarre nightmares. He was going to try one more time, because if he didn't, he would never be able to forget her.

He felt a swell of confidence. It was the right thing to do. It was the perfect thing to do.

He *knew* it.

In her herbarium in the Dakota, Harriet stood back, smiling. Her ametrine still glowed, dark-purple threads throbbing through the yellow-and-violet crystal, fading gently as its energy was expended. The pungent smoke from the herbs she had burned—dried rosemary and Saint-John's-wort, to ease inner struggles, wild carrot and bishop's wort for calmness and understanding—wafted up to dissipate against the high ceiling.

Beside the candle and her amulet rested a strand of Annis's dark hair, retrieved from the apron she wore during their sessions together. There was also a pressed field rose, plucked from the Seabeck woods, to represent James, Marquess of Rosefield.

It was very early in New York, dawn not yet breaking over the park. Grace was still sleeping, and Harriet assumed Annis was, too. She estimated the time in Dorset to be just after one in the afternoon.

This rite—this cantrip—was her secret. Annis would have objected out of pride, and James—James still had no idea of the forces that had been at work on him.

Harriet would never compel the young people together, not as Frances had tried to do. She had created no philter, no potion, and certainly no manikins. The strand of hair, the pressed field rose, were merely tokens, symbols of Annis and James.

She had sent her intention, the most innocent of all intentions, out into the world. It was her wish and her prayer that, if the two would be happy together, they would find each other again. She used her rite to invite James to America. If he no longer thought of Annis, if his feelings had been created only by the *maleficia*, he would decline. He wouldn't even know he was doing it.

But if, as she suspected, he had fallen in love—if, like Annis, he was treasuring the small tokens they had given each other—he would come. If Annis's name came to his lips often, as his did to hers, if he thought of her when he looked at his Andalusians, as she thought of him when she looked at Black Satin, then he would come.

Love was its own kind of magic. It needed no help from witchcraft. It required only opportunity.

She touched the pressed flower with her fingers and murmured one more time, as if she were whispering in someone's ear,

Don't delay.
Come today.

Harriet was certain Annis would be overjoyed to see James again. She was certain, also, that the marquess would accept her magical invitation. As her rite ended, in that powerful moment when the stone shimmered and the smoke curled around her and the electric tingle of magic flowed through her body, she *knew*.

40

Annis

Annis rode Black Satin every day during the cool, bright days of autumn.

She spoiled him so much that Robbie scolded her, warning her that too many treats would not help the stallion's health, and that too much indulgence would ruin the exacting training routine they had always employed.

"No need to make up for the harm," Robbie said. "He's forgotten it, even if you haven't."

Robbie was wrong, though Annis didn't try to explain that to him. She sensed the horse's need to see her every day, as if their enforced separation, ending in his being taken away from his home, had really hurt him. She thought he must be like a child who couldn't understand why a parent had abandoned him and didn't trust in that parent's return.

She had known from the moment of his homecoming how distressed he had been.

She had been waiting in the breakfast room, where a window gave a view of the drive and the stableyard at the corner of the house. She saw Neufeld's stableman ride up on a thick-legged cart horse, with Bits and Sally on halter leads. Gentle Sally followed the cart horse in her customary docile fashion, although her neck was stretched to its limit as she tried to keep up on her short legs. Bits, however, was anything but docile. His head was high, and even from the window Annis could see how he jerked the halter lead so hard she feared he would dislocate the stableman's shoulder. Bits stamped and sidestepped, blowing spittle and switching his tail.

It must have seemed to the stableman like bad temper, but Annis knew better. Anxiety and fear were making her beloved horse behave in such a way. One of his best qualities, which brought many mares to him, was his easy disposition, but only if Annis was there to manage him. He would not, in the end, have pleased Mr. Neufeld or his customers.

She flew from the breakfast room and cut across the shrubbery to the stableyard. She slowed as she approached the party, not wanting to startle the horses, but she called out, "Bits! Bits, easy, easy. I'm here. It's all right now. I'm here."

He whirled, finally succeeding in ripping the halter lead from the stableman's hand. He stood for a moment, trembling, staring, then trotted toward her with a strong, high step. The stableman cried, "Miss, have a care!"

It must have looked as if Black Satin were going to trample her, but he stopped when his feet were just inches from her own. He blew a noisy breath and lowered his head as she put up her arms. He pressed his warm forehead to her chest, and she hugged him to her, shedding two hot tears of relief. When she pulled back to look into his deep dark eyes, she thought that if horses could cry, he would be weeping, too.

The stableman dismounted and stood, clearly mystified by this display. He shuffled his feet and fiddled with his stained cloth cap until Annis turned to him.

"Thank you for bringing Black Satin home," she said. "And Sally. I'll take them now." She picked up the end of Bits's dragging lead and held out her hand for Sally's.

He handed it to her with some reluctance. "Miss, I'm supposed to take the payment back. For the horses, I mean."

"Oh yes, of course. There's a check for you. I forgot to bring it out." She stroked Bits's cheek. "Let me just stable these two, and I'll be right back."

Belatedly Robbie appeared, hurrying across the stableyard. "Here, Miss Annis. I'll take 'em."

Annis handed the two leads to Robbie, but not before planting an unabashed kiss on Bits's wide, smooth cheek. Neufeld's stableman gasped at such behavior with a breeding stallion. Robbie only chuckled.

Annis had worried that when the effects of their cantrip wore off, her father would be angry at having been manipulated into buying back the two horses, but he wasn't. He shrugged and said, "It wasn't that much money, and now I don't have to fork over a big dowry."

"I wasn't aware you objected to paying my dowry."

"Your stepmother gave me no peace until I agreed to it. That's all over now."

Frances herself made no comment. She continued mute and unresponsive.

Velma had transferred all her devotion to Frances. She seemed content to be the one to feed her, bathe her, dress and undress her. Annis, seeing this, ordered a cot moved into Frances's room so Velma could sleep when Frances did. Velma brought all her few belongings and stowed them in a wardrobe Frances no longer used. Annis was touched to see the cut-glass swan candleholder resting on a little stool beside her cot. It held a candle that had never been burned. It was as pristine as the day she had bought it in the shop near the *strega*'s.

Once, when Annis asked Velma if she wanted to continue her unrelenting care of Frances, the maid said simply, "Mrs. Frances needs me. You never did."

It was true. Annis had never wanted a lady's maid and was content to be free of Velma's anxieties and clumsy ministrations. Still, she felt Velma deserved better pay for her constant attention to Frances, and risked angering her father to ask for it.

"I suppose I'll have to pay the girl more," he said. "It seems I'm a widower again, but still with the responsibility of supporting a wife."

"Have you been to see her, Papa? Even one time?" They had been home for weeks.

"What's the point?" he growled and refused to discuss it again.

As the sultry summer melted into a cooler autumn, Annis divided her time between riding Black Satin and helping Robbie in the stables and her work with Aunt Harriet at the Dakota. The doorman of the Dakota scowled at first over a young lady arriving alone and going up the corner staircase to Miss Bishop's apartment, but in time he became accustomed to it. Now when she hurried in, flushed and bright eyed from the walk from Riverside Drive, he tipped his cap, greeted her by name, and gestured to the staircase as if he were one of her own servants. If she had a basket with her, he sometimes asked if she needed help carrying it up the stairs. When she departed, he tipped his cap again and wished her a good afternoon.

She loved working with Aunt Harriet. It was good work, more practical than magical. She was thrilled the day she was allowed to compound a tincture all by herself, for a patient named Dora Schuyler, who suffered from painful menses. Annis took careful notes for the book of remedies she was steadily filling, writing down the elements of the tincture—cramp bark, poppy flowers, cohosh and burdock root. She learned the technique of macerating the tincture in alcohol and wrote down the proportions before she placed everything in a jar.

It had to sit for two weeks. Harriet had made an appointment by mail with the patient to come for the remedy, and she allowed Annis to be present as she handed the medicine to Mrs. Schuyler, who was a well-dressed, fragile-looking woman.

When Mrs. Schuyler had paid her fee and departed, Annis said, "Mrs. Schuyler seems terribly sad. Is that because of her pain?"

"In a way," Harriet said. "She is sad, and there's little we can do to help her with that."

"She doesn't seem to mind the cost of her remedy."

"No. Money is not one of her concerns. I don't hesitate to charge a full price for my patients who can afford it. It helps subsidize my patients who can't."

"You've seen Mrs. Schuyler before."

"I have, but on principle I can't speak to you about it. I will teach you, though, in time, and without mentioning names, how we help women who come to us with a certain problem."

Harriet wielded knowledge and experience and wisdom in her herbarium in equal measures. Annis watched her chop and dice and pound, her face intent, her steady instructions so full of information Annis had to rush to write everything down. It hardly seemed possible, watching Harriet go about the quotidian work of an herbalist, that she had once watched her great-aunt wield a magic so powerful she had literally lifted from the ground.

Only two things marred Annis's contentment. One was, of course, Frances's failure to recover from the effects of the *maleficia*. Harriet asked, each time Annis appeared, if there was any change. There never was. Annis worried that Harriet blamed herself, but when she tried to talk about it, Harriet put up her hand and said, "Frances brought this on herself. I only wish it would not cost her whole life." She turned away, muttering under her breath, "Such a waste."

The second thing was one Annis never spoke of to anyone. She thought that if she didn't talk about it, in time she wouldn't think about it. Even better, she hoped, she would stop dreaming of it. Of him. Of James.

It was embarrassing, really. She had been so adamant, both with him and with Lady Eleanor, that she had no interest in marriage. She knew her rejection had hurt him, and she hoped his feelings had been soothed by her care for him after the crisis. She never told him what had really happened the night Frances magicked him. She knew he didn't remember any of it and would be aghast if he did. She didn't want that. It would only hurt him further.

But she thought about him all the time. She couldn't help it.

When she went to the stables, she imagined the foals Black Satin would throw with Dancer or Breeze. When she walked from Riverside Drive to Harriet's apartment, she thought how simple and elegant Rosefield Hall was, compared with the ostentation of the Dakota. When she and Harriet foraged in the park, she remembered with a pang of nostalgia the riches of the woods and fields of Seabeck. She had placed the daguerreotype of Seastar on her dressing table, and each time it caught her eye she pictured James's lanky figure, easy in the saddle at the trot and the canter, less comfortable in formal clothes. She remembered his disapproving expression as he looked down on her in Regent's Park, offended by the American girl with no manners. She recalled his stiff proposal and his pain at her refusal.

She supposed she would never know if he might have come to like her for herself. If his feelings had been left unaffected by the *maleficia*, would he have changed his mind? She doubted it. His first reactions to her, before Frances magicked him, were no doubt his true feelings. They had parted on friendly terms, but he had not tried to stop her from leaving. No doubt by now, healed from the effects of the *maleficia*, he had forgotten her completely. Perhaps he had met a more suitable bride and was even now planning his marriage. She tried to pretend to herself she wouldn't mind that, but without much success. The truth was that she minded very much indeed.

She had sent a formal letter of thanks to Lady Eleanor and James for their hospitality and kindness in the face of Frances's illness. A brief note came to Allington House a month later, asking after Frances and wishing Annis well. Lady Eleanor had signed it. There was nothing from James.

She still had the manikins. She had carried them home in the bottom of her jewel case, then wrapped them in an old chemise and tucked them beneath a pile of winter nightdresses. Twice she took them out, laid them on her dressing table, and gazed at them.

They were supposed to be destroyed by the one who had made them, Harriet had said. One day soon, Annis told herself, she would take Frances's hands in hers and guide them in destroying the manikin that represented herself, tear off the fluff of hair, wipe away that strangely red mouth.

But James's figure, crude though it was—somehow she didn't want to see it ruined.

She convinced herself Aunt Harriet had forgotten about the manikins. As time passed, she was more and more reluctant to admit to her great-aunt—to confess, rather—that she still had them in her keeping. The secret nagged at her, like a pebble in her shoe that she was trying to ignore. It was all tangled up with her feelings for James, her nostalgia for Seabeck and Rosefield Hall and the Andalusians. She even missed Lady Eleanor's cool glance and efficient ways. All of these thoughts left her confused. Unfamiliar emotions swept over her at the oddest times so that she felt by turns weepy and exhilarated, thrilled by her work with Harriet but lonely in her bed at night.

In early November, as the first chill of winter crept through Central Park and caused Robbie to light the oil stove in the stables, Annis turned eighteen. Mrs. King baked an enormous cake, enough for all the staff to share. Robbie gave her a lovely new bridle for Bits, one he had been laboring over in secret for months. She hugged him, making him blush and turn his cap in his hands. Her father gave her a gold bracelet and the papers that told her she had come into a small inheritance left by her mother. Harriet gave her a beautiful book of herbs, so large and heavy she almost couldn't carry it home.

She didn't expect anything from Frances, of course, nor did she receive anything.

Frances disappeared that very day.

Annis had insisted Velma leave Frances for a time to join the kitchen staff for a piece of birthday cake. Velma resisted at first, but Annis could see how gratified she was at her welcome in the kitchen. The maids had hardly seen her since her return from England. Velma blushed and gave the maids a shy wave, and Mrs. King cut her a generous slice of cake with a dollop of thick cream.

When she was finished, Mrs. King cut a tiny slice of cake for Frances. "Mrs. Frances won't eat it, probably," Velma said.

"We can only try," Mrs. King said. Velma took the plate, with a sliver of cake arranged on a doily, and carried it back upstairs.

Moments later Velma's cries of alarm carried down the staircase and into the dining room where Annis and her father sat over their coffee. George didn't move, but dropped his chin onto his chest as if that would shut out Velma's shrieks.

Annis jumped up, letting her napkin slip to the floor, and dashed toward the stairs. She found Velma on the landing, tears streaming down her red cheeks. "She ain't there, miss, she ain't anywhere!"

Annis took the stairs two at a time. On the landing she took Velma's arm and steered her up the second flight. As they walked she said, "Now, Velma, calm down. Don't cry anymore. Frances must have wandered off. I'll help you look."

"She ain't never done that, miss, not in all this time!"

"I know. Perhaps she's feeling better?"

Even Velma knew better than that, and didn't bother answering. Together they went to Frances's bedroom, checked her dressing room, looked in her bathroom. They peered into all the other bedrooms, George's, Annis's, where Annis surreptitiously checked that the manikins were where she had left them. They climbed the back staircase to look in the servants' rooms. Annis was startled at how small and cold these were. She didn't think she had ever been in one of them before, and their paucity of comforts bothered her.

She and Velma flew back down the stairs to the kitchen, the

pantry, the storeroom, both parlors and the breakfast room, even the little room beside the servants' entrance at the back of the house where coats and umbrellas were hung and a rack held muddy boots awaiting cleaning. There was no sign of Frances.

Annis escorted a still-weepy Velma back to the kitchen, where she turned her over to Mrs. King for a cup of tea. "We'll find her, Velma," Annis said. "Stop crying. It wasn't your fault."

"I've got Velma, Miss Annis," Mrs. King said. "I've sent Robbie and Freddie out to look in the stables and the garden shed, just in case. You go tell your father what's happened."

It was odd, Annis thought, as she started back to the dining room, that her father had stayed where he was, as if he couldn't hear the uproar around the house, the clatter of feet, the calling voices, the slamming of doors. She half expected to see he had finally left the table to join the search.

He hadn't. He sat in his heavy armchair, staring at his coffee as it grew cold. He hadn't touched the slice of cake resting in front of him.

"Papa?" Annis said uneasily. Instinctively she put her hand to her collar, where the moonstone nestled against her throat. Her father looked up at her, his eyes heavy with misery. With guilt. The moonstone throbbed under her fingers, and she knew. Suddenly, without the slightest doubt, she *knew*.

"Papa! You—you sent her away!"

"I had the doctor come for her."

"Where did she go?"

"She's in a better place. A place she can be cared for."

"What place?"

"I don't see what difference it makes, Annis. She won't notice anyway."

"Papa—" Annis gasped as the moonstone vibrated against her skin and a knowledge was borne in her mind, knowledge she didn't want and couldn't accept. "Papa, I can't believe—you sent her *there*?"

He blinked at the force of her voice. "How could you possibly know where I sent her?"

Annis ignored the question. Her heart began to pound, and her throat constricted. "That place! It's horrible. The way they treat people—I can't believe you would be so cruel!"

"She's lost her mind," he said, his voice like gravel.

"You don't know that!"

"I don't—I can't stand looking at her like that."

"You never see her as it is!"

He shoved himself to his feet and thundered, "But I know she's there! Drooling, mindless—it's horrible! I'm not having that in my house!"

He spun away from her and stamped toward the door. Mrs. King was in the doorway, and in his haste George stepped on the cook's trailing hem, knocking her off balance so she stumbled. Annis leaped to steady her before she fell.

Mrs. King, wide-eyed and wordless, stared after her employer. Annis patted her shoulder, but she had no words, either. She knew her father could be ruthless in business. She knew any affection between him and his second wife had died long ago. But this—this was too horrible to contemplate. Pretty Frances, who loved nice clothes and hairstyles and beautiful jewelry— poor, ill Frances, in that place!

Whatever she had done, she didn't deserve this.

Mrs. King recovered herself enough to croak, "Miss Annis, what's happened? Do you know where Mrs. Frances is?"

"I do, Mrs. King," Annis said, her voice barely steadier than Mrs. King's. "I'm sorry to say I do. Papa sent her to Blackwell's Island. To the asylum."

"Oh no! Surely he did not," Mrs. King protested. "Did he tell you that?"

Annis shook her head. "No. But I know."

Mrs. King's answer was interrupted by the clang of the iron knocker at the front door. She threw up her hands in frustration and went to answer it. Annis, at a loss for what to do next, followed her.

On the doorstep, with his manservant waiting beside a hired carriage in the drive, stood James, Marquess of Rosefield. He was in the act of bowing slightly to Mrs. King when he caught sight of Annis, and she of him.

"Miss Allington," he said, snatching off his top hat and bowing from the waist. "I do hope my arrival isn't spoiling your birthday party."

41

James

His timing could not have been worse, but he didn't realize that straightaway. At first he simply thought he had made a ghastly mistake in coming.

There seemed to be some sort of disruption in the house. He heard pounding feet, raised voices, a door slamming. Worse, behind the slender woman in a cook's apron who had opened the door, Annis looked as if she had suffered a shock. Her face was white except for two scarlet spots on her cheeks. Her mouth opened when she saw him, but it seemed she couldn't speak.

It was his worst fear. Annis was not pleased to see him, not at all happy about his unannounced arrival.

He stood on the step, feeling tall and awkward and out of place. Perry, behind him, gave a choked sound of embarrassment. The woman in the apron stared up at him in dismay as Annis closed her mouth, opened it again, closed it again. For long, miserable seconds no one moved.

Finally James spoke in a hollow voice. "It seems I have misjudged my moment."

At that the tableau burst apart like an ice jam cracking into pieces. Annis cried, "Oh, James, no, not at all! I am so glad to see you! So very glad!"

The woman in the apron stood back, holding the door wide and saying, "Do come in, sir, come in out of the cold. Your man, too."

Perry breathed a sigh of relief so gusty James thought it might penetrate right into the house.

James himself, with his hat in his hand, took the step over the sill. Annis seized his free hand in both of hers and drew him into an elegant, high-ceilinged foyer. He took in the polish of the tiled floor and the brilliance of the large electrified chandelier overhead as Annis said, "Mrs. King, can you send for Robbie? He'll see to the carriage and horse."

Perry, coming in behind James, said, "It's only hired."

"Oh yes, but the horse will need a bit of mash and some water. And Mrs. King, perhaps the driver could use a cup of something."

This set the aproned woman scurrying off. The slamming of doors and pounding of feet had ceased, leaving only the clink of dishes being moved from a room somewhere beyond the staircase. Annis said, "Perry, it's good to see you again. Do bring in the valises, and pull the door closed, could you? It's icy out tonight."

Perry lifted the valises and carried them inside, then turned back to close the door against the night air. James looked around him, trying to regain his balance after the nasty moment on the doorstep. For an awful few seconds he had thought he and Perry might need to turn right around and go back to the ship's terminal. Now he was being greeted with all the enthusiasm a welcome guest might expect. It was disorienting.

Annis had still not released his gloved hand. He looked down at her long, strong fingers gripping his, and the wave of relief that swept over him was almost more bewildering than the strangeness upon which the front door of Allington House had opened. He struggled to find words that would not sound foolish, and could think only of, "Thank you for letting us in."

Her color was returning, the scarlet spots in her cheeks subsiding. "Oh, James! There was never any doubt of your coming in, but—oh, I'm so glad you've come, and it's the perfect time, the most perfect time!"

For Annis, this was indeed effusive. He turned his hand to catch hers and carry it to his lips. The gesture felt completely natural. "Have you had a happy birthday? A good day?"

"It was, until—until just before you arrived. I'll explain. It's all a terrible mess." She reached for a bell that rested on a side table and rang it. "Mrs. King will get someone to help Perry with the bags. There's a guest room just to the left at the top of the stairs. Perry, you may have to share a room. I do hope you won't mind."

James was impressed by the efficiency with which Annis directed the servants. In no time someone had taken his hat and coat and gloves. Annis led him to a charming small parlor, and Mrs. King, the aproned woman, came in with a tray of coffee and what seemed to be the remains of a birthday cake. Annis stirred up the fire herself and added a small pine log, which smelled wonderful as it caught and began to burn. She pointed James to a well-cushioned armchair, and she pulled up a hassock near it for herself.

Perched there, her linked hands on one knee, she said, "Is coffee and cake enough? Have you had supper?"

"Coffee and cake is lovely," he said. "I'm delighted to share in your celebration."

She wrinkled her nose, making the freckles dance. "The celebration rather fell apart, I'm afraid."

"So I gather. I do hope everyone is well."

"Everyone except Frances."

"Ah. My mother told me there was no improvement in her condition."

"What's happened is ugly, James. Horrible. I'm ashamed to tell you."

She waited until he had sipped some warming coffee and taken a taste of Mrs. King's confection. As she told her story, his appetite disappeared, and he laid down his fork. He hadn't been susceptible to Mrs. Allington's charms, but the thought of that lively woman consigned to a madhouse turned his stomach.

It developed, also, that the eruption between Annis and her father meant he would not meet George Allington that night. She explained that her father had stormed out of the house and would probably sleep at his factory.

James said uncomfortably, "Perhaps, if your father is not here, it's not appropriate that you invite me to stay."

Her expression hardened, and she thrust out her chin. "I don't give a fig for 'appropriate,' James, as I think you know. You're my guest, not Papa's. I'm eighteen. I'm not a child."

"No. No, I suppose you're an adult now."

"Officially. I've always been mature for my years, everyone says so."

"Indeed."

"I've come into my inheritance, too."

James hated himself for feeling a flicker of optimism over this news. "Your—your inheritance? Really?"

The optimism was considerably tempered when she said, "My

mother left me some money. It's not much, but it's enough to buy at least two mares for my bloodline."

James nodded. It was better that way. She would understand it was not her money that had brought him to New York. "Congratulations, then, Annis. I'm happy for you."

"And you, James?" she asked, giving him that direct forget-me-not look that had at first disturbed him and which now he loved. "Are you happy?"

"I'm happy to be here with you," he said simply.

She reached up her hand, and he took it. They sat that way for a few moments, not speaking. The fire crackled and sent up a little shower of festive sparks. James thought he would never smell burning pine again without thinking of this tender fragment of time, with Annis's hand in his and her strong profile glowing in the firelight. They were, at the very least, friends. Good friends, who could sit together in silence, hands linked, content just to be together. That was no small thing, after the months of misery.

It even seemed possible, in this moment, that his heart need not break after all.

42

Harriet

Harriet had seen the Marquess of Rosefield only from a distance, but she recognized him immediately. She had been expecting him.

Grace answered the door, and Harriet emerged from the herbarium just in time to see Grace stop and stare, startled by the sight of the tall, thin young man at Annis's side.

Annis said, "Good morning, Grace. This is James. I know it's early, but I need to see Aunt Harriet as soon as possible."

"This is—oh my, Miss Annis, of course it is!" Grace astounded Harriet by dropping a perfect curtsy. "Lord Rosefield, I believe, is your proper title, sir, is it not? What a great pleasure to see you here in America! Miss Harriet will be delighted—why, I'll fetch her right now—but I do hope, my lord, you had a most pleasant journey, and that you'll find our country as beautiful as your own. Miss Annis has told us all about it, and—"

Harriet saw the young man's eyes widen at this flood of conversation. She stepped out into the hallway so he and Annis could see her and said, "Thank you, Grace," cutting through the tide of words as gently as she could.

Annis brushed past Grace and hurried down the hallway. James hesitated, then handed his hat and coat to Grace with a little nod of acknowledgment and followed. "Aunt Harriet!" Annis exclaimed. "I have to talk to you, to tell you—"

Harriet interrupted her. "Of course, Annis, we'll talk. But first, do please introduce me properly."

"Oh yes. Sorry. This is James. James, this is my great-aunt, Harriet Bishop."

The marquess inclined his head. "Miss Bishop."

She liked him at once, but was not tempted, as Grace had been, to curtsy. She put out her hand in the American style, and he took it. "Marquess, I'm glad to meet you at last. I've heard a great deal about you."

"And I about you," he said, shaking and then releasing her hand. "I will be happy to postpone pleasantries, as Annis is quite upset about her stepmother."

"Is she?" Harriet led the way toward the parlor. "Grace, some coffee, I think, as it's so early. Marquess Rosefield, do come this way. Annis, tell me what's happened."

Annis began speaking even before they had taken seats. Harriet bent her head to listen, even as she noticed that the marquess took a straight chair as close to Annis as he could.

"Blackwell's Island, Aunt Harriet!" Annis finished. "My father—I can't believe he would be so cruel. It's true she seems— I can't argue that it seems her mind is gone, but I know—" She caught herself and only just managed to stop herself from casting a guilty glance James's way. "That is, I—I worry—that she's still there, trapped."

The marquess asked, "Is this place so terrible? We have lunatic asylums in England, of course, and while they were appalling in years past, I understand they have improved greatly."

"It *is* terrible!" Annis said. "There was a book about Blackwell's Island, and a great public outcry, but very little has been done."

"I'm afraid Annis is right," Harriet said. "Blackwell's calls itself an asylum, but it is in effect a prison, simply a place to put people away. I'm shocked Mr. Allington would allow this to happen to Frances, no matter how ill she is."

"You are related to Mrs. Allington, I believe," the marquess said.

"We are distant cousins."

"Then it's only natural for you to be concerned with her well-being."

"We all are!" Annis assured him.

"Are you quite sure Frances is in Blackwell's?" Harriet asked Annis.

"I suspected, when we found she had disappeared. Then Papa admitted it." Annis's eyes met Harriet's in a glance full of meaning, and Harriet understood. Annis hadn't had to guess where Frances had been taken.

Grace came in with a tray. "Here we are," she said. "I do hope, my lord, that you like our coffee. I believe it's different from the sort you're used to. There's fresh cream, and some bread and butter, in case you haven't had your breakfast yet. I brought some of my own almond cookies, too, what Miss Annis is so fond of. Please help yourself if you're hungry. And you can..." She was still talking as she left the tray on the low table in front of the divan and bustled back to the kitchen.

Despite the grimness of their visit, Annis and James shared an amused glance. Harriet was pleased to see a twinkle come into James's eyes and a smile curve his lips. She much preferred a man with a sense of humor.

"Annis," she said, "I'll do everything I can. For now, do have a cup of coffee, both of you, and a bite to eat. Grace is a great talker, but she's also a wonderful baker."

The marquess said, "You're fortunate in your housekeeper, I see, Miss Bishop."

"I don't know what I would do without her."

When the coffee had been poured and the plates passed around, Harriet leaned back in the divan, her cup and saucer on her knee. The three of them made polite conversation, very little of which Harriet would later remember. Her mind was circling around the problem that loomed before her, distracting her from pleasantries and small talk. Annis, seeing this, cut the visit short, saying she and James were going to ride in the park if it didn't rain.

Before she left, however, she used the excuse of an embrace to whisper in Harriet's ear. "Send for me when you're ready. I want to help."

When they had gone, Harriet helped Grace carry the teacups and the tray back to the kitchen. Grace said, "Now, there's a nice young man for Miss Annis, isn't it? Is this the one, do you think? How lovely that would be, and she would be Lady Rosefield! Wouldn't that be a thing, now? I was that surprised to see him with her this morning. I had no idea he was coming, did you? You didn't mention it at all."

As usual, no response was needed to Grace's chatter, and Harriet didn't try to give one. She was laying plans. She had no appointments for the day, which was fortunate. Despite the threatening rain, she would have to go out for supplies. It wasn't a good time of year to forage in the park, but with luck the *strega* would have what she needed.

Perhaps the old Italian witch would have a word of advice. She needed that, too.

Signora Carcano rummaged in her back room for many minutes. Harriet, restive and tense, roamed the shop, examining shelves of jars and vials, racks of scissors and knives, a counter spread with stones of various colors. She picked one up, a rough-edged stone she thought was black but that turned out to be so thick with dust it stained her glove gray. Beneath the dust the stone was a deep blue shot through with black veins. An amethyst, in its raw form. She blew it clean and took off her glove to cradle it in her palm.

The *strega* spoke from the door to the back room. "You will buy that," she announced. "It is right for you."

Harriet glanced back at her and nodded. "Yes, it is."

"Also, I found the *uovo di serpente*. The egg of the snake." The old woman held up a small bag of what looked like burlap, with a bit of brown string holding the neck together.

Harriet moved back to the counter as Signora Carcano set the bag down and pulled the string to open it. With careful fingers Harriet lifted out the old stone and set it in the nest of fraying burlap. It was small and oval, black and gray, pierced through by a single hole, an opening created over centuries by the force of water.

"This is it," Harriet said. "It's perfect."

"Is very old," the *strega* said. "Roman. I bring from Italy."

"We call it an adder stone," Harriet said. "I'm grateful you had this. I'm in need of it, to help someone."

"The younger witch," the *strega* said, and she tapped her nose with her finger. "The pretty one. Much *buio* she has. Darkness."

"Yes." Harriet touched the stone with her finger. "My grandmother had one of these, though I don't know what became of it. She used it to cast a glamour, just once."

"Glamour?" The signora put her head to one side, her gray eyebrows lifting.

"I don't know the Italian. In English, it means a deception. A trick of magic, to hide something—or in this case someone—in plain sight."

"Is very dangerous."

"Yes."

"*Sì.* This glamour—we would call it *fascino.* It is fragile. It can break, *subito.* You have a lamen, to protect you?"

Harriet knew the word, though she hadn't heard it in years. She didn't usually show her amulet to people, but in this case it seemed the right thing to do. She tugged the chain out from beneath her shirtwaist and lifted the ametrine into the light.

Signora Carcano held out her wrinkled hand, palm up. Harriet felt a twinge of reluctance, but it subsided as she unclasped the chain to lay the amulet in the old woman's hand.

"Ametrine," the old witch murmured. "Amethyst and citrine together. Healing and clarity, very good. Someone gave you this with much love."

"My grandmother."

"Makes you powerful. Your *nonna*'s power joined with yours." The *strega* handed back the amulet. "I wish you don't do this."

"I must. She's in trouble, and it's partly my fault."

The old woman thought for a moment, pursing her wrinkled lips. "I advise?" she said.

"Please."

"Before you create this—this glamour—call on your *nonna* to help you. To protect you. You have an apprentice?"

"I do."

"She, too, must help you. I give you a citrine, to keep with the amethyst. You put them together, for balance."

"Do you have a moonstone in the shop?"

The *strega* paused, a finger on her chin, then made her way to the cluttered counter where the stones lay in a tumble. She stirred the pile, plucked out one tiny, pearly gem, and brought it back. "Your apprentice?" she asked.

"Yes."

"Is good. All three stones together for your work. To gather the power."

"Thank you, signora."

"*Prego.*" Signora Carcano replaced the adder stone in its bag and wrapped the three crystals in a twist of paper. "You return the *uovo di serpente*, after."

"Yes, of course."

Harriet paid her and tucked her purchases into her handbag. As she left the shop, she heard the *strega* muttering to herself. She glanced back and saw that Signora Carcano had brought her own lamen out into the dim light. It looked like it might be a large cross, silver perhaps, but gone black with age. She was murmuring a prayer, or an intention.

Harriet hoped it was for success in the task that lay ahead of her.

43

Harriet

"How does it work?" Annis asked.

Harriet blew an anxious breath. "I don't know for certain that it *will* work," she admitted. "I've never done this before. Grandmother Beryl only did it once, and she never wanted to do it a second time."

"Just tell me what to do."

Harriet's nervousness eased in the presence of Annis's trust and courage. She had told her about the *strega*'s warning. She understood the risk they were taking.

"We'll put the stones together, where the candle flame will shine on them."

Annis accepted Harriet's ametrine from her hand and removed her own moonstone from around her neck. She set them on the worktable, where the amethyst and citrine and the little moonstone from the *strega* waited. "Why do stones have such power?"

"They're the stuff of the earth," Harriet said. "Try to imagine how old they are, how long they lay waiting to be found. They carry the energy of eons inside them."

Harriet had spent the previous evening preparing an incense.

She had chopped several sprigs of thyme, for courage, and added shavings of sandalwood and ground cedar needles for protection. She explained the mixture to Annis. "The incense is to help us draw on our best selves, our strength and our boldness. Once we begin we must not look back, and we must act quickly, before the glamour fades."

"Will they really not be able to see her?"

"If we are successful." She took the little burlap bag from her pocket and slid out the adder stone.

"Oh!" Annis said softly. "Is that it?"

"It is. Signora Carcano says it's Roman, very old. I believe we can trust her."

"May I touch it?"

"Of course." She handed the cool bit of stone to Annis, who took it in both hands, cupping it between them. She closed her eyes, and her lips parted in wonder.

"It's very old, Aunt Harriet. So many hands have touched it. They—they leave an imprint. I can almost see them."

Harriet accepted the adder stone back into her own hand. "I don't feel it," she said ruefully.

"Perhaps I'm imagining it," Annis hastened to say.

"No, no, Annis. Trust yourself. Part of what we do *is* imagination, of course, but it's also instinct. Ignoring your instinct, your intuition, will make it shrivel and die. It will atrophy, and that would be a terrible waste of your ability."

Harriet drew the blinds so she and Annis could focus on the candle flame and the answering light in the stones. She gave the adder stone back to Annis. "It speaks to you," she said. "It's better you hold it. And now we must concentrate. The words of the cantrip don't matter nearly so much as the strength of our intention."

Annis folded her hands around the adder stone and held it just in front of her solar plexus. Harriet set a match to the candle wick and then to the incense in its burner. As the pungent smoke began to curl upward, they both closed their eyes.

Harriet had not felt the resonance with the adder stone that Annis did, but as the herbarium filled with the scents of sandalwood and cedar and thyme, she felt something else, something just as powerful. She sensed Beryl's presence first, and then others of her kind, the ones who had come before. She felt the touch of her ancestresses, no longer in the body but still present with her. Present with Annis, who represented this new age of witches. They were all bound together by blood, by love, by pain, by magic.

The power of ageless warmth and infinite energy made her sway on her feet. She had to remind herself to breathe. When she spoke her cantrip, the words seemed to echo down the years as if she had spoken them before, as if she remembered them from long, long ago.

Guide us both in heart and mind.
Our missing sister help us find.
Hide her face and hide her form
So we can bring her safely home.

She didn't repeat it. It was complete upon the instant. Her bones sang with the knowledge, and her blood tingled with it, the electrical thrill of accomplished magic coursing through her body.

She opened her eyes.

And saw that she was floating several inches above the floor of the herbarium.

How many times, she wondered, as she settled slowly, gently down, *how many times have I done this, and never realized?*

She glanced to her left to see Annis still rapt, eyes closed, adder stone pressed close. Harriet had been slightly dismayed that Annis felt the vibrations of the adder stone and she did not, but this—this levitation—this was a testament to her power. It was vanity, but she was proud of it just the same.

She whispered to Annis, "It's done. We must go while the magic is strong."

Annis opened her eyes, nodded, and held up the adder stone. "Do we take it?"

"We need it with us. Can you secrete it in your bodice? Are you wearing a corset?"

"I never wear corsets if I can help it," Annis said matter-of-factly. "Frances used to buy them for me, then never noticed if I didn't put them on." She opened the top button of her shirt-waist and slid the adder stone under the sprigged cotton. "It will be safe in my chemise."

Moments later, in coats and hats and boots, they were on their way. Annis had come in the Allington carriage, with Robbie at the reins. The carriage impressed the Dakota doorman, who gave the two ladies an elegant bow as they crossed the courtyard.

As the carriage wound out of the courtyard and into the park, Harriet said, "I see your driver knows the quickest way to the East River. You're sure he won't mind our destination?"

"No. I've told him we're going to visit Frances, but that we have to do it in secrecy, so Papa won't complain." She gave a wry smile. "Robbie is accustomed to helping me keep secrets from Papa."

"I hope he can find the place. This won't be much of a dock."

Her friend Tom, the shepherd, had found a boat and a boatman for her without asking any questions. "It won't be much of a boat, either, Tom says. I hope you're not subject to seasickness."

"Not in the least."

Both dock and boat lived up perfectly to Tom's warning. The dock was of the floating sort, splintered gray wood loosely attached to two rickety, waterlogged pilings, with a single bollard at the end. The boat itself was a rowboat, without amenities of any kind, but it proved to be river-worthy. It was hardly a pleasant cruise, but it was a blessedly brief one. The boatman, pressed into service by the faithful Tom, tied the boat up at the commercial pier just north of the asylum and helped both ladies out, all without speaking a word.

Harriet told him they would return as soon as possible, and he nodded acknowledgment.

As they made their way toward the asylum, Harriet said, "I will remind you, Annis. Once we begin—both of us holding Frances between us—we mustn't break the contact. If the glamour should fade, you and I would be trapped."

"I know."

"It could be hard for anyone to extricate us. Visitors are rare at Blackwell's, and women who go there are assumed to be insane. No one questions it."

"I know that, too. I read Nellie Bly's book."

"You're not afraid?"

"I am, a bit."

"Good. Because I am, too."

44

Annis

Annis hadn't told Harriet that she had seen her float again after she pronounced her cantrip. She hadn't meant to spy, but the adder stone had begun to tremble in her hands, and her body to tingle from head to foot, as if she had touched lightning. She felt the room tilt around her, spun by the power of the magic, and she feared she would lose her balance.

Her eyelids had fluttered open just as Harriet lifted from the floor. Annis saw the tiles shining with candlelight beneath Harriet's feet. Her shadow floated like the silhouette of a ghost.

The moment Harriet began to settle to earth again, Annis squeezed her eyelids shut and gripped the adder stone harder, pressing it against her. Strands of her hair stirred against her forehead, and she shivered with wonder.

Her aunt Harriet, she thought, must be the most powerful witch of the age.

The day before, Annis and James had enjoyed a long ride through the park, and returned pink cheeked and tousled from being out in the cold sunshine all afternoon. The note from Aunt Harriet had been waiting when they came in from the stables. Annis read it with James standing at her shoulder.

It helped that James had already met Harriet and knew her to be a sober and intelligent person. "I need to go with her," Annis said. "It's a terrible place, and she shouldn't go alone."

"I shall accompany you," he said gallantly.

"Oh no, James. Thank you, but it's best you don't. She's in a wing for female inmates, and by all accounts the women are in shocking conditions. Frances would hate you to see her like that. We will be fine together, my great-aunt and I. I promise you."

He tried, but didn't quite succeed, to hide the relief he felt at that. He protested again, but without much conviction. They were about to separate, to go and dress for dinner, when she remembered to warn him. "Don't mention this to Papa, will you, James? He will scowl and tell me I should leave well enough alone."

"He may be right."

"He can't change my mind," she said. "I will simply ignore his objections. But he would spoil our dinner, and that would be a shame. Mrs. King is a wonderful cook."

"Very well," he said, with an indulgent smile. "Let us not ruin Mrs. King's dinner. And at dinner, I can thank him for the loan of his horse today."

"Oh, that's hardly necessary. It was good for Chessie to get out of the stables for a change. Papa hardly ever rides anymore."

"All the same," James said. "I want to be on the best terms with your father."

"Why?" Annis said, without thinking. A heartbeat later she felt the flame of embarrassment in her cheeks. "Oh. Oh, that."

He took her hand and pressed it between his. "Oh yes, Annis. That. And soon."

Bemused, she had mounted the staircase, trying not to imagine the conversation James and her father might have.

On their way to meet the boatman, Annis told Harriet that Velma had been upset not to be included in their visit. "It wasn't easy, talking her out of it," she said.

"I find that touching. It can't be easy, caring for Frances all the time."

"I'm sure it's not. Velma is not terribly bright, but she's loyal, and she seems to have transferred her loyalty from me to Frances."

"Frances needs her more."

Annis smiled. "That's what Velma said."

"Perhaps she's brighter than you think."

"Maybe she is, at that." Annis leaned toward the window to watch the city spin by. "Aunt Harriet, I should tell you, too—well, the thing is—it's about James."

"Would you like to tell me about James? About how you feel?"

Annis twisted back to gaze at her aunt. "You've guessed, I think."

"I suspect your heart and your mind are divided."

"Yes. For one thing, I still worry that he's under the influence of the *maleficia*."

"I doubt that very much. It's my opinion that he's made a full recovery."

"I also want to stay in New York, to study with you, to breed horses."

"You are fortunate in having choices. So many young women don't."

"Oh, I know. I do know that." Annis bit her lip. "It's hard to think about."

"Tell me, Annis. Do you love your James as much as you love Black Satin?"

Annis hesitated, then gave Harriet a rueful, slightly guilty smile. "I can assure you I love James *as much* as I love Black Satin."

"Well." Harriet smiled back. "I suppose that's enough."

"James is going to speak to Papa today, while we're out."

"I don't envy him having to speak to George," Harriet said mildly.

"He insists on doing it." Annis worried at her moonstone with her fingers. "I don't know what Papa will say. Now the dowry money has been paid back to Mr. Neufeld, and...it shouldn't be all about money, should it?"

"I hope it won't be. But you must put it out of your mind for now," Harriet admonished. "Distractions are dangerous."

Annis bit her lip, ashamed of her selfishness. "Yes. Sorry." She released the moonstone and shifted her hand to the adder stone, safe beneath her chemise. Her worries about her future faded as she felt the silhouette of the ancient stone under her hand. The magic of the herbarium returned in full force, swirling through the inside of the carriage, uniting her with Harriet and reminding her of their purpose. "Yes," she said again. "I will focus."

The exterior of the Women's Lunatic Asylum on Blackwell's Island was as bleak as any place Annis had ever seen. There was almost no landscaping, no decent walkways, nothing to look at except the gray walls and the small barred windows that trapped the unfortunates within.

The interior was infinitely worse.

The smell that struck them when they walked through the double doors of the entrance made Annis want to pinch her nose shut. She was used to the smells of refuse often dumped on the city streets, but this air was thick with the stench of urine, of spoiled meat, of gas and kerosene and unwashed bodies. The odors seemed to have permeated the walls and soaked into the lobby furniture, only to be exhaled by oil heaters struggling to warm the cavernous place.

Harriet was wearing her single fur, a beaver cape with a standing collar, and a matching hat on her upswept hair. Stern faced, she strode through the lobby to the superintendent's office as if she knew exactly where she was going.

She pushed through the door without knocking. A thin woman behind a wide desk looked up. "I want to see my cousin," Harriet declared, as if she was not accustomed to being refused. "It's Frances Allington. I'm in a hurry."

Annis marveled at the aura of magic that surrounded Harriet as she infused her voice with a tone of command, sending the woman scurrying into the office behind her.

A moment later a stout man in shirtsleeves, with ink protectors reaching to his elbows, emerged. Scowling, he stamped around the desk to the spot where Harriet stood, her booted foot tapping with impatience.

As he drew near her, the man's expression altered. Irritation gave way to confusion, and then, by the time he had reached her, to deference. He inclined his head and said politely, "Stephen Beaufort, at your service. I don't believe you gave my secretary your name, Mrs. . . . ?"

"Harriet Bishop." Harriet made a show of pulling back her lapel to glance at the gold watch pinned to her shirtwaist. "You are the medical superintendent, are you not?"

"Yes," Beaufort said warily.

"Your name is known to me from the hearings. The *Times* covered them extensively."

"Oh yes, yes. Of course, the hearings were—that is, we've been trying to—"

"Never mind that now. I'll speak to the mayor if I have questions. In the meantime, if you don't mind," Harriet said, with an aristocratic sniff, "I have so little time. We've brought Mrs. Allington some things, and I wish to deliver them personally."

She gestured to Annis. Obediently Annis held up a linen bag holding a piece of cake from Mrs. King and a chemise and night-dress Velma had begged Annis to bring.

Mr. Beaufort said, with an apologetic air, "I'm afraid we'll have to look inside the bag, Mrs. Bishop."

"Indeed?" Harriet raised one haughty eyebrow and nodded permission to Annis. Annis pulled the neck of the bag open and held it out so Mr. Beaufort could peer inside.

He leaned forward, though he kept his hands behind his back, and peeked into the bag. He nodded approval and straightened. "I'll send for a nurse to accompany you."

"We won't need a nurse," Harriet began, but Mr. Beaufort gave an apologetic shake of his head.

"I'm sorry, Mrs. Bishop. It's not safe for a lady like yourself to go in there alone. The poor wretches can be unpredictable. The worst of them are, I'm afraid, often violent."

"I don't believe my cousin is violent. Or insane, for that matter, Mr. Beaufort."

His mouth turned down in a look of feigned sadness. "Not to doubt you, ma'am, but I'm afraid they all say that. It don't make it true."

Harriet sniffed again. "Send for the nurse, then. But do, I beg of you, hurry."

Mr. Beaufort nodded to his secretary, and the woman bolted out of the office as if she had been stung. Mr. Beaufort said to Harriet, speaking as if Annis weren't there, "Won't you have a seat? I'm sure it won't take long to find a nurse."

"I won't, thank you," Harriet answered.

He nodded again, looking uncomfortable and not a little perplexed at having been so quickly and completely mastered by a woman whom he had never met and whose name he didn't recognize. Luckily, the nurse appeared almost immediately, giving him no time to reconsider his capitulation.

The nurse was a woman who, had she been able to stand straight, would probably have been as tall as Harriet, but her back was rounded, as if she hadn't grown up with enough sunshine. Her thin neck jutted out from between her shoulders, making her look a bit like an underfed and poorly bred horse. Mr. Beaufort said, "Fleming, take Mrs. Bishop along to see Frances Allington. A quick visit, mind you! We don't want the ward upset."

There was a moment of fuss over whether Annis, whom they obviously believed to be the lady's maid, would be allowed to accompany Harriet. It was soon settled with another impatient tapping of Harriet's foot and another glance at her watch. These actions seemed to roil the magic that clung to her, to make her every wish irresistible.

The asylum lobby had been bad, but the ward itself was a nightmare. The smell of urine intensified as the nurse opened the door, and moans and wails rose from rows of hard benches where women in various states of dress sat or slumped or, in some cases, were collapsed completely. Those who weren't groaning stared blankly, hopelessly, at the walls. One woman stood facing a corner, tearing at her hair and shouting something at regular intervals, as if it were her task to do it.

There must have been forty or fifty women, and Annis knew this was not the only building housing females. Gaslights cast a sickly glow but left the room mostly in shadow. The floor felt sticky underfoot. Two women whose hair looked as if it had not been washed in weeks limped toward the newcomers, hands out in supplication.

Annis couldn't help shrinking back a little as the women approached. One of them tried to snatch the linen bag from her hand. Harriet set her feet, folded her arms, and glared as Fleming herded the women back to their bench, muttering threats of punishment until she had them settled again.

"I believe," Harriet said, when the nurse returned, "that there were supposed to have been improvements in the living conditions here."

"Oh yes, ma'am," Fleming said. "There's been plenty improvements. They get an extra meal now, and every one of 'em sees a doctor once a year."

"Once a year." Harriet spoke with the same disgust Annis felt. "You call that an improvement?" Annis wondered if Harriet experienced the queasiness that churned in her own belly. She wanted to touch the adder stone, to hurry this along, to escape into the fresh air. She gritted her teeth against her weakness.

The nurse didn't respond to Harriet's remark. She peered around the room, then wound her way through the benches to lift someone ungently by one arm. She yanked the woman forward, half dragging her down the aisle, and pushed her forward so they could see her. "This the one? Allington?"

Annis nearly cried out in horror. Her stepmother's grimy face was nearly unrecognizable. Her hair hung in ragged hanks around her face, obviously sliced off with the dullest of shears and without thought for cosmetic effect. Her complexion was sallow and bruised, and her eyes were as dull as if she had gone blind.

Her father had said Frances would be better off here. Gazing upon this ruined, ragged figure, it was tempting to believe him.

Harriet took the bag from Annis's hands and held it out to Frances. Frances, gazing at some point past Harriet's shoulder, didn't reach for it, nor so much as blink in recognition.

The nurse said, "Ain't any good giving this one anything. She don't know nor care."

"On what grounds do you make that claim, Fleming? Have you tried to talk to her?"

"No point," Fleming said. "Just another crazy."

"I object to your choice of words."

The nurse shrugged. "Just the way things is, ma'am."

Harriet sniffed. "I believe I read from the transcripts of the hearings that you're keeping your patients dosed on chloral. Have you been drugging Mrs. Allington?"

"No need," Fleming answered. "This one don't give no trouble at all. Just sits and stares."

"And you do nothing for her?"

"What do you want I should do? Won't do no good."

"This place is an abomination," Harriet said crisply. "As a nurse, I should think you'd be ashamed to work here."

"Got to work somewheres," Fleming said. She peered at Harriet, her thrust-out neck wobbling. "Not everybody can do it."

"I can imagine." Harriet pressed the linen bag into Frances's limp hand, and in the process, despite her cousin's unwashed and decidedly noisome condition, put her long, strong arm around Frances's shoulders.

It was the signal. Annis stepped swiftly forward, elbowing Fleming aside, and linked her arm with Frances. Now, at last, she pressed the adder stone beneath her bodice as the two of them, she and Harriet, held Frances between them.

The glamour enveloped Frances, rendering her instantly invisible. No one but Annis and Harriet could see her. Even to Annis's eye she looked shadowy and vague, a figure half-seen.

Harriet said, in a voice that rang with authority, "Fleming, that will be all. Thank you."

The nurse stared at them in confusion. "What—you mean you're done now? Visit over?"

"Yes. We won't need you further. You may stay with your patients."

Fleming's mouth opened and stayed that way. She stared at them, her eyes narrowing as if she were trying to remember something, a chore she was supposed to do, an order she was supposed to be following.

Harriet said, under her breath, "Now, Annis. Let us go."

As quickly as they could, they moved out of the dimness of the ward and into the brighter light of the corridor. It was difficult, urging Frances to walk between them. Her steps were uncoordinated, as if her feet were numb. It made for an awkward progress, but they had to remain in contact to close the circle of magic.

It was an agonizing walk down the hallway and around the corner. It helped that Frances weighed almost nothing, but they had to half carry her, not daring to release her arm or her shoulders for even a moment. Once or twice her feet simply stopped moving, and they found themselves literally dragging her. As they labored across the lobby, Annis felt as if the distance to the doors had tripled, but it seemed they were going to make it without interference.

"Wait! Mrs. Bishop!"

Harriet muttered, "Damn."

It was Beaufort, trotting across the lobby toward them, his round belly bobbing as he ran. "Mrs. Bishop, a moment, please!"

Annis couldn't see a way out of it. She and Harriet exchanged a glance above Frances's head and slowed their steps. Frances slumped against Harriet as they came to a stop and waited for Beaufort to reach them. They must have looked odd, with Harriet's arm around Frances's shoulders, and Annis with an arm around her waist, holding her up as best she could. To her own eyes they made a suspiciously awkward trio, an unnatural formation of bodies.

Annis could hardly breathe with tension as Beaufort walked around to stand in front of them. He didn't look at Annis, which was no surprise, since he believed her to be Harriet's maid. He didn't look at Frances, either. The glamour was holding.

Harriet said, in a haughty tone Annis had never heard her use, "Yes, Mr. Beaufort? I believe I made clear that I am in a great hurry this morning."

"Oh, I won't keep you," he said hastily. "I simply wanted to make certain everything is to your liking in the ward. You will tell Mr. Allington—that's George Allington of the Allington Iron Stove Company, is it not? I looked it up. Please tell him we will take the best possible care of his wife. I'll see to it personally."

"He will be glad to hear that, Mr. Beaufort," Harriet said. "And no, I did not find everything to my liking. It's far too cold in that room, and many of those women need warm baths and fresh clothes."

"Oh yes, ma'am, yes indeed. I'll speak to Fleming about it."

"Mr. Allington will expect no less," Harriet said. She shifted her feet, as if she were about to walk on to the door.

Annis, alert to this move, shifted her own feet. Frances, now sagging under her supporting hand, did not. Instead she drooped farther. Her knees buckled, and her head lolled as she crumpled all the way to the floor. Annis lost her grip on Frances's waist, and Frances slipped from under Harriet's arm. As they lost contact, the glamour broke.

The lights in the lobby seemed to flicker, as if the gas had flared high and then dropped. Frances appeared as if through a mist, an untidy specter huddled on the bare wooden floor.

Beaufort's eyes went wide, his eyebrows lifting impossibly high. His swarthy face blanched, and he tottered back on his heels. "What—" he choked. "What has—"

Annis swiftly bent to slide her hands beneath Frances's armpits. At the same moment, Harriet grasped Frances's shoulder and slid her hand down to grip a handful of her ill-fitting dress. They were connected again, the three of them enclosed by magic. The lights in the lobby steadied. Frances disappeared.

Beaufort's mouth hung open for a long, painful instant. When he closed it, he rubbed his eyes as if he thought his vision had failed.

"Are you quite well, Mr. Beaufort?" Harriet said in a silky tone.

"Oh, I—yes, I think—took a turn there for a moment. I'm all right now."

Harriet said, "Very good. Thank you, Mr. Beaufort. We will return soon, and I expect to see the women in Mrs. Allington's ward in far better condition."

They were on their way again. Hauling Frances between them was like trying to move a piece of furniture. Annis managed to get an arm around her back, her hand still under her armpit. Through the flimsy fabric of her dress, Frances's skin felt like ice. Harriet, the linen bag in her left hand, kept her grip on Frances's dress in her right. They pushed through the front doors and staggered down the steps, Frances's feet missing every other tread.

They were exhausted by the time they reached the boat. They let the glamour fade as they maneuvered Frances into it. The air around the three of them shimmered, as if a ray of sunshine had broken through the clouds, and there she was, drooping, dirty, as if they had picked her out of a gutter.

The startled boatman's shaggy eyebrows rose. "Where'd that one come from?"

"She is leaving the asylum. We're taking her home."

"But she—I dint see her before."

"Did you not? How odd," Harriet said. "The light must be bad."

He stared at Frances for a moment, then turned his grizzled face to Harriet. "One more fare, missus."

"Very well. I will pay it. Now hurry, please."

He nodded, settled onto the bench seat to unship his oars, and began to row without another word. Annis took a last look back at Blackwell's Island, shuddered, and vowed she would never set foot on it again.

Robbie was waiting at the horses' heads when they disembarked from the rowboat. When he caught sight of them, he gave an exclamation and hurried to help lift Frances out of the boat and onto the unsteady dock. Annis and Harriet between them managed to get Frances off the dock and up the little slope to the carriage. As they settled her inside, she slumped, unaware, in the corner. Robbie stood by the door, wringing his hands.

"Poor Mrs. Frances," he said. "Poor lady. Whatever did they do to her? Are we taking her home? Did Mr. Allington—"

Annis interrupted. "No, Robbie. Papa doesn't know, and we're not going to tell him."

Robbie froze for a moment, his hand on the carriage door, his cap in his other hand. "Miss Annis—"

Annis said, "Please, Robbie. He'll never know you helped us."

Harriet said, "It's for Mrs. Allington's sake, Robbie. That place is unbearable."

Robbie's stiff posture began to relax. Slowly, as if it were part of his making a decision, he replaced his cap on his head and pulled the brim low over his forehead. He gave Frances a sorrowful look. "I've heard that," he said. "I was hoping—that is, I sure didn't think Mr. Allington would—"

"Nor did I," Annis said crisply. "It wasn't right, but we're fixing it as best we can."

"Well done, Miss Annis," he said. He closed the door of the carriage but still lingered, looking in at Frances's inert figure. "Poor lady," he repeated. "A terrible thing."

"Yes," Annis said. "Terrible. Thank you, Robbie, for understanding. I'm grateful. Let's start for the Dakota, shall we? This has been a difficult day."

He tapped the carriage door once with his fingers, giving his assent, and climbed up onto the driver's seat. Annis breathed a great sigh of relief and heard her aunt do the same. The carriage began to move, the steady hoofbeats of the horse taking them away to safety.

Frances's eyes didn't flicker as the scenery changed. Her bosom, shrunken nearly to nothing, barely moved with her breath. She seemed hardly alive, but Annis knew the truth. Her stepmother's mind still functioned, though the link with her body had been irretrievably broken. The tragedy of it was beyond bearing, and she turned her face to the window so Harriet would not see the tears on her cheeks.

45

James

James took a final look in the mirror. His jacket was impeccably brushed, thanks to Perry. His hair was trimmed, and he was clean shaven. His boots were polished. He swished some eau de cologne around his mouth and spit, then straightened and made a minute adjustment to his tie. He was ready.

It was, he had discovered, a day when George Allington worked on correspondence at home instead of at the factory. He would be in his study until luncheon. James wasn't sure where his study might be, but after smoothing his hair one last time, he set out in search of it.

For someone who had so recently consigned his ailing wife to an asylum, he found Mr. Allington remarkably cheerful. When James knocked, he greeted him jovially, invited him in, offered him a chair opposite his desk, and rang for coffee.

A neat pile of letters awaited his attention on his desk, and a sheet of stationery, half-covered in small, tidy script, lay on the blotter. Mr. Allington set his pen at an angle across it and pushed it aside. He leaned back, steepling his fingers. "So, young man," he said. "How are you finding New York? Had a good ride yesterday?"

"I did, sir, and thank you very much for the loan of your horse. He has a fine gait, and an easy disposition."

"So I recall. Haven't ridden in a while. Leave all that to my daughter."

"Your daughter is an impressive horsewoman."

"So I'm told! I'm no expert, I'm afraid. I suppose you find her not very ladylike."

James crossed one leg over the other and rested his linked hands on his knee, striving to look relaxed. "I find her most amicable, sir," he said. "And completely charming. I've met any number of ladylike girls and found them dull. Miss Allington is never dull."

George Allington grinned. "That's high praise for my handful of a girl."

"I am very fond of her," James said. "And that's why I'm here."

"Glad to hear you speak plainly, son," Allington said. "I'm a blunt man myself."

"Very well." James uncrossed and recrossed his legs, then realized, with warmth growing in his cheeks, that he wasn't behaving in a relaxed fashion at all. *Damn it all*, he thought. Like a green lad with no experience. A boy, when he wanted to be seen as a man.

He cleared his throat, then wished he hadn't. He said, "I will endeavor to speak plainly, since you encourage it. I believe you know a bit about my circumstances, sir, and—"

"You mean, impoverished nobility and all that?"

For a moment James was struck dumb. Allington had said he was a blunt sort of man, but James had not been prepared for just how blunt he might be. He was startled by how offensive he found it. He shifted in his chair and told himself to let it pass, for Annis's sake. "Uh, well, sir, I'm afraid—yes. You see, my father, the previous marquess, passed away unexpectedly, and he—there are certain debts—"

"Oh, of course, my boy. There are always debts! God forbid I should die just now and leave Annis with my debts to settle!" Allington gave a hoot of laughter, pushed his chair back, and propped his booted feet on his desk. "So what's your plan? Sell some land? I understand your estate is extensive."

"Yes. There is a parcel of land, bordering a neighbor's property. He has asked to purchase it many times, and now I feel I will have to do that."

"Got anything else? Livestock? Horses?"

James swallowed, trying to hold in his temper. He had not expected such tactless questions. He didn't like them, and he wasn't sure how to respond. It was no wonder, he reflected, that Annis wasn't particularly ladylike. She was her father's daughter.

Allington seemed to sense he had stepped too close to the line. He brought his feet down from his desk, letting them fall to the floor with a bang. "Sorry, my lord," he said. "That's the proper address, isn't it? I'm a businessman, always have been. Came up the hard way. I think in numbers. No offense."

"None taken, sir," James said. He drew a long breath through his nostrils and settled his own feet firmly on the floor. "I admit, I had not expected our conversation to take this turn."

"Ah." Allington tipped his head to one side and gave him a look reminiscent of Annis's penetrating one. "Please tell me what you intended for us to talk about. I'll listen. Always ready with free advice, though!" He gave a snort of laughter and then, with obvious effort, fell silent.

The moment had arrived. James said, "Thank you, sir. I will come to the point, if you don't mind. I've come to ask your permission to marry your daughter. To make Annis my marchioness. I'm sorry about the indebtedness of Rosefield, but I'm a healthy man, well educated, reasonably well thought of among my friends and family. I will do my best to make her a good husband."

George Allington raised one graying eyebrow. "That's why you're in New York, eh?"

"Yes, sir." James heard the aristocratic accent dominating his voice and tried to soften it. "Yes, I came to New York for this express purpose."

"Well," Allington said thoughtfully. "Well, well, well." His gaze dropped to his desk. He picked up his pen—a beautiful pen, carved of some dark wood, ebony perhaps—and tapped it against his hand. "I can't say I'm completely surprised. My wife was quite set on Annis marrying someone like yourself. Actually, she wired me that an engagement had been arranged." He glanced up and seemed, for the first time, unsure of himself. "Perhaps I shouldn't have said that. It appears not to have been true."

"It's quite all right, sir," James said. "It is not true yet, but the dowager marchioness—my mother, that is—and Mrs. Allington very much wanted it to happen. Your daughter and I have discussed this quite frankly."

"Oh, you've discussed it, have you?" Allington now tapped his blunt chin with his pen, so hard James was afraid he would spatter his white linen collar. "And what does Annis have to say about all of this? About becoming your marchioness?"

"She has not said yes, sir. But except in the case of one rather clumsy effort on my part some months ago, which I have taken care not to repeat, she has not said no, either."

"That doesn't sound like Annis. She's a girl who has always known her own mind."

"If I receive your permission, I intend to speak to her again this evening."

"Hmmm. What about the money?" Allington asked.

Another shock clenched James's belly. In his circle it was rare to speak directly about money. He quite understood that this was an affectation, a pretense made possible by privilege. His friends could afford to pretend money didn't concern them. He had done it himself, until his father died. He wondered if he could learn to face the question of money as squarely as this plainspoken man did.

He drew a breath and met Allington's gaze. The eyes that were forget-me-not blue in Annis were the blue of polished steel in her father. For all the jollity of his address and the laughter, James had no doubt Allington was a hardheaded businessman. He might claim he had debts, but James would have wagered they were not heavy ones.

"Well, sir," he said, as evenly as he could. He didn't clear his throat, and he didn't look away from those hard eyes. "As I've confessed to you, money is an issue at Rosefield Hall. However, there are steps I will be taking to pay down my father's debts, and I will salvage what I can. I wish to marry your daughter because I care for her. My mother also is quite taken with her and admires her spirit and her independence. I believe I can make your daughter happy, and I know my mother will support us in our marriage, which is no small thing."

"Indeed it is not," Allington said. He laid down the pen, and his gaze drifted to the view of the river beyond the Allington gardens. "I was quite happily married to Annis's mother. She died of a fever when Annis was tiny, but I know how good marriages can be."

James noticed that Allington didn't speak of his second marriage. It seemed odd, but perhaps it was an American belief that illness should be hidden away.

"I would like my daughter to be happy, of course," Allington went on. "As long as we're laying our cards on the table, I will tell you I agreed to a large dowry under pressure from her stepmother. That pressure is gone, and I'm no longer inclined to do that."

James set his jaw. "I understand, sir. I want to marry Miss Allington just the same, and I would like your permission to press my suit."

Allington's grin returned. "As we don't have to talk about money, you have my permission. My blessing." His grin widened. "I wish you luck, son. No idea what she'll say."

He didn't add, until James was already at the door, "Better watch out, my lord. Annis knows things, things she shouldn't. She's a hard girl to deceive."

The thought did nothing to improve James's confidence. Fortunately, he had no intention of deceiving Annis about anything.

46

Harriet

The Dakota's doorman looked shocked at the sight of Harriet and Annis lifting a dirty, unkempt wretch down from the Allington carriage. His earlier deference disappeared, and he thrust his hands into the pockets of his uniform as if to make clear he would not touch the person Miss Bishop had inexplicably chosen to bring to his establishment.

Harriet glared at him. "We will need the elevator," she said, in a tone that meant she had no expectation of being refused. Annis, wide-eyed, watched the man back away, his mouth pulled down in distaste. The aura of magic had dissipated, evidently. The doorman did, however, lead the way to the elevator and open the gate to it, though he scowled throughout the operation.

Harriet did not thank him. She and Annis bundled Frances into the elevator, and Harriet operated the device on her own.

"He can't stop you from having her here, can he?" Annis asked.

"No. He's only the sentry, but he's the biggest snob in a building full of snobs." The elevator clanked to a stop on her floor, and Harriet unlatched the gate. They maneuvered Frances to the door of Harriet's apartment.

Harriet pulled out her key and inserted it into the lock. "Go back to Robbie, Annis. It's best I handle introducing Grace to Frances on my own."

"Are you sure?"

"Oh yes." Harriet pushed the door open and drew Frances through it. "You should go home. I'm sure James is waiting for you."

"Yes."

"Do you know what you're going to say to him?"

"No."

"Do you want to be a marchioness?"

"I wouldn't mind. Seabeck is wonderful, and the horses—"

Grace's quick footsteps sounded in the hall on the way to the front door. Their conversation would have to wait. "Go now," Harriet said. "Before Grace gets here. I'll expect you tomorrow morning. But send Velma tonight, will you? Assuming she's willing."

By the time Grace reached the door, Annis had disappeared down the staircase. Grace exclaimed, "Oh! My goodness gracious, Miss Harriet, you've brought Mrs. Allington. What a surprise! Dear me, poor Mrs. Allington, you don't look at all well. Are you going to stay? I had no idea. I would have aired the spare bedroom." Harriet had a good grip on Frances's left arm, and Grace hurried to take her right.

As they made an awkward progress down the corridor, Grace chattered on. "I would say the first thing for poor Mrs. Allington is a warm bath and a good hair wash. Mrs. Allington, wouldn't you like that? A nice long bath and some fresh clothes will make you feel ever so much better. Then some soup, I think. I've made a nice thick chicken soup, the kind Miss Harriet loves, and..."

Grace was one person, at least, who would not mind Frances's failure to answer questions. Harriet helped her to guide Frances into the spare bedroom. They settled her safely in an armchair, and Grace hurried to begin filling a tub. When she returned, leaving the taps running, Harriet said, "I'd better stay with you, Grace. I'm afraid Frances is unable to do anything much for herself."

As if to dramatize the problem, Frances slumped over the arm of the chair, and her head fell back as if she could no longer hold it up.

"Oh dear, oh dear," Grace said. "What are we going to do with her?"

"We have to keep her here, I'm afraid. I couldn't leave her in that place."

"Keep her—forever?" Grace's usual pleasant expression faltered.

"I'm sorry, Grace, but yes. Annis's maid is coming. She has been caring for Frances since their return from England."

"Velma? That one?"

"That's the one."

Grace was silent for a full minute, which was something of an achievement. She fiddled with her apron, folded and unfolded her arms, and finally put her hands on her hips as she gazed down at Frances's blank face. "Velma will have to share the bedroom."

"Yes. I believe she has done that for months."

"Will Mrs. Allington get any better?"

"I will do what I can, but I fear not."

Grace clicked her tongue, smoothed her apron, and went to turn off the taps in the bath. As she came back, she signaled her acceptance of the situation by beginning to talk. "Well, I must say, Miss Harriet, that Velma isn't going to be very good company. I expect she's glad of a secure place, and it's a thankless sort of task she's taking on, but she's not much of a talker, is she? And really, it's hard to imagine Mrs. Allington with a maid like that, after that fancy Frenchie she had for so long..."

On and on it went, as between them they stripped off Frances's filthy dress and the shift under it that was not one bit cleaner. The clothes went into the dustbin, and Grace carried the bin outside in case the clothes were infested. They managed to get Frances into the bath, and Grace, saying, "Just this once, mind. I'm not a nurse," sat beside the tub to make certain Frances didn't slip under the water and drown.

"I know that, of course. Just do your best, Grace, just for now," Harriet said mildly, and made her escape.

Harriet bathed, too, both because of their visit to that awful ward and because, before performing a rite, she wanted to be perfectly clean. As she dried and dressed, she heard Grace murmuring from the spare bedroom, then still muttering as she made her way along the corridor to the kitchen. Harriet let herself into the herbarium, closing the door on the homely sounds of clattering dishes and banging pot lids.

She pulled the drape back on the long window to allow the clear wintry light to fall on her worktable. She moved swiftly, knowing exactly what she needed. White willow bark for clarity of thought. Thyme for courage. Golden ginkgo leaves for confidence. She added a twig of witch hazel twined with a sprig of rosemary to ease communication. She spread everything out on a wooden block, leaving each herb in its natural form. She set the moonstone, for Annis, on her left, and the amethyst, for James, on her right. The citrine, for light in the darkness, she laid in the center. At the foot of the candle she nestled her amulet into the witch hazel and rosemary branches, then set a match to the candle wick.

It felt good to be doing this. She was healing herself as much as she was trying to support James and Annis as they made a big decision. The *maleficia* had taken more out of her soul than she liked to think about, but this—this magic of blessing and harmony—might help to restore some balance.

It might also, she knew, cost her an apprentice. Harriet would be alone again, but she had been alone for two and a half decades. She was resigned to it.

She took up a vial of salt water and sprinkled it over the herbs, taking care that drops fell on the stones, too. Before she spoke her cantrip, she bent her head for a moment, thinking of Alexander, remembering the day he had asked her to marry him and how full of joy and hope and optimism they had both been. They had been so young! Full of dreams, sure of themselves, devoted to each other, confident of the future.

Would those feelings have lasted? She would never know, of course. Those emotions were trapped in that long-ago moment, crystallized as if suspended in amber. The affection between the two of them had no chance to grow and deepen nor to fade and die.

Annis and James had a chance, if they decided to take it. She wouldn't make the decision for them, but she could help them to see what was possible.

She opened her eyes, stretched out her hands, and murmured,

Surely know, clearly see
The future you desire to be.

Be not afraid, do not delay,
Seize your chance while yet you may.

The candle flame flickered higher, and the ametrine began to glow, its deep-purple threads shining from the golden stone. Harriet smiled to see it and nearly laughed aloud when the knowing swept over her.

"Oh, Alexander," she whispered. "I am so glad. I am so very glad for them."

47

Annis

Annis, like Harriet, felt in need of a bath the moment she reached home. She dashed up the stairs without seeing anyone and ran her own bath. She stripped off her clothes and piled them on the floor. As she sank into the scented, soapy water, it occurred to her that when Velma went off to the Dakota, there would be no one to pick up her things, to clean them, to put them away when she tossed them about. Perhaps having a lady's maid wasn't such a bad idea after all.

She scrubbed herself from head to toe, even washing her hair, though it would take hours to dry. When she emerged from her bathroom, she found a dejected Velma gathering up her dropped shirtwaist and skirt and lingerie and stuffing them into a laundry bag.

Velma straightened, and it was obvious from her swollen eyelids and reddened cheeks that she had been crying.

"Velma," Annis said, as gently as she could. "It's going to be all right."

Velma shook her head. "It ain't. Mrs. Frances all alone in that place? Not all right."

"I have very good news about that, Velma, but it means a big change for you. A different opportunity. You can say no if you wish, and no one would hold it against you."

Velma stood dumbly, holding the laundry bag, gazing at her without understanding.

"Mrs. Frances is out of the asylum. She's safe with my aunt Harriet. You will soon meet my aunt, Miss Harriet Bishop."

Velma nodded, her lips a little apart, her dull eyes beginning to brighten. "Miss Harriet got Mrs. Frances?"

"Yes. At the Dakota, across from Central Park. We're hoping you will go to be Mrs. Frances's maid. Well, her nurse. She's no better than she was, I'm afraid."

Velma's eyes brightened more. "That's my job now? At Miss Harriet's?"

"If you're willing to take it."

Velma nodded, and more tears filled her eyes, tears of relief and hope. Annis felt a twist of empathy in her breast over Velma's misery and constant anxiety. She said as gently as she knew how, "Go and pack your things, then. They're expecting you tonight."

Annis had only just finished dressing and toweling her damp hair when Velma returned. Annis exclaimed aloud over her transformed appearance. The swollen eyelids were gone, and she had washed away the blotches of tears on her cheeks. She was wearing her best shirtwaist and newest skirt. She had brushed her thin hair into a passable chignon and perched her flat straw hat on top. She held a cardboard valise in one hand and her short woolen coat in another.

Annis said, "You look—why, Velma, you look very nice."

"The Dakota," Velma said, as if that explained the effort she had made.

"Yes, indeed. I hope you'll like it there."

They were already downstairs, with Robbie waiting in the drive, when Velma said, "Oh! I forgot!" She dropped her valise and her coat on the floor and turned to run, rather clumsily, back upstairs. When she returned she was carrying the cut-glass swan, carefully cupped in her hands.

Annis picked up the maid's valise and coat and carried them for her. She assisted Velma up into the carriage and saw her safely settled, her most precious possession cradled in her lap.

"Robbie," Annis said as he picked up the reins. "Don't let that doorman send you down to the servants' level. Tell him Velma is to go right up the stairs, just as a lady's maid does."

Robbie grinned. "Yes, Miss Annis." He touched his cap and set off for the Dakota. Annis stood in the gravel drive, waving farewell to her former maid.

Annis, hairbrush in her hand, knelt before a lively fire in the small parlor to dry her hair. James found her there and held out his hand for the brush. "Allow me," he said.

Startled, Annis gave him the hairbrush and bent her head. With patient hands he untangled the strands of damp hair and began to brush. It was an oddly intimate experience, the heat of the fire against her scalp, the firm, slow strokes of the hairbrush, the occasional grazing of her cheek by James's long fingers. Annis's breathing quickened, and her heart beat a little faster at his nearness.

When his elbow grazed her shoulder, she had a sudden flash of that awful night in her bedroom in Rosefield Hall, when he was under the influence of the *maleficia*. She caught a horrified breath at the memory, then resolutely thrust it away.

This moment wasn't anything like that night of bewitchment. These feelings were thrilling, but they were natural. She liked him so very much. She knew him to be a kind man behind his self-conscious facade, and to be a man of integrity and honesty. Now that the *maleficia* no longer interfered, they could be friends. Perhaps even more than friends.

When her hair, though still damp, was free of tangles, she lifted her head. James helped her drape the heavy strands of hair back from her face.

"I like your hair around your shoulders that way," he said. He was blushing, but his gaze was steady. He hadn't cleared his throat once. He put a hand under her arm to help her up, and they sat together on the divan before the fire.

"Annis," he began. "I spoke to your father today."

"You didn't need to. I'm eighteen now. I can make my own decisions."

His mouth turned down in that priggish way that made her want to laugh. "It's the proper way to go about things."

"All right, James," she said. She still felt the laugh bubbling up in her throat. She covered her lips with her fingers to prevent it escaping. "Tell me what Papa said."

"He gave me permission to propose to you. He gave us his blessing."

"His blessing? I haven't said yes yet."

His lips relaxed to their normal pleasant line. "I think you're going to," he said.

Her eyebrows shot up. It wasn't like James to jump ahead that way, to make an assumption. It was—it was confident. She found it charming.

She said, "Do you?"

"Yes. Because I'm going to persuade you." Surprising her even further, he bent and kissed her mouth. There was nothing offensive in it, but neither was it a hesitant kiss. His lips were closed and firm, utterly unlike his awful attempt when he was driven by the *maleficia*. He pressed his mouth to hers for just the right amount of time, enough to make her breath quicken in her throat and her solar plexus quiver. When he straightened, he said, "That's my first argument."

She gazed at him, her lips a little apart, her cheeks warming. All she knew of actual kissing was what her schoolmates had said, and she had never been sure they weren't making things up. The actual event made her suspect she was going to like kisses.

James said, "I have other inducements." He reached into the pocket of his jacket and brought out a small black velvet box. He opened it with one finger and held it out for her to see. The ring inside was a simple one, gold, a ruby surrounded by pavé diamonds. It glittered temptingly in the firelight.

Annis buried her hands in her skirt to stop herself from touching it. "Are you sure you want to marry me, James? I'm not a proper sort of girl at all, not the sort you're used to."

He smiled. "I already know that, of course."

"Did Papa say anything about my dowry?"

James gave a wry chuckle. "Your father made it clear there wouldn't be one. He said, 'I don't want to talk about money.' So we didn't."

"You mean—there's to be no money, but you still want to marry me?"

He gave her a gentle, very James-like smile. "I do, Annis. I do, very much. It's too bad about the money, of course. I'll just have to find another way out of our difficulties."

"Are they very bad, those difficulties?"

"They're serious, I'm afraid, and my mother isn't going to like the solutions. She loves the London house, for example. And I love High Point, but there's no help for that. It's a big debt, and we must be free of it."

"I'm so sorry, James. I wish I could do something."

"Well, it's not really your problem, is it? I will manage," he said. His smile faltered, and his jaw tightened. "I must manage, actually, whatever it costs. People are depending on me."

"Yes, I see that." She sighed and looked away, into the jolly little fire. "There's something else, James. I don't know how you're going to feel about it." He found her hand and held it. "I want to complete my studies with Aunt Harriet. To be an herbalist."

"What does that mean?"

She took a breath. "I will have to spend several months a year in New York."

His hand tightened on hers. "But what about Black Satin?"

Startled, she glanced up at him. "Sorry?"

He brought her hand to his lips and kissed it lightly. "It's my idea, Annis, that you marry me, and spend your bit of inheritance to ship your stallion to Liverpool."

"Oh!" She blinked at the new thought. "And could I hire Robbie to work with Jermyn at Seabeck? I've always promised his job would be safe, and he could see that Black Satin makes it safely to England."

"Of course, although you must warn him Jermyn won't like it."

"Jermyn doesn't like much, it seems."

"He's a touchy, old-fashioned sort, but that doesn't matter. You

can start your bloodline at Seabeck, with my Andalusian mares."
James's sudden grin made him look young and rather dashing.
"It's a cracking good plan, don't you think? Black Satin is just the
fresh blood the Seabeck line needs. We may even turn a profit."

"And my studies with Aunt Harriet?"

His grin faded. "That could be a problem, Annis. You'll be the
Marchioness of Rosefield. There are privileges that come with
the title, but there are also obligations. Duties. You can hardly
discharge them if you're not present."

"But as an herbalist, there is so much I can do at Seabeck. Not
just for the horses, but for the people." *And being a witch will be
even better.*

"But that won't be necessary. We have a doctor." He frowned
at her with real puzzlement, as if he couldn't understand what
she was saying.

The good feeling between them evaporated, all at once. She
couldn't think how to argue her point. It didn't seem fair she
should have to.

Not knowing what to say, she pushed herself up. "I'm going to
change for dinner."

"Wait, Annis—" James stood, too, the box with its beautiful
ring still in his hand, his face full of dismay at his proposal going
awry yet again. "You haven't—aren't you going to give me an
answer?"

"Not now. I have to think." She picked up the hairbrush from
the footstool and turned toward the door.

"If I—wait, Annis, don't go—if I say it's fine to come to New
York and study with your aunt, then will you say yes?"

She paused in the doorway, the hairbrush gripped too tightly
between her hands. She couldn't look at him. "I don't think I

should marry you, James. I don't think I should marry anyone." The words hurt her throat and made her heart ache, but she rushed ahead, wanting to get them out. "I can't bear the thought of being told by a husband what I may or may not do."

He said, "But, Annis—that's just the way—"

"Don't say that's just the way it is!" she cried. "That's no excuse!"

She looked at him then, and her heart ached at the sight. He looked almost as vulnerable as when he had been ill, holding the elegant little ring box as if it had his heart inside. "Oh, James," she murmured.

He took three long strides to reach her. He drew her close with one arm, tipping up her still-damp head with the other hand so he could look into her eyes, deeply, as if he wanted to see into her very soul. "You're right," he said, his voice coming from deep in his throat. "I shouldn't tell you what you can and cannot do, whether you marry me or you do not."

"Oh, James," she repeated. "Are you sure? You won't regret saying that?"

"I will not regret it," he said. "And you will learn that I am, for all my other failings, a man of my word." He pulled her closer and bent to kiss her once more, which felt very nice indeed. He murmured, his lips close to her ear, "Say yes, dear Annis. Lovely, strong-minded, independent Annis. Say you'll be my marchioness, and I won't ask you to be obedient."

"Oh! Oh, James, when you hold me like this it's so hard—I just don't—"

He pulled back a little, just enough to lift the ring out of its box. He found her left hand with his right, and slid the ring onto her finger, where it fit as if it had been made for her.

"Oh, James," she breathed. "It's beautiful." She couldn't bear to think of taking it off. Indeed, she could barely think at all, but then, it wasn't a moment for thinking. It was a golden moment for pure emotion. A rare, singular moment in time, for touching, for sensation, for joy.

"Say yes," he whispered.

Annis said, "Yes. Yes!" and turned up her face to be kissed again.

He obliged, with a sincerity she felt as clearly as if she could touch it. He kissed her again, and then once more, until they were both breathless.

When he released her at last, he smiled and pressed her hand with its lovely new ring to his heart. "Lady Rosefield," he said.

She laughed and pulled her hand free so she could hold it out and admire the sparkle of the ring in the firelight. "I'll never get used to being called that," she said.

"You will when you learn how effective it can be at getting things done."

She flicked her fingers, watching the ruby's glow change in the light, and thought about how nice it was going to be to give orders of her own and have them obeyed. She could tell Jermyn to saddle whichever horse she wanted to ride. She could visit the farmers and take gifts for their children and find out what their crops were like. She could forage for herbs wherever on Seabeck's wide lands she cared to. She could breed horses and care for them, and see that Black Satin's line was the best it could possibly be.

If all of that was what being a marchioness meant, she was going to like it. She was going to like it very much indeed.

48

Harriet

"Did you bring them?"

"Yes." Annis set a small covered basket on the worktable in the herbarium. As she stripped off her gloves, Harriet saw her surreptitious glance at the shining ring on her left hand. Self-consciously Annis adjusted it on her finger, and a small, furtive smile curved her lips.

Good. She was happy. No one had coerced her. Indeed, knowing Annis, they probably couldn't have even if they had tried.

Harriet's own lips curled, but she didn't say anything. She had already formally congratulated Annis and James, sent them a small silver tea service as a wedding gift, and accepted the invitation to their wedding.

She watched as Annis folded back the bit of linen that covered the little objects. In the bright morning light, the manikins looked crude and sinister. It would be a relief when they were disposed of.

Annis said, "I know this thing doesn't really look like me, and of course I didn't create it. Still, when I touch it, I *feel* something. Something nasty. Shameful."

"And the other one?"

Annis glanced up, and there was something in those clear blue eyes that made Harriet pause in the act of tying on her apron. "What is it?" she asked her.

Annis's eyelids dropped, as if she knew her eyes revealed too much. She wasn't smiling now, but thoughtful. Grave. She put out a finger to graze the top of James's manikin, and withdrew it again as if the thing were hot and might burn her.

"Annis?"

"I want to keep it," Annis blurted. She folded her arms in a defensive gesture and thrust out her chin. "In case I need it."

"Need it!" Harriet stared at Annis. "Have I not been clear about this? The *maleficia*—"

"Oh, I know, Aunt Harriet, I know! I wouldn't use the *maleficia*, or do anything to hurt James. It's just—"

Harriet, dismayed and disturbed, managed to hold her tongue as she watched Annis struggle to find a way to express herself.

Annis breathed a long, gusty sigh. "You know how fond I am of James. And I have no doubt he's fond of me, at least for now—"

"Ah. You're thinking of your father, and Frances."

Annis nodded but didn't look up. "Papa and Frances made all the promises, the same ones James and I will make, but they broke them. What if James breaks his promise?"

"Which one are you worried about?"

"He promised he wouldn't tell me what I can and can't do. What if he changes his mind? What power will I have except—" She unfolded her arms and swept them around the herbarium with its shelves of jars and bottles and candles, its bunches of herbs hanging overhead. "This is the only real power I have, Aunt Harriet. I'm afraid of losing it when I'm only just learning it."

Harriet finished tying her apron and walked away to stand at the window and gaze out at her beloved park. She touched the amulet where it hung on her breast and thought of Alexander. For just a moment, a few heartbeats, she felt him at her shoulder, and it was such a distinct sensation that she closed her eyes to feel the warmth of his body behind hers. She might have stood that way a long time, but Annis came to stand beside her, and the impression of Alexander's presence evaporated.

Harriet released the amulet and leaned forward to take in the winter vista of the park, the bare trees rimed with ice, the grass crisp with frost. "There are risks in all our relationships, Annis. In love. In friendship. Even in a relationship like ours, which is— well, I don't know what to call it exactly, but it requires trust to make it work."

"I trust you, of course, Aunt Harriet."

Harriet straightened and turned her head to look directly into Annis's eyes. "Then you must trust me in this, Annis. The manikin must be destroyed. There is no good in it. No benefit."

"Are you sure? I thought perhaps—the bit of magic that clings to it—"

"I am sure, to my sorrow," Harriet said heavily. "I don't want you to make the same mistake I made, long ago."

"What mistake was that? You didn't—you didn't use the *maleficia*?"

"I did. It was my greatest mistake, and it cost me everything." Before she knew it was going to happen, before she could stop them, tears began to trickle down her face, the second time she had wept in the space of a few months. She didn't sob or sniffle. Her weeping was just tears, a steady, slow stream of them, as if a dam had broken and released a flood. They dripped down her chin and onto the bib of her long apron.

"Aunt Harriet!" Annis seized her hand and pressed it between hers. "Tell me. I can't believe it's as bad as you think." She freed one hand and dug in her pocket to bring out a clean handkerchief. As Harriet pressed it to her eyes, Annis circled her aunt's waist with one arm and led her toward the two stools at the far end of the worktable. She urged her to sit on one, and she took the other. She stayed close, one hand on Harriet's back, the other holding her arm, as if she were afraid Harriet might topple off the stool.

Harriet wept for a time. Annis waited, not speaking, not moving from her side. The handkerchief was soaked through by the time Harriet's tears stopped, and she realized Annis was patting her back, gently, as you might pat the back of a crying child. It was surprisingly comforting.

She gave up trying to dry her cheeks with the already-wet handkerchief. They would dry on their own in time, she supposed, although she would look a sight. No doubt she already did. She took one deep, shuddery breath and straightened her spine. "I'm going to tell you," she said, in a voice thready with tears. "But please know I've regretted it for twenty-five years, and the thought of it has never failed to cause me pain."

Annis took the wet handkerchief from her and produced a fresh, dry one. Harriet accepted it gratefully.

"When I was young," Harriet began, "I met the most wonderful man in the world. His name was Alexander."

She told her tale as clearly and briefly as she could. Annis listened, rapt, watching her face as she spoke. "And so," she finished, feeling the gravity of her story afresh, so that her shoulders slumped despite her, "I tried to dissuade Alexander from going to war, but all I succeeded in doing was distracting him so he was vulnerable. He didn't protect himself. He died because I interfered."

"Aunt Harriet," Annis said, speaking for the first time since the recitation began. "Your Alexander might have died anyway. It was the war. So many people died."

"I shouldn't have done it, Annis. I knew better. Grandmother Beryl taught me better. We should never toy with the *maleficia*. Alexander paid the price for my selfishness." She made herself pull her shoulders back and her spine straight. "It was a long time ago, and there's nothing to be done about it now except advise you never to make the same mistake."

Annis sat silently, looking toward the frosty scene beyond the window, her lower lip caught between her teeth. Harriet said, "Annis, do you understand? Employing the *maleficia* is imposing your will upon someone else. It's precisely what you don't want a husband to do to you. In the end it redounds upon the practitioner, as poor Frances learned. The outcome is inevitable."

Several minutes passed while Annis's brow creased with thought and Harriet, believing she had said all she could, sat in tense silence. Finally, with a long exhalation, Annis broke the moment. "I understand, Aunt Harriet. Of course you're right. We can go ahead."

"I'm relieved to hear that." Harriet stood up. "Wrap up the manikins, will you? We'll have to take them to Frances. She never leaves her room."

Grace was in the kitchen, murmuring to herself. Harriet and Annis went down the hall to Frances's bedroom. The door was open, and they could see Velma dusting the bureaus and windowsills with a large dust cloth. Frances was seated in an armchair, which Velma had turned to allow the winter sun to shine on her face.

With Velma's cot added to the room's furniture, the room felt crowded. Harriet knocked on the door frame, and Velma, dust cloth in hand, turned to see her former mistress. "Oh!" she said. "Miss Annis! Am I coming back?"

"No, Velma," Annis said gently. "No, we've just come to see Frances. Are you well?"

Velma didn't answer the question. "You're not gonna take away Mrs. Frances?"

"No," Annis said. "She's best here, with Aunt Harriet. With you, I should say."

The creases of anxiety in Velma's forehead eased. "She wants me here."

"Do you think so? Then I'm so glad you're willing to stay."

"Velma," Harriet said, "why don't you go have a cup of tea? I think Grace is baking scones, and you can have one while it's hot."

When Velma hesitated, casting an anxious look at Frances, Annis spoke again. "She'll be fine for a little while. We won't leave her until you come back."

When she was gone, Harriet said, "She's devoted to Frances."

"She always worries about everything under the sun. Now I'm afraid she'll worry about Frances."

"Did you notice what she said, Annis?"

"What?"

"She said Frances wants her here. Now, how do you think she knows that?"

Annis caught a breath, and her clear blue eyes sparkled with sudden understanding. "She senses her, as I do."

"I think she must. It's a sign of her good heart, Annis. You may miss her more than you think."

Annis smiled and crossed the room to pick up something from the bureau Velma had been dusting.

"What's that?"

"This," Annis said, "is Velma's treasure." She held up the cut-glass swan.

"It's very pretty."

"It is, isn't it?" Annis set it down again, taking care to position it just as it had been. "I was so surprised when I found how much she liked it. Now I'm surprised again."

"Has George noticed Velma is gone?"

"No. He hardly ever saw her. We'll just let him go on paying her wages until . . . well, until we see what's going to happen."

"You have ways of managing your father, I see."

Annis smiled. "I think our little bit of magic has not completely faded."

Frances had not moved at all since they came in. She had gained a bit of weight since coming to the Dakota. She was freshly washed, her hair brushed and pinned up, but her pretty face was as blank as a statue's. Her lips drooped open, and with Velma not there, a drop of saliva rolled from the corner of her mouth.

Harriet had become accustomed to the stab of remorse in her breast when she saw her cousin like this. It was all too easy to leave her in the care of Velma, to avoid confronting the result of their battle, but she sometimes felt guilty about that, too.

She took the wrapped bundle from Annis and knelt beside the armchair. "Frances, I hope you can hear me. These are the manikins you made. They need to be destroyed, and you're the only one who can do it." She laid the bundle in Frances's lap and folded back the linen.

She had no expectation of a response, but she waited a moment just the same, in case one might come. Annis came to stand behind her, first bending to dab at Frances's chin with a towel.

Harriet was about to pick up Frances's hand, to move her fingers for her, when Frances blinked and took a quick, gasping breath, as if someone had pinched her. A strange sound emerged from her throat, a moan, or a whimper.

Harriet whispered, "Frances?"

The cool sunlight illuminated Frances's still-white cheeks, her drooping eyelids, her slack mouth. It didn't seem possible she might actually speak. It didn't seem likely she was conscious of what was happening, but her hands moved in her lap, lifting and falling like injured birds. The fingers flexed, as if they were searching for something. Annis, standing behind the chair, pressed a hand to her breast as if her heart hurt.

Harriet lifted the manikin that represented Annis and placed it under Frances's hand. "Undo it, Frances," she murmured. "No magic today. No cantrip. Just undo it."

The moan came again, a pitiful, helpless sound. Frances's fingers touched the little simulacrum, grazing the tuft of hair, feeling the makeshift dress. She smoothed it with uncertain fingers before, feebly, she began to take it apart.

First the cloth came free and fell to the floor. Harriet's stomach contracted at the crude shape of the body beneath, the legs, the arms, so clumsy and yet so terrifyingly human.

Frances, her gaze as blank as ever, began to crumble the wax beneath her fingers. She started with the legs, then the arms. Tears began to trickle weakly down her cheeks.

Annis said, "She's crying. Frances is crying."

"I see," Harriet said. "That hasn't happened before, has it?"

"No, but…Oh dear God, Aunt Harriet. It's so awful. She's aware. She knows what's happening, but she can't—she can't do anything about it."

They watched, helpless, as Frances scrabbled at the torso of the poppet, unsteadily crumbling it into bits. When Frances reached the head, Annis gasped.

Harriet peered at her. "Do you feel something, Annis?"

Annis's voice was thin. "In a way I do. I feel—it's odd, Aunt Harriet, but I feel her sorrow." Her fingers fluttered up to her throat, where the moonstone rested. "It hurts her," she said. "She has lost everything, and it hurts her."

"Oh, Frances," Harriet said, shaking her head. "Poor Frances."

Frances gave another moan, a thin, formless sob. Her tears were tiny dull droplets that carved crooked paths down her face. With a convulsive movement, she tore the tuft of hair from the wooden bead that formed the manikin's head and dropped the bead into her lap.

There was no human shape left at all now, no hint of what the figure had been, nothing left but a little gray mound of shredded wax. Annis gently wiped the tears from Frances's cheeks.

The second manikin soon followed. It seemed Frances needed no prompting, though her fingers fumbled blindly at the task. Her whimpers grew louder, and Harriet had the sickening feeling she wanted to speak, to say something about what she was doing, perhaps about what she had done. The sounds never became words. Frances was locked in her body as surely as if she were shut into a prison cell.

It must be, Harriet thought, a living hell.

They watched Frances pull apart James's manikin, much as she had Annis's. She fumbled the bead that represented his head, with its painted eyes and curl of fair hair, dropping it to the floor. It rolled out of sight under the bed.

When it was done, Frances's head lolled against the high back of her armchair. Her tears had stopped. Her eyelids drooped as before, and her mouth sagged open, as if the brief moment of energy had never happened.

"Can you help her, Aunt Harriet?" Annis asked in a small voice.

"I don't know," she answered. "I'll do all I can."

"I'll be back to help," Annis said. "We're going to Seabeck after the wedding, but I'll be back in the fall to work with you."

"I will look forward to that." Harriet struggled a bit to get to her feet, feeling stiff and old and tired. "Why don't you gather up all that wax, and we'll dispose of it in the herbarium. I'll fetch Velma so we can get to work."

She found Velma hovering in the corridor, awaiting her summons. When they came back into the bedroom, Annis was just folding the linen over the remains of the manikins.

Harriet forgot all about the bead that had rolled under the bed. When she came back for it, later in the day, it was gone.

49

Annis

James wired his mother, and Lady Eleanor sailed posthaste to New York to be present for the wedding, arriving at Allington House with all the dignity and fuss of a great ocean liner claiming her berth. A lady's maid and a footman and dozens of trunks and hatboxes and suitcases trailed in her wake, a show of status that would have made Frances weep with envy. Lady Eleanor held out one black-gloved hand to George Allington, and in a gesture that made Annis's eyes widen, he bent over it as if they were in Victoria's court.

Lady Eleanor began her visit with her customary icy demeanor but thawed swiftly in the warmth of her host's easygoing hospitality. Annis, though she was up to her chin in dressmakers and florists and bakers, watched this with bemusement.

"My father," she told James, on a day when they managed to escape for a ride through the park, "is quite taken with Her Ladyship."

"My mother has that effect on people," he answered. "When she chooses."

"I like her very much," Annis said. "I believe, once we're married, I will address her as you do, as Mother."

He smiled. "I expect she'll be pleased."

"She's not upset that there will be no money?"

His smile faded, and he glanced away, into the bare limbs of the trees stretching into the wintry sky.

Annis said, "James?"

He cleared his throat, something she hadn't heard him do in a long time. "I'm sorry, Annis, but I—it seemed best to—"

"James! You haven't told her!"

He looked ahead to the curving drive where it wound through the trees, their silvery limbs laid bare by winter. "It doesn't matter, Annis," he said.

"Doesn't matter! Of course it matters."

She was watching his profile, and she saw his chin jut in a way that reminded her of her father. Of herself, for that matter. It made him look older. Harder.

He said in a grim tone, "It's my problem now, Annis. It falls to me to save Seabeck, not to my mother. The decisions will have to be mine, no matter how difficult."

She chewed her lip, contemplating this. "You mean about the London house."

"The London house, the High Point parcel, and more. There's no way out of it." He drew a ragged breath through his nostrils. "Seabeck will never be what it was, I fear, but it will survive. I mean to see to it."

She reached out and put her gloved hand on his sleeve. "We'll see to it together, James."

He looked at her then, his autumn-hazel eyes glistening in the thin sunshine. "I'm grateful you'll be at my side, Annis, but I warn you—it may not be easy."

She smiled affectionately at him. "Any task is easier when shared, I believe."

"Indeed." He smiled back. "Easier when shared."

"I do hope your mother won't resent me, James. You could have married a real heiress, one with a decent settlement, one who could have saved you all of this trouble."

"I could have done that, it's true." He grinned, and the look of worry left his eyes. "But she wouldn't have been you, Miss Annis Allington. I should never have been happy!"

Annis had spoken to her father about the subject of her dowry, but he had been unmoved. "Proves he really wants you," he said. "Never liked Frances putting you on the market that way."

"You didn't stop her from doing it."

"I got tired of her complaints."

"You were willing to let me be married off just to make her happy?"

He said, as he had before, "You had to marry someone."

It was the same old argument, and she didn't have the energy to pursue it. Her father had a reputation for being tight with money, and in the past, she had admired it. Now—she didn't care so much for herself, but she could see the weight that lay on dear James's shoulders, and there seemed to be nothing she could do to lighten it.

It was a busy time. She was occupied from morning till night, either with Harriet in the herbarium, entertaining James, or dealing with the issue of a trousseau.

One of the first things Lady Eleanor had done, upon learning that Annis no longer had a maid, was to engage one for her. She knew well how to go about these things, quickly producing a woman of middle age called Myra, already trained by an elderly lady in Manhattan. Myra was a marvel with a sewing needle, quick with a cup of tea or broth or cocoa when it was needed, and willing to travel across the Atlantic with her new young mistress. She took on the task of supervising the trousseau, and Annis surrendered all decisions regarding clothes, lingerie, shoes, and hats to her.

The idea came to her one afternoon, bursting into her brain all at once, like one of the fireworks going off over the park in the summer. Simmering with suppressed excitement, Annis persuaded Myra to go to the milliner's shop without her. It would give her a couple of hours of freedom. Lady Eleanor was resting. James, at her father's invitation, had gone in the carriage to visit the Allington Iron Stove Factory. She could be alone.

She had no herbarium, of course. She had only her corner of Mrs. King's pantry, though she hadn't used it in months. She hurried there now and found her space as tidy as ever, her stores of herbs and ointments still in their jars. Of course she had a great deal still to learn, but she had been working with Harriet nearly every day since their return. She thought she knew enough to do this one small thing.

She remembered the day in the herbarium when she and Harriet had made, and magicked, the salve that brought Bits home. She had everything she needed, the rosemary, the wormwood, the mandrake, and a bit of honey.

She could have asked Harriet to help her, but what if Harriet refused? Then, if she had the result she wanted, Harriet would suspect what she had done. If Aunt Harriet said not to do this, then doing it anyway would be a betrayal of her trust. She meant—with one possible exception—never to betray Harriet's trust.

She chopped and pounded until her ingredients were smooth, then rolled them into a small, perfect ball. She found an unburned candle and carried it and the electuary up to her bedroom. She laid her moonstone at the base of the candle and set the ball of herbs and honey next to it. She recited the cantrip from her memory, pleased it was still so clear in her mind, changing only one word.

The touch of this remedy will move the heart
So kindness is the better part.
Leaf and root and flower bless
The heart that always answers, Yes.

It made her smile to remember how easy it had been to persuade Mr. Neufeld to return Black Satin and Sally to the Allington stables. It had been even more simple to beg Papa, under the effect of the salve, to return the price Neufeld had paid.

And now—now, she would change her father's mind one final time. James would be relieved. Lady Eleanor, so proud of her son having won his chosen bride, would never need to know there had been any question about it.

And she, Annis, would know she had the power of the Bishop witches in her own hands.

She did everything the way her mentor had taught her. When she spoke the cantrip, she stood before her array of candle, moonstone, and remedy, and waited.

With a thrill of pride, she watched the moonstone begin to glow, its surface turning as pearly as the face of a full moon in

a cloudless sky. She felt the power flow up through her feet and
legs, into her body, out through her arms to her hands and up
into her throat. It was that now-familiar sense of having touched
lightning, that almost pain that made her feel more alive than
should be possible. It filled her, and it surrounded her, and it
charged her electuary with magic.

She was just about to blow out the candle when the other feeling struck. It rolled up from her belly into her chest, thrilled
through her throat and into her skull, where it bloomed like a
flower in midsummer. The room rocked around her, beneath
her. She felt as if something had taken over her body and her
mind, and she was powerless to resist it.

The knowing.

She must go to Harriet, as soon as possible. She had something
to tell her.

50

Harriet

Harriet was standing on a footstool in the herbarium, in the midst of her winter task of scrubbing shelves, when the knock on her door came. It wouldn't be Grace, of course, who was trained never to disturb her. It could only be Annis, though she wasn't expecting her. The wedding was set for tomorrow. The bride-to-be should be busy with a hundred pressing tasks. She frowned as she climbed down from the footstool, hoping nothing was amiss.

She unlocked the door and opened it to a beaming Annis, pink-cheeked from the December cold, swathed in a white fur that made her eyes look like sapphires. "Annis! Whatever are you doing here?"

Annis laughed and said, "I have something to tell you, Aunt Harriet, something so—so important I don't have words for it. I wouldn't have interrupted you otherwise." She peered past Harriet's shoulder at the scoured counters and empty worktable. "It doesn't look like you're working."

"Just cleaning. It's too cold for foraging."

"It's snowing now. So pretty, but I did come in the carriage."

"What a surprise!" Harriet caught sight of Grace hovering in the hallway and said, "Oh, Grace, good. Perhaps you could make some tea for us. I'll take Annis into the parlor."

Grace bustled toward Annis. "Now, here, Miss Annis, you just give me those furs. Aren't they lovely? From your trousseau, I suppose. Beautiful. Perfect for this December weather. You'll be too warm inside, though. I've just stirred up the fire in the parlor, and I have some scones for you, not today's, but yesterday's, they're still fresh as can be just the same. I'll just give them a bit of a warm in the oven. There you are now, you go and sit down and I'll have your tea in a moment." She was still chattering as she hung the furs on the coatrack and trotted off toward the kitchen.

Harriet led the way to the parlor, and she and Annis sat close to the fire. Annis looked as if she were going to burst with excitement, literally bouncing on the seat of the divan, and Harriet couldn't help laughing. "You look like a child about to open her Christmas presents!"

"Oh, Aunt Harriet, I feel that way!"

"Because your wedding is tomorrow?"

"Oh no! I mean yes, of course, and dear James is excited, too—but just let me explain."

"Very well. Shall we wait for the tea?"

"Oh no, I can't wait another minute! I wanted to come last night, but it was so late, and it looked like snow, so..."

Annis bounced off the divan and came to sit next to Harriet. She seized her hand and squeezed it. "First, Aunt Harriet, just imagine! Papa has decided to dower me after all, and a very nice dowry it is, enough to pay off the old marquess's debts. It means James doesn't have to worry so much, and he doesn't have to tell his mother about selling the London house."

Harriet raised her eyebrows. "Indeed. That's quite generous of George. I never think of him as a generous man."

"Oh, he's not, not in the least!" Annis said. "He says he's going to save all kinds of money, now that he won't have to support me and my horses and…" Her voice trailed off, and her blush deepened.

Harriet tilted her head to one side as she regarded her great-niece with a measuring glance. "You worked a bit of magic, didn't you? All on your own."

"I—well, yes, I did. Because poor James was so worried, and he was going to have to sell his favorite part of Seabeck. I couldn't bear to see him unhappy, and I know perfectly well Papa can afford it! I understand his financial position every bit as well as he does. He thinks females don't understand money, but he's wrong."

"He certainly is. I have always managed my own money without the slightest difficulty."

Annis twinkled at her, laughing. "It was the same rite you and I did together, except I made an electuary and popped it into Papa's glass before dinner. He takes ice in his whiskey, and he never even noticed."

"Well done, dear Annis. Very well done indeed. It was creative to use an electuary."

"Thank you! I thought it was quite a successful effort, myself."

Harriet smiled, pleased that Annis didn't bother to feign modesty. It was a notable achievement for an untried practitioner. She couldn't help wishing Annis's studies weren't going to be interrupted, but she had resigned herself to it. "There's something else, you said?"

Annis stopped bouncing. Grace came in with the tea tray,

floating on her usual tide of chatter. Annis didn't say anything more until the tea had been poured and the scones presented and Grace had withdrawn. She didn't pick up her teacup or take a scone. She touched the moonstone at her throat and said, "I used the same cantrip you did before. I knew the magic was there because the moonstone told me, and then—"

She dropped her hand and reached for Harriet's once again. "Aunt Harriet, it was the knowing. It was so strong, I felt as if my head might burst." Her voice throbbed with intensity, and she was no longer the excited girl. She was a mature woman. An experienced witch, sure of herself and her practice. She said, with such gravity Harriet could not doubt her, "Aunt Harriet, you were not the cause of Alexander's death."

Harriet couldn't restrain her gasp. A sudden faintness came over her, dimming the light in the room, disorienting her. She found herself gripping Annis's hand, a lifeline in a sea of confusion. She whispered, "What? What do you mean?"

"It was his own reluctance," Annis said, softly but firmly. "I felt it all, as clearly as if I were inside his mind. Alexander didn't want to kill. Couldn't bring himself to do it. He hesitated because he didn't want to be there, didn't want the promotion, didn't want to shoot at his fellow Americans. He thought of them as his brothers of the opposition, and that was what made him vulnerable. It was not the *maleficia*. It was his own nature. It was not your fault."

"Not my fault," Harriet repeated. She could hardly take it in. All the years of regret and guilt and grief—could they simply melt away? Leave her with a clear conscience at last?

"There's no doubt," Annis said, squeezing her hand between both of hers. "There is absolutely no doubt at all, Aunt Harriet."

Harriet believed her. Not just because she wanted to, which she did, but because the magic was so strong in this girl, the Bishop magic.

She supposed it would take a long time for her to absorb this moment, but she would do it. She would come to understand, to accept, and ultimately to be free. Annis was leaving her, but she had given her a priceless gift.

She leaned forward and kissed Annis's smooth, rosy cheek.

"I suppose now I have to address you as *my lady*," Harriet said.

Annis wrinkled her nose at her and laughed. "If you do, I'll never speak to you again!"

She looked achingly lovely in her wedding dress of cream brocade and ivory silk. Her pearls were around her neck, the moonstone gleaming in the hollow of her throat. Her eyes sparkled, and her cheeks glowed above the swaths of creamy fabric. Her new lady's maid had done something wonderful with her hair, pinning it up into a flattering, subtle shape. When Harriet complimented it, Annis had groaned. "It took an hour, Aunt Harriet! A whole hour! I could barely sit still. I won't be doing that very often."

Between them Myra and Mrs. King had created a wonderland out of the rarely used Allington House ballroom. It was just what Frances had dreamed of, banks of lilies and white hothouse roses, a long table set with china and silver and crystal for the wedding breakfast, chairs draped in snow-white linen, her stepdaughter acquiring a title. Frances, of course, was not here, nor had Harriet been able to persuade Velma to leave Frances's side long enough to attend.

None of the Four Hundred were here, either. They had not been invited.

Several of Annis's school friends had come with their parents. George, looking by turns proud and restless, had invited a few of his business associates, and they and their wives were clearly enjoying the luxury of an expensive wedding breakfast. Mrs. King, with Lady Eleanor interfering at every stage, had produced a magnificent cake, all in white, like Queen Victoria's wedding cake. She brought Annis to see it and wept into her handkerchief while Annis praised the confection and assured her she would return to New York in just a few months.

The ceremony itself was modest and brief, but the festivities after were surprisingly enjoyable. Even the dowager marchioness unbent, accepting the less formal American customs.

And now it was done. James and Annis were the Marquess and Marchioness of Rosefield. The photographers from the *Times* and the *Tribune* had come and gone. Mrs. King's lovely cake had been dismantled and devoured. The guests were gathering at one end of the ballroom in readiness to bid the newlyweds farewell as they started off on their wedding journey.

Annis went up to her bedroom, with Myra in tow, to change her dress. Harriet lingered near the arch of vines and flowers where the couple had spoken their vows, thinking she might steal one or two blossoms and press them to give to Annis as a memento. She was just reaching for a sprig of jasmine when she saw that the tiny pochette bag that had been part of Annis's wedding ensemble had fallen behind the arch, its ribbons tangled in the vines.

Harriet crouched to untangle it and picked it up. It was made of creamy silk, with seed pearls sewn in a floral design on the outside. She smoothed it with her fingers, admiring the artistry of the needlework, then paused.

There was something in the little bag, something more than the obligatory handkerchief. It was hard, and round, and it felt familiar to her searching fingers.

She glanced around to be certain no one was paying attention before she slipped behind the arch. Half-hidden, she pulled the ribbons to open the pochette. She reached inside and pulled the thing out between two fingers.

It was the wooden bead that had formed the head of James's manikin. The curl of fair hair was still glued to it, and the eyes and mouth, though the ink had faded, were just as Frances had made them. The magic still clung to this artifact, like moss clings to a stone.

Harriet gazed down at the bead in her palm. Why had Annis kept it? What should she do now that she had found it?

She turned away from the festive scene behind her. Still hidden by the floral arch, she held the bead in one hand and pressed the other palm over the amulet beneath her bodice. She closed her eyes, bent her head, and whispered,

Bishop mothers, swiftly speak,
Elder wisdom now I seek.

How long since she had spoken that cantrip? She believed it had been with Grandmother Beryl, when they were deciding what to do about Frances. Beryl had spoken it long before that, in some other confused situation, as she tried to discern her duty.

Harriet drew a long, steady breath and opened her eyes. She opened the pochette bag again and dropped the bead inside. She pulled the ribbons to close the little bag before she emerged from behind the bridal arch. With the long strides she used when she was foraging in the park, she crossed the ballroom, wound her way through the crowd of people, and hurried around the corridor to Annis's room.

Annis was seated at her dressing table, and Myra, with a handful of pins, was adjusting her hat. It was a rather complicated affair, small, with a profusion of ivory ribbons, obviously made more for fashion than for warmth. Myra bent forward to insert a long hat pin through the confection of silk and straw. Annis, tilting her head to help, caught sight of Harriet in the doorway, and the pochette cupped in her hand.

The color instantly drained from Annis's cheeks. She said faintly, "Oh. Aunt Harriet."

Myra glanced up and, not understanding, smiled. "We're almost ready, Miss Bishop. Just the hat and the fur cape. Doesn't Lady Annis look pretty?"

"Beautiful," Harriet said. "Myra, could you excuse us, just for a moment?"

Myra paused, looked down at her young mistress, then back at Harriet's solemn face. She muttered something about more pins and scuttled out of the bedroom.

Harriet closed the door when she had gone and walked to the dressing table. Annis rose, and Harriet held out the pochette for her to take.

"Aunt Harriet, I just—" Annis began.

Harriet put up a hand. "Dearest Annis, don't tell me. I can imagine."

Annis pressed the pochette between her hands. "It's still there," she whispered.

"It is."

"Why didn't you take it?"

"It's not my decision, dear heart. It's yours. I've taught you what I can, and I see no darkness in you. I see quite the opposite. I see light, and love, and courage."

"I think of it as—a protection, I suppose. In case..." Her voice trailed off, and her eyes filled with tears that shone blue in the afternoon light.

"Are you sorry you married your James?"

Annis shook her head. "No."

"But you still thought you needed protection?"

Annis blinked away her tears. Her mouth firmed, and she thrust out her chin. "Men change too easily, Aunt Harriet. Even the best of men. They change their minds. They regret their promises. What if, now that we're married—"

"Ah." Harriet met Annis's eyes in the mirror. "I would say, dear heart, that no one can predict the challenges they will face. You and James have everything before you, wonderful things, hard things, sad things, happy things. I hope you will meet them as equals."

"That's what I want," Annis said. "Equals."

Harriet gave a tiny shrug and smiled. Annis let her chin drop again and smiled back. She thrust the pochette out, back into Harriet's hand. "You're right, Aunt Harriet," she said. "If I use magic, we're not exactly equal, are we? Please take it. I have—" She hesitated, then grinned, an impish expression that made Harriet laugh aloud. "I believe I have other persuasions."

Harriet said, still laughing, "I am sure you do!" She tucked the pochette into her own handbag, to deal with later.

In far too short a time, Harriet was standing at the top of the curved gravel drive, waving goodbye to the bride and groom as the carriage bore them away to the Battery. There they would board the *Teutonic*, with Robbie and Black Satin on one of the lower decks. They would sail away toward their new life together.

The symbolism, Harriet thought, was perfect. Just the same, it was a wrench to see Annis depart from her, to strain for a final glimpse of her gay, beribboned hat and her white furs ruffling in the breeze as she waved from the carriage window.

Indoors, as servants scurried this way and that with hats and coats and walking sticks, Harriet bid Lady Eleanor farewell and congratulated her on her son's marriage. The dowager marchioness was clearly pleased by the whole event.

"Shall you have a carriage to fetch you?" Lady Eleanor asked as Harriet was helped into her coat.

"No, it's not a long walk to the Dakota. I'll be glad of the exercise."

"You will come and visit us at Rosefield Hall, of course, Miss Bishop," Lady Eleanor said. "And do come to our London house during the season. There will be concerts and exhibits, most delightful, and you can visit with your great-niece."

"What a kind invitation, Lady Eleanor. I look forward to both those things."

With her coat buttoned around her and her hands tucked into a beaver muff, Harriet set off, ready for the peace of her own apartment and Grace's soothing chatter. She was uncomfortably aware of Annis's pochette inside her handbag. The magicked bead made her feel as if she were carrying a hot coal.

She could hardly wait to be rid of it. She would put it in Frances's hands, have her strip off the curl of hair, scrub away the inked eyes and mouth. That would put an end to the *maleficia* that clung to it.

After she had been fussed over by Grace and warmed by the

fire, and had checked in on Velma and Frances in their room, she carried the pochette into her herbarium. She rolled the bead out onto her worktable and stared at it. It gazed back at her, blind and mute and helpless.

In a few short years, Harriet reflected, a new century would begin. Would it be better for women, or worse? Would they have more independence, or would there be a backlash to undo a hundred years of progress? Any answer she had would be no more than a guess. It would not affect her so much, at her advanced age. It was Annis, and the young women like her, who would have to deal with whatever was to come.

Despite Annis's brave words, she had a point. She was a married woman now. To some people that meant her husband was her master. Harriet couldn't imagine anyone being Annis's master, but she would be in a strange country, in a place with different customs. Who knew what might lie ahead for her?

Harriet clicked her tongue. "I didn't create you," she muttered at the wooden bead. "But you're here now, and my girl is far away. I'll just—just put you someplace safe."

She picked up the bead, dropped it back into the pochette, and tightly knotted the ribbons at its neck. She pulled her footstool to the far end of the herbarium and climbed up on it to reach for an empty jar resting on a top shelf. She pulled down the jar, lifted its lid, and dropped the pochette with its fragment of *maleficia* inside.

She pushed the jar as far to the back of the shelf as it would go. When she had climbed down from the footstool, she looked up to assure herself the jar was invisible from the floor.

It was well hidden. She could forget all about it.

For now.

Acknowledgments

My most heartfelt thanks go to Alex Bird Tillson, my friend and colleague, for being the first reader for this book. I'm also indebted to the wonderful novelists Anna Quinn and Erica Bauermeister for their exacting critiques. The feedback from these three gifted writers was invaluable in the development of this novel, and I'll always be grateful for that, and for their friendship.

Thanks also to Sarah Guan, my patient editor, and to Peter Rubie, my faithful agent and the dedicatee of this book. You were both wonderful throughout.

The team at Orbit/Redhook is terrific, and I appreciate their hard work and enthusiastic support more than I can say. Not every writer is so lucky. The cover art, the promotional efforts under Ellen Wright's able guidance, and the quick responses to all my concerns—these are gifts to an author, and I accept them with gratitude.

Last, but most important, thank you to my remarkable family. Faithful husband, talented son, wonderful sisters, brother, and brothers-in-law—I turn to you all at the oddest times, and I'm so lucky you're there when I need you. I love you all.

Look out for

A
Secret
HISTORY
of
WITCHES

also by

Louisa Morgan

Brittany, 1821. After Grand-mère Ursule gives her life to save her family, their magic seems to die with her. Even so, the Orchires fight to keep the old ways alive, practising half-remembered spells and arcane rites in hopes of a revival. And when their youngest daughter comes of age, magic flows anew. The lineage continues, though new generations struggle not only to master their power, but also to keep it hidden.

But when World War II looms on the horizon, magic is needed more urgently than ever – not for simple potions or visions, but to change the entire course of history.

extras

www.orbitbooks.net

about the author

Louisa Morgan is a pseudonym for award-winning author Louise Marley. Louise lives in the Pacific Northwest where she and her Border Terrier, Oscar, ramble the beaches and paths of Washington State.

Find out more about Louisa Morgan and other Orbit authors by registering online for the free monthly newsletter at www.orbitbooks.net.

if you enjoyed
THE AGE OF WITCHES

look out for

THE TEN THOUSAND DOORS OF JANUARY

by

Alix E. Harrow

ACCORDING TO JANUARY SCALLER, THERE'S ONLY ONE WAY TO RUN AWAY FROM YOUR OWN STORY, AND THAT'S TO SNEAK INTO SOMEONE ELSE'S . . .

In a sprawling mansion filled with peculiar treasures, January Scaller is a curiosity herself. As the ward of the wealthy Mr Locke, she feels little different from the artefacts that decorate the halls: carefully maintained, largely ignored and utterly out of place.

But her quiet existence is shattered when she stumbles across a strange book. A book that carries the scent of other worlds and tells a tale of secret doors, of love, adventure and danger. Each page reveals more impossible truths about the world, and January discovers a story increasingly entwined with her own.

The Blue Door

When I was seven, I found a door. I suspect I should capitalize that word, so you understand I'm not talking
about your garden- or common-variety door that leads reliably
to a white-tiled kitchen or a bedroom closet.

When I was seven, I found a Door. There—look how tall
and proud the word stands on the page now, the belly of that
D like a black archway leading into white nothing. When you
see that word, I imagine a little prickle of familiarity makes the
hairs on the back of your neck stand up. You don't know a thing
about me; you can't see me sitting at this yellow-wood desk, the
salt-sweet breeze riffling these pages like a reader looking for
her bookmark. You can't see the scars that twist and knot across
my skin. You don't even know my name (it's January Scaller;

so now I suppose you do know a little something about me and I've ruined my point).

But you know what it means when you see the word *Door*. Maybe you've even seen one for yourself, standing half-ajar and rotted in an old church, or oiled and shining in a brick wall. Maybe, if you're one of those fanciful persons who find their feet running toward unexpected places, you've even walked through one and found yourself in a very unexpected place indeed.

Or maybe you've never so much as glimpsed a Door in your life. There aren't as many of them as there used to be.

But you still know about Doors, don't you? Because there are ten thousand stories about ten thousand Doors, and we know them as well as we know our names. They lead to Faerie, to Valhalla, Atlantis and Lemuria, Heaven and Hell, to all the directions a compass could never take you, to *elsewhere*. My father—who is a true scholar and not just a young lady with an ink pen and a series of things she has to say—puts it much better: "If we address stories as archaeological sites, and dust through their layers with meticulous care, we find at some level there is always a doorway. A dividing point between *here* and *there*, us and them, mundane and magical. It is at the moments when the doors open, when things flow between the worlds, that stories happen."

He never capitalized doors. But perhaps scholars don't capitalize words just because of the shapes they make on the page.

It was the summer of 1901, although the arrangement of four numbers on a page didn't mean much to me then. I think of it now as a swaggering, full-of-itself sort of year, shining with the gold-plated promises of a new century. It had shed all the mess and fuss of the nineteenth century—all those wars and revolutions and uncertainties, all those imperial growing pains—and now there was nothing but peace and prosperity wherever one looked. Mr. J. P. Morgan had recently become the richest man in the entire history of the world; Queen Victoria had finally expired and left her vast empire to her kingly-looking son; those unruly Boxers had been subdued in China; and Cuba had been tucked neatly beneath America's civilized wing. Reason and rationality reigned supreme, and there was no room for magic or mystery.

There was no room, it turned out, for little girls who wandered off the edge of the map and told the truth about the mad, impossible things they found there.

I found it on the raggedy western edge of Kentucky, right where the state dips its toe into the Mississippi. It's not the kind of place you'd expect to find anything mysterious or even mildly interesting: it's flat and scrubby-looking, populated by flat, scrubby-looking people. The sun hangs twice as hot and three times as bright as it does in the rest of the country, even at the very end of August, and everything feels damp and sticky, like the soap scum left on your skin when you're the last one to use the bath.

But Doors, like murder suspects in cheap mysteries, are often where you least expect them.

I was only in Kentucky at all because Mr. Locke had taken me along on one of his business trips. He said it was a "real treat" and a "chance to see how things are done," but really it was because my nursemaid was teetering on the edge of hysteria and had threatened to quit at least four times in the last month. I was a difficult child, back then.

Or maybe it was because Mr. Locke was trying to cheer me up. A postcard had arrived last week from my father. It had a picture of a brown girl wearing a pointy gold hat and a resentful expression, with the words *AUTHENTIC BURMESE COSTUME* stamped alongside her. On the back were three lines in tidy brown ink: *Extending my stay, back in October. Thinking of you. JS.* Mr. Locke had read it over my shoulder and patted my arm in a clumsy, keep-your-chin-up sort of way.

A week later I was stuffed in the velvet and wood-paneled coffin of a Pullman sleeper car reading *The Rover Boys in the Jungle* while Mr. Locke read the business section of the *Times* and Mr. Stirling stared into space with a valet's professional blankness.

I ought to introduce Mr. Locke properly; he'd hate to wander into the story in such a casual, slantwise way. Allow me to present Mr. William Cornelius Locke, self-made not-quite-billionaire, head of W. C. Locke & Co., owner of no less than three stately homes along the Eastern Seaboard, proponent of the virtues of Order and Propriety (words that he certainly would prefer to see capitalized—see that *P*, like a woman with her hand on her hip?), and chairman of the New England Archaeological Society, a sort of social club for rich, powerful men who were also amateur collectors. I say "amateur" only because it was fashionable for wealthy men to refer to their passions in this dismissive way, with a little flick of their fingers, as if admitting to a profession other than moneymaking might sully their reputations.

In truth, I sometimes suspected that all Locke's moneymaking was specifically designed to fuel his collecting hobby. His home in Vermont—the one we actually lived in, as opposed to the two other pristine structures intended mainly to impress his significance upon the world—was a vast, private Smithsonian packed so tightly it seemed to be constructed of artifacts rather than mortar and stones. There was little organization: limestone figures of wide-hipped women kept company with Indonesian screens carved like lace, and obsidian arrowheads shared a glass case with the taxidermied arm of an Edo warrior (I hated that arm but couldn't stop looking at it, wondering what it had looked like alive and muscled, how its owner would have felt about a little girl in America looking at his paper-dry flesh without even knowing his name).

My father was one of Mr. Locke's field agents, hired when I was nothing but an eggplant-sized bundle wrapped in an old traveling coat. "Your mother had just died, you know, very sad case," Mr. Locke liked to recite to me, "and there was your father—this odd-colored, scarecrow-looking fellow with God-help-him *tattoos* up and down his arms—in the absolute middle of nowhere with a baby. I said to myself: Cornelius, there's a man in need of a little charity!"

Father was hired before dusk. Now he gallivants around the world collecting objects "of particular unique value" and mailing them to Mr. Locke so he can put them in glass cases with brass plaques and shout at me when I touch them or play with them or steal the Aztec coins to re-create scenes from *Treasure Island*. And I stay in my little gray room in Locke House and harass the nursemaids Locke hires to civilize me and wait for Father to come home.

At seven, I'd spent considerably more time with Mr. Locke than with my own biological father, and insofar as it was possible to love someone so naturally comfortable in three-piece suits, I loved him.

As was his custom, Mr. Locke had taken rooms for us in the nicest establishment available; in Kentucky, that translated to a sprawling pinewood hotel on the edge of the Mississippi, clearly built by someone who wanted to open a grand hotel but hadn't ever met one in real life. There were candy-striped wallpaper and electric chandeliers, but a sour catfish smell seeped up from the floorboards.

Mr. Locke waved past the manager with a fly-swatting gesture, told him to "Keep an eye on the girl, that's a good fellow," and swept into the lobby with Mr. Stirling trailing like a man-shaped dog at his heels. Locke greeted a bow-tied man waiting on one of the flowery couches. "Governor Dockery, a pleasure! I read your last missive with greatest attention, I assure you—and how is your cranium collection coming?"

Ah. So that was why we came: Mr. Locke was meeting one of his Archaeological Society pals for an evening of drinking, cigar smoking, and boasting. They had an annual Society meeting every summer at Locke House—a fancy party followed by a stuffy, members-only affair that neither I nor my father was permitted to attend—but some of the real enthusiasts couldn't wait the full year and sought one another out wherever they could.

The manager smiled at me in that forced, panicky way of childless adults, and I smiled toothily back. "I'm going out," I told him confidently. He smiled a little harder, blinking with uncertainty. People are always uncertain about me: my skin is sort of coppery-red, as if it's covered all over with cedar sawdust, but my eyes are round and light and my clothes are expensive. Was I a pampered pet or a serving girl? Should the poor manager serve me tea or toss me in the kitchens with the maids? I was what Mr. Locke called "an in-between sort of thing."

I tipped over a tall vase of flowers, gasped an insincere "oh *dear*," and slunk away while the manager swore and mopped at the mess with his coat. I escaped outdoors (see how that word slips into even the most mundane of stories? Sometimes I feel there are doors lurking in the creases of every sentence, with periods for knobs and verbs for hinges).

The streets were nothing but sunbaked stripes crisscrossing themselves before they ended in the muddy river, but the people of Ninley, Kentucky, seemed inclined to stroll along them as if they were proper city streets. They stared and muttered as I went by.

An idle dockworker pointed and nudged his companion.

"That's a little Chickasaw girl, I'll bet you." His workmate shook his head, citing his extensive personal experience with Indian girls, and speculated, "West Indian, maybe. Or a half-breed."

I kept walking. People were always guessing like that, categorizing me as one thing or another, but Mr. Locke assured me they were all equally incorrect. "A perfectly unique specimen," he called me. Once after a comment from one of the maids I'd asked him if I was colored and he'd snorted. "Odd-colored, perhaps, but hardly *colored*." I didn't really know what made a person colored or not, but the way he said it made me glad I wasn't.

The speculating was worse when my father was with me. His skin is darker than mine, a lustrous red-black, and his eyes are so black even the whites are threaded with brown. Once you factor in the tattoos—ink spirals twisting up both wrists—and the shabby suit and the spectacles and the muddled-up accent and—well. People stared.

I still wished he were with me.

I was so busy walking and not looking back at all those white faces that I thudded into someone. "Sorry, ma'am, I—" An old woman, hunched and seamed like a pale walnut, glared down at me. It was a practiced, grandmotherly glare, especially made for children who moved too fast and knocked into her. "Sorry," I said again.

She didn't answer, but something shifted in her eyes like a chasm cleaving open. Her mouth hung open, and her filmy eyes went wide as shutters. "Who—just who the hell are you?" she hissed at me. People don't like in-between things, I suppose.

I should have scurried back to the catfish-smelling hotel and huddled in Mr. Locke's safe, moneyed shadow, where none of these damn people could reach me; it would have been the proper thing to do. But, as Mr. Locke so often complained, I could sometimes be quite improper, willful, and temerarious (a word I assumed was unflattering from the company it kept).

So I ran away.

I ran until my stick-thin legs shook and my chest heaved against the fine seams of my dress. I ran until the street turned to a winding lane and the buildings behind me were swallowed up by wisteria and honeysuckle. I ran and tried not to think about the old woman's eyes on my face, or how much trouble I would be in for disappearing.

My feet stopped their churning only once they realized the dirt beneath them had turned to laid-over grasses. I found myself in a lonely, overgrown field beneath a sky so blue it reminded me of the tiles my father brought back from Persia: a majestic, world-swallowing blue you could fall into. Tall, rust-colored grasses rolled beneath it, and a few scattered cedars spiraled up toward it.

Something in the shape of the scene—the rich smell of dry cedar in the sun, the grass swaying against the sky like a tigress in orange and blue—made me want to curl into the dry stems like a fawn waiting for her mother. I waded deeper, wandering, letting my hands trail through the frilled tops of wild grains.

I almost didn't notice the Door at all. All Doors are like that, half-shadowed and sideways until someone looks at them in just the right way.

This one was nothing but an old timber frame arranged in a shape like the start of a house of cards. Rust stains spotted the wood where hinges and nails had bled into nothing, and only a few brave planks remained of the door itself. Flaking paint still clung to it, the same royal blue as the sky.

Now, I didn't know about Doors at the time, and wouldn't have believed you even if you'd handed me an annotated three-volume collection of eyewitness reports. But when I saw that raggedy blue door standing so lonesome in the field, I wanted it to lead someplace else. Someplace other than Ninley, Kentucky, someplace new and unseen and so vast I would never come to the end of it.

I pushed my palm against the blue paint. The hinges groaned, just like the doors to haunted houses in all my penny papers and adventure stories. My heart *pat-pat*ted in my chest, and some naive corner of my soul was holding its breath in expectation, waiting for something magical to happen.

There was nothing on the other side of the Door, of course: just the cobalt and cinnamon colors of my own world, sky and field. And—God knows why—the sight of it broke my heart. I sat down in my nice linen dress and wept with the loss of it. What had I expected? One of those magical passages children are always stumbling across in my books?

If Samuel had been there, we could've at least played pretend. Samuel Zappia was my only nonfictional friend: a dark-eyed boy with a clinical addiction to pulpy story papers and the faraway expression of a sailor watching the horizon. He visited Locke House twice a week in a red wagon with *ZAPPIA FAMILY GROCERIES, INC.* painted on the side in curlicued gold lettering, and usually contrived to sneak me the latest issue of *The Argosy All-Story Weekly* or *The Halfpenny Marvel* along with the flour and onions. On weekends he escaped his family's shop to join me in elaborate games of make-believe involving ghosts and dragons on the lakeshore. *Sognatore*, his mother called him, which Samuel said was Italian for good-for-nothing-boy-who-breaks-his-mother's-heart-by-dreaming-all-the-time.

But Samuel wasn't with me that day in the field. So I pulled out my little pocket diary and wrote a story instead.

When I was seven, that diary was the most precious thing I had ever owned, although whether I technically owned it is legally questionable. I hadn't bought it, and no one had given it to me—I'd found it. I was playing in the Pharaoh Room just before I turned seven, opening and closing all the urns and trying on the jewelry, and I happened to open a pretty blue treasure chest (*Box with vaulted lid, decorated with ivory, ebony, blue faience, Egypt; originally matched pair*). And in the bottom of the chest was this diary: leather the color of burnt butter, creamy cotton pages as blank and inviting as fresh snow.

It seemed likely that Mr. Locke had left it for me to find, a secret gift he was too gruff to give directly, so I took it without hesitation. I wrote in it whenever I was lonely or lost-feeling, or when my father was away and Mr. Locke was busy and the nursemaid was being horrible. I wrote a lot.

Mostly I wrote stories like the ones I read in Samuel's copies of *The Argosy*, about brave little boys with blond hair and names like Jack or Dick or Buddy. I spent a lot of time thinking of bloodcurdling titles and copying them out with extraswirly lines ("The Mystery of the Skeleton Key"; "The Golden Dagger Society"; "The Flying Orphan Girl"), and no time at all worrying about plot. That afternoon, sitting in that lonely field beside the Door that didn't lead anywhere, I wanted to write a different kind of story. A true kind of story, something I could crawl into if only I believed it hard enough.

Once there was a brave and temeraryous (sp?) girl who found a Door. It was a magic Door that's why it has a capital D. She opened the Door.

For a single second—a stretched-out slice of time that began on the sinuous curve of the *S* and ended when my pencil made its final swirl around the period—I believed it. Not in the half-pretending way that children believe in Santa Claus or fairies, but in the marrow-deep way you believe in gravity or rain.

Something in the world shifted. I know that's a shit description, pardon my unladylike language, but I don't know how else to say it. It was like an earthquake that didn't disturb a single blade of grass, an eclipse that didn't cast a single shadow, a vast but invisible change. A sudden breeze plucked the edge of the diary. It smelled of salt and warm stone and a dozen faraway scents that did not belong in a scrubby field beside the Mississippi.

I tucked my diary back in my skirts and stood. My legs shivered beneath me like birch trees in the wind, shaking with exhaustion, but I ignored them because the Door seemed to be murmuring in a soft, clattering language made of wood rot and peeling paint. I reached toward it again, hesitated, and then—

I opened the Door, and stepped through.

I wasn't anywhere at all. An echoing in-betweenness pressed against my eardrums, as if I'd swum to the bottom of a vast lake. My reaching hand disappeared into the emptiness; my boot swung in an arc that never ended.

I call that in-between place the threshold now (Threshold, the line of the *T* splitting two empty spaces). Thresholds are dangerous places, neither here nor there, and walking across one is like stepping off the edge of a cliff in the naive faith that you'll sprout wings halfway down. You can't hesitate, or doubt. You can't fear the in-between.

My foot landed on the other side of the door. The cedar and sunlight smell was replaced by a coppery taste in my mouth. I opened my eyes.

It was a world made of salt water and stone. I stood on a high bluff surrounded on all sides by an endless silver sea. Far below me, cupped by the curving shore of the island like a pebble in a palm, was a city.

At least, I supposed it was a city. It didn't have any of the usual trappings of one: no streetcars hummed and buzzed through it, and no haze of coal smoke curtained above it. Instead, there were whitewashed stone buildings arranged in artful spirals, dotted with open windows like black eyes. A few towers raised their heads above the crowd and the masts of small ships made a tiny forest along the coast.

I was crying again. Without theater or flair, just—crying, as if there were something I badly wanted and couldn't have. As my father did sometimes when he thought he was alone.

"January! *January!*" My name sounded like it was coming from a cheap gramophone several miles away, but I recognized Mr. Locke's voice echoing after me through the doorway. I didn't know how he'd found me, but I knew I was in trouble.

Oh, I can't tell you how much I didn't want to go back. How the sea smelled so full of promise, how the coiling streets in the city below seemed to make a kind of script. If it hadn't been Mr. Locke calling me—the man who let me ride in fancy train cars and bought me nice linen dresses, the man who patted my arm when my father disappointed me and left pocket diaries for me to find—I might have stayed.

But I turned back to the Door. It looked different on this side, a tumbled-down arch of weathered basalt, without even the dignity of wooden planks to serve as a door. A gray curtain fluttered in the opening instead. I drew it aside.

Just before I stepped back through the arch, a glint of silver shimmered at my feet: a round coin lay half-buried in the soil, stamped with several words in a foreign language and the profile of a crowned woman. It felt warm in my palm. I slipped it into my dress pocket.

This time the threshold passed over me like the brief shadow of a bird's wing. The dry smell of grass and sun returned.

"Janua—oh, there you are." Mr. Locke stood in his shirt-sleeves and vest, huffing a little, his mustache bristling like the tail of a recently offended cat. "Where were you? Been out here shouting myself hoarse, had to interrupt my meeting with Alexander—what's this?" He was staring at the blue-flecked Door, his face gone slack.

"Nothing, sir."

His eyes snapped away from the Door and onto me, ice-sharp. "January. Tell me what you've been doing."

I should've lied. It would have saved so much heartache. But you have to understand: when Mr. Locke looks at you in this particular way of his, with his moon-pale eyes, you mostly end up doing what he wants you to. I suspect it's the reason W. C. Locke & Co. is so profitable.

I swallowed. "I—I was just playing and I went through this door, see, and it leads to someplace else. There was a white city by the sea." If I'd been older, I might've said: *It smelled of salt and age and adventure. It smelled like another world, and I want to return right this minute and walk those strange streets.* Instead, I added articulately, "I liked it."

"Tell the *truth*." His eyes pressed me flat.

"I am, I swear!"

He stared for another long moment. I watched the muscles of his jaw roll and unroll. "And where did this door come from? Did you—did you build it? Stick it together out of this rubbish?" He gestured and I noticed the overgrown pile of rotted lumber behind the Door, the scattered bones of a house.

"No, sir. I just found it. And wrote a story about it."

"A story?" I could see him stumbling over each unlikely twist in our conversation and hating it; he liked to be in control of any given exchange.

I fumbled for my pocket diary and pressed it into his hands. "Look right there, see? I wrote a little story, and then the door was, was sort of open. It's true, I swear it's true."

His eyes flicked over the page many more times than was necessary to read a three-sentence story. Then he removed a cigar stub from his coat pocket and struck a match, puffing until the end glowed at me like the hot orange eye of a dragon.

He sighed, the way he sighed when he was forced to deliver some bad news to his investors, and closed my diary. "What fanciful nonsense, January. How often have I tried to cure you of it?"

He ran his thumb across the cover of my diary and then deliberately, almost mournfully, tossed it into the messy heap of lumber behind him.

"*No!* You can't—"

"I'm sorry, January. Truly." He met my eyes and made an abortive movement with his hand, as if he wanted to reach toward me. "But this is simply what must be done, for your sake. I'll expect you at dinner."

I wanted to fight him. To argue, to snatch my diary out of the dirt—but I couldn't.

I ran away instead. Back across the field, back up winding dirt roads, back into the sour-smelling hotel lobby.

And so the very beginning of my story features a skinny-legged girl on the run twice in the space of a few hours. It's not a very heroic introduction, is it? But—if you're an in-between sort of creature with no family and no money, with nothing but your own two legs and a silver coin—sometimes running away is the only thing you can do.

And anyway, if I hadn't been the kind of girl who ran away, I wouldn't have found the blue Door. And there wouldn't be much of a story to tell.

The fear of God and Mr. Locke kept me quiet that evening and the following day. I was well watched by Mr. Stirling and the nervous hotel manager, who herded me the way you might handle a valuable but dangerous zoo animal. I amused myself for a while by slamming the keys on the grand piano and watching him flinch, but eventually I was shepherded back into my room and advised to go to sleep.

I was out the low window and dodging through the alley before the sun had fully set. The road was scattered with shadows like shallow black pools, and by the time I reached the field, stars were shimmering through the hot haze of smoke and tobacco that hung over Ninley. I stumbled through the grass, squinting into the gloom for that house-of-cards shape.

The blue Door wasn't there.

Instead, I found a ragged black circle in the grass. Ash and char were all that remained of my Door. My pocket diary lay among the coals, curled and blackened. I left it there.

When I stumbled back into the sagging, not-very-grand hotel, the sky was tar-black and my knee socks were stained. Mr. Locke was sitting in an oily blue cloud of smoke in the lobby with his ledgers and papers spread before him and his favorite jade tumbler full of evening scotch.

"And where have you been this evening? Did you walk back through that door and find yourself on Mars? Or the moon, perhaps?" But his tone was gentle. The thing about Mr. Locke is that he really was kind to me. Even during the worst of it, he was always kind.

"No," I admitted. "But I bet there are more Doors just like it. I bet I could find them and write about them and they'd all open. And I don't care if you don't believe me." Why didn't I just keep my stupid mouth closed? Why didn't I shake my head and apologize with a hint of tears in my voice, and slink off to bed with the memory of the blue Door like a secret talisman in my pocket? Because I was seven and stubborn, and didn't yet understand the cost of true stories.

"Is that so," was all Mr. Locke said, and I marched to my room under the impression that I'd evaded more severe punishment.

It wasn't until we arrived back in Vermont a week later that I realized I was wrong.

Locke House was an immense red stone castle perched at the edge of Lake Champlain, topped with a forest of chimneys and copper-roofed towers. Its innards were wood-paneled and labyrinthine, bristling with the strange and rare and valuable; a *Boston Herald* columnist had once described it as "architecturally fanciful, more reminiscent of *Ivanhoe* than a modern man's abode." It was rumored that a mad Scotsman had commissioned it in the 1790s, spent a week living in it, and then vanished forevermore. Mr. Locke bought it at auction in the 1880s and began filling it with the world's wonders.

Father and I were stuffed into two rooms on the third story: a tidy, square office for him, with a big desk and a single window, and a gray, musty-smelling room with two narrow beds for me and my nursemaid. The newest one was a German immigrant named Miss Wilda, who wore heavy black woolen gowns and an expression that said she hadn't seen much of the twentieth century yet but heartily disapproved of it thus far. She liked hymns and freshly folded laundry, and detested fuss, mess, and cheek. We were natural enemies.

Upon our return, Wilda and Mr. Locke had a hurried conversation in the hall. Her eyes glittered at me like overshined coat buttons.

"Mr. Locke tells me you've been overstimulated lately, nearly hysterical, little dove." Miss Wilda often called me *little dove*; she was a believer in the power of suggestion.

"No, ma'am."

"Ah, poor dear. We'll have you right as the rain in no time at all."

The cure for overstimulation was a calm, structured environment without distraction; my room was therefore summarily stripped of everything colorful or whimsical or dear. The curtains were drawn and the bookshelf cleared of anything more exciting than *A Child's Illustrated Bible*. My favorite pink-and-gold bedspread—Father had sent it to me from Bangalore the previous year—was exchanged for starched white sheets. Samuel was forbidden to visit.

Miss Wilda's key slid and thunked in the keyhole, and I was alone.

At first I imagined myself a prisoner of war resisting the redcoats or rebels and practiced my expression of stoic resistance. But by the second day the silence was like two thumbs pressing against my eardrums and my legs shuddered and shook with the desire to run and keep running, back to that cedar-spiraled field, through the ashes of the blue Door to some other world.

On the third day, my room became a cell, which became a cage, which became a coffin, and I discovered the very deepest fear that swam through my heart like eels in undersea caves: to be locked away, trapped and alone.

Something in the center of me cracked. I tore at the curtains with clawed nails, I ripped the knobs from dresser drawers, I beat my small fists against the locked door, and then I sat on the floor and wept great hiccuping rivers of tears until Miss Wilda returned with a syrupy spoonful of something that took me away from myself for a while. My muscles turned to oiled, languorous rivers and my head bobbed loosely along the surface. The creep of shadows across the rugs became a terrible drama so absorbing there wasn't room for anything else in my head until I fell asleep.

When I woke, Mr. Locke was sitting at the side of my bed reading a newspaper. "Morning, my dear. And how are you feeling?"

I swallowed sour spit. "Better, sir."

"I'm glad." He folded his paper with architectural precision. "Listen to me very carefully, January. You are a girl of very great potential—immense, even!—but you've got to learn to behave yourself. From now on there will be no more fanciful nonsense, or running off, or doors that lead places they shouldn't."

His expression as he surveyed me made me think of old-timey

illustrations of God: severely paternal, bestowing the kind of love that weighs and measures before it finds you worthy. His eyes were stones, pressing down. "You are going to *mind your place* and *be a good girl.*"

I wanted desperately to be worthy of Mr. Locke's love. "Yes, sir," I whispered. And I was.

My father didn't return until November, looking as creased and tired as his luggage. His arrival followed its usual pattern: the wagon crunched its way up the drive and stopped before the stone majesty of Locke House. Mr. Locke went out to offer congratulatory backslapping and I waited in the front hall with Miss Wilda, dressed in a jumper so starched I felt like a turtle in an overlarge shell.

The door opened and he stood silhouetted, looking very dark and foreign in the pale November light. He paused on the threshold because this was generally the moment fifty pounds of excited young girl rocketed into his kneecaps.

But I didn't move. For the first time in my life, I didn't run to him. The silhouette's shoulders sagged.

It seems cruel to you, doesn't it? A sullen child punishing her father for his absence. But I assure you my intentions at the time were thoroughly muddled; there was just something about the shape of him in the doorway that made me dizzy with anger. Maybe because he smelled like jungles and steamships and adventures, like shadowed caves and unseen wonders, and my world was so ferociously mundane. Or maybe just because I'd been locked away and he hadn't been there to open the door.

He took three hesitant steps and crouched before me in the foyer. He looked older than I remembered, the stubble on his chin shining dull silver instead of black, as if every day he spent away from me were three days in his world. The sadness was the same as it always was, though, like a veil drawn over his eyes.

He rested a hand on my shoulder, black snakes of tattoos twisting around his wrists. "January, is something wrong?"

The familiar sound of my name in his mouth, his strange-but-not-strange accent, almost undid me. I wanted to tell him the truth—*I stumbled over something grand and wild, something that rips a hole in the shape of the world. I wrote something and it was true*—but I'd learned better. I was a good girl now.

"Everything is fine, sir," I answered, and watched the cool grown-up-ness of my voice hit my father like a slap.

I didn't speak to him over the dinner table that evening, and I didn't sneak into his room that night to beg stories from him (and he was a champion storyteller, let me tell you; he always said ninety-nine percent of his job was following the stories and seeing where they led).

But I was done with that fanciful nonsense. No more doors or Doors, no more dreams of silver seas and whitewashed cities. No more stories. I imagined this was just one of those lessons implicit in the process of growing up, which everyone learns eventually.

I'll tell you a secret, though: I still had that silver coin with the portrait of the strange queen on it. I kept it in a tiny pocket sewed in my underskirt, flesh-warm against my waist, and when I held it I could smell the sea.

It was my most precious possession for ten years. Until I turned seventeen, and found *The Ten Thousand Doors*.